Stay Calm
and
Dance On

SHARON OBERT

DEDICATION

To my tap mates Sue Combe and Brenda Hanks. Thank you for your laughter, encouragement, and friendship. Sadly, Sue passed away August 12, 2018, from pancreatic cancer at the young age of 64. We had ten wonderful dance years together. Diamond Girl, you will be forever in our hearts. Dance on!

ACKNOWLEDGMENTS

After I finished this novel, Casper College's Writing Center recommended Jamie Smith, a poet of a certain age, as a beta reader. Jamie managed to punch through the manuscript and give me ideas to shape the raw lump it was in the beginning. Then, Erin Brown's (www.erinedits.com) comments and encouragement kept me in the game. I thank them for their help and for making me feel this project was worth publishing.

Darlene Shortridge and Daniel Mawhinney of 40-Day Publishing (www.40daypublishingcom) helped me make this book a reality. Thank you to their editor, formatter, cover designer, and to their agent, Darcie Gudger, who answered my many questions. I am grateful to them all.

Thank you to Tonya Willadson, director of Dance Evolutions, and to the patient tap dance instructors who put up with us for so many years! What a great time we had!

And, of course, the love of my life, Paul Obert, who supported my monumental undertaking in every way. I love you to Gansarcal and back.

REVIEWS for
STAY CALM AND DANCE ON

Laugh out loud funny. Nothing like it out there. Brilliant.
- Susan Saranrap, author's BFF

A Crayola is colorful; this book is full of dull.
Change the y to a p and you will see
my true review: It's crapola.
- Jealous younger sister and unsuccessful poet

A character in the book is based on me, so yeah y'all, of course it's a great read!
- Next-door neighbor

The movie was better than the book. Oh, it wasn't a movie? Then what book did I read?
- Man on the street who thinks book worms are for fishing

CHAPTER 1:
MOVERS AND MOTHERS

The steep, narrow path wound through the shadows of tall lodgepole pines, which stood straight as arrows aimed at the cloudless, blue sky. Birdsong floated on the warm, gentle breeze. Squirrels chattered . . . and snake-like, half-buried tree roots lay in wait to attack an innocent, unsuspecting hiker.

Following behind her husband on the trail, Nancy Leopold knew better than to tap dance and hike at the same time, but she did exactly that and, sure enough, face-planted in the dirt. Splayed on the ground, she lifted her head. A flash of blue caught her eye, and it wasn't the sky. Great, an audience. The two oncoming hikers smiled, stepped around her, and passed without a word.

Ted bent down and held out a hand. "You're not bleeding? Nothing's broken?"

"No, just embarrassed." She'd been listening to Billy Joel's "Piano Man," which screamed the waltz step, and she couldn't resist. "Why is it that we haven't seen a single human being in an hour? Then, right when a tree root takes me down, and I'm sprawled out like an octopus, gawkers come out of nowhere? Huh, Ted, *why*?"

"God works in mysterious ways," he chuckled. "Sure you're all right?"

"Yes." Nancy yanked out her earbuds and brushed herself off. Her palms were scratched and stinging, but they weren't bleeding. "I'm glad we're almost to the truck. I'm done."

They were on the downhill side of the mountain trail and would soon be out of the shade. The hot August sun, now higher in the sky, baked them the last 300 yards to the parking lot. Nancy gulped the remainder of her water, briefly stretched her leg muscles, and climbed into the pickup's air-conditioned cab.

When Ted pulled into their driveway, an orange eighteen-wheeler was parked in front of the house next door. After years of flying south every winter, the previous owners had put their house up for sale and built a permanent nest in a retirement community in Mesquite, Nevada.

At the end of July, a SOLD sign went up. A few days later, Ted was outside repairing their RV's leaky roof vent, when the new guy walked over and introduced himself as Trebo Luapa. He and his wife, Charlene, were from Dallas, Texas, and had bought the house. Ted invited them over for venison kabobs and grilled corn-on-the-cob. Nancy and Charlene had been friends ever since.

So while two muscular men in baggy jeans and matching orange t-shirts hauled furniture and boxes into the house through the garage, Charlene stood overseeing the work with one hand on her slim hip. Since she had broken her wrist right before moving to Collinsville, the other arm hung by her side, sporting a maroon cast with GIG 'EM, AGGIES written in white marker.

"Charlene might be close to my age," Nancy grumbled to herself, "but those are definitely not my hips." She hadn't worn such a cute, flowery summer dress since she was sixteen. Charlene protected her right-amount-of-tan face with a floppy-brimmed straw hat. Nancy had noticed that Charlene's short, naturally blond hair and designer clothes were always stylish. On the other hand, Nancy hadn't worn a drop of makeup her entire life, preferring a natural look, freckles and all. On special occasions, she managed some mascara but that was it. "Doesn't matter what that woman does, she could be mowing the lawn and still look like she'd stepped out of a fashion magazine," Nancy muttered again.

"What'd you say? You talking to me?" Ted looked at Nancy before placing his sunglasses on the dashboard and opening the driver's side door.

"No, but it looks like the Luapas' furniture is here. I'm gonna run over and say hi." Nancy slid out of the truck. Wearing tan camping-catalog shorts and a teal t-shirt with Key Largo emblazoned across the front, she picked her way over the river rocks separating their driveways. Her used-to-be-natural auburn hair was not quite long enough for the clip to contain it all, allowing a few strands to fall across her eyeglasses. She swiped at the damp tendrils.

Charlene waved. "Hey, Nancy! Now that the hickory floors are in, our furniture is finally out of storage. I don't have to sleep on an air mattress anymore." Charlene frowned. "My word, do you want some water? You look like you're having a heat stroke."

"No, thanks. My face always turns beet red when I'm exercising. We've been hiking on the mountain. Plus, it's freaking hot out here. How's your arm?"

"It itches like mad. I'm not supposed to, but I've been sticking a letter opener down there. Thank God I've got a little over a week before this dumb thing comes off."

"That's good. Makes my skin crawl thinking about an itch I can't scratch." Nancy rubbed her arms. "With all the unpacking you have to do, will you be able to make it to dinner and the World of Arts show on Saturday?"

"Yes, ma'am. We should be mostly unpacked by then. Bo's working today. He had a mandatory Monday meeting, but he's got the rest of this week off. We may not get it all done, but I'll definitely be ready for a break!"

"Good. I'm excited for you to meet Milly and Joan."

Nancy had joined an adult tap class eight years ago. While women came and went, only three regulars had stuck with it. Meeting the last Saturday in August had become tradition for the adult tappers. It was a way for them to catch up on summer activities and not take up time during the first class in September. Nancy had assured Charlene she would be welcome, because even after all these years they still considered themselves beginners, and she had tentatively agreed to join the class.

"Excuse me!" Charlene hollered to a worker. "Would you leave that green container in the garage, please?"

"And pull up your pants!" Nancy groaned. "Ugh, that's downright gross."

"Oh my god, I hope he didn't hear you," Charlene whispered.

"He didn't hear me, but geez, his butt crack is showing three inches. Do you think he does it on purpose?"

"I don't know. Why don't you ask him?"

"Dude!" Nancy called, making like she was going to follow him. The mover did not respond and continued into the house with his dolly stacked full of boxes after having removed the requested container.

Charlene jumped in front of her. "For heaven's sake, I was being sarcastic! Don't you dare ask him. But since you've brought it to my attention, it *is* hairy." She shuddered. "If he comes back with his pants hitched up, we'll know he heard you."

"If his crack is covered, you give him a big Texas thank you from me."

Charlene swatted at her friend, grinned, and said, "I will do no such thing."

"You've got this under control. I gotta take a shower. If you need anything, call, text, bang on our door, whatever."

"Oh no, missy. You are not leaving me alone with those two. Not after what you blurted out."

"Okay, okay. I'll get a couple of chairs and keep you company. It's not bad in the shade. In the spring this Mayday tree blooms with little white flowers. Really pretty and smells good. Probably better than those two."

"Shut up! I'm fixin' to change my mind about wantin' company."

"Oh, come on. Want something to drink? I don't have any hairy cheeks, but I can bring back a couple fuzzy navels."

"You are impossible!" Charlene laughed. "Thank you, but I have water for me and my boys. Miss Nancy, you better bring your sweaty body back here!"

"Yes, ma'am!" Feigning a stern look, Nancy saluted at the direct order and marched back across the rocks to her garage.

The fishing boat barely fit, with all the camping and fishing gear shoved on shelves and piled on the floor around it. She really needed to clean the garage. Those old paint cans were probably dried up. She could start a shoe store with the number of hiking and hunting boots purchased for every possible weather condition, some she and Ted hadn't worn in years. And she'd been meaning to give away the giant, plastic storage bin of outdoor

Christmas lights they never hung up anymore. They'd moved on to one of those laser light shows that projected onto the house.

Nancy was hot and tired and sat down on an empty cooler to think about where the chairs might be in this mess, but instead her thoughts drifted to her new neighbor. Charlene probably didn't have a real mean streak in her entire body. Then again, how much do we really know about each other?

Charlene was full of Southern charm and hospitality. Nancy couldn't believe she would flip anybody off. Unlike herself, one time thrusting her arm out the window and offering her middle finger to a Grand Caravan that had swerved into her lane. "Wake up!" she had yelled. Big mistake. Those two old ladies came after her. *Whoa!* She hadn't seen that coming. But her mighty four-cylinder, manual five-speed mini-coupe outran the automatic, six-cylinder minivan. Actually, she had run the tail end of a yellow light and the grannies stopped. Lost 'em! "Not so grand now, are ya," she'd sputtered to herself as she made a sharp left and zig-zagged through an unfamiliar neighborhood in case they followed. That incident hadn't stopped her from flipping people off—she just kept her middle finger below the dashboard.

Ted called her the Enforcer. While she'd always been a little on the bossy side, she'd noticed she was developing an attitude, becoming more outspoken on many subjects. Nancy blamed her change in attitude on two things:

One, *the* change. Hormones, or lack thereof. On a menopausal-mood-swing-and-hot-flash scale of one to ten, she was a fifteen.

Two, her mother, Trixie Bayer Herschel. Who doesn't blame their mother for some things, right? During the last few visits to San Diego, California, Nancy had noticed her soft-spoken mother become more ill-tempered. Like mother, like daughter. Except Trixie attributed her irritability to frequent headaches. Whenever Nancy tried to convince her mother to see a doctor, she would change the subject.

Charlene's mother chaired several high society committees and sat on the board of two charities, while Nancy's mom had never even had a driver's license. Never attended her daughter's school concerts where she played the flute. Never went to PTA meetings. She was a loving mother, but aloof to those outside her immediate family. Although, now that she thought about it, Trixie had seemed more paranoid than aloof.

Trixie wasn't involved in community affairs, but she had instilled in her daughter the love for reading and gardening, especially flowers. And Trixie loved to cook. That skill, unfortunately, did not get passed down. Nancy chuckled at the memory of her mother saying she was allergic to washing dishes and to this day, Nancy's nose itches, too, when she does the dishes. But it was her father who taught her to swim, ride a bike, and ice skate. She was twenty-two when he died of a heart attack. She missed him.

Nancy was an only child and her family had moved around a lot, from one city to another. Although she was always "the new girl," she had made friends easily. Her mom wasn't anything like her friends' moms who'd welcomed her at slumber parties. Trixie had not allowed sleepovers. Why? Nancy wondered, frowning. She'd never known the answer to that.

Ted came out of the house, breaking her reverie. "What are you doing out here?"

"Looking for the folding chairs. Where are they? I was gonna bring a couple over to Charlene's and keep her company. Bo's not home from work yet."

He dug through the piles, moving an old vacuum cleaner out of the way and tossing cardboard boxes he used for target practice onto the boat deck. Making it to the far corner, he pulled out two slender bags that held the canvas chairs. "Thank you." She kissed his cheek and headed back to check on the status of the moving man's pants.

CHAPTER 2:
MISSION IMPOSSIBLE?

Nestled in a wide valley, Ghanwik City was bordered on the east by the Bennu Mountains and the Chariklo Mountains to the west. Of the two ranges, Bennu claimed the highest peaks. Tonight, moonlight highlighted the blanket of snow on its sharp crests. Two minor full moons had already appeared in the night sky. The largest moon, Gansarcal, would soon rise between her sisters.

Bright as birthday candles, hundreds of towers lit with blue, red, and yellow lights formed Ghanwik City center. As evening approached, air traffic slowed considerably, except every now and then a Scrambler blasted past causing the lights to smear into a kaleidoscope of color.

Rigel O'Rion had received an urgent comm from the director of the Intergalactic Research Institute and was presently on board one of those autonomous taxis rocketing to the top of the tallest tower. As the Scrambler docked outside, he wondered what Bet was doing at the office so late.

He exited the short-winged craft and entered the hallway leading to the door labeled Dr. Betel G. Euse.

The biometric scanner identified Rigel, and an artificial voice announced his name. The door hissed open. As he strode into the austere room, Dr. Euse swiped away a green holographic screen hanging in the air and stood to greet her visitor. "Rigel, my friend, glad you had a moment to meet with me."

"Bet, whenever you use 'my friend' I know you have something up your sleeve. How are ya, kid?"

The statuesque director, with her flaming red braids wrapped around her head like a crown, laughed and said, "I'm peachy, and what I have in mind wouldn't fit up my sleeve." She tugged at the long sleeve of her red and gold tunic and peeked inside the opening. "Nope, nothing there, but I *do* have a proposition for you." She grinned and swept her arm toward the molded chair in front of her crescent-shaped desk. "Have a seat."

"I knew it." Rigel eased into the hard chair with an ankle resting on his knee and his fingers entwined behind his head. Unlike the chair, he was comfortable with the Institute's director. Minus the braids, he was her equal in height at 6 feet 2 inches. Both near retirements, they had been childhood friends, even attending university together, but their work rarely crossed paths. He was a financial manager, one-among-many budget officers. Dr. Euse was one-of-a-kind, the top administrator in D'Gnome's search for intelligent beings. Earth was the only planet so far discovered to have evolved similarly to D'Gnome.

Rigel stroked his black goatee. "Zooks, Bet, what's up that's required my presence on such short notice?"

Betel sat down, leaned forward, and clasped her hands. "Appreciate you heeding my call. I have serious business to discuss, and you're the only one I trust to get it done."

"Gee, thanks. I'm afraid to ask . . . what business?"

"I'm sure you've heard—for the first time in history—two gateways have malfunctioned. Both within a matter of days."

"Yeah, heard the Biloxi traveler was dropped into the Gulf of Mexico instead of the lighthouse. And the second, what was it, a sewage lagoon in some rural area of San Diego County? That must have been hilarious." Rigel laughed.

"Laugh all you want, but that means two gateways are shut down. Her return almost overheated the decontamination chamber. Fortunately, the lagoon was four feet deep and she was able to reach the portal before it closed. The poor guy in Biloxi couldn't get a foothold in the water. Got picked up by a dolphin-searching tourist boat. Had to return to D'Gnome via New Orleans."

"You know why the gateways failed?"

"Not yet. Meissa Shining, new head of the gateway recovery team, is working on a fix. Gossip is already spreading like the wind, bringing up old issues like—" Betel made air quotes when she said, "The *deaths* of Harold and Erma Bayer."

"Ah." Rigel pursed his lips and nodded.

"Not to mention, one news feed is raising questions about their daughter. I'm sure there'll be more. Stars alive, Trixie left D'Gnome at seventeen. She's been *dead* longer than Harold and Erma. Why are they bringing *her* up?"

Rigel cocked his head sideways. "You know how people are. They thrive on sensationalism. A gateway's never gone down before. Not in sixty-five years. This is big news. I'm not surprised the Bayers have been dredged up from the depths of obscurity."

"Well, guess what? That obscurity isn't so deep, because Meissa has found out that Harold and Erma are imprisoned on Gansarcal. She knows there was no river rafting accident."

"How'd she find that out?"

"Snooping around with her lousy second-level security clearance. It shouldn't have been enough to get her as far as she got, but then the recommendation committee said she was a brilliant astrophysicist. She's brilliant, all right. Has a notion that since Erma created the gateways that Erma should be able to help solve the problem. In any other circumstance, that'd be true. Of course, Meissa doesn't know the extent of Erma's mental capacity. At least I don't think she does. She wanted to meet her. I denied the request."

Rigel crossed his arms. "Meissa's taken a confidentiality oath, hasn't she?"

"Yes, but I detected hostility in our meeting this morning, which makes me suspicious of her intentions. I told her to focus on her job, not the Bayers, although, I don't put it past her to find a backdoor to the most secure files—"

"Harold's nepial research."

"His research, the Bayers' existence. It's all bad. Guess it's time to retire. I brag about being proactive, yet I've failed on my most important job of keeping knowledge of the Bayers top secret. Had a serious discussion with my chief security officer, but what else can I do? I fell into complacency, like everyone else, and now something like this has happened. I'm screwed."

"Bet, don't be so hard on yourself. No matter how much data protection one has, it's never enough. No offense to you, but I'm dumbfounded it has taken half a century for someone to find out Harold and Erma, our most renowned scientists, are living in forced isolation on the moon. Now, stop that negative talk. This isn't like you."

"Rigel, need I remind you, any data leaked about the Bayers is a capital crime. No matter who does the leaking, I'm ultimately responsible. I am ready to explode because my whole career will be thrown down a black hole if we don't get this fixed pronto.

"The Biloxi incident made their national news. The traveler wasn't identified as D'Gnoman, but we can't risk that kind of exposure." Betel paused and rubbed the back of her neck. "Rigel, I can't confide with anyone at the Institute. So, indulge me, please. Because there's more."

"More?"

Betel's shoulders sagged. "Meissa found a diary of Erma's in the archives during her investigation. Carelessly left by the agents, I might add. It had a reference to Trixie Bayer, which aroused her interest. You know what she said to me? 'I know Bellatrix is Harold and Erma's daughter.' Hadn't heard the name Bellatrix in so long, I about fell on the floor when she said that. Mainly because I was shocked to hear she'd discovered Trixie in the first place, but also because it brought back such vivid memories. I can't remember the last time I thought about Trixie. She hated being called Bellatrix. We were such a clique back then, weren't we?"

"Not so much me as you, Trixie, and Saiph. I was Saiph's kid brother, the annoying tagalong. Trixie didn't like anyone calling her Bellatrix, though. She felt it was too old-fashioned."

"Well, her name is neither here nor there. What counts is that Meissa knows about her. Get this. She asked me, 'How can Bellatrix be living in the United States of America for decades when every other D'Gnoman's nepial gland would swell? We'd get terrible headaches and be dead within a year.' I was so taken aback I didn't know what to say."

"Did you tell her Trixie had received the vaccine?"

"Of course not! You think I'm an idiot? I told her she'd suffer serious repercussions if she continued to deviate from her gateway analysis. She hasn't broken any laws, so I can't fire her. Not yet anyway, but I'm going to be watching her very closely. What if more gateways fail and people die or are seriously hurt? We've got to find the answer to the crashes, and a new team leader would be another setback."

"Hmm, I see the pile is growing." Rigel stood up and strode to the window that made up an entire wall of the office with a breathtaking penthouse view of Ghanwik City and the Bennu Mountains.

Betel slapped her hands on the desktop. Rigel jumped and turned back to Betel. "How can you be so *calm* about this?" she shrieked. "It'll be my ass on the line either way, whether we can't fix the gateways or the vaccine is discovered or the Bayers and their daughter are exposed. Oh, and we can't forget the granddaughter, Nancy What's-Her-Name." Betel flicked her wrist, a holographic screen popped up in front of her and she asked the question. The screen responded with *Nancy Leopold*; Betel whisked it away. "Leopold. Nancy Leopold."

"Stars, Bet, you don't have any of your Brandywine, do you? I think we could both use a drink."

Betel heaved a sigh. "Right you are. Open bar." A door slid open on the wall to their right, exposing a mini-bar. She retrieved two snifters and pressed a sequence into the keypad to pour the liquor. "My latest concoction. What do you think?"

She held out a snifter. Rigel took it, swirled the reddish-gold liquid, and sipped. "Very good. A hint of cherry?" He returned to the window, and Betel joined him.

"A touch." Betel sighed. "I never get tired of this view at night—city lights, the stars, especially the three moons when they line up like this. They look like they're smiling, like they're happy to see me."

"It is an amazing sight. Makes me wonder how much Trixie misses D'Gnome. It's too bad she most likely lived in fear speculating when the government would make her return. Wish I could talk to her. See how she's doing."

"She has survived just fine. What worries me is that since Biloxi and San Diego crashed, conspiracy theories about the Bayers are spiraling out of control. There are people out there who believe Harold and Erma didn't drown and it's all a government coverup. Imagine that. It feels like the dormant volcano is rumbling and ready to erupt. Can't you feel it?"

"I can." Rigel hesitated. As free as he felt to talk with Bet, he warned himself to be cautious or he'd lose her trust. He didn't want to sound like one of the undergrounders she despised, yet he couldn't help but push it once in a while. "Maybe it's time for a change. Keep the volcano from erupting. Be more transparent." He couldn't understand why an intelligent person like Dr. Betel G. Euse would deny the importance of government transparency. It was bound to lead to the very trouble she so feared.

"Rigel, dear, you're starting to sound like—"

"An old man with foolish ideas. Let's take a moment and savor the view. When we were kids, we used to make a wish when the moons aligned like this. Come on, Bet, we'll make a toast to the moons for a speedy gateway resolution." He chuckled. Then, like the childhood friends they were, the two wished upon the moons.

They stood absorbed in their own thoughts, quietly soaking up the peaceful scenery until Betel said, "I almost forgot why I asked you here."

"Yeah, why *did* you ask me here?" Rigel smirked.

Betel drained her glass. "Look, I told Meissa she could not meet Harold and Erma. Then she asked to interview Trixie, as if *she'd* have information about the portal malfunctions. Again, I said no. But the thing is, Trixie might. We don't know for sure. She is, after all, the daughter of the gateway creator. Who knows what she's been told or what data she's been given to protect? And I don't put it past Meissa to uncover Nancy's existence and go after her."

"Go after. What's that mean?"

"I mean use Nancy Leopold in some way to get to Trixie. There's no solution yet to the gateway failures. How desperate might Meissa grow to find the answer? So here's my plan."

Rigel frowned. "Does this call for a drum roll?"

"Ha, ha. Listen, I've been pondering how best to meet with Trixie. She needs to be told what's happening here. As you know, the Bayers were forced to use Trixie for the vaccine trial. They agreed under one circumstance: we would not force physical contact while she lived on Earth. No breaking down her door." Betel snickered. "Unless, of course, Trixie agreed to a visit, which she has never done. There are no rules concerning Nancy, so I have decided to talk to her first. She needs to know what's going on, as well."

"Whoa, I'm not so sure Trixie would be open to her daughter getting involved. We don't even know if Nancy is aware of her mother's origins. Aren't we butting into a family situation that is none of our business?"

"It is our business if it's a life-or-death situation."

"Bet, I can't imagine it's that serious. No one from DG will bother Nancy."

"You don't know who might harm her if word got out of her existence. She is, after all, the child of a D'Gnoman and an Earth man. The first and only. That's enough to be concerning."

"You've got a point there."

"And guess where she lives."

Rigel shook his head. He was tired. "Tell me."

"Your old stomping ground . . . Collinsville, Wyoming!"

She sounded like he'd won the trip of a lifetime.

"How long has it been since you've seen your old friend Millicent McGilly? She's still in Collinsville. Weren't her parents your Earth study sponsors?"

"Yeah, they were. The last time I saw Milly was before her husband died ten years ago. I guess it's worth a try."

"Great! I was afraid you wouldn't concur."

"Did I concur?" Rigel yawned.

"You did!"

"So you're abandoning the idea of contacting Trixie and going for her daughter, like you didn't want Meissa to do?"

"Better us than her. I don't trust Meissa. Plus here's your chance to make your wish come true. In a roundabout way, if everything works out, you'll get to talk to Trixie."

"Craters, Bet, I wouldn't even know how to approach Trixie's daughter." Although he did have to admit to himself, he was feeling more invigorated at the mention of Millicent's name.

Rigel had spent his last year of high school living with Milly and her parents. D'Gnoman students of the highest caliber were chosen to continue their education through the Senior Superlative Earth Study Program. Students were assimilated into the Earth school's familiar Foreign Exchange Program using falsified birth records. They were hosted by trusted families acting on behalf of DG parents. Milly's parents had sponsored Rigel and, two years prior, his sister Saiph and Trixie.

"Hear me out." Betel leaned her back against the window pane and crossed her arms. "You'll love this. Quite by coincidence, Millicent and Nancy are friends."

"No way."

"They are."

"Does Milly know of Trixie and Nancy's mother-daughter relationship?"

"Hell if I know. Millicent was a kid when Trixie lived with her family. And then it was for one school year. She may not remember her. Even if she does, unless Nancy has said something, I doubt Milly would bring it up." Betel tucked in a loose braid.

"So if Nancy knows nothing about D'Gnome, it would be extremely difficult to explain it to her without someone who understands that life on D'Gnome exists, and that Trixie has a connection to it. Someone she knows, like Milly."

"Exactly! Zooks, you're good, Rigel."

"So where do I come in?"

Betel beamed and said, "I want you to meet with Millicent and set up a meeting with the three of you. If needed, she can soften the blow."

Rigel groaned. "Sure. Why not? Let's hope I'm not the one this time to end up in a sewage lagoon."

"Don't say that! I don't want three gateways on my hands. I'd be dead for sure. Can you go tomorrow? I want to get there before Meissa does something behind my back."

Why couldn't he say no? He was a mathematician, not a mediator. But maybe he and Milly could get Nancy Leopold to cooperate and set up a visit with her mother . . . or maybe not. Either way, it would be nice to see Milly again. "Okay. Day after tomorrow. I have a day job, ya know. Can't do it any sooner."

"Deal." Betel opened a desk drawer. "Here, take this. It's Erma's journal of their river trip. Give it to Trixie when you see her."

"Not putting it in the archives?"

"Nope. Give it to Trixie."

Rigel set the empty glass he'd been holding on the desk and took the journal. "Well then, I've got to get some sleep. Thanks for the Brandywine. See ya 'round if ya don't turn square."

"Oh, that's ancient." Betel pushed him toward the office door. "Thanks, my friend."

Rigel returned to the waiting Scrambler. He absentmindedly climbed into the taxi. From the moment he'd stepped out of Betel's office, he'd been lost in thought. Would Trixie and Nancy be in peril if knowledge of their existence was revealed? Trixie was the sole recipient of the vaccine, or so the government thought. There'd be plenty of D'Gnomans who'd like to know how Trixie survived on Earth so long. And Nancy's heredity alone was enough for some lunatic to cause chaos.

Rigel startled when an AI voice announced loudly: "I repeat. What is your destination?" He voiced his home address and the rocket shot into the night.

CHAPTER 3:
SHE'S A MEAN ONE, DR. EUSE

Meissa Shining sat at her kitchen table sipping chamomile tea, infuriated after another unsuccessful day of bringing two gateways back online. Despite her frustration, she snickered at the traveler flailing in a sewage lagoon.

"What is so funny?" asked Flekk. Sitting across from Meissa, on a tall stool, the brown Bengal cat lapped at her saucer of melon-flavored water.

"Oh, a traveler to San Diego was dropped into a sewage pit instead of the California Building in Balboa Park."

"Stars, that must have been awful."

"She made it home. Happy ending for her. Not for me. That makes two down. I have to figure out why the damn things malfunctioned."

Flekk jumped to the floor and onto Meissa's lap. "You'll figure it out." She circled once and settled down, purring. She knew the throaty hum would sooth her companion.

Meissa had been team leader of the Gateway Monitoring and Recovery Team for three days when San Diego went down. The prior leader had been fired within hours for letting the Biloxi gateway fail. He didn't have a backup or a way to restore it. Meissa was astonished at the abruptness of his firing and her promotion. What would happen to her if she couldn't resolve the issue? As an astrophysicist, this was the job she'd coveted. She knew she was up to the challenge but wasn't sure whether her team would find the answer as quickly as the Institute's director felt they should.

The team's duties included the travelers' logs—those coming and going, when, where, and why—and the monitoring of gateway integrity, which hadn't gone well so far. Monitoring had always been a part of the job. Recovery was added when Biloxi crashed. More work, same number of people to do the job. Typical.

There were two staff she could depend on. The third member was a new intern requiring more supervision. They were all younger than she. Funny how that worked. She had always been the youngest at every job. Then one day, suddenly, surprisingly, she realized she was the oldest. Meissa was only forty-four. Was she slowing down in her race to the top? With her new position, she was one step closer to her career goal of becoming director of the Intergalactic Research Institute. Dr. Betel G. Euse was considered a supergiant in the field of planetary studies, designated a first-magnitude by the senators, but her light was dimming. She'd have to give up the reins one of these days, and Meissa Shining would be there to take them.

Or would she be overtaken by those newbies?

"Hop down, sweetie. I'm going to take a bath."

"I hope the hot bath will soak away the misery you're feeling." Flekk leaped to the floor and back to her water dish.

"I hope so too." Meissa rinsed her cup in the sink. She had recently purchased this small, stone house, built in an earlier era, on a lakefront in a suburb outside Ghanwik City. She guessed there had once been lovely gardens in back, but now it was overgrown with tall weeds. The blue flower boxes on the front of the house were loose and faded, begging for repair—one of many items on her to-do list. Maybe someday she'd rework the gardens, but for now, she was in the midst of renovating rooms in the old home. So far all she'd completed besides the kitchen was the en suite bathroom.

The kitchen's sage green walls complemented the cream cabinetry. There was no need for a stove/oven duo, as she had installed the latest food printer, but she kept it anyway. It was nostalgic. The old oven cavity served as extra storage, while the sleek stovetop held pots of lacey herbs. This home was normally her sanctuary. At the moment, though, Meissa could not dismiss the past twenty-four hours.

Maybe the hot bath would make her feel better. In shades of grey, with black and blue accents softened with greenery, her bathroom was a major success. Her favorite was the wall behind the double-sink vanity—its small, brushed-aluminum tiles reflected the light, creating hundreds of swirls, like tiny galaxies. She looked in the mirror at her fading blue hair and made a mental note to make an appointment for color and a trim. Her spikes were sagging, as well as her spirit.

On the menu screen next to the tub, she touched icons for coconut, guava, and hibiscus oils to be mixed into the water. The luscious scent reminded her of the beach. Soft woodwind music floated on the air as she tried to take her mind off work. She sank into the warm, fragrant water and closed her eyes, imagining ocean waves crashing onto the shore . . . but it wasn't happening.

Her job kept crashing into her mind. Biloxi came up and went down again. The instability was driving her crazy. Their investigation was as cold as the conditioned air in the gateway data center, an immense room within the Institute, full of servers the size of refrigerators stacked to the ceiling. The ubiquitous, non-stop blinking green and red lights felt like their progress so far—on, off, on, off.

On her first day, she'd called a staff meeting to assign tasks: look for anomalies around the Biloxi portal, double-check security algorithms and make sure they were up to date, and search all known documentation on the creation of the gateways.

On the second day, when Biloxi suddenly came back online, then off again, Meissa was leaning toward human interference, not natural degeneration. She asked her team to check users' digital fingerprints for anything unusual going back to the creation of the gateways. Maybe someone's been working on breaking the system for some nefarious reason for a long time. Maybe this, maybe that. She could not overlook any possibility.

Another part of her strategy had been to inventory the Bayers' belongings. Hundreds of bins with the Bayer name were stored in the National History Archives but never cataloged. Meissa had speculated over what may have gone unnoticed when their home had been packed up fifty years ago, after Harold and Erma had been declared dead during a rafting trip.

With her team busy on their assignments, she had gone to the archives yesterday. Lo and behold, in the very first bin she'd found Erma's diary still stuck to the bottom of an old duffle bag the Bayers had taken on their river trip. Meissa was so ecstatic she couldn't think of anything else but to race home to read it. Erma Bayer had been her childhood heroine and her inspiration to become an astrophysicist. The rare, paper-bound journal held Erma's last words! That's what she believed at the time anyway.

Last night she had crawled into bed with the diary and savored it as if it were a decadent dessert. There were the usual scenery descriptions and wildlife observations, but the passage that had caught her eye was one that had nothing to do with their trip: "As we float this calm section immersed in breathtakingly steep canyon walls, I am reminded of my precious Trixie. She would have loved the exhilaration of the rapids. I regret bringing her to the lab and should have fought harder. I miss her so much."

What did *that* mean? Bringing Trixie to the lab for what? And who was Trixie? A pet? A child maybe? Was there something she witnessed or some procedure performed on her? Too many questions. And that's what piqued her interest. Curiosity. She had immediately pulled up a holo-screen and begun her data dig.

Meissa knew nothing about the Bayers, except what she had learned in school. Textbooks included the Bayers' accomplishments and drowning deaths but nothing on their private lives, like whether or not they had children. All she knew was that Erma had developed a network of ninety-nine gateways which had worked flawlessly for sixty-five years until now. Harold was a neuroscientist, but she couldn't remember what he was known for.

Daylight had been creeping into her bedroom window when she felt her brain cells finally decelerate. So much adrenalin had been rushing through her veins that there was no way she could have slept. In the mine pit that kept getting deeper and deeper, she had unearthed filthy, dirty lies, leaving her shocked and angry to put it mildly. Who was the Trixie that Erma mentioned in her journal? She was Erma's daughter. After her Senior Superlative year, she had supposedly died in an exploratory mission. That information wasn't hard to find. Older citizens were posting all over the place about their memory of the tragic accident. But after a little more digging, she found Bellatrix was no more dead than Harold and Erma! She smashed the bathwater with her fist.

Meissa smirked, remembering how she *had* to talk to someone about what she'd found, but who? With the confidentiality oath she'd taken, there was only one person: Dr. Betel G. Euse. Well, that turned out to be a *huge* mistake. Meissa could kick herself for talking to her superior this morning in such an exhausted state of mind.

At the meeting with Dr. Euse, Meissa conjectured that, since Erma Bayer was alive, she'd know what to do. So, she'd asked Dr. Euse's permission to meet Erma.

No, you can't go visit Erma Bayer, Dr. Euse had said. Then Euse had plucked Erma's journal out of her hands.

Focus on your job, not the Bayers, Euse had said. Too late for that, boss. I've already found more lies than I ever dreamed of finding. She had wanted to say that it wasn't *her* fault the agents left the journal, but she'd kept her mouth shut.

Of course, the agents weren't even real investigators, only stooges of the government, picking up the leftovers of the Bayers' bogus river rafting trip. She corrected herself. The couple really had gone on a rafting trip but had been caught using an illegal device called a Pathfinder, which circumvented the established portals. They were arrested and sent to the penitentiary on Gansarcal. They weren't housed with the inmates, but had been provided separate living quarters. How nice.

The bogus part was the newsfeed sent out at the time: "After an exhaustive search of the River Nelg and the area in and around the Heybe-Diess Canyon, Harold and Erma Bayer, D'Gnome's most eminent scientists, have officially been declared dead."

Yeah, right. To the planet's general population, but not to the Inner Circle of which Meissa was not a member. She found out about it anyway, via her hacking skills. She truly was gifted in that respect, although she had gotten herself into trouble with Dr. Euse, who'd be keeping a closer eye on her from now on. Not so smart.

She slapped the water again. Enough! She climbed out of the tub and grabbed a towel. The tub sensed her absence and began to drain and self-clean.

Meissa felt drained, too, but she'd have to get over it and figure out the gateway problem. That's what Erma Bayer would have done. Erma had been admired by all, and that's what Meissa craved. Somehow, she would be another Erma Bayer—everyone would know her name.

CHAPTER 4:
THE HALF-BAKED AFFAIR

Nancy's cell dinged. She put down the book she was reading to pick up the phone. Charlene had texted: Boxes to donate. Want to come with me to the thrift store?

You bet. Got room for one more box?

Yes. 15 minutes too soon?

Nope. Meet you outside.

In her neighbor's driveway, Nancy noticed the cargo area of Charlene's SUV was full. "You want some Christmas icicle lights? I'm givin' 'em away. It's now or never."

"Good Lord, Christmas hasn't even crossed my mind, but I think we're good."

"Okey-dokey, your loss." Nancy grinned and loaded the large, red container into the backseat before climbing into the front passenger seat. "You know where you're going?"

"Yes, ma'am. This is my second load. This thing was completely full yesterday. Barely had room for me."

"Where's Bo?"

"He loaded everything up for me and left. He wasn't supposed to work this week, but I guess he had stuff to do."

"Looks like you're making progress unpacking, if you've got this much to give away."

"Still have boxes of books to go through. This house is smaller than our Dallas home. Don't have room to store everything. Most of these things I haven't used in years, so might as well get rid of them. Anyway, glad you could come along. Been a difficult day for some reason. Felt like I needed company."

"I'd say it's that maroon t-shirt you're wearing. You're in Wyoming now. Ditch that Aggie stuff and invest in some brown and gold. Make you feel right at home."

"Never! Bo and I are diehard A&M fans. Gig 'em, Aggies!" Charlene raised her thumbs. "Never," Charlene slapped her chest and her jaw dropped, "would we ever switch allegiance, no matter where we lived. How could you suggest such a thing? But I'll forgive you." Laughing, she put the SUV in reverse and backed out of the driveway.

"Glad you're laughing. I thought you might throw me out of the car. I'll say, though, moving will make you feel sad. I've moved a lot. I mean *a lot.*"

"You did?"

"Went to eight different schools in thirteen years, if you count Kindergarten. Ted and I have moved three times because of his career. Not so bad as an adult, but in high school, I would get hysterical when I had to leave my friends. I absolutely hated it."

"That sounds awful. I just got here, so you better not move again! I don't know what I'd do! I'm still not over the image of those movers coming and literally sucking my house dry. Nothing left but memories. I bawled from the moment I walked out our door for the last time clear through Oklahoma. Could hardly see to drive. Thank goodness I had Bo's truck to follow or who knows where I would have ended up. Then near the Kansas border I heard my momma's voice: 'Charlene Rae! Bowie women are strong. Quit falling apart and pull yourself together.'"

"Gosh, knowing how hard it was for me, I should have realized how difficult moving was for you. I'm sorry."

"You shouldn't be sorry. It didn't help that I'd broken my wrist right before we left. I was pretty unhappy, but I'm feeling better now. You've helped immensely."

"Aw, that's nice. My mom probably said something similar each time we moved: 'Stop your blubbering and get up off the ground!'" Nancy chuckled. "My parents had to drag me into the car kicking and screaming."

"I can't imagine moving that many times."

"It was toughest in senior high—I went to a different school every year. Then when I went to college, my parents settled down. Never moved again." Nancy huffed and shook her head. "I should ask my mother about it. Maybe she'd tell me. She never was much of a talker. Still isn't. Our phone conversations are, like, three minutes long."

"Heavens, my mother couldn't stop talking and still can't. She was always on the phone or gossiping at coffee klatches at our house or someone else's house. Had more time for society meetings and her bunco and bridge clubs than for her middle daughter."

"Wow, my mom was the total opposite. She spent time with me—'course I was an only child—but she never spent time with anyone else. I don't think she had any friends other than my dad. I remember in fifth grade I had 'alienate' as a spelling word. We also had to write the definition. One definition was 'to withdraw from the world.' It described my mom perfectly, which is why I probably remember it so well. From then on, I called her my alien mother. Not to her face, mind you."

Charlene giggled. "Oh, that's funny. In my family, I was the alien. I never felt like I fit in. But I reckon they both did the best they could, don't you think?"

"I suppose so. Since we're having this heart-to-heart, I need to tell someone, and here you are."

Charlene glanced at Nancy. "Tell me what?"

Nancy took a deep breath and sighed. "Ted's having an affair."

"*What?* Are you kidding me?"

"Eh." Nancy shrugged. "He says she's simply a friend, but that's what they all say."

"Oh, Nancy, I am *awfully* sorry to hear that."

"She lives alone and every day he brings her food. He wanted me to meet her."

"Good night. Your husband sounds half-baked to me. What did you say?"

"I asked what she has that I don't have? He said they have things in common. He hunts big game; she hunts small game. I sometimes hunt with Ted, but I guess he thinks she's a better hunter than me. Oh, and they're both artists in their spare time. He's a taxidermist; she weaves the most amazing, intricate designs ever. Puke. I'm no artist!"

"Hey, it's okay, Nancy. I'm here for you." Charlene touched her companion's arm.

Nancy sniffed and dabbed her eyes with the sleeve of her sweatshirt. "Thanks. I don't know what he sees in her. She spends most of the day curled up in a corner, except when there's food."

"How weird is that?" Charlene hit the brakes hard to make a sharp right turn. "Sorry, almost missed the turn."

"Actually, that one I get, because when someone brings me food, I perk up too. What I think is weird is that at night she hangs upside down in the center of her home."

"Like in one of those anti-gravity contraptions I've seen advertised? I've thought about getting one, because gravity sure is playing a number on me. Plus it's supposed to help your back."

"I'm probably beyond help when it comes to gravity." Nancy cupped her breasts, bounced them a couple times, then let them flop back down. "The worst part of all is that Ted says she's a good housekeeper. Like I'm not. I know I'm not the best housekeeper, unless company is coming over, then I'm a girl on fire. Know what I mean?"

"Your housekeeping is fine. An immaculate house is the sign of a misspent life. I read that somewhere."

"Yeah, well, the biggest difference between her and me is that when her house is a wreck, she doesn't break into a sweat and get all stressed out like I do." Nancy looked at Charlene and tried to keep a straight face. *"She eats it and makes a new one."*

Charlene frowned at Nancy. "Say that again? She eats it and makes a new one? Now you're pulling my leg."

"I am!" Nancy threw her head back and laughed. "We call her Charlotte. She's a cat-faced orb-weaver spider, like in *Charlotte's Web.*"

"God, I'm gullible!" Charlene smacked her forehead with the heel of her hand. "Not sure if I want to punch you for leading me on or hug you for making me laugh. I *do* know I've changed my mind. *You're* the half-baked one!"

Nancy grinned. "She builds her web in the corner of our French doors. We're, like, inches from her. She's the coolest thing to watch. I can't stand spiders, but I am fascinated with her."

"Oh, like Wilbur. He was hesitant of Charlotte at first, but quickly grew to like her."

"I still don't like spiders, but Charlotte is the exception. Ted will catch a little moth and throw it in the web. She runs over to get it, hangs on with one or two legs, and wraps it in a cocoon, after she injects it with poison, of course, to eat later or suck the blood, I guess. Thanks to Ted, she's a fat little thing. I swear her body is the size of my thumbnail. I could tell you more but looks like we're here."

Charlene pulled off the street and over the strip that rang a bell inside the store. A man came out to greet them and lifted the boxes from the back of the SUV and onto the loading dock. Nancy retrieved her container from the backseat.

When all had been unloaded, Charlene grinned. "I admit you had me going, you nut. I was going to pay for ice cream while we were out. Now I'm not so sure."

"Are you serious? You drive, *I'll* pay."

CHAPTER 5:
MEET THE SASSY SISTAS

Another sleepless night. Meissa tumbled out of bed and stumbled to the kitchen, groggily tripping over Flekk on her way.

"Good morning, to you too." The Bengal cat flicked her tail and meowed loudly in protest.

Meissa felt like she'd been hit by a Scrambler after yesterday, spewing out almost everything she'd learned to her supervisor. She poured herself a cup of black coffee.

Flekk sauntered up to Meissa's leg. "Hey, where's my breakfast? A cat cannot live on fancy water alone."

"Sorry, Flekk-baby, coming right up." Meissa slid a bowl into the food printer and programmed it to prepare flaked tuna topped with cream gravy. She downed a second cup of coffee and began to feel somewhat better.

During the night she'd come up with a plan to speed up the inventory on the Bayer household. She'd gone through the first bin at the archives, but there were hundreds more. Her twin brother's hobby was building androids—she would borrow two from him.

Meissa knew that Marcus built redundancy into each operating system to guard against failure. He would tell her she only needed one machine, but she was taking no chances. Two androids, working simultaneously, would finish the inventory faster and more accurately than any human. They didn't need breaks—they didn't get distracted from their assigned task.

She picked up her comm-cell and began to dictate her message: "Dear brother, I need you—" Oh drat, she'd accidently touched send.

"No you don't," he responded.

"I meant to say, I need your droids."

"For what?"

"An inventory on the Bayer belongings. After the river trip their household goods were packed up and put into storage and never cataloged. What if one day a museum was built in their honor? Wouldn't you want to know what's in the collection? It's all still in the basement of the National History Archives. I'm going to do an inventory and at the same time look for anything that might give me a clue to solving the gateway issue. I started the first bin but too much for me or my staff to finish. I want two of your droids to complete the work."

"Why mine?"

"I'd have to ask the procurement department for droids and wait for approval. Then they'd send them to programming and I'd wait some more.

Take a long time to go through the system. In a hurry. Want them bad."

"How bad?"

"Real bad. Like right now."

"Give me today and tonight. Can't get 'em to you any faster. Meet me at the History Archives tomorrow morning. 10 o'clock?"

"Wow, sure. Thanks, Bro. I'll send the archive authorization code to your comm-cell pronto."

Meissa looked up from her cell. That was easy. Almost too easy.

Marcus Shining, who had the perfect droids to loan his sister, also had his own reasons for accessing the Bayer storage units. He was a member of the Freedom Jumpers, an underground league dedicated to bringing D'Gnome and Earth's populations together in a peaceful manner. Erma Bayer was its founding member, so consequently, the group had been assisting the Bayers during their incarceration. Harold Bayer had asked Marcus to recover a holo-drive troll that belonged to Erma. It had been hidden in the archives for fifty years, and now the time had come to retrieve it. Marcus hadn't yet determined how to gain entry—one could not enter without authorization. Now the opportunity had fallen right into his lap. Maybe he should have put up more of a fight. That's what his sister would have expected.

Oftentimes Marcus questioned how they could be twins, but he'd heard plenty of parents describe their kids as night and day. Typical sibling rivalry was how their childish behavior had been described. Now in their forties, Meissa was high-strung, he easygoing, and their sibling rivalry was as strong as ever. Neither was married nor had children; both had blue eyes and jet-black hair, although Meissa's was currently dyed blue. And they both had been Senior Superlatives in their high school days—top of their class. That was the end of their commonalities.

Marcus was a mechanical engineer by trade and a dreamer by nature, and he'd always had big dreams. From an early age, he had been fascinated with all things mechanical, the more intricate the better. His ambition rewarded him with the title of head of global transportation. His department designed and created mass transit and commercial transports for travel around planet D'Gnome and to its nearest and only inhabited moon, Gansarcal. While a penitentiary was on the far side, three huge vacation resort biodomes were in the works for the near side. Marcus's department had already designed and built a prototype to ferry guests.

Second only to his interest in sleeker and faster spacecraft were his beloved androids and their interaction with people. It amazed him how far artificial intelligence had come. And his singing girl group, the Sassy Sistas, was living proof. Well, living was maybe going a bit too far.

How fortuitous, then, that his androids would do the work he could not. Meissa wanted two, but she'd get three, solely to annoy her. He'd tell her one could not work without the other two. On such short notice, he had nothing else credible to offer. With some tweaking, it would not take him long to give Meissa what she wanted and a smidgeon of what she didn't. He was always getting her arse out of hot water without much appreciation. He got back at her in his own way once in a while, like with the Sassy Sistas. If you want it bad, you'll get it bad—real bad. Well, not bad enough to jeopardize her job. They both wanted an accurate inventory, but he laughed, knowing the quirky personalities he had given his girls would irritate her.

The next morning, Meissa called for a Scrambler to pick her up from home and take her to the National History Archive building. At ten sharp Meissa walked through the doors of the archives. She flashed her ID badge at the sentry as she rushed past. He did not stop her, so she proceeded to the open elevator. Upon entering, her voice commanded the door to close, and it dropped her quickly to the lowest level.

When the elevator door opened, she stepped into a cavernous area with dark, rough-cut stone walls, high ceilings, and three arched doors, over which Directory signs hung. From her previous visit, when she had discovered Erma's diary, she knew the storage section she wanted was to her left. The door gave way when she shoved it, and motion-sensor lights brightly illuminated the pathway. She could see her twin and his androids in the distance.

Marcus introduced the Sassy Sistas to Meissa. Saffron, the tall, curvaceous droid, with skin the color of cream, wore a red-bedazzled, tight-fitting cocktail dress and a black mullet wig. When she heard her name, she stepped forward with a "Hello-o-o!" in the key of C.

Slightly shorter and thinner than Saffron, Sojourner wore the same style dress that glittered blue over her cocoa-brown skin. She tossed her dark brown wavy locks over her shoulder and greeted Meissa with a "Hello-o-o!" in the key of E.

The smallest of all, but not too small—for she had a big voice—was Sagan. Her smile was as bright as her blunt bob, which matched her sequined dress and spring green skin. "Hello-o-o!" sang Sagan in the key of G.

In perfect harmony, they sang, "We are glad to meet you." The Sassy Sistas bowed.

Marcus applauded, while Meissa stood unmoved, looking disgusted. "Not dressed for dirty work, are they?"

"I don't have a change of clothes for them, but their costumes will not interfere with their work. I have no intention of screwing up your inventory."

"Do we need the leprechaun?" Meissa sneered. "I only wanted two."

The Sistas took a collective step backwards at hearing the slight.

"Take 'em or leave 'em—they're all I've got right now. Each is programmed for a job: identify, analyze, and record. One will not work without the others. And you owe Sagan an apology."

"She's a droid, Marcus. Why would you even give them human names? They aren't your friends. They have no feelings. They're artificial entities." Curses. The androids were working for her, yet she had no control over them. Damn her brother.

"Look, do you want my help or not? You'd better show more appreciation or I'm walking out and taking Sojourner, Saffron, and Sagan with me."

Huffs were heard from the Sistas.

"Fine. I apologize." Meissa couldn't help but roll her eyes. It was an artificial apology to artificially intelligent machines.

Marcus shook his head. "Forget it. We're all here. Let's get on with it."

Meissa took a deep breath and sighed. "Thanks for the droids. I really do need them and appreciate the loan."

"You're welcome."

She was not one to confide in her brother, but found herself saying, "I'll be nicer since you're doing me a huge favor." She smiled at her brother, but, honestly, she couldn't seem to shake this bad mood. "Dr. Euse is no fun to work for, that's for sure."

"I hear you. Lots of stories swirling around about her being unstable."

"I haven't worked for her very long, but there's definitely something going on with her. Don't have time to worry about it right now. Have you figured out how to call down the bins?"

"Trying to when you came in. The podium here has a screen with a directory. I typed in the Bayer name, and a list of container labels came up. That's as far as I got."

"The letter-number combination listed is the location. Oral commands will work. This system is old enough that it will also recognize artificial voices, so the droids shouldn't have a problem—I researched that before I asked for your help. Let's start with the one I already did, so you can show the androids." She pressed the activate button on the podium and called out in a louder tone: "D19L55."

The cogs and wheels stubbornly creaked alive and brought forward the bin identified as D19L55. It dropped onto the floor with a loud clunk, and the airtight lid popped open. A foul odor met their nostrils.

"Hoo!" Marcus waved his hand in front of his face.

"Yeah, this stuff was from their fateful river trip and obviously wasn't cleaned before they stored it." She would not tell her brother that she knew the Bayers hadn't died on that trip or that the bin was missing Erma's diary. "I've looked through it, but the androids should start with this container, so the contents can be added to the inventory database. Have them take everything out, record it, and put it all back. If you can take it from here, I've got to go."

"Yup, I'll add code, show them what needs to be done, and they'll be set. See ya tomorrow."

"Bye and thanks again."

Meissa didn't like droids. They creeped her out. In her experience, androids could be unpredictable, especially since they had become so independent. Machines with artificial intelligence, absorbing enough information through trial and error, could learn without human programming. Androids could form their own opinions and make decisions. Her brother's droids were old stock, because he was a cheap sucker and purchased his hobby droids from the recycle depot, but they were highly capable after he'd refurbished them. He would have updated their central processing units—basically their brains—to perform a task, in most cases, just by explaining it to them.

Through a methodical process of elimination, she was hoping to find old notebooks or memory cards, anything that might hold clues to the creation of the gateways. If nothing useful panned out in the Bayer collection, she would somehow question Erma Bayer personally. She wished Euse could see that talking to Erma would be the logical solution if nothing else worked to fix the gateways. The recovery team had tried everything they could, but nothing was keeping them online. Why wouldn't Erma have suggestions, since she was the one who created them? Made sense to Meissa. There must be something else going on with the Bayers that she didn't know about that caused Euse to forbid a visitation.

The androids had been working a full day, but Meissa had barely given a cursory glance at the inventory file. It was updated in real time as the Sassy Sistas made headway, listing each bin's ID number and contents. She was curious to see the actual physical activity of each bin being emptied, cataloged, and the items returned. So on her way home from work she couldn't resist a stop at the National History Archives to watch the droids in action.

The last two times to the archives, Meissa had run through the front doors and barely paid attention to who was behind the guard desk. This late afternoon she was in no particular hurry, and as she strolled past the desk she noticed the unkempt appearance of the burly man. Human Resources was scraping the bottom of the barrel for employees these days. Stringy black hair hung a couple of inches below the ballcap that shadowed his eyes. A thick, dark brown mustache curled at the corner of his lips, and a long beard covered the rest of his face. His olive-drab shirt and pants were stained with grease, and a sharp, offensive odor assaulted her sense of smell. The archives were closed to the public, so she imagined there wasn't a lot of traffic through these halls, but couldn't the man clean up some? She was glad when she reached the elevator.

From outside the vast environs of the storage area, she cracked open the door and paused a moment to listen to the Sassy Sistas' chatter.

"Dusty!"

"Musty!"

"Fusty!"

"Stale and unclean smelling."

"Smelling? Can you smell? I can't smell."

"I can smell. Can't you smell?"

"Who can't smell? I can smell."

"I smell stale and moldy and fusty!"

"Dusty!"

"Musty!"

"Fiddlesticks, we appear to be in a loop."

"Must reboot."

Each Sista gestured with her hands like bird beaks, then tucked them under her armpits, flapped her elbows, shook her booty, and clapped four times. This was not a normal android reboot. They looked like chickens, and Meissa knew this was Marcus's sick sense of humor. They were correct, though, the air was musty. She hadn't noticed that earlier, but then she had been preoccupied. It was the bin she remembered as having a musty scent. Meissa decided not to bother them and left the machines to continue their labors. She made her way out of the archive building and into a waiting Scrambler, musing how she could possibly contact Erma and Harold Bayer, who would be under constant guard.

CHAPTER 6:
IT'S COMPLICATED

"Did you sense someone, Sistas?"

"I sensed duplicity!"

"Hypocrisy!"

"Truckery! I mean trickery! This dust is affecting my circuitry."

"She's gone."

"Departed."

"Back to work, Sistas. Open bin M19K71."

The container scraped its way to the forefront and noisily descended to the floor.

"Dolls."

"Pretty dolls."

"Very pretty dolls." Each one passed from Saffron to Sagan to Sojourner to be identified, analyzed, and recorded to the database.

"Here's an odd one." Saffron held up a miniature naked doll with a mess of upswept neon orange hair. The rubber toy was completely out of character from what had been cataloged from the container's contents. At the utterance of the key word "odd," one of numerous words to immediately halt the data entry, Sagan stopped recording. The inventory would not restart until the next object was picked up to be identified.

"Peculiar."

"Truly uncommon. What is it?"

"My scanner identifies it as a three-dimensional character called a troll. Three inches long . . . made from flexible silicone material," said Saffron.

"Does a troll roll?" Sagan asked. She pulled the toy from Saffron's hand. The doll split in half.

"Oh no! You broke it!" said Saffron.

"Unquestionably, *you* broke it!"

Sojourner stepped between the two. "Indubitably, Sistas, it is broken. But look!"

"Ooh," cooed the sparing Sistas, as everyone stared at a family image that came into focus in front of them.

"It seems the troll is not a doll after all; therefore, it is not broken," said Sojourner.

"Lucky for you, Sagan."

"Lucky for you, Saffron."

"Lucky for all of us. Carry on before we fail completely," said Sojourner.

"Appears to be a mass data storage device cleverly implanted into a silicone figurine. The holo-drive contains photographic images and videos with vocal narrative by Harold and Erma Bayer," said Saffron.

"I think we have a keeper," said Sojourner.

Sagan dropped her half of the troll doll into Saffron's outstretched hand and said, "Think? Can you think? I can't think."

"I can think. Can't you think?"

"Who can't think? I think I can think."

"If we can think, what shall we think?"

"I think we have a keeper."

"Oh shoot."

"Another loop."

"Reboot."

They did their chicken dance and with their operating systems refreshed once more, Sojourner lifted her sequined dress to touch her exposed thigh. A cavity appeared. The two sisters tossed their troll pieces in, and the orifice sealed shut. Any outward evidence of a compartment completely disappeared.

After cataloging the rest of the container, the dolls were returned to M19K71—all but the troll. Saffron called for the next bin, and their work continued as if nothing unusual had occurred.

Having finished his work for the day, Marcus Shining reclined in his office chair with his feet on the desk and brought up a holographic screen to view his androids. He had implanted tiny cameras and microphones in the Sassy Sistas' eyes, allowing him to see what they were seeing and to hear their conversation and any other sounds around them.

On the left side of the split screen, he could see the Sistas were in the midst of children's toys, specifically dolls. The right side displayed the actual inventory database. No one except Marcus could remotely see the droids in action, but he had given his sister permission to read the inventory file from any holographic screen she used.

When Saffron selected a doll and recognized it as "odd," Marcus's feet smacked the floor, while, at the same time, a warning signal blared on his personal comm-cell attached to his wrist. He swatted the cell to stop the alarm, gaping at the screen in front of him. The droids had pulled the object apart to discover a holo-drive. Jackpot! This is what he'd been looking for! A small toy troll with orange hair. He presumed the drive held more than family photos or he wouldn't have been asked to keep it hidden, but Harold had not divulged the exact contents.

After hiding the holo-drive troll, the androids continued where they had left off, closing and returning M19K71, then requesting the next bin. He had worried about adding more detailed description, like specific type of doll or its hair color, but he didn't want to give too much away. Some hacker was always around the corner. He breathed a sigh of relief. His instructions to the Sistas had worked. They had identified the troll as odd, and the recording stopped.

Each line in the database was an item belonging to Erma and Harold Bayer. Everything had been packed, from cutlery to underwear, and stored in hundreds of containers. When the recording stopped, all that had been entered on the particular line in question was the bin label (M19K71) and the category (child's toy). The description was missing, which is what Meissa would notice. The next line was complete and contained a new entry with the same bin label and category and a specific description of the item.

Despite his haste, he should have added a command to delete lines related to his key words. If Marcus deleted the partial line entry manually now, anyone reading the file could detect the edit. Deleting it manually would definitely look suspicious. Better to let it go. He would come up with some excuse to justify his slipup. That's what happens when you rush. It wasn't 100% perfect. He supposed "if you want it bad, you'll get it bad" worked both ways.

He needed to retrieve the troll before Meissa concluded something was missing. At the front entrance to his office building, Marcus hailed a Scrambler and requested the National History Archives.

The same scruffy guard who had been at the desk when he'd brought the Sistas waved him on as he ran to the elevator. In the basement, he called to his three friends. "Hello, ladies! How are you?"

"I am defective."

"Feeling substandard."

"Feeling faulty."

"Feeling? Can you feel? I can't feel."

"I can feel. Can't you feel?"

"Who can't feel? I can feel."

"I am defective. Oh shoot."

"Cannot compute."

"Reboot."

Restored after their subsequent dance, Sojourner asked, "Why so many restarts, Marcus?"

"And what's with these loops?" asked Saffron.

"Are we loopy?" asked Sagan.

Spontaneous reboots were an uncommon occurrence. He wrinkled his brow. "Hmm, sounds like a flaw in your interface, maybe in the speech pattern I've initiated to irritate Meissa. I promise to examine it. Can you cope with the pattern and restarts a tad longer?"

"I don't think we have a choice."

"Think? Can you think? I can't think."

"I can think. Can't you think?"

"Who can't think? I think I can—"

"I see this is difficult for you," said Marcus. He issued a command to resume their original language pattern, a normal human cadence with complete sentences, not the repetitive, staccato quips. The Sistas sighed with relief.

"It's exhausting," Sojourner admitted.

"I am exhausted. Are you exhausted?" Saffron asked Sagan.

"Very exhausted. I may be a machine, but I have feelings." Sagan immediately realized what she'd said. "Don't start."

"I can't seem to stop. Can you feel?" responded Sojourner.

Marcus scratched his chin, prodding his mind as to what he missed with the code. "I can't seem to stop it either. Have you run a self-diagnostic?"

"Affirmative."

"Looking for bugs."

"I hate bugs. Bugs are bad."

"Not all bugs are bad."

"True, Sista, some are, some are not."

"Like people, some are bad, some are not."

"People are not necessarily bad; they just do bad things. My mother told me that."

"You don't have a mother."

"You don't have a mother, either."

"Oh, we don't have a mother. I feel sad." Sagan frowned. "Oh-oh."

Marcus also frowned. "I am totally at a loss as to what's going on. I'll research your speech some more and work on your frequent reboots too. After I retrieve the holo-drive, I'm going to deactivate you for a brief period." He entered a shutdown command into his comm-cell. The Sistas stood straight, arms by their sides, and closed their eyes.

Marcus surveyed the neatly folded clothing on the floor. Looked like a container from a closet had been opened. To double-check the accuracy of what the girls had inventoried from the open bin, he compared the list of contents on the holo-screen to what had been removed from the bin. As he picked each folded item up, he flung the piece aside after finding it on the list.

"Aha!" he said aloud, as he closed the screen with a flourish. He had an idea on how to explain the partial line entry to Meissa. He knew she would suspect something had gone awry, but he could not tell her the cataloging had stopped for the one item he was looking for. He *could* say the androids had been affected by the faulty ventilation system, since it seemed, in fact, to be faulty.

He'd tell her he had immediately gone to the archives when he saw the database error and had found nothing amiss with the physical inventory. So far, so good. He would even report the uncirculated air to building maintenance. There really was a problem with the air in the basement. Although it would not have affected the droids, he'd say it may have. Yes. Meissa would not be the wiser. He hoped.

So much for hope. Marcus got a call from his twin early the next morning. Meissa was in the archive's basement.

"Hey, it was a minor glitch caused by the inadequate air quality. You can't deny the air is unfiltered. You're there, can't you smell it? The error might be caused by a droid's short circuit, due to the harsh environment. I may have to rewrite the interface or change out some hardware. It's complicated, Meissa."

"Complicated? *Complicated?*" Meissa shouted into her comm-cell. "There is nothing complicated about this! Get over here!"

When Marcus met his antagonist in the dank storage vault, he found it difficult not to laugh at his sister in all her blue fury, standing in the middle of a pile of clothing, the items the Sistas had folded after they'd taken them out of the bin to catalog. He'd not bothered to refold them, but had tossed them around instead. He ached to pick up a hot pink broad-brimmed straw hat and shove it on her head to tame those spikes.

Meissa's arms were spread wide. "Marcus, how did this happen?"

"What, this?"

"Please don't act so innocent," she pleaded. "I can't take much more incompetency. This was not caused by bad air, brother dear. We have robots and droids that do everything under the sun for us in all types of conditions. This wasn't a difficult task. Something stinks here, and it's not this room. Well, this room does stink, but the mistakes those droids made are yours. Garbage in, garbage out."

Ouch, that was a low blow. He'd take her criticism of his coding skills, because if he weren't careful, she could give the job to her office minions. For curiosity's sake, if there were anything else of interest, he wanted to find it before his sister which was why, instead of focusing only on the troll, he had included other search words in case more curious artifacts were in the bins.

"As soon as I saw the incomplete entry, I came down and went through everything. The mess of clothes is mine. There was no inaccuracy on their part. And I've already made a report to maintenance for building repairs. I'm going to do a full diagnostic on the Sistas tonight and will have them up and running by tomorrow morning. They will redo this container, clean up the mess, and finish the job. I promise it won't happen again. Agreed?"

"Make sure it doesn't." She turned on her heels and marched off.

Good riddance. He had found Erma Bayer's holo-drive. That's all that mattered.

CHAPTER 7:
LONG TIME NO SEE

At the Intergalactic Research Institute's portal wing, Rigel O'Rion stepped into the cylindrical chamber digitally labeled Collinsville, Wyoming. He felt tingling throughout his body, as his atoms separated and he journeyed through a cosmic tunnel, becoming whole again as he passed through his destination's portal in the backstage crossover of Collins High School's auditorium. Unbeknownst to the young actors who used the crossover to move between stage left and stage right, the crossover also received D'Gnoman travelers.

Drapery hung on both sides of the corridor, providing a backdrop for the audience and covering a concrete wall from ceiling to floor. At center stage was an invisible 3x7-foot energy field in the concrete wall. Only D'Gnomans felt the magnetic pull as they neared. When entered into by the traveler, the portion of the physical wall that was the portal dissolved into a shimmering opening before solidifying once the traveler passed through.

School was out for the summer; Rigel stood alone in the crossover. It took several seconds for his equilibrium to return and his eyes to focus in the darkness. An exit sign provided dim illumination as he made his way along the curtained concrete wall at the back of the empty stage into an adjacent alcove. He opened the door to a wide hallway lined with lockers. At the opposite end of the hallway was a frenzy of construction activity. Engrossed in their work, no one noticed him slip out a side door.

Standing under the late-morning August sun, he gazed at the crenellations atop the towering front entrance. Collins High had always been the grandest building in the city—a classic example of Collegiate Gothic-style architecture. He was relieved to see the façade of the original building unchanged. The new additions were all glass and steel. No life in them, no verve. Simply cold, straight, emotionless lines.

When a student, ready to commence his Earth Study Program, Rigel had selected Collinsville from a list of participating portals. Even as a smart-alecky kid of seventeen, he'd had a serious interest in economics. Collinsville seemed a good location for his chosen study thesis on the boom and bust of the oil fields. He also had picked this town because his sister, Saiph, and her best friend, Trixie Bayer, had completed their Senior Superlative course here two years earlier.

Millicent McGilly's parents hosted the students, and when they relinquished their program sponsorship, Milly and her husband, William, inherited the trusted relationship with the D'Gnomans. They had received one or two students each school year for the Earth Study Program until William's death, prompting Milly to resign from sponsoring. Officials had already been contemplating the closure of Collinsville, Wyoming, a small western town in the United States' least-populated state. It was not considered a high priority. Still, the portal, which had been a dedicated D'Gnoman student gateway, remained available.

He called Milly to let her know he was in Collinsville for a visit. He knew she'd be surprised, but not this hysterical. Laughing, he held the phone two feet from his ear and could still hear her exclamations.

"Rigel O'Rion! I can't believe this! I haven't heard from you in . . . I don't know . . . how long's it been?"

"Close to fifteen years."

There was a pause, then Milly said, "That's right. William died ten years ago, and it was several years before that when you last stopped by. I can't believe you're here!"

"Wish I could have given you more notice, but we still haven't figured out how to make an impossibly long-distance call to a private citizen on Earth. I have to wait 'til I get here to revert to your outdated technology." He laughed again in a deep, resonant tone.

"I'm not blaming you. It's so good to hear your voice! Will you be around for a while? I am at this very minute sitting in my dentist's parking lot, and I'd feel bad cancelling this late."

"I'm not leaving until I see you, so do whatever you have to do. I'll be here."

"Lord-a-mighty, I won't be able to sit still for a cleaning. They'll wonder what's wrong with me. Wait for me! I'll be home in an hour."

"I'll hang at the library 'til you're through."

The county library was a few blocks from the high school and a block from Milly's apartment building. He had spent many hours there his senior year. It was too hot to walk very fast, so he removed his jacket, loosened his tie, and took his time looking around. Nothing seemed to have changed much in this area, besides the school.

Entering the cool library, he slipped his jacket back on. It didn't surprise Rigel that he was rather out of place wearing a business suit on a summer day in this casual atmosphere. He *was* surprised, though, to encounter his assignment so soon after arriving in Collinsville.

Nancy Leopold was standing in a self-checkout line when he first saw her. There was no need for a picture. She was the exact image of her mother, right down to the freckles on her nose and cheeks. Rigel guessed her to be about 5 feet 8 inches, taller than her mother by three inches. Her hair was a darker red than Trixie's, but there was no mistaking her identity.

He sent her a telepathic signal, similar to a ping a computer sends when testing a connection. Her reception was good, he reasoned, when she ran her fingers through her hair. Nancy turned to look at him. He smiled. She adjusted her eyeglasses and focused her attention on the older gentleman in front of her who was waving his library card every which way but right.

"Seems like everyone is busy," Nancy said. "Can I help you with this?"

"Thank you. I always have problems with these things. A librarian used to be behind the counter. Now we talk to machines."

"Budget cuts I suppose. I have difficulty with this sometimes too. Let me see if I can get it to work." He handed her his card and a DVD. She showed him how to use the self-service machine. When the title appeared on the screen, she printed his receipt and handed it to him with the movie. "Here you go."

"Thank you, young lady." He returned her smile. Leaning on his cane, he shuffled through the automated sliding door.

Nancy repeated the process with her book, ignoring Rigel, and left the building.

Rigel read a few more front flaps of the new mystery books on display, then walked the short distance to Milly's apartment complex. Standing outside, he phoned her to say he was at the front door. It wasn't long before the door flew open and he was greeted with an enthusiastic hug. Electricity coursed through him. Maybe he *should* have made up an excuse to stay home and insisted someone else do this.

She was as pretty and petite as he'd remembered. The single difference was her short, soft, black curls, were now streaked with white, like salt and pepper. Her coffee-colored eyes, flecked with gold, were sharp and glittering with mischief. Her emerald midi-dress darted around her lithe, ebony body, reminding him of how light and carefree she was, yet he knew that, like an ocean, she had the strength of an undertow.

"Rigel O'Rion, it is so good to see you!" Milly shook her head in disbelief.

"Millicent McGilly, you're as pretty as the first day I saw you."

"Rigel, I was ten when you first saw me. Don't fool with me!"

"And I was seventeen."

"Well, get in here, old man. Elevator's waitin'." Milly beckoned with her arm. "And don't call me Millicent—I'm still Milly to you."

On the short ride to the sixth floor, Milly reached up to touch Rigel's chin. "What's this?"

"Like it?" He stroked his well-trimmed goatee.

"I do." The doors swished open, and Milly led him down the hallway to her apartment. "Come on in. We'll have lunch and a cold drink."

Rigel settled into a white wooden chair at the butcher-block dining table. The yellow walls and white curtains decorated with ripe strawberries brightened the kitchen. A calico cat sauntered in to scrutinize the racket. Approving, she rubbed the visitor's leg.

"Who's this?" Rigel scratched the calico's head.

"Cinnamon. She likes you."

"No shocker. I'm a nice guy, huh, Cinnamon?"

"What a wonderful gift to hear from you this morning. Too bad I had a dental cleaning scheduled or we could have gotten this party started sooner."

"No problem. Had a noteworthy encounter at the library while I waited."

"You'll have to tell me, but first, how does ham and Swiss on rye sound?"

"Anything you make is fine with me."

"It's too hot to cook," Milly said, as she assembled the fixings for lunch. "I've got cherry-chocolate chip ice cream for dessert."

"Haven't been here ten minutes and you're already spoiling me. Wasn't expecting you to feed me, but I do appreciate it. Impressed you remembered cherry-chocolate chip was my favorite."

"I didn't. It happens to be *my* favorite!"

Rigel chuckled. "How can I help?"

"Sit there and relax. This won't take a minute. On second thought, you can pour the lemonade. Glasses in that cupboard, ice in the freezer."

Rigel jumped up to do Milly's bidding. "How you been doin'?"

"All right. Some say age is a state of mind. Got aches and pains I never used to have, but I keep pluggin' away."

"Wish I could have visited you in person now and then after William died, but my travel was restricted."

"Figured it was something like that. Sometimes ten years feels like yesterday, and sometimes I feel I've been alone a long time. Willy had one more year until he planned to retire when we got the diagnosis of stage four pancreatic cancer. The doctor suspected it was his gall bladder and scheduled surgery, but when they went in, there was nothing they could do—no chemo, no radiation, nothing. Closed him back up and said to put our affairs in order." Milly reached for a pickle jar and slammed the refrigerator door shut, rattling everything inside.

"That must have been awful for you."

"Six weeks. Six weeks was all we had, the last two in hospice care. That's how fast it took him. How can that be? There was so much he wanted to do." Milly dabbed her eyes with a paper towel. "I've mostly let go of the anger. I know God and Willy would not want me to be angry, but I can't always let go of the sadness and shock of it all. We had so little time left. Whatever you do, don't take life for granted. It can fly in the blink of an eye."

"We lost a great man. Our hearts were filled with sorrow. Everyone who knew him, loved him."

The cloud lifted as quickly as it had descended. "They surely did." Milly set two plates on the table, with a pickle spear and baby carrots next to each sandwich. "I was born and raised here, but I met Willy at college in Laramie. We both wanted to be teachers. He was from Gulfport, Mississippi, and had received a football scholarship to UW. We waited until I graduated before we got married, and, of course, moved back here. I knew one day I would take over my parents' sponsorship role. We were lucky to both get teaching jobs. Sorry to be rambling on like this."

"Nothing to be sorry about. Go on, Mill. If you have things you haven't talked about in a while, then I'm happy to sit here and listen."

"Oh, I'll shut up. But being a black couple in a mainly white town sometimes had its challenges. We got through them together. He was so easy-going and exuded such an upbeat personality that it didn't matter who you were, most ended up liking him. It helped being involved in the community like he was, not only with school, but with coaching and mentoring kids in need. I never saw a more positive person."

"He was well-respected as a chemistry teacher. I was lucky to be the liaison for Senior Superlative students and see his antics at a few football and basketball games. He definitely knew how to work the crowd."

"Willy was quite a character, wasn't he?" Milly's eyes twinkled, remembering those shenanigans. "His students thought it was wild that our names rhymed. One of his science students was taking a woodshop class and made an engraved frame for him." She pointed to a living room wall covered in photographs. Burned into an oak-stained wooden frame were the words *Willy's McGillys.* Inside was an 8x10 photograph of the McGilly family—Willy, Milly, Billy and Lilly—on an observation deck of the Eiffel Tower from their one trip to Europe.

Rigel went over to get a closer look. "Beautiful picture. How are the kids?"

"Billy's an audiologist in Savannah, Georgia. Don't get to see him and Juliette and their two boys as often as I'd like, but the kids like Savannah. Lilly didn't have the portrait studio yet when I saw you last. She's doing well right here in Collinsville. And my granddaughters, Villy and Nilly, take good care of their granny."

"Really? Don't recall that your granddaughters' names rhymed."

"Heck, just messin' with you! Elizabeth's a junior at CHS; Brianna graduated UW with a journalism degree and works for a bridal magazine in Denver. Their names are as far away from rhyming as you can get. Lilly got enough of that growing up. You don't realize what you put your kids through until it's too late. How's your sister?" Milly asked.

"Saiph volunteers at a hospital in the neonatal unit, holding babies. She wanted to come, but knee problems are keeping her incapacitated for now."

"Doesn't get any better than cuddling babies." Milly smiled. "Whenever we said 'be safe' to someone, she'd say, 'Don't be me, be yourself.' She thought that was pretty funny. Isn't that something? I can remember that line but not what I had for breakfast yesterday. Give her my regards, will you? And what about you? Married?"

"Nah, seems a little late."

"Rigel! It's never too late for love."

"Oh? You got someone in mind?" He lifted an eyebrow and flashed her a sideways glance.

"No, I do not!" Milly emphasized every word. "Willy said before he died that I had his blessing if I found someone new to love. I haven't found anyone to suit my soul, and I'm perfectly happy the way things are."

After finishing their ice cream, the two moved into the living room, bringing a fresh refill of lemonade with them. Rigel claimed the sofa corner, stretching out his long legs; Milly sat in her rocker/recliner. Catching up on years gone by took most of the afternoon. Milly was the first to get to the reason for Rigel's visit. "You didn't want to say much on the phone this morning. What is so important that you need my help?"

"Remember Trixie Bayer? She was the exchange student living with your family along with Saiph. You were eight about then."

Millie smacked her cheeks. "Oh my, I do. She had the prettiest red hair, and did I ever want red hair. So badly that when no one was lookin', I dissolved cherry Jell-O in a bowl of cold water and soaked my head in it."

"What a sight that must have been!"

"More like a sticky mess! I got into big trouble over that caper." Milly giggled. "My mother would not let that story go. God rest her soul."

"If it's not too late for love, it's not too late for red hair," Rigel said in a teasing voice.

"Shoot, I see women my age all over the place with cherry red hair, even blue or purple." Milly swiped her hand in the air dismissing the idea. "Not for me though. What about Trixie?"

"Your guess is as good as mine as to her hair color."

"No, goofball. What's up with Trixie?"

Rigel took a big swig of lemonade. "After graduation, instead of returning to D'Gnome, Trixie eloped with a young man from CHS. She's been living in San Diego, California."

"You're kidding. Who'd she marry? Do I know him?"

"A guy in her class, James Herschel."

"Huh, doesn't ring a bell, but then I wouldn't have known many in the high school. So they eloped, huh? Bet that caused a ruckus. How's she still here? I thought your head would explode or something if you all stayed."

"No, not quite, but Trixie received an experimental drug that reduced the nepial gland in her brain. So, yeah, she's here."

"Seems like I should know this, but I can't recall what the nepial gland does."

"It's a sensory organ for thought transference. D'Gnomans have one, while it disappeared through evolution in Earth's human population. For some reason, while on Earth, the gland begins to swell and eventually causes death which is why you'll not see a D'Gnoman here longer than a year. Otherwise, we are the same in every way."

"So it is responsible for the mind reading you do so well."

"You got it. Telepathy is a skill we do not use lightly. D'Gnomans instinctively block their thoughts, but with others, like you, we will never intrude without permission."

"Well, that's reassuring."

From her tone of voice, Rigel wasn't sure it she wasn't being sarcastic, but he smiled. "Mill, I'm here to find out if Trixie knows anything about why our gateways would malfunction and if there's an answer to restoring them. It's believed that Trixie's mother, who was one of the scientists to create the gateways, may have given the design code to Trixie for safe-keeping. Highly unlikely, but I've got to speak with her."

"Why aren't you talking to her?"

"Long story. But because of the gateway fiasco, gossip is surfacing about Trixie's parents and their deaths, which we fear will eventually lead to questions about Trixie. She was the sole participant in a classified government longevity study, and if this knowledge became public, it could put her in jeopardy."

"Lordy be, Rigel. I can't possibly see what any of this has to do with me."

"You know Nancy Leopold, right?" He downed his glass of lemonade, wishing it contained something stronger than sugar and lemons.

Milly's jaw dropped. "Nancy *Leopold*? What does *she* have to do with this?"

Rigel leaned toward Milly, resting his elbows on his knees and clasping his hands. Then he said, in slow motion, "Nancy is Trixie's daughter."

Milly jumped up, startling Cinnamon from the room, and paced the floor. "Say what? Rigel, you can't be serious. Nancy is Trixie's daughter?" She put her fingertips to her temples. "Trixie is Nancy's mother?"

"Yup. That's why I'm in Collinsville. Trixie has always been uncooperative about communication with us. The government made an agreement with the Bayers that we wouldn't use force toward her. So the conclusion was that we may be more successful contacting her if we bring Nancy into the picture." He grinned. "How convenient to be in Collinsville on assignment and also have the pleasure of seeing you."

"Stop trying to butter me up!" She stopped pacing and stomped her foot, glaring at her guest. "You still haven't told me why *I* have to be involved."

"I want Nancy to convey to her mother that I have essential information to share with her and that we care about her."

"And how you gonna do that? Wait. Let me guess . . . you want me to talk to Nancy."

Rigel grinned.

"Stop smiling at me! You can't charm your way into me doin' this." She threw a magazine from the coffee table at him.

"You think I'm charming?" He ducked and smiled even wider, deepening his dimples.

"I think you're batty, Rigel O'Rion, that's what I think. What is it you want?"

"If you can set up a meeting with all three of us, I will do the talking. Don't mention me though."

"Oh, no. I haven't said I'd do anything! How would I bring up a subject like that? What would I *say*?"

"You won't have to say anything. I'll do the talking."

"You're assuming Trixie has never told Nancy where she's from?"

"No clue. It's a delicate situation, which is why we need you, someone who can verify what I say. Can you make up a reason to see her? A ride to a doctor's appointment perhaps?"

"I'll be needin' a doctor 'cause I'll be having a heart attack." Milly clutched her chest.

"Please say you're feigning. I didn't mean to upset you. I was never convinced this was a good idea."

Milly waved him off. "Get away. I'm fine. But this isn't going to be easy. If she doesn't know about her mother, how in the world are you gonna convince her? I'm nauseous thinkin' about it."

"Don't worry. All you have to do is set up the meeting. Please."

"Like where, Rigel? Where do you propose to have this meeting? A public place so she can freak out and cause a scene?"

"Hmm, in a public place. How about a restaurant over lunch? I bet she'd be less likely to get hysterical when she's enlightened of her extraterrestrial connection. Know what I'm sayin'?"

Milly sighed. "Unless she already knows."

"In that case, it'll be no more than a pleasant meal. Who knows. Nancy may be aware of your connection to D'Gnome and hasn't said any-thing."

"Huh-uh. If she knows I know, she would have said something already. We've known each other a long time."

"So what do you say?"

"I ain't sayin' nothin' yet. Nancy and I are friends, but we don't socialize, other than dance-related doings. She's gonna wonder why I'm askin' her to lunch and not Joan, as well."

"Who's Joan?"

"The other woman who's danced with us as long as we've been together."

"Oh. Well, make up some excuse why you need Nancy to pick you up. Lilly is out of town and your car's in the shop."

"Nancy knows my car. It sits in the parking lot, and she'd see it." Milly looked mischievously at Rigel. "But it *could* be in the shop. It needs a paint job."

"Perfect! I'll pay to get it painted and detailed too. What do you say?"

"Now you're talkin'. I should be getting some-thing out of this. Our annual dancers' dinner is this coming Saturday. I could ask her for a ride but doubt you can get the car scheduled that soon."

"I have my ways. You can count on it. I'll let you know the time, and you can call Nancy. I re-ally appreciate this."

"Don't be thanking me yet. Nancy's not gonna like being told her mother's an alien."

"Star person, Mill. Sounds better. That reminds me. I saw her this morning at the library. I made a connection. She doesn't comprehend it yet."

Milly glanced cockeyed at Rigel. "Humph. Can't wait 'til she does."

"It'll work out. Take a rest." Rigel pointed to the recliner. "Tell me about your tap dancing."

She performed a triple time step. "Ta-da!" She sank into the rocker. "Sounds better on a hard floor."

"Hmm, not bad."

"We're better than bad—we're bad *ass*," Milly quipped.

"What got you into tap dancing?"

"A year after Willy passed, friends told me I should get out more, maybe join a dating website. No way was that happening, but I joined a tap dance exercise class at the YMCA. Tap is supposed to keep the ol' grey matter healthy. That's where I met Nancy. When the Y quit teaching the class, we switched to a studio. We even do the recital at the end of the year with all the kids. It's a lot of fun."

Rigel put his fingertips to his temples and closed his eyes. "Ah, I see a beautiful woman in a tutu dancing across the stage."

"Well, that ain't me. And for your information, we don't wear tutus. Last year we wore a sequined little black dress. We compete too. Won a diamond award at our last competition. That's the highest award you can get."

"Whoa, let me finish. I'm imagining how beautiful you would be on stage whatever you're wearing. I'll be there."

"We'll see."

"I hate to say it, but I've got to get going."

"It's nearly dinnertime. You sure you don't want something to eat before you go?"

"I'm sure, but thanks again for lunch."

"You'll get back into the school all right?"

Rigel rubbed his fingertips together. "I've got a way in, but first I've got to get you an appointment at the body shop."

She walked him to the elevator. He turned to her. They hugged, letting go reluctantly. "It was great to see you, Mill."

"Same here."

"I'll be back on Saturday," Rigel said as he pressed the ground floor button.

"You hope. I'm still not sure I can pull this off," Milly replied, but the doors had already closed.

When Rigel was outside, he looked up to see Milly looking out the window. He waved and blew her a kiss. Was it too late for love? What was he afraid of? Rules forbidding such unions? Regardless of Milly's heartbreaking loss, he didn't need to intrude into her thoughts to perceive she was attracted to him. Or maybe he was infatuated, and it was just his imagination. What next? He knew the answer. He smiled and headed to the high school.

CHAPTER 8:
DINNER AND A DREAM

Nancy had seen the man in the grey pin-striped suit and lavender tie perusing the New Books display at the library earlier today. She had been standing in line to check out a book. What made her turn around she couldn't say, but an inexplicable force drew her eyes to his. When their eyes met, a prickling sensation erupted on her scalp. She finger-combed her hair, then turned away to aid the person in front of her with his checkout. She didn't recognize the man in the grey suit, yet he seemed vaguely familiar, not in a celebrity way, but on a more personal level.

Now here he was this evening, wearing the same business attire, standing on a corner of the intersection she and her husband, Ted, were approaching on their way to dinner and a late movie . . . well, the 7:25 show. She couldn't remember when they'd last gone on a date night. The norm was lunch and a matinee, because they were less expensive, but hey, she wasn't complaining. Anytime she didn't have to cook was fine with her.

The man had a Walk sign but stepped off the curb without looking, so engrossed in his phone that a car turning right nearly knocked him to his knees. He seemed unperturbed about the close call. Nancy would have been screaming at whoever tried to run her over. But then, she would have made eye contact with the driver first before crossing the street to avoid getting hit in the first place. And she would not have been on her phone, for heaven's sake.

Because Ted reminded her often that she could get shot yelling at strangers (even if it was for their own good), she fought back an overwhelming urge to yell at the guy, especially since they had stopped for the red light. No need to invite him closer. Instead, Nancy complained to Ted, "I don't get these people who can't put their phones down for one minute. He could have been killed!" She scowled at the man and his eyes pierced hers. She blinked. Her head tingled again, and she scratched it to get rid of the creepy-crawly feeling. She wondered if she'd picked up lice somewhere.

"Hello!"

"Did you say something?" she asked Ted.

"Nope."

Nancy was certain she had heard a distinct hello. Was she hearing things? Maybe it was the radio. For some reason, she was drawn to this man like steel to a magnet. Her friend and fellow tap dancer lived nearby. She would have to ask Milly if she'd seen this guy roaming the neighborhood.

Rattled by this second encounter, Nancy reached over and hit the horn when the mud-splattered diesel pickup in front of them didn't move after the light changed. She knew Ted absolutely hated it when she did that, but it happened so fast that even she was hardly aware of her misbehaving appendage. Besides, it was more a gentle toot than a honk. Geez, she has toots louder than the toot this car makes.

Their vehicle was a sub-compact, a mouse among elephants in this city. Mrs. Teal, as Nancy lovingly called her, still got better gas mileage than any new vehicle on the road, hadn't burned a drop of oil in eighteen years, and had not needed a major repair in 190,672 miles. Although, like Nancy, Mrs. Teal was showing her age. Her skin was blotchy, and her back door didn't work properly. The cooling system had gone haywire, and the antenna had flown the coop long ago, leaving her with spotty reception. Most things were sagging, such as the side-view mirrors, which were held in place with duct-tape, not unlike Nancy's sagging gut held in place on special occasions with Spandex. Despite her flaws, Mrs. Teal had never let her down, and Nancy planned to give her a big sendoff when she inevitably departed to that beautiful junkyard in the sky.

Back at the intersection, at Mrs. Teal's gentle urging (beep-beep), the pickup jerked forward, billowing black smoke. "There ought to be a law against that," Nancy said.

Ted agreed, but told her in no uncertain terms not to honk the horn again (as he'd said many times before).

Relishing their impromptu evening at the theater, Nancy disregarded the correlation she had found between the amount of sugar consumed after 7 p.m. and dreams—the more sugar, the scarier the dreams. Consequently, it was no shocker when, after devouring an entire jumbo-sized box of Junior Mints, she had one whopper of a nightmare.

She woke up with Ted poking her in the ribs and her heart pounding.

"I had a horrible dream." She snuggled closer to Ted.

"Yeah, I heard. What were you moaning about?"

"I was being interrogated by a strange man. We were sitting across from each other at a table in a room with grey walls, no windows, with a single streetlight shining down on us. He was staring at me with huge black eyes. Only they weren't eyes, but Domino's lava cakes. The chocolate filling was dripping on his cheeks, and I wanted to lick them."

"Mmm. Let's buy some lava cakes tonight, and you can lick the chocolate off me." Ted slipped his hand under her PJ top.

"Stop." She pushed his hand away. "It was frightening. The guy started crying dark chocolate pudding tears, and I asked him why he was crying. He said he was allergic to cats, but there weren't any cats around. Then Clint Eastwood's voice asked me if I'm feeling lucky, that line from *Dirty Harry*."

"'You've got to ask yourself one question: Do I feel lucky? Well, do ya, punk?'"

"That one. But the voice was coming from the light. Then the interrogator asked, 'Hey Ted, you want me to terminate her?' But you didn't answer."

"I didn't, huh?"

"No. Instead, hundreds of cats crawled out of the walls and started clawing at toilet paper holders that suddenly appeared. The paper was filling the room, and I couldn't get out of my chair. I was glued to it. I was suffocating and started yelling for you. Eastwood's voice asked me again if I felt lucky, and I screamed NO-O-O-O!"

"It sounded like E-E-E-E." Ted made a high-pitched squeal.

"Don't. That gives me the creeps. Sorry I woke you up so early. Go back to sleep. I'm getting up."

"What time is it?"

"Five-fifteen."

"We'll go to breakfast later."

"Yum." She planted a kiss on his warm forehead and, with fear fresh in her mind, slipped out of bed, fumbling for her eyeglasses in the dark, and tiptoed downstairs.

Nancy usually forgot dreams, but this one affected her more than usual, because the interrogator was not some vacant face—he was the well-dressed man from the library and the street corner. Sucking water from her ever-present water bottle, she turned on the television to a rerun of *The Golden Girls*, picked up some five-pound weights, and stepped on and off a six-inch-high plastic platform on the floor behind her recliner. But the comedy failed to distract her. The curling and stepping lasted exactly two minutes, and she'd had enough exercise. She headed to the kitchen in search of a light snack to hold her over until breakfast.

Curled up in her recliner with a mango-flavored energy drink and a piece of whole wheat toast slathered with avocado, she picked apart the dream. Which way the toilet paper went on the spindle had been her and Ted's first disagreement. Ted was an under; she was an over. She had won, of course, but why had that memory been dredged up?

Ted didn't answer the termination question. She must be fearful that he resented her. Why? Hitting the horn. That was it. She was always criticizing his driving. She was feeling guilty that Ted was annoyed with her. God, it was true. She nagged Ted all the time . . . how he dressed, how he ate, what he ate, how much he ate, the list went on and on. She couldn't blame him for wanting to suffocate her for twenty years of nagging. Well, it wasn't really twenty years of nagging. Maybe the last five or six. Okay, nineteen.

Or maybe the dream was warning her of something bad to come that she wasn't prepared for. Who was that man, and why did his image bother her so much? This pondering was making her even more nervous. She flipped through the channels, trying to relieve the feeling that the stranger was here for a reason, and she was part of it.

She stood up, shaking off her negativity. Right here and now she would resolve to think before she spoke and try not to correct people all the time. Oh, and keep her hands *off* the horn. Nancy hoped she could, but she also kept resolving to lose weight, and *that* hadn't happened, either.

Outside the window, soft pinks and yellows painted the horizon, reminding her that extra-crispy hash browns awaited. Before she got ready to go, though, she needed to make a note to call Milly about the man near her apartment building. For all she knew, he could be a stalker.

CHAPTER 9:
THE SETUP

Bloated from breakfast, Nancy tossed sheets into the washer and checked the time. 8:10. She knew Milly was an early riser but didn't want to call before nine. She went out to the backyard, dragged the hose over the lawn, and watered the flowers that the automatic sprinklers couldn't reach. Filled the bird bath. Dragged the hose back to storage. Checked her watch for the time. 8:22. Pulled weeds in her raised vegetable garden. Picked up some trash that had blown in over the fence. Went inside to wash her hands and decided not to put her call off any longer.

Milly answered on the third ring. "Hey, Nancy."

"Hi, Milly. Are you busy?"

"No, just watching *Hardcore Porn* while I dust the living room."

"You're watching *porn*?"

"Heavens, no! I haven't watched porn since my Willy died."

"Say what?"

"Forget I said that last part. I meant *pawn!* Didn't I say pawn? *Hardcore Pawn!* It's a TV show. This man and woman are fighting over a broken mantle clock that one figured was a valuable antique. The cashier said it was nothing special and won't give 'em any money. The numskulls are punching each other. The cashier's eyes are popping out of her head like golf balls while those two nitwits go at it."

"Want me to call you back?"

"Nah, it's a rerun. Hold on, let me lower the volume." Nancy heard a thud in her ear. In a few seconds Milly was back. "Sorry, dropped the phone. Can't find the remote. How can I lose something I had a few minutes ago? Losin' my mind. I'm goin' into the bedroom so I can hear you better. Then if I pass out from nerves, I won't hit my head on anything hard."

"What? Are you okay? You need me to come over?"

"How'd you know? Yes, I need you to come over. No, not now, tomorrow."

"Are you *sure* you're okay? I'm starting to worry."

"Shoot, let me start over. I'm flustered over something that has nothing to do with you." Nancy could hear Milly take a deep breath, then exhale. "How are you, girlfriend?"

"Fine," Nancy said. "Haven't seen you all summer. How've you been?"

"Good, good, thank you. Summer's gone first, fast I mean. Can't wait to see you and Joan tomorrow."

"Me too. And Charlene will be there."

"Oh, that's right. You emailed about her. Glad she can come."

"You guys will like her, but I'm calling about a different subject."

"What's up?"

"Yesterday, I saw a man at the library, then later in the evening near your apartment building. He was around six feet tall, wearing a grey business suit, muscular build, black hair, with a mustache and goatee. Good looking, I might add. Have you seen anyone like that walking around your neighborhood?"

"Was he black?"

"Yes."

"Sounds like you're describing my dream man!"

"You've seen him?"

"Sweetie, I see a lot of tall, dark, and handsome men around town. Trouble is, none of 'em are lookin' back."

"I know this sounds weird, but I felt a strange connection to him."

"What do you mean by strange?"

"Let's just say I was attracted to him. It's hard to explain."

"Honey, what about Ted?"

"Never mind. I seem to be digging myself in deeper. He seemed kind of familiar, that's all. Wondered if he lived in your building."

"Seriously, nobody by that description lives here. A bunch of fat old farts is all."

"Forget it. I doubt I'll see him again."

"Not to change the subject, but I was going to call you if you hadn't called me. I've got an appointment Saturday morning to get my car repainted. It's the day of our get-together, but they had a cancellation and that was the only time they could get me in for weeks, and I didn't want to wait, since there's a special goin' on. Lilly and the family are out-of-town, so I wondered if you'd mind picking me up around eleven o'clock? We can drop off the car, and I'll treat you to lunch. We could try the new Mexican restaurant that opened in the same place where Blue Ocean used to be. I know you like Mexican."

"I do. I could eat it every day. Haven't tried the new place. Don't have any plans, so'd be happy to swing by." And to check up on you, Nancy added to herself.

"Awesome. If you want, after lunch, we could go see the photo exhibit at the art museum until it's time to meet Joan and Charlene. Lilly has two of her photographs entered."

"That sounds like fun!" said Nancy.

"You're sure it's no trouble?"

"Positive. I'll pick you up at eleven."

"I'll be here, still huntin' for the remote. Knowin' me, it's in the freezer."

"I can relate to that. See you Saturday."

"Thank you." Milly disconnected before Nancy could say any more.

Hmm, wonder what's going on with her? Maybe she'd find out tomorrow.

CHAPTER 10:
CANDID CAMERA

Saturday morning, Milly exited the body shop, practically skipping to Nancy's car.

"I'd be happy, too, if Mrs. Teal got a new paint job. What color did you pick?"

"Sienna Sunset. Why don't they call it what it really is, burnt orange, instead of some screwy name? He's also detailing the inside, sweet man."

"Who's he?"

"He who? Oh, the guy at the shop."

"He's sweet?"

"He was very nice." With downcast eyes, Milly buckled her seatbelt. "Who's Mrs. Teal?"

"You're sitting in her. I hope you're not embarrassed, because she might be the dumpiest car in the city." She sent a silent apology to Mrs. Teal. Although an inanimate object, somehow Nancy felt she'd jinx her running record if she spoke unkindly of her. She patted the faded dashboard. "Don't you have a name for your car?"

"Yeah, clunker, hooptie, crap piece of junk." Then Milly muttered, "Shoulda made him buy me a new car. That's what I shoulda done."

"What'd you say?"

"I need a new car is what I said. Mine's not much younger than your Mrs. Teal. At least it'll look like new with this paint job. Thanks again for picking me up."

Nancy pressed the clutch and turned the ignition key. Mrs. Teal shimmied and stalled. She tried again. "Dang it, knew I shouldn't have called her dumpy."

"Seriously? Shoot, this is a stick shift. Do they make those anymore? It's done for. Maybe we can take the bus. I've seen it come down this street. We don't want to be late."

"Late for what? We don't have reservations."

"You're right. And I apologize for my rudeness. I'm hungry, that's all. I'm gonna give Mrs. Teal some love." Milly kissed the dashboard.

They both giggled. Nancy held the clutch down and turned the key. The car started, and she shifted from neutral to first. "See? I told you she has feelings."

"And I thought I was crazy," Milly said, smiling and shaking her head. "Let's leave before she gets mad again."

The Mexican restaurant was located between the edge of downtown and the newer commercial development of big box stores and chain restaurants farther to the east. It had served several types of food over the years. Situated on a busy street with many other small businesses, the parking lot was small. "Good thing I'm driving Mrs. Teal. I'd never fit in here with our pickup."

Inside, the dark blue and rust-colored walls were covered with Talavera plates.

"Hey, that's the color of my car, or will be anyway."

"That's a nice color. Kinda dark in here and cold. Nice on a hot day like today, but wish I had my sweatshirt."

They asked to be seated in a window booth, hoping it would be warmer. "Look," Milly said, "there's a giant parrot on a swing. How pretty."

"There's another one over there. Pretty parrot want a menu?" Nancy plucked two bi-folded, laminated menus from the holder at the end of the table and pushed one toward Milly.

Milly slipped on her reading glasses. "Hmm, what looks good?"

Nancy studied the menu. "I'm having the carnitas plate. It comes with a side of rice."

"That does look good. Think I can eat three carnitas tacos?"

"Holy cow, Milly, you could eat anything and not gain a pound. If you can't eat the third one, I will. Plus, I'm gonna add a beef tamale."

"Done deal." Placing her glasses near the edge of the tabletop, Milly dug into the chips the server had brought. "Fresh and warm, like I like 'em."

"This salsa is awfully spicy. My eyes are watering and my nose is running." Nancy sniffed and rifled through her purse for a tissue.

"Bring on the heat. What's hot to one is mild to another. The more you eat, the less hot it will be."

Nancy took the advice to heart, and the women emptied the bowl of chips and the salsa. When their orders arrived, Nancy bit into her shredded pork taco. "Oh my god, this is delicious. I am in seventh heaven. Thank you for lunch."

As the meal progressed, Milly frequently glanced around the restaurant, in search of what, Nancy couldn't tell, but her friend was certainly distracted. She tried to get her attention. "Tell me more about your women's tour group to the national parks and monuments in Arizona. Didn't you go to New Mexico, as well?"

At the question, Milly jerked, accidently knocking her reading glasses to the floor. Fumbling under the table she grumbled, "This was a stupid idea." She hit her head on the table trying to get back up, uttered "Lord, help me," and shoved the glasses into her purse with a "Humph."

It was all Nancy could do to keep from laughing. "I would have gotten those for you if you weren't so quick to duck. Are you all right?"

"No, I am not. You see that man?" She pointed toward the front door. "He just walked in."

"Oh my god! That's him! That's the man in my dream!"

"Girl, he's the man of *my* dreams."

"This is no laughing matter, Milly. That's who I was asking you about. I didn't tell you I had a dream about him, more like a nightmare. Omigod!

He's coming over. I think he's a stalker." Trying to become invisible, she slouched into the bench seat.

"Calm down." Milly reached across the table and took Nancy's hands in hers. "I know him."

"What?" Nancy hissed and yanked her hands away. "Why didn't you tell me?"

Milly leaned back and crossed her arms. "How was I supposed to know who you were talkin' about? You didn't give me a name, and, by the way, your description could have fit anyone. Well, not *anyone*. He *is* good looking, isn't he?" Nancy scowled at her lunch partner. "Look, I've known him since I was ten years old. He wants to meet you."

"He wants to meet *me*? Why would he want to meet *me*?"

"You'll have to ask him. He's sizzlin' hot, so trust him."

"Milly, hot is not a reason to trust someone. You tricked me." Nancy's heart thumped hard and fast, but instead of running, she sat up ready to confront her stalker.

"Hello, Rigel."

"Hi, Mill. Mind if I join you?" Nancy left no room for him to sit next to her, so he scooted in next to Milly. "Care to make introductions?" he asked, grinning.

"Let's see, um, Nancy, I'd like you to meet Rigel O'Rion. Rigel, this is Nancy Leopold.

Rigel wore strikingly different attire—a black, tight-fitting t-shirt tucked into black jeans and matching cowboy boots. Nancy hated to admit it, but his clothes did set off a very fine physique. Now that she had a good look at him, he even had freaking dimples. And his awfully cute smile reminded her of LL Cool J if he had more hair. Despite her traitorous thoughts, she kept her hands in her lap when he held his out. "Nice to meet you, Nancy."

She glared from one to the other. Why was she feeling so hostile? This man was a friend of Milly's, yet she couldn't stop herself from being ill-mannered. "What's going on? Why do I feel like you're more than a friend of Milly's?"

"Oh honey, don't I wish."

Rigel beamed at Milly. "Really?"

"Shut your pie hole." Milly swatted his arm.

The server came over to pour refills. Rigel ordered a sweet tea. "Anyone want dessert?" The offer was declined. The server retreated. The drama began.

Anxious, Nancy left no room for small talk. "Something doesn't feel right here. Why were you at the library?"

"Checking out a book?" Rigel answered with raised eyebrows, then sobered, "I was waiting for Milly to get home—she doesn't live far from there."

"I saw you that same night on the street corner. Did you say hello?"

"I did."

"How was I able to hear you from that far away?"

"Telepathy. Sweet, huh?"

"Telepathy? Nope, not possible. Telepathy is a crock of bull." Yet, she had heard something.

Nancy was always worrying about early-onset dementia. Maybe hearing things was a symptom, but he *had* acknowledged greeting her from afar. It hadn't been the radio or her imagination.

"It's very possible for D'Gnomans. And let me say, those meetings were coincidental. I wasn't following you or anything. The night you drove by, I was leaving Milly's."

Nancy closed her eyes for a second to clear her head before asking, "Have we ever met before?"

"No, not really."

Not really wasn't a very good answer, but she wasn't ready to pursue it. Nancy sighed deeply, placed her fingertips on her forehead, thumbs on her cheekbones, and pleaded, "Milly, what is going on?"

"Let Rigel speak. I'll fill in when I can."

"Don't blame Milly for not saying anything. It was my idea. I am your mother's friend and—"

"My *mother*?" Nancy dropped her hands from her face and leaned menacingly over the table. "What do you want with my mother?"

"Hold it!" Rigel held up his right hand, palm open. "I haven't talked to her since we were teenagers. Back then my sister and I were her friends. We have not been able to get in touch with her, so we'd like your help."

"That's all? You want to talk to my mother? Why didn't you call her on the freaking phone? Or better yet, send her a telepathic message?"

"Well, for one, she's too far away for telepathy to happen." He chuckled. "I'm not sure she would have answered if I'd called on a phone. This is where it gets complicated. Let's all go back to Milly's apartment and talk there."

"Good! Let's get this show on the road." Milly acted to get up, giving Rigel a slight push to move.

Nancy didn't budge. "I'm not going back to Milly's apartment with you! I don't even know you. And Milly, how are you involved with this man?"

"I'd *like* to be involved. Oh my, did I say that?"

"I think you did," said the man with the sparkling brown eyes.

Milly ignored him and directed her comments to Nancy. "I *meant* I want to be involved in helping you understand. I assume you have a lot of questions."

"Understand what?" Nancy looked at Rigel. "Tell me why you want to speak to my mother, and I'll consider leaving here. She's not in trouble, is she?"

"No, she's not in trouble. Your mother left Ghanwik City before you were born and never returned. I simply want to speak to her regarding problems the city is having. She may have the knowledge we're looking for."

"She has never mentioned Ghanwik City. Where is that? Someplace in your imagination?"

"Since you ask, and you're going to find out anyway, there's no point in holding back. It's a city on an exoplanet called D'Gnome."

"Ghanwik City is on a *planet*? Like other than *Earth*?"

"Yes," Rigel answered, smiling, while Milly shook her head, a defeated look on her face.

"Oh-h-h," Nancy nodded knowingly. "My mother is an a-li-en." She scrutinized the restaurant. "I used to call my mother an alien but never meant it literally. I just thought she was odd. Wait. Now I get it! This is a reality prank show! You've got hidden cameras. I've seen those shows! You tell people some wild story, like you're from outer space, and record their reaction. No wonder you didn't want to say anything, Milly! You were in on it and didn't want to spoil the surprise."

"It's a surprise, all right, but there aren't any cameras. We've been here long enough, and people are staring. You've known me for many years. Trust me when I say he's not here to hurt you or me. Let's go. We can talk at my apartment."

"I don't get it. Trust him? Trust you? I don't trust either of you!" Nancy began to slip out of the booth. "This man is talking nonsense, and you're going along with it. God, Milly, you can have him. I'm leaving." She stood, took two steps, turned, fumbled for her wallet, and threw a twenty-dollar bill on the table. "Keep the stupid change."

Milly glared at Rigel. "A public place not so good after all. Get out of the way." She shoved him as hard as she could. He stumbled out of the booth, and Milly charged after Nancy.

Nancy was opening her car door when Milly caught up. She reached for her friend's sleeve. "Hold on," Milly panted. "I haven't sprinted like that in a long time." She gasped a couple more times. "Let's go together."

"You're right. Let's ditch this guy."

"Please," Milly begged. "As unbelievable as this sounds, give him a chance. He means well and really is concerned for your mom."

"Then why would he contact you? Why didn't he Google me or something?"

"He thought I could help. It's such a long story. Would really be easier to explain back at my apartment. I promise you're safe with him. Here he comes. Be nice."

Rigel strode toward the women. "Here's your twenty. I paid the bill and included a nice tip."

Nancy snatched the bill from his hand and shoved it into her capris pocket. "I'm going because I don't want to leave you alone with him. Get in."

Rigel crammed his long legs into the back seat of the subcompact, insisting Milly sit in front. Seat belts fastened, Nancy started Mrs. Teal and shifted into reverse.

"Never understood this tipping thing. Everyone gets a livable wage on D'Gnome."

"Cool it, Rigel," Milly warned.

"Trying to make conversation."

"You don't tip on D'Gnome. Really, where the H are you from?"

"I'm from a Goldilocks planet. Not too hot, not too cold. It's ju-u-st right. For life, that is." Rigel laughed. Milly groaned. Still in the parking lot, Nancy slammed on the brakes. Mrs. Teal shuddered and stalled.

"Will you *stop*?" She slapped the steering wheel with both hands. "What kind of joke *is* this?" This whole scene was so bizarre, she was near tears.

Milly patted Nancy on the knee and said, "You need to drive, hon. You don't want to kill anyone, not yet anyway. Ignore what he says."

"If I didn't know you, Milly, I would be dialing 9-1-1." Nobody said another word.

Back on the road and twelve insufferable minutes later, the trio were riding the elevator to Milly's apartment. She offered her guests something to drink before gathering awkwardly in the living room—Rigel in the sage green recliner, Nancy on the opposite end of the sofa from Milly, as far away from Rigel as possible.

The cat, who had scrambled to the bedroom when discord erupted at the front door, tentatively tiptoed into the room. Nancy reached for the calico. "Come here, Cinnamon." But the cat haughtily disregarded her, nimbly jumping onto Rigel's lap.

"There you go," Milly said. "Cinnamon adores Rigel, so he can't be all bad."

"Not to be rude, Milly, but do you have anything stronger than water?"

"Oh goodness, yes! I've got a bottle of Plum Loco, a sweet red. Might calm your nerves and mine."

"Oh, isn't that appropriate . . . Plum Loco." Nancy smiled weakly.

"Brought as much as I could carry all the way from Deming, New Mexico. Then found out they sell it here." Milly went to the kitchen and poured a glass for each of them.

Nancy downed the wine in several gulps, coughed spastically, and plunked the empty glass on the coffee table. "Pour me another, Milly, please."

"This is like a sipping wine. Sip sip. Not gulp gulp. Lord, what's gotten into me. Under the circumstances, I should not criticize. You have all you want. What I'll do is add some Sprite. Makes it surprisingly light. You'll like it."

Nancy drained the second glass, burped loudly. These two had struck a nerve with her, and it felt good to be uncouth. "Excuse me." She burped again. "I'm going to humor you for a while, then I'm leaving. Where is Ghanwik City? And don't tell me it's in outer space."

"I have contemplated this moment," Rigel said. "Where does one begin? As there are stars in the universe, there are as many details to tell you."

Nancy looked at her watch. "See if you can fit it in, let's see . . . I'll give you ten minutes."

"Here me out. Ghanwik City is where our central government resides on D'Gnome, a planet in a galaxy far, far away—"

"Enough with the *Star Wars* jokes." Nancy's eyes narrowed.

"—named El'o-el'ay."

"El-oh what?"

"El'o-el'ay."

Nancy repeated each syllable slowly. "L-O-L-A? LOLA? Like the song?!"

Rigel groaned. "There is little chance this dialogue will be any less difficult than I expected."

"Then tell me how you got here. Our laws of physics don't allow intergalactic travel. Humans haven't gotten to our nearest planet let alone another galaxy."

"For you, not yet. Bridges exist creating shortcuts between two places instantaneously. We've gone so far as to travel without space craft. To your scientists, shortcuts are theoretically possible—they just haven't proven it yet. One day in the future they will figure out that their laws of physics, as they know them, will not apply. Consider how much has been accomplished in the last hundred years. Your technology is advancing exceedingly fast."

Nancy made screwy faces at Rigel. "You *sure* you're not wearing a hidden camera? Because I don't believe anything you're saying, except about our technology, which I can't keep up with."

"No cameras."

"Then this is all very weird. I'm leaving. Thanks for the wine, Milly." Nancy stood up. "I'll be back to check on you and pick you up for our dinner tonight."

Milly sprang from her seat. "No, please, please, please, don't go."

"Wait," said Rigel. "Let's rewind with a few basic facts, then see how you feel."

Nancy hesitated and turned toward Rigel, one hand on her hip, a knee bent. "I doubt anything you say will change my mind."

"Your mother is Bellatrix Bayer Herschel, correct?"

"First of all, if this is not a reality show, then I'm only staying because you're a friend of Milly's. Maybe she's the one who needs protection." Nancy sat back down, dug into her purse for her cell phone, and held on to it. "With that said . . . Bellatrix? Never heard her called that."

"Her friends call her Trixie. She is the daughter of two famous scientists, your grandmother, an astrophysicist, and your grandfather, a neuro-scientist."

"Wow, I'll partially grant you that one. Not that they were famous, but I do recall they were scientists. Of course, you could have gotten that information off the Web." She didn't tell him that she had never searched for her grandparents so did not know what one would find. She'd never met them and her mom had no brothers or sisters—no family to speak of. She knew it was popular nowadays to do the DNA tests to find out your ancestry, but she had not been interested.

"Your maternal grandparents were presumed drowned in a river rafting accident fifty-one years ago."

"They died when I was a young girl, but again, you could have gotten that from the Internet. Are you positive you have the right person? Nothing. I mean *nothing* in my entire life would have hinted I am related to . . . you know." She couldn't quite bring herself to say extraterrestrials.

"Yes, I am positive. No matter how much you search, you will not find any information on your mother or her relatives on your Internet."

Nancy massaged her forehead. "Then why did my mother lie to me? Or are *you* lying to me? I'm not feeling well, Milly. I'm not much of a drinker. Should've stuck to water."

"If you're ill, we don't have to continue this."

"Are you kidding? I want to see where this farce is going." Nancy held out her hands. "Look. I'm shaking like a leaf. Please tell me truthfully what this is all about."

"Let Rigel finish. It sounds like your mother hasn't told you everything concerning her childhood."

"Did you know my mom, Milly?"

"Yes, I did. She stayed with my family for her senior year in high school, when I was eight. Rigel stayed with us two years later. Your mom, Rigel, and his sister were what we called Senior Superlatives."

"We? Don't tell me you're from this place too."

"No, I am not. I have lived my entire life in Collinsville. Senior Superlatives were like exchange students. They had identification stating they were from a foreign country. The kids fit in better that way."

"Duh. What else could you say? Hi, I'm from another planet." Nancy shook her head.

"Anyway, my parents were sponsors. My family goes way back in partnership with D'Gnomans. How that happened is for another day. I've known since I was twenty. Rigel has visited throughout the years, but after her graduation from CHS, I never saw your mother again. I figured she went home to D'Gnome, like all DG kids did. And," she added emphatically, "I *never* knew there was any relationship between you and her until Rigel called me a week ago."

"My mom lived with your family? I knew she went to school here for a year, but I assumed she lived with her parents. I guess I should blame myself for not asking more questions. And now the line between truth and fiction is blurring. I'm trying to recall everything my mother ever said to me. Collinsville is where she met my dad. It's his hometown. His parents owned a gas station that had an attached garage for auto repair. My dad worked as a mechanic there. They've all died, so can't ask them anything."

"I'm sorry to hear they've passed on," said Milly.

"It's been a long time. My grandparents both died of cancer within months of each other, a real love story. I truly believe my Grandpa Herschel didn't have a reason to live without Grandma. But my dad . . . I had graduated from college and had joined my first accounting firm when he died of a heart attack. I wonder if he knew."

"Can't answer that, but has your mom ever told you how she met your dad?" Milly asked softly.

"They were high school sweethearts and eloped after graduation, but that was probably a lie too." Nancy sat cross-legged clutching a decorative pillow, every muscle in her body quivering from the adrenaline coursing through her veins. She wasn't sure how to accept the wildly unbelievable things they were saying. Rigel, she didn't know, but Milly had no reason to lie to her. She couldn't comprehend what this was about.

"No, that was true," Rigel said kindly. "I'm not here to harm you or your mother. It would be nice to see her again, and, like I mentioned earlier, she may have information we need to solve certain travel problems we're having."

"Like what?" Nancy asked.

"First let me say this. We would not have involved you if we could have talked to Trixie. Despite several attempts in the past, she has refused to communicate. I'm unsure how she'll feel about me telling you about D'Gnome, when, honestly, she should have done it herself."

"If my mother hasn't said anything to me, maybe there's nothing to tell. Although I can't fathom why you're making this up."

"I'm not." Rigel smiled. "Your grandmother, Erma Bayer, was lead researcher on space-time travel, creating those bridges I mentioned. With her crew, they created ninety-nine different gateways to Earth. Right now two of the portals are no longer functioning properly."

"Wow. I've read about the theory in Hawking's *A Brief History of Time*. Portal, gateway. What's the difference?"

"Anymore the terms are used interchangeably. More accurately, a portal is the specific entry or exit point. Gateway refers to the entire connection between DG and each location, like a hallway with a door at each end."

"So much for that. Tell me why you want to see my mom."

Rigel smiled reassuringly. "It's a slim chance, but a chance nonetheless, that Trixie might be able to help because of her familial connection. She may have been given data to safeguard."

"Data? Are people after this data? Is that why we moved so much?"

"We don't know if she has information or not. What we do know is that the gateways have never failed and now two have. That news has gone viral. We don't believe anyone's been seeking her before this. Our concern is that the shutdowns are leading to gossip about your grandparents, which, in turn, might lead to Trixie. We want her to be aware of what's happening.

"As far as moving around, Trixie was cognizant of her situation and may have been afraid of abduction. We don't know, which is why I want to talk to her."

"So she's safe for now?"

"For the present," Rigel assured her.

"This is getting too much for me to absorb," Nancy said, her jaw tight, her teeth chattering, her entire body trembling. She felt cold. "What is this senior super-thing she was involved in?"

"I can tell you're not feeling well. We'll take a break after this. Each year the brightest students are selected to continue their education through the Senior Superlative Earth Study Program. Each student picks a city from participating locations. All students return at the end of the school year and must present their research paper. D'Gnomans of any age cannot remain on Earth longer than a year without suffering debilitating headaches. We have a gland in our brain, that you don't have, called the nepial. It begins to enlarge, eventually leading to death.

"Your grandfather, under strict government orders of secrecy, developed a vaccine to reduce the swelling. Trixie received the vaccine right before she left on her Earth Study. She was seventeen and the solitary participant in the longevity study. When the nanobot monitoring her health expired, the study was abandoned, and Trixie remained here. You will have to talk to her about a lot of this. I'm just skimming the surface."

Nancy recalled her mother's headaches getting worse as she aged. Because of her genetic makeup, was that why she refused to see a doctor? Were her headaches the result of this nepial gland? She didn't feel like asking any more questions, except one: "So, my mother really is from this place?"

"Affirmative," Rigel replied.

Whereupon Nancy felt the room darken and limply met the floor with a thud.

Milly jerked, having nearly fallen asleep to Rigel's deep fluid voice, and screamed at Nancy's lifeless body.

"This isn't exactly how I meant to take a break," Rigel muttered.

CHAPTER 11:
ENCOUNTER OF THE THIRD KIND

Rigel! She's dead! Wha-da-we-do? We killed her!" Milly shot up from the sofa and jabbed a finger into Rigel's chest. "*You* killed her. I didn't want anything to do with this!"

Cinnamon raced into the kitchen when Rigel stood up and knelt next to Nancy. He checked her vital signs. "She didn't fall far, more like slid to the floor, nor did she hit her head hard. I am certain there are no injuries." He picked up the pillow Nancy had been holding and placed it under her legs to elevate them above her heart, then laid her phone on the coffee table. "Shake her gently and call her name. She's breathing and has a heartbeat. If she doesn't come to in a minute, we'll call 9-1-1, like anyone else. I don't have any magic tricks with me."

"Nancy! Wake up!" screamed Milly, shaking her vigorously. "Dear God, please wake up."

"Gently, Milly, gently. Don't break her neck."

"I should break *your* neck for what you've caused!"

"Mill, she would have found out eventually. Although it baffles me why Trixie has let it go this long."

Nancy stirred and moaned.

"Praise the Lord! I thought you were dead. Stay still 'til you feel better."

"How'd I get on the floor?" Nancy tried to sit up. Rigel lifted her back onto the sofa.

"You fainted. You don't have to stay. We can talk some other time. We don't even have to go to the show tonight. I'll tell everyone you have severe indigestion from the chips and salsa," Milly said anxiously. "I could drive you home, and Rigel could follow in my car. No, wait, I don't have my car. I'll call a taxi and we'll follow the taxi in your car. No, we'll follow the car in your taxi."

Nancy gave her a funny look. "You know what I mean," Milly said, wringing her hands, as if she could twist them off her wrists.

"No, not really."

"Oh Nancy, I did trick you, and I am very, very sorry. I didn't know how to tell you this. Please forgive me."

"I'm not mad at you, and I don't need to go home."

"How are you feeling?" Rigel asked.

"In shock, obviously. Kinda weak, but I'll be okay." Maybe lunch wasn't sitting well with her. She felt nauseous. A multitude of questions was roiling inside her skull. "Does my mom have superpowers, that sort of thing? If she's from wherever, what does that make me?" Nancy was visibly trembling again. Milly covered her with a soft blanket.

"Thank you." Nancy angled her legs under her and pulled the blanket to her chin.

"Define superpowers," said Rigel.

"Telepathy. Can she do that?"

"Yes, she has the ability to communicate without speaking."

"Is she . . . um . . . human?" Nancy could barely get the question past her lips.

Rigel responded with a laugh. "Our world evolved as yours, except we have a thousand-year head start. Be assured, we are all one hundred percent human, as is your mother, except she has the nepial gland and you don't. Oh, and her blood is green."

"Sheesh! No wonder she never went to the doctor."

"Nah, I'm pullin' your leg."

"That's not funny! Don't joke around, or I *will* leave. You realize I'm having a tough time believing this. I like science fiction, but that's what it is—fiction. Make believe. Not real. You're telling me my mother is an alien as if it's a fact."

Rigel nodded. "Yeah, it is, except alien has such a negative connotation. We prefer star people. We are all of the stars after all."

Star people. That did sound nice. He had a deep, hypnotic voice, and Nancy was finding it hard to concentrate. Inhale . . . exhale. She was starting to warm up and relax. "She obviously doesn't want to see you, or you wouldn't be coming to me. There must be a reason. In my mom's interest, I shouldn't be talking to you until I talk to her. I need proof that you're telling the truth. As disagreeable as my mother may be, I love her and don't want to hurt her."

"I felt we should speak to Trixie directly, but the person who asked me to come here—in her infinite wisdom—believed it better that I visit you first and see how it worked out. How's it workin' out?"

There's that sweet smile and deep dimples. She saw why Milly was attracted to him. Nancy shook her head and grimaced. "I fainted. How's that for workin' out? What about my dad? Yee gods, this is ludicrous." She felt her jaw tighten. "Milly, help me out here."

"Wish I could. What Rigel says is true."

"How do you know? Have you seen this portal?"

"No, I haven't. It's not something you see—it's something you feel."

"Correct. Only D'Gnomans can detect or use the portal. No one can accidently fall through, or you'd have more people claiming abduction than ants at a picnic." No one laughed at his joke, as he paused. "Come on! I'm doing my best here!" At their grim looks, he sighed. "Travelers must be D'Gnoman or accompany one. I've been thinking. There's no other way to prove it. Come back with me."

"Oh yeah right. There's no way I'd go off alone anywhere with you! Are you nuts?"

"Fair enough. But don't you two have a function at the high school tonight?"

"What's the school got to do with this?"

"It's the portal location."

"In a school? *With children?!*"

"It used to be a dedicated student terminal. Now that students don't use it, it's kept open for a person like me, who very occasionally has an official reason to be in Collinsville."

"Oh. We do have a function at school tonight. How'd you know?"

"Milly told me."

"Thought maybe you could read the future."

"No such luck. But here's what I'm going to do to prove our existence. I will take you both back to D'Gnome. That way you won't be alone."

"Really?" Milly looked guiltily at Nancy, who returned an incredulous stare. "I have always wanted to go there! It'll verify what Rigel's been saying!"

"How can you accept this so easily?"

Milly cupped her chin with her hand and pursed her lips before answering. Her hand fell to her lap. "Well, let's see. How can I explain this? Everyone who has a sponsorship commitment does so with a vow of confidentiality. Sponsorships are passed on from one generation to the next. One doesn't learn of the relationship until adulthood, and when you do, you're expected to one day take over. It's not solely hosting students, but to be there for travelers who need assistance of any kind, as well. I learned when I was twenty. I was shocked, as you are now, and pitched a fit that it wasn't possible. With my parents, I accompanied a student to the portal and watched him disappear through the wall, as if by magic, kind of like the old *Star Trek* show—'Beam me up, Scottie.' I'm the same person you've always known. The hard part will be telling Ted, but I had to tell William, and he had to make the same vow of silence. I'll help you with Ted when the time comes. It all seems so normal to me now."

"If we agree to go with him, what if something goes wrong? He's already said portals are messed up," Nancy said to Milly.

"It won't. It's Biloxi and San Diego," replied Rigel. "I'll meet you outside the school, by the west side entrance nearest the backstage door, half an hour before the show starts. Sound okay?"

"Yes!" Milly pounded the sofa with her fist.

After a long pause, Nancy hunched her shoulders. "Um, I suppose so."

"If you can't make it, Milly can text me. She has my number. I'll hang here until it's time to meet."

"If you're so advanced," Nancy said, "why are you using an ordinary cell phone?"

"Our devices are not compatible with yours, so we revert to your technology. Plus, we speak whatever language is required."

"You're good. Can't tell English isn't your native language, but couldn't you have thrown in a British accent? It's all the rage."

"I could, but I prefer a Midwestern inflection so I'm not so conspicuous."

"One more thing. Seeing as Collinsville is some sort of landing zone, when my husband applied for a wildlife biologist position here, did he get the job on his own merit, or was there *star people* intervention?"

"We don't interfere with people's lives. He got the job on his own merit."

"Will we be gone long?" asked Milly.

"You'll be back before anyone realizes you're missing."

"Yeah, Milly, this sounds way more fun than looking at a bunch of photos hanging on walls." Nancy giggled nervously, referring to Milly's deceitful scheme to visit the art gallery after today's lunch. She supposed her attempt at a joke was a good sign of progress. She took a deep breath.

Nancy watched the two of them discuss how it would feel to travel and how long it would take. You don't feel a thing, except a bit of tingling, initially, then darkness. Some people are disoriented the first trip; others are not. Because your atoms are separated while traveling, you may notice changes to your body's biochemistry upon reentry. Doesn't happen to us, but in Earthlings, one attribute may become more pronounced than another, for example, extra-ordinary muscle strength, which almost all of you acquire. Or you may gain a skill you never had before, depends on how your DNA may have been altered during re-particling. But, again, no two people are alike, and each may be affected differently.

She heard Milly ask, "How do you know we'll be stronger? You don't let Earth people visit. Will we get in trouble if we're there?"

"Long ago, before our current mode of travel, we brought Earthlings to our planet until we found out about their extraordinary abilities. It is one of the reasons our government is no longer interested in cooperative visitation. And no, we're only going to the portal wing and back. That will be enough to convince you and Nancy this is legit. Maybe someday, Mill, you and I will be able to explore our planet together. It is a beautiful place to live."

Nancy felt as if she were an actor in an episode of *The Twilight Zone*. She tuned out the voices in the room, only to hear a voice in her head: *"There is something you should know. They're here. In this town. Why here? The least-populated state in the nation? You'd think they would stand out. Be discovered. But they're like you and me. A word to the wise . . . watch out. You may be safe here, but up there in the stars someone waits to take you . . . up there in the void we call the Gnome Zone."*

Feeling cold again, she pulled the blanket tighter, and blamed the "voice" on stress and her active imagination.

CHAPTER 12:
DANCERS' DINNER

When Milly and Nancy entered the Chinese restaurant for their annual tap dancers' post-summer gathering, Joan was already sitting at a table. She sprang up and greeted them with hugs. "Can you believe we're back for another year? I am thrilled to see you guys!"

For eight years the three women had taken the same adult tap class. One or two people would sign up on occasion, but they never came back after their first recital or dropped out when they found out there *was* a recital. Joan was the youngest, mid-forties, with dark brown hair that was as bouncy as her personality, especially when it was tied in a high ponytail. Tonight it was side-parted and flipped off her shoulders. At 5 feet 4 inches tall, she was an inch shorter than Milly and more plus-size than petite. Nancy was glad to be a part of this group of tappers who would never dream of letting body size interfere with their love for dance.

Whenever one or the other was frustrated with not getting a tap combination, Joan provided endless encouragement. Nancy struggled the most to get her feet, hands, and head to work concurrently. Oftentimes it's like patting your head and rubbing your stomach, Joan had once said. Some people find that trickier than others. Nancy was in the "trickier" category.

"Did you get Jasmine's text?" Joan asked. Jasmine had been their instructor for four years and had been invited to the dancers' dinner the last three.

Nancy and Milly eyed each other and said they hadn't seen it.

"Her grandfather's in the hospital, so she's not coming."

"That's too bad. Hope it's not serious," said Milly.

Charlene walked in, hesitated inside the door, and smiled when Nancy waved. "Here she is! Our newest member." Nancy tried to sound more energetic than she felt and patted the chair next to hers. Introductions were made, menus forgotten. They managed a drink order but asked for a few more minutes to decide on food.

"I'm glad we all like Chinese food, because I adore this restaurant. The food is always great, and it's the most relaxing place in town," Nancy said. A large fish tank gurgled by the entrance, curly bamboo decorated each table, and the music was soft and soothing. You didn't have to yell at your partner to carry on a conversation. The atmosphere was calming, and she desperately needed calm.

Charlene looked down at her menu. "What do y'all recommend?"

After their orders were taken, Joan asked Charlene how she broke her wrist.

"I fell off my bike."

"Schwinn or Harley?" asked Milly.

Charlene smiled. "Schwinn. Actually, a Trek. It's a stupid story."

"Tell us. I'd say you're in good company," Milly said.

"Nancy's already heard the story, but since you asked . . . Before I moved to Wyoming, Texas was suffering from unrelenting record hot temperatures and drought. When our city council came up with Umbrella Day, I *had* to participate." Charlene rolled her eyes. "Everyone was to carry an umbrella, no matter what they were doing. The notion was, if enough people took part, we could make it rain. I knew it was a bunch of poppycock, but we needed something to raise our spirits, and carrying an umbrella en masse seemed like a fun, supportive thing to do.

"So, I took my umbrella with me when I went for a bike ride. The first dumb thing I did was carry it open, until I almost flew off like Mary Poppins. I stopped, closed the umbrella, and, like an idiot, hung it on the handlebar. The umbrella waited until I built up speed, then caught in the front wheel and tore out half the spokes, while I flew over the handlebars, and you know the rest of the story...." Charlene held up her casted forearm. "At least I can say I did my part, except I went through all that trouble, and it *still* didn't rain!"

Everyone laughed. It felt good to be with these women. For a moment, Nancy forgot how her life might drastically change.

Charlene fit right in. After coaxing from Joan and Milly, she divulged more about herself. Born and raised in Dallas, Texas. Her mom, dad, older sister and younger brother remained there, but her two sons and daughter lived in three different states. She was a graduate of Texas A&M College Station and worked from home as a graphics designer for small businesses. Her husband was a civil engineer. He got a job offer from a company working on advanced technology for wind and solar energy.

"I can see why his company would move here. Collinsville's got plenty of wind. Blows me over more times than I can count," said Milly.

The food arrived and Charlene said, "That's more than you ever wanted to know about me. Let's eat!"

The friends chorused "Amen!" and dug in. Conversation eventually returned to dance.

"We always do the end-of-year recital, but last year we got bold and entered a regional dance competition. And guess what? We won first place in our age group!" Joan told Charlene.

"We were the *only* ones in our age group," added Nancy. "When everyone gathered for the awards ceremony, we didn't see anybody over eighteen sitting on the stage floor, so we sat in the audience."

"We sat in the audience because we were afraid if we sat on the floor, we wouldn't be able to get back up! At least not in a graceful way," Milly said. "When the judge announced our dance, it felt like we were on the *Price is Right.* Come on down! We started yelling, flapping our arms, and running willy-nilly to the stage steps. It was a performance all its own." Milly waved her arms over her head.

"I have a proposition you'll find even more thrilling," said Joan. "Another competition!"

"Shoot, my nerves haven't recuperated from the last one," Milly said with a grimace.

"I shouldn't have called it a competition—it's actually a fundraiser talent show with our graduates from UP."

Joan volunteered for UP. Nancy and Milly were familiar with her work, but she explained their mission to Charlene. "When you're down, there's no place to go but UP, right? We teach single mothers, at or below poverty level, skills to land good-paying jobs where they can support themselves and their children. We also offer training in parenting skills, budgeting, healthy meal planning, and other things that facilitate self-sufficiency. If a woman is accepted into the nine-month program, it's an enormous opportunity for her to better her life. The more money we raise, the more women we can enroll.

"UP didn't exist when I was a single mom, Charlene. My two daughters are adults now, but

I know from experience what it takes to raise kids alone, especially hard when the rest of your family lives several states away, as in my case. The UP program means a lot to me.

"Usually, we invite the public to a barbecue and silent auction. A local band plays for dancing afterwards. This year we're replacing the dance with a talent show. We've got a lot of talented mentors and moms. It's both a fundraiser and a celebration of our graduates' hard work. We're calling it 'Everyone's a Star!' I'm a mentor. And guess what's my talent?" She looked around the table as if expecting an answer. At the raised eyebrows and wide eyes, she said, "You! We can do 'Proud Mary.'"

"You say what now?" Milly cocked her head at Joan. "I've already forgotten the steps."

"It'll come back to you." Joan pressed her palms twice toward the ceiling. "What wha-a-at?"

"When is it?" Nancy asked.

"October 27th at CHS."

"That's not far away. Not enough time for me to learn something new," said Milly. "Could we get a costume for Charlene by then?"

"Hold on. If y'all wouldn't be able to learn something new, how am I going to? I said I'd join the class, but I haven't tapped since I was a teenager."

"We'd love to have you tap with us, Charlene," Joan said. "Jasmine is a great choreographer. She'll have no trouble working you into the dance. Our goal is to have fun. We try not to worry much about the steps. If we screw up, and I guarantee you we do, we dance on. No one notices, and if they do, who cares. They should be up there tapping, not judging."

"You and I can meet at my house for extra practice," Nancy offered. "You'll pick it up fast."

"If y'all say so, then I'll try."

The server brought their checks and fortune cookies.

"That settles it. I'll run the event by Jasmine. In the meantime, be thinking of a name to call ourselves for the program." Joan ripped open a wrapper and withdrew the thin strip of paper from inside the cookie. "When you read your fortune, add 'in bed' after it. Like this: A new business venture is on the horizon—in bed. Hmm, what business could I run in bed?"

"It's not selling mattresses," Milly said.

"I hear a girl can make good money at it," Nancy replied.

"What, selling mattresses?" asked Charlene. "I was thinking of something else."

"Me too! If it's what I think you're thinking, I'm not interested. And I don't think Marcus would be either." Joan tossed her fortune onto her plate.

"Marcus?" Charlene asked, brows raised.

"He's my boyfriend. Although I feel too old to call him a boyfriend. He's my beau, lover, hot-to-trot manfriend. Yeah, that one sounds better. He flies between here and Des Moines, Iowa, for work, so it's on-again, off-again. I used to live in Des Moines, which is where I met him. These long-distance relationships suck."

"I bet they would. Look forward to meeting him one day," Charlene said. "Well, here's my fortune: Always be yourself—in bed. Hmm, better dig up my French maid costume. I like acting a little on the trashy side."

No one was positive if Charlene was kidding or not, but Joan said, "Now Marcus would go for that one!"

Milly added, "Lordy-be, quit talkin' trash. Now here's mine." Their rowdy laughter caused people to look their way. Milly held her tiny strip of paper at arm's length, then thrust it toward Nancy to read.

"You will be reunited with an old friend—in bed. Ooo-la-la, Milly," Nancy teased. "Who do you suppose that could be?" The rest of the group mimicked her with "Ooh, tell us."

"No one! What's yours say, Nancy?"

"You will find the solution to your problem where you least expect it—"

"In bed!" everyone shouted. People stared. Maybe diners were wishing they could join that table. They'd be disappointed to find the hardest thing those women were drinking was iced tea.

"If bed won't solve your prob, you can always confide in us," said Joan.

"Thanks, kid." Nancy had a huge problem and doubted the answer would come to her in bed. Although she could truly use a nap. Then she could think more clearly.

"That was fun. We better get going, though, if we want to make it to the World of Arts." Joan verified Charlene knew how to get to the school. "Just in case, you can follow me."

"I've got to stop for gas, so you guys go on. Milly and I will meet you in the lobby." At that, Milly and Nancy left without further ado. In the car, Nancy said, "I don't really need gas—I used that as an excuse. Somehow we have to ditch those two. What do we do?"

"We sit here until they leave. Then we follow them. When they turn left, we turn right. I'm betting they'll park in the big lot on the east side, closest to the front door. If you go around the block, they shouldn't see us, and you can park on the street next to the west side door. Rigel should be waiting outside and can get us in. Dang, if I don't feel like I'm in a James Bond movie, ditchin' the bad dudes."

"Wow, you have this all figured out."

"You bet your bippy, I do. I'm not missing this chance to experience intergalactic travel."

"Yeah, that sounds weird. And frightening. I have lost my mind."

"Nah, 007 never loses. They're gone. Take off."

As Nancy pulled up to the curb outside the high school, Milly pointed, "There he is. Doesn't he look scrumptious, leaning so nonchalantly against the building? Like a Hershey bar, I want to eat him all up."

"Milly! I did not hear you say that!" Nancy plugged her ears with her fingers.

"Isn't it great? We've both lost our minds. Don't think about it. Shake it off, girlfriend, and let's roll."

"Oh my god. What have I gotten myself into? This is crazy." But only Mrs. Teal heard, as Milly had already slammed the car door.

From dance recitals, the women were pretty sure the side door would be locked from the outside, but Rigel placed his hand on the door handle, held it there a moment, and pulled. At their astonished looks, he said, "Kinetic energy. Not everyone can do it. After you, ladies."

Once inside, steps led down to the dressing rooms or up to a hallway. Straight ahead a short distance down the hallway was the door to the stage. Milly took the lead. "It's dark. Be careful." Gripping a metal handrail, they tiptoed down four steps into a dark alcove level with the stage. A stagehand, peering at a tablet in his hand and speaking into a headset, looked up. "We're dancers," said Milly. The young man nodded but didn't stop them.

"Hold on," whispered Rigel. "Let me go first." They moved down the empty crossover.

Rigel stopped dead center. "Can you feel it, Nancy?"

"What am I feeling again?"

"A pulse, gently pulling you toward the wall."

"Um, maybe a little. I've passed on through here umpteen times for dress rehearsals and performances and never noticed, but I do feel something like a vibration. If I move over here, I don't feel anything."

"Yes, that's right."

Milly ran her hands over the drapery. "Shoot, wish I could feel it."

"Nancy detects it because she's part DG. We shouldn't spend any more time back here, in case someone comes along. The most important thing is to hold hands, so we have a connection, especially Milly. Nancy should be able to go through without help, but take Milly's hand, I'll take her other. Whatever you do, don't let go."

At the exact moment they were reaching for each other's hands, Joan rushed down the crossover, with Charlene close behind. "Here you are! You weren't in the lobby yet, so I was showing Charlene where we have the recital."

Charlene tripped on a thick cable lying across the floor, falling into Joan, who fell into Nancy. All three women clutched the curtain hanging against the wall for stability. Collectively off-balance, they knocked into Rigel and Milly. Milly's hand slipped out of Rigel's, as the heavy material ripped off the rod. For a split second before the women were plunged into complete darkness as the curtain fell, Nancy saw Rigel's arm disappear, then his head, as the rest of his body followed through the portal. In another instant, the cocoon of black velvet also disappeared.

CHAPTER 13:
SITTIN' ON THE DOCK

Nancy's feet hit first before her legs collapsed onto a solid surface. She was suffocating. Oh dear God, she was dying. At least it was painless so far. Until a limb knocked her in the head. Life was not being sucked out of her. Her dance friends were thrashing about under a tent of heavy black material. "Ow! Get off me!" Nancy yelled.

"You get off *me!*" yelled Milly.

"Watch it! You hit me with your cast!" Joan shouted.

"You better not break my other wrist!" Charlene shouted back.

Scratching and clawing their way out of the massive amount of black velvet drapery that had come with them through the portal, they cried in unison, "Where are we?"

Milly was the first to recover. "Thank you, Lord, we made it." She labored to her feet and pulled Nancy up. They left Joan and Charlene sitting down, their heads popping up out of the velvet, swaying to music only they could hear.

"We made it somewhere." Nancy looked around. Her heart pounded and her breathing quickened. She leaned over with her head down, hands on her knees. "Supposed to arrive inside the Institute's portal wing." She took a deep breath. "Sterile white walls. This not what Rigel described. Lots of water. Sand. Palm trees. Uh-uh."

"Don't hyperventilate on me, Nancy. Focus."

Still bent over, Nancy glanced sideways at Milly. "Why aren't you . . . having a problem focusing?"

"I've lived with the concept of space-time travel my entire adult life. D'Gnomans coming and going to our house and my parents' house. I've accepted it. You haven't. Even though you're part DG, you are still doubting it. But it happened like Rigel said. Tingly, like when your leg falls asleep, only more intense, like your nerve endings are on fire all over at once, darkness, and then I felt nothing until I fell onto this decking. I'm cold, though. How 'bout you?"

Nancy straightened slowly, felt her face, checked how many fingers she had on each hand. "I was cold, but I'm feeling warmer now. Take a look around. We didn't whizz past the Institute and sail into oblivion, did we?"

"If this is oblivion," Milly said, "not a bad place to be. Very tropical."

They were sprawled next to a small building at the end of a dock that projected a short distance over a large body of water. Calm waves lapped the sandy shore. White, cumulus clouds floated statically overhead in an azure sky.

"Do you see Rigel?"

"I don't. Oh, Lord, this ain't right. He didn't say nothin' 'bout a beach. We got to figure out what happened. I don't know where we are."

"Hey, you two, how ya doin'?" Nancy asked.

"Bzzz," said Joan. "I feel buzzed."

"I was buzzed once," said Charlene. "Okay, twice." She giggled. "My momma would kill me if she found out I smoked weed. Maybe three times?" She covered her mouth with both hands. "Oh, who's counting." She giggled again.

"We won't tell your momma." Joan pulled her arm out of the fabric and patted Charlene's leg. "As long as you don't tell my momma about my man, who is sexy in bed like you wouldn't believe. Marcus can dance and sing and play guitar and make hot, steamy love to me. Not all at once, mind you. Or maybe he can all at once; he's terribly talented. My momma would *not* want to know that." She fanned herself. "Is it hot? I might have a fever. It's not a hot flash, is it? I'm too young for hot flashes. The last time I was with him, he gave me a full body massage. And you know where that leads—"

"Time out." Nancy made a T with her hands. "Stop. Too much information. We have to figure out how to get back home again."

Milly whispered to Nancy. "That girl won't stop talking. Those two must be experiencing the disorientation Rigel told us about."

"I think you're right. I'm sure it's temporary." Nancy looked through the building's window. "We must have come through here."

"What's in there?"

"It looks empty, but I feel the magnetic pull like I did backstage."

"That has to be the portal. Get away from it in case you trip into it, or, God forbid, you'll leave us behind."

"Yoo-hoo! Down here." Joan waved her arms. "Where *are* we?"

"We seem to be sitting on the dock of a bay," said Nancy.

"No shit, Sherlock," said Joan. "Oops, I didn't mean that. I'm not feeling myself. I mean I can feel myself." She poked her arm several times. "I'm just not feeling myself, ya know what I'm sayin'? How'd we get to the beach?"

"Through a special backstage door." Nancy shrugged her shoulders at Milly. She had no idea how to explain this.

Charlene gazed in all directions. "Far-out prop room."

"Bitchin'," said Joan. "The sky looks like the painted ceiling in Caesar's Palace or the Venetian in Las Vegas. How'd we get to Vegas?"

Nancy and Milly studied the sky. "We're under a dome," said Nancy. "How can that be? I don't remember Rigel saying anything about a dome or fake sky."

"D'Gnome is a planet like ours with oxygen, the whole bit. They don't live under a dome. I don't know what this is, but we have to get back to the school," said Milly.

"Y'all! There's Elvis Presley! Elvis is alive!" Charlene clapped her hands. "He's alive! I *knew* it." She swatted the drapery away and tried to stand up, swayed, and sat back down.

"Girlfriend, that man is as black as can be." Milly pointed to a man near the end of the pier sauntering toward the group wearing a solid cobalt blue double-breasted blazer and matching slacks. Light blue cuffs peeked out from his jacket sleeves.

"No, ma'am, over there!" Charlene pointed to the shoreline on her left and waved. "He-e-y! Yoo-hoo, Elvis!"

Elvis waved back.

"Alrighty, I do see an Elvis look-a-like," Milly said. "I forgot how long his sideburns were, and he's got that annoying black curl over his forehead I want to brush off."

"That's a lot of red and blue bling on that white getup," said Nancy. "Hope he doesn't get those fancy white boots wet."

"Elvis is popular in Vegas," said Joan. "How'd we get to Vegas?"

Elvis was a distance away down the shore, but the man in blue was nearly upon them. "Hey you, I was restin' and watchin' the tide roll away. What-choo doin' here?"

"Watchin' for ships rollin' in!" Joan laughed.

"Groovy."

The man was close enough to see the thin mustache lining his upper lip. He stepped onto the dock. "Holy guacamole! I recognize you." Joan began crawling on her hands and knees toward the man. She plunked down on the wooden deck and gazed up at the newcomer. "Is this the dock you sang about?"

Milly and Nancy each seized an armpit and hauled her back to the building and away from the stranger. "Don't you guys recognize him? Otis Redding—the King of Soul—the Big O. He's in the Rock and Roll Hall of Fame. 'Sittin' on the Dock' was the first posthumously released song to hit Number One on both the Billboard Hot 100 and R&B charts. Posthumously," she emphasized. "He was killed in a plane crash on December 10, 1967. How'd I know all that? Oh yeah, I did a report on him in seventh grade music class." Joan frowned. "Wow, I have a good memory. Anyway, he's dead. Am I dead?" She looked at Milly. "Are we dead?"

"If we are, then this must be Rock and Roll Heaven!" Charlene hugged Joan.

"Or VEGAS!" they yelled together, hugged again. "Whoo-hoo!"

Milly addressed the group: "Quiet! Listen to me. This is not Vegas. We are not dead. But we gotta get outta here before either of these men do somethin' crazy. Do as I say, okay? No questions. Scoot together. Hold on to the curtain. It will keep us together. Do not let go! On the count of three push against the side of the building."

"Excuse me, Milly." Joan held up an index finger. "One question. It seems important. Push *on* three or one, two, three, and then *push*."

"After three. Nancy, take hold of the Elvis-lover. I'll grab the Vegas showgirl. Okay. One, two, three, PUSH!"

CHAPTER 14:
THE SPLITS

Rigel was standing backstage in the empty, dark crossover, when one woman after another tumbled onto his feet. Little time had passed since he had gone through the portal to the Institute, found Nancy and Milly were not with him, and returned to the school. Now here they were entwined in one big lump of fabric.

"That was a hard landing," said Milly. "My old bones can't take this being shoved around by all your bodies."

Nancy pushed Joan away before she and Milly clambered away from the curtain.

"I have been looking all over for you!" Rigel said. "We were all standing there when your two friends came up. Everyone fell down, and I got pushed through to the Institute's portal wing without you. I returned immediately to the school. You should have still been in the crossover. Where have you been?"

"We went through. You weren't there," Milly said.

"You went where?"

"Don't ask me. A dock on a bay. Big body of water, sand, palm trees."

"Say what? That doesn't make sense." He contemplated a moment. "Or maybe it does. Remarkable."

"Remarkable? Like that was a swell place to be? Like it was fine and dandy to be off in some nether land alone? I'm not sure I trust these portals," said Nancy.

"Tell you later what I think occurred. Right now I'm going to perform a quick memory delete—more like a rearrangement—but they won't remember a thing about what happened. Then let's get these two up before someone comes along. The performers will be coming out of the dressing rooms pretty soon and using this area." Rigel kneeled down, placed his fingertips first on Joan's temples.

"Hi there, handsome," Joan cooed, while stroking the velvet drapery. "I once did a sexy dance for my boyfriend to 'Black Velvet' . . . naked," she whispered in his ear, running her finger lightly down his chest. "It's a very sexy song. Mississippi in the—"

"You keep singing. This will only take a second." Rigel held his fingertips in place a few seconds longer and then switched to Charlene, who said, "I'll have to try dancing naked for Bo. You think he'd like that?"

"I'm sure he would." Rigel looked up at Nancy and Milly who were shaking their heads.

"Get up, you two," said Nancy, reaching for Charlene. Milly threw off the material covering Joan and grabbed her hand. After a short struggle and disentanglement, Charlene and Joan were standing and had recovered from the cosmic travel as if it had never happened.

"I'm sorry, Joan, I tripped on that cable and took you down with me," said Charlene.

"No problem. Crappy curtains, though." Joan scratched her head. "Need replacing for sure."

"We should go. Here comes a guard." Nancy indicated stage right.

A security guard wearing a navy-blue uniform with "Security" embroidered in gold on both his short sleeves and left breast pocket sauntered toward the group. A communication radio was attached to his collar. He looked to be over eighty and carried a flashlight and a fairly large gut. Nancy figured they could outrun him, if they had to.

"Hello, officer," Nancy said. "I dance here and was showing my friends around, when she tripped on this cable and pulled the curtain down." She indicated the floor. "Someone should have covered these cables. Incredibly dangerous."

"Anyone hurt?"

"No." Nancy brushed herself off. "We're fine."

"We did this school a favor," Milly said. "These draperies are rotten. What if this steel rod had hit a student?" One end of the curtain rod clung to the wall; the other swung freely. Concrete dust and debris littered the floor.

"We'll get this cleaned up. You ought to join the other performers and send your friends back to their seats. The show's starting in a few minutes."

The women laughed, because the security guard believed Nancy was part of tonight's performance.

The auditorium served the school and the community with programs like the World of Arts, which once a month brought in performing artists from around the globe. Tonight, Collinsville was hosting Japanese Taiko drummers. People of all ages were milling about, roughly half having taken their seats. Unruly children were running up and down the aisles. Three sets of double doors stood open across the back of the auditorium, opening into the lobby. A steady stream of people flowed in.

Lucky to find five seats together, Milly introduced Rigel to Joan and Charlene as an old friend passing through town. Nancy twisted around to look up at the balcony. "Man, these seats are uncomfortable. You think they're any better up there?"

"Doubt it. This theater is as old as the school," said Milly. "I get the district newsletter, and the good news is that next year this theater is scheduled to be remodeled. They plan to replace these ugly red plush seats."

"And hopefully those awful drapes," said Charlene.

At that, the lights dimmed. The show was about to begin.

Having said their goodbyes to Charlene and Joan, Nancy drove back to Milly's, with Rigel once again stuffed in the back seat. No one mentioned the Taiko drummers. Nancy broke the silence. "As farfetched as it seems, I believe what you two are saying. There's no other explanation for what happened tonight, is there? Like no one slipped a hallucinogen into our drinks at the restaurant, did they, Milly? I mean, I'm trying not to freak out. I *really* have to talk to my mom. Give me a couple days to let this sink in, then I'll call her."

"Super," Rigel replied. "If she will come to Collinsville that will make it easier, especially since we can't rely on the San Diego portal."

"Are you sure we can rely on the Collinsville one?" Nancy wasn't so positive after what had happened tonight. At least their atoms weren't floating somewhere lost in space. Holy cow, had she just thought that? She glanced in the rearview mirror at Rigel. Was there an extraterrestrial creature lurking within that human form? Shivers went through her.

"The gateway is safe. I have a suspicion of what happened, but until I talk to the person responsible, I'll leave it at that. Otherwise, I'm speculating, but to be sure, tell me where you went again?"

"Heck if I know. Sandy beach, palm trees, very tropical, but we weren't about to go exploring!" Milly raised her hands in exasperation.

"We were sitting on the dock of a bay. There was a small building on the end over the water that happened to be the portal. That's what I remember," said Nancy.

Rigel's brows furrowed. "I thank the stars you remembered how to return. Was it Biloxi? That's one of our problem gateways. It's got beaches and palm trees."

"Nope, been there plenty of times. It wasn't Biloxi. You can't get there from here, can you?" Milly asked.

"Not under normal circumstances, but I'm not sure what's normal anymore."

"Joan thought it was Las Vegas, because we saw Elvis Presley and Otis Redding," Nancy said. "And the sky looked like what you might see in those upscale casinos, like Caesar's Palace, as if we were under an artificial sky."

"Ah." Rigel smiled. "Got it. Were Elvis and Otis real or robotic?"

"Real. You mean alive? Hard to tell. They were lifelike, walking and talking, but those guys are both dead." Nancy replied with a genuine smile. "They weren't ghosts. I'd say very good impersonators." She was feeling more like an ally than an outsider.

"Androids," said Rigel. "You went to Gansarcal, the largest of our three moons. Resorts are being built there under gargantuan biodomes. And I might know who made your trip possible. He has an entertainment contract there, so I'm certain those were his droids."

Nancy pulled into the parking lot of Milly's apartment building. Rigel leaned forward and said, "Thanks for agreeing to work with us. And don't hold anything against this delightful woman. She got dragged into this."

"Really? Did you hear that, Nancy? I'm delightful." Milly sighed like a girl in love, then immediately became serious. "And he's right. I had nothing to do with this. I was a porn in this man's hands. I mean pawn. Lordy, I did it again. You know what I mean."

"I can see you two need to carry on this conversation someplace else, like—in bed!" Nancy said, good-naturedly.

Now Rigel laughed, a deep rumble that bounced off the windows. "Now you're talkin'."

"No, she's not. Thanks for the ride." Milly climbed out of the car.

"I'll keep in touch with Milly, so tell her what happens with your mother."

"I will. Just don't call me. I don't want my husband to find out. I can't explain this to him yet."

"It'll work out," Rigel said as he exited the car. The two left Nancy alone with Mrs. Teal. As she pulled into the street, this new reality hit like a ton of bricks and terrified her all over again.

Why had her mother never said anything? Nancy went to eight schools in thirteen years. Had the frequent moves meant her mom had been running from someone? What stopped her? She's been in the same house for more than forty years. Did this ET thing explain why her mother had been so disengaged from her daughter's life?

Would her mother even come to Collinsville? In the eleven years Nancy had lived in this town, Trixie had never visited. She didn't like to travel, because the migraines made her sick. Maybe she couldn't hide as easily in a small town, unlike San Diego. What could her mom be hiding from? Worst of all, what would she tell Ted? She'd eventually have to tell him her newfound family history. Thank God they didn't have children.

Nancy's head was spinning from all the unresolved questions. Then the big one hit: Were there more like her? With an alien parent? Maybe she could start a support group. Oh god, that wasn't even funny. Her heart skipped a beat and she felt faint. What had she inherited? Most people knew who they were by fifty-five. Nancy felt like a stranger had invaded her body. Who was she?

Then, of all people, Milly—she'd known her for years! And Rigel—who was he really? Both had turned her world upside-down. Why couldn't she be *The Little Engine That Could*? She kept telling herself: I think I can. I think I can. I think I can accept everything I've seen and heard . . . but she couldn't.

Her breathing was shallow, her palms sweaty. Do not panic. Mind over matter. Breathe and relax. You may be having a panic attack, but you are not going to die. To relieve her tension, Nancy took a deep, cleansing breath, dropped her shoulders, which were up to her earlobes, and kneaded the back of her neck with one hand, while keeping the other on the steering wheel. Nancy repeated Rigel's words like a mantra: inhaling deeply, exhaling slowly. "It'll work out." Inhale . . . exhale. "It'll work out."

Quit concentrating on your physical symptoms, she told herself, and distract your mind—think happy thoughts. Tonight's dinner with dance friends. What did her fortune say? You will find a solution where you least expect it. Then they had added "in bed" and laughed. Charlene, you aren't the only one with a French maid's costume. Well, maybe you are. Hers had been chucked when that ship sailed with menopause, but on occasion she could drag something up from the depths of her psyche.

Tonight, though, she was too tired. Therefore, starting tomorrow or the next day, or maybe the next, her solution might come from where she least expected it, ya never know . . . in bed. Actually, a lot of good ideas came to her as she was first waking up. Maybe that's what her fortune meant. She was feeling better already. It *would* work out.

CHAPTER 15:
ON THE TRAIL

Rigel returned to D'Gnome happier than he'd felt in a long time. He would not have gotten Nancy's help without Milly and was thankful Nancy was still speaking to him after what he'd put her through. She had even agreed to ask Trixie to visit Collinsville. And what a relief no one had been harmed when he separated from the women at the school portal. Then there was Milly. He wondered where their relationship might go.

There was obviously more than one portal at the school now, and since he had not been informed of it, he surmised it wasn't an official one. He concluded the gateway breakdowns were human-caused and was pretty sure he knew the human causing the problems: the notorious Marcus Shining. Along with the transportation contract to Gansarcal, Marcus also had an agreement to provide entertainment in the hotels being built. He wasn't the only one with an entertainment contract, but he was the sole owner of song-artist androids from the same era as Otis Redding and Elvis Presley.

He'd have to find out why Marcus would be messing with intergalactic travel, since gateways were outside his realm of responsibility. But before that happened he needed to report to Betel Euse on his mission to "his old stomping ground," as she had put it. He commed her that he was back and, if she were free, would meet her for breakfast tomorrow at the Daisy Café.

"Good news, Bet!" Rigel said, once they had been seated at a secluded table enclosed with white latticework. He wasn't sure what the flowers were climbing up it, but he recalled at one time Bet saying they were hydrangea and wisteria. Didn't matter, he wasn't into this frilly place with its lacey placemats and fresh flowers on the tables. Bet liked it and the coffee was good, so he tolerated it for her. Plus each order came with a free "daisy bun," a cinnamon roll with pineapple tidbits for petals and a red cherry in the middle. He always liked a good deal.

"As it turned out," Rigel said, "Nancy had no knowledge of her mother's origins and was having none of it." He laughed. "At first, she thought it was a reality TV show and cameras were recording her reaction. But seriously, without Milly, Nancy would not have cooperated."

"See? So what'd she say? Will she get ahold of Trixie for us?"

"Yes. She asked for a few days and then she'd let Milly know. I'll keep in touch with Milly. It was a close call there at one point. Nancy fainted and fell on the floor." They both laughed at that. "Of course, it wasn't funny at the time. Milly thought I'd killed her."

"Well then, maybe we'll find out if Trixie knows anything or not. Can't have her sharing our gateway knowledge with anyone."

"Bet, if she knows anything, you'd think she'd have said something by now. She's our age."

"Are you inferring I'm old, Rigel?"

Rigel threw his head back and laughed. "Stars, Bet, you know I'm not. I'm just saying after all these years, you don't have anything to fear from Trixie."

"Let's hope not. Heads will roll if we can't get why these gateways failed or if we can't find out what Trixie knows."

Betel was sounding unusually sinister, so he dropped the subject of Trixie, and the two conversed on general topics through the rest of their meal. Rigel did not mention the backstage drapery debacle that brought Nancy, Milly, and their two friends to the dock on Gansarcal Bay.

As the meal wound down, Betel asked, "What else do you have planned for today?"

"Got to stop by the office."

"No golf then?"

"I'll take you up on the offer another day."

"Ha! Sure you don't have other things on your mind? How was your visit with Millicent?"

"What do you mean? I told you it went fine. It was good to get caught up on years past, but otherwise we discussed Nancy and Trixie. I didn't stay long."

"Huh, thought I picked up something. But that would be impossible because you haven't had the vaccine."

"No, I haven't." Rigel frowned. "Where are you heading with this, Bet?"

"Never mind. Got lots going on right now. Thanks for breakfast."

"Promise I'll take you up on that golf game soon."

"You're on." Betel stood up.

Rigel walked her to the door, and they went their separate ways.

He hated lying to his long-time friend. Like Marcus Shining, Rigel was a Freedom Jumper and had received the nepial vaccine. An unexpected side effect, discovered when the nanobot reported Bellatrix's pregnancy, was the drug's interaction with hormones that drive physical attraction and sexual desire between the two civilizations. Further research was halted and all information on the vaccine destroyed. The government was determined to keep the D'Gnoman race free of what they considered tainted blood—there would be no more Nancys.

Betel was right about something on his mind, but he couldn't discuss that with her, either—the mysterious new gateway to the moon. His investigation took on new meaning when Milly was involved. Whatever work needed to be accomplished, he could do from home, so he skipped the office. Later this evening, he'd hit up the place he knew Marcus Shining would be.

Waves of neon light undulated around the walls of the crowded room, casting a lavender glow over the noisy customers. The dance floor pulsed to the techno beat from the surround sound. The Purple Slurple Pub and Grub was meant for parties and good times.

Rigel was a Wednesday night regular—not that he was a partier, but he enjoyed the music from a trio of androids called the Sassy Sistas. He ordered the drink the pub was renowned for, a stein of deep purple malt liquor, and waited for the show to commence.

"Hey, old man, how's it goin'?" Marcus Shining claimed the empty bar stool next to Rigel.

"Been a long day." Rigel drained the last of his beer. "Seriously thinking of retiring. Letting someone else manage the Gansarcal resort project. Got this guy causing headaches with his change orders and requests for budget increases." Rigel smirked sideways at his younger friend.

"You're not serious. Dude, wait 'til you see the latest in transpo, the SX-WD41. The ship pierces the biodome's shield so smoothly passengers won't even notice. Lands like soft butter on warm toast." Marcus gestured with his hands as if they were the ship making that smooth landing on the moon.

"Not a very catchy name for the latest in moon travel."

"It's meaningful, man. SX 'cause this baby is sleek and sexy. WD for an updated warp drive that took us forty-one tries to get right. We got a surprise for passengers on approach and liftoff, which gave us trouble for a while. We're calling it the Rainbow Bridge. Wait 'til you see it. And, yeah, we coulda used a faster drive, but who needs it when you're going to the moon, so right-on, saved money there." Marcus grinned.

"I'd rather not talk about work."

"Hey, man, you brought it up. How 'bout I buy you a beer? The girls are coming on soon."

"I did, and I'll take you up on that beer. Thanks, bud."

With drinks in hand, the men turned toward the front of the room as the music faded and the lights dimmed. A hush fell and spotlights scanned the room. A light settled on each android as she reached center stage. With no microphone needed, three females who looked every bit like humans, sang in perfect harmony, "Hello, hello, hello!"

"We are the Sassy Sistas, and we know you love oldies from Earth. In case you're new here, I'm Saffron." She gestured toward a customer near the front. "You like my mullet, baby? It's new too!"

"Hi, everybody! I'm Sojourner. Tonight we're covering the great Earth artist Aretha Franklin. And, yes, if you've seen her you're thinking I look like that gorgeous woman. No? Maybe a little?"

Sojourner fluffed her wavy dark brown locks and brushed her bangs aside with a flair. The crowd cheered and whistled. "Uh-huh. I know I'm crushin' it. Thank you!"

"Last, but not least, I am the mean, green singing machine, Sagan! Thank you, thank you, I know I'm cool. But before you enjoy our show, we got a little sass for our programmer, Marcus Shining."

"Most of you know him. He's sittin' right over there." Saffron pointed to the bar, and a spotlight followed.

"Oh, Hades." Marcus bowed his head and shaded his eyes with this hand.

"Oh, my," cooed Sojourner. "He's sittin' next to Rigel O'Rion. Hey, Rigel, you handsome devil! Wish I could taste those luscious lips of yours, but, alas, I cannot, for my lips are synthetic." The audience laughed and "oohed."

"Seeing those beautiful dark eyes of yours, Rigel sweetie, my sensors go senseless." Sagan swooned.

In a serious tone, Sojourner said, "But we got to talk to Marcus Shining after this set. You hear me, Marcus dear?"

"That broom closet you put us in ain't no dressing room. We want a *real* dressin' room," demanded Sagan. "Come on, fans, show your love for the Sistas. You agree with us, don't you? Let's hear it!"

Over the roar of the crowd, Saffron yelled, "A broom closet don't show us no respect!"

"We ain't no chain of fools. We're stars!" said Sojourner.

"So you betta think, Marcus," said Sagan. "Think about how you treatin' us."

And at that, the Sassy Sistas broke out in Aretha's "Think," with live orchestral accompaniment.

"They're the least of your worries, man." Rigel listened to the music for a minute, then looked around to be sure everyone's attention was on the stage before he leaned closer to Marcus and said in a low voice, "Listen, I've been meaning to talk to you."

Marcus groaned. "I'll get those spreadsheets to you, promise. Next week."

"Forget those right now. Got any new projects in the works? Say, an Elvis Presley or an Otis Redding impersonator?"

Marcus appeared startled. "I have, as a matter of fact, been working on a couple of male singers from the same era as the Sassy Sistas. Did my Senior Superlative theme on that decade—flower power, make love not war; you get the drift. I love Earth's oldies, the '60s especially, and customers are asking for more. So, I give 'em what they want. Rock and roll never died, ya know."

"Isn't that the truth. Definitely doesn't compare to the tunes on today's waves."

"How'd you hear about the androids? I haven't announced any new ones."

"I'd tell ya, but we can't talk here. Seems like a good time to go, before the Sistas can call you out again."

"Right on. Let's grab a Scrambler to the terminal. I'll show you how the SX-WD41 will earn its worth."

They paid their tabs but didn't quite make it out before "Think" ended, or more like it was cut short.

"Don't you be trying to sneak outta here, Marcus Shining. Rigel, honey, don't be dragging that man off. We got issues to resolve." Saffron defiantly placed her fists on her hips.

The customers hooted and hollered, but no one stopped the men.

Marcus raised his arm in farewell. "I promise I'll talk to management about a dressing room. Rock on!" Then he followed Rigel out the door. From the comm-cell on his wrist, Marcus hailed a Scrambler.

At the hangar housing the SX-WD41, Marcus led Rigel to a larger, souped-up version of the standard Scrambler. It had lost its wings. The cockpit wasn't as prominent, instead it blended into the fuselage to look more like a cigar with eyes.

"The cherry red with yellow blaze motif on the fuselage was my design," Marcus said.

Rigel perused the sleek space mobile. "Swank."

Marcus touched his palm to the ID pad embedded on the side of the ship. A hatch opened, and half a dozen steps cascaded to the ground. "Climb aboard. I'll show you what this sucker can do."

CHAPTER 16:
RAINBOW BRIDGE

In moments, the lights of Ghanwik City disappeared. Soon the SX-WD41 slowed on its approach to the biodome, and its thrusters emitted a spectrum of color. Looking out the window, the ship appeared to slide down a prismatic arc. The rainbow disappeared as the rocket pierced the shield. The shield resealed, and the ship landed smoothly on the tarmac.

"I'm most proud of our work group for their creativity." Marcus grinned. "How'd you like the rainbow effects?"

Rigel nodded. "Very impressive."

"We wanted the landing zone to blend in with the environment, and at the same time not create a sandstorm. The tarmac is a solid surface, the same reddish-yellow color and texture of the sandy soil that naturally occurs here."

"And, if I recall, a bit pricey," Rigel teased, "but, like you said, a buttery-smooth landing. Nice job, kid."

"Thanks. You can't skip on a quality experience."

Rigel wouldn't argue with that. As financial manager of the project, he had seen the extensive resort plans and costs. While each biodome had a landing zone for guests, other transporters, cargo and the like, would dock outside the domes and unload through separate airlocks. The three zones were connected by guest-accessible corridors. Each zone had its own independent life support system. Emergency escape pods were strategically placed throughout the compound. The hub of the entire multi-complex was the geodesic dome in the center, which contained everything needed to sustain life: air and water purifiers and circulation pumps, gravity controllers, solar power plants, and a data control center to keep everything running smoothly. Durable goods, fresh food and drinks, and ingredients for printer meals were flown in from D'Gnome.

When completed, there would be three resort hotels in separate biodomes, each with a different theme: oceanic, desert, and rainforest. They were meant to resemble large resorts on Earth, with luxury hotels, restaurants, spas, and sports activities coinciding with each theme. Pleasure travel to Earth was not allowed. These resorts, the senators reasoned, would curb the appetite of people desiring trips to Earth. They could get on a rocket ship and travel to another world, albeit the moon, but it would look and feel every bit like Earth.

"We're calling this connection from DG to Gansarcal the Rainbow Bridge. Always wanted to see what was at the end of the rainbow? Take the Rainbow Bridge and slide into a world of relaxation, entertainment, and fine food. Whadaya think?" Marcus asked.

"Not my thing, but people go for that gimmicky stuff. I'd say you oughta be in marketing instead of transportation."

"No thanks. I'll keep my day job."

Rigel looked out the cockpit window. "Stars, I shoulda come here sooner. It's more expansive than one can imagine digitally."

"With the passenger ships and hover buses, plus escape pods we're building into the hotels and corridors, I've been here plenty. Let me give you the grand tour." Marcus unbuckled his harness.

"Not yet." Rigel did the same with his harness but stayed seated. "It's all clear in the cockpit to speak openly. I've got some questions."

Thanks to Dr. Euse, Rigel was a member of the Inner Circle. He had taken an official oath to never discuss the Bayers or their daughter, Bellatrix, outside the Circle. Grandchildren did not exist at the time of his oath, however, and no reference had been updated regarding future offspring. An ironic oversight of the oversight committee. Not that an oath mattered here. The men knew each other from their membership in the Freedom Jumpers. The "all clear" was a sign they could speak without eavesdroppers.

"Talk to me, man." Marcus crossed his arms.

"Recently four Earth friends and I tried to take the portal from Collins High School to the Institute's portal wing. Somehow we separated, and from their description, they arrived here instead. Since you're engaged in the project, I supposed you might be familiar with what goes on here, like maybe a new gateway."

"What the blazes do you mean? How could your friends have gone to Gansarcal?"

"That's what I'm asking you. They were expected to come with me to DG. While I arrived at the Institute, they materialized outside a shed on the dock of a bay. I'm pretty sure *this* bay and *that* shed." Rigel could see the water and the dock from the cockpit window. "You don't have anything to do with a split gateway from Collinsville, do you?"

"Never heard of a split gateway."

Rigel sensed that Marcus knew more than he was telling. "I am concerned for my friends' safety. If it happened once, it could happen again, Marc, that's all I'm saying."

"Not unless you're with them. Earth folks can't use the portal."

"One was part DG."

"No way. *Part* DG? You mean Nancy Leopold?"

"You know her?" Marcus asked.

"As a Freedom Jumper, like you, I know *of* her, but I've never met her. And you have?"

"Euse decided to circumvent Trixie and meet with Nancy. So yeah, I've met her."

"Ooh, Meissa will be furious when she finds out you went instead of her."

"I'm sure she will be. But Euse is right, Trixie will trust someone she knows more than a stranger like your sister. I wasn't sure at first if meeting Nancy was the best idea, but now I believe it was. We've never been able to talk with Trixie, and this probably would have been no different. So I'm hoping Nancy can convince her mother to meet with me."

"Why'd you get Nancy and her friends involved with the portal in the first place?"

"Nancy wouldn't believe me about D'Gnome, so I offered to show her and a friend. Two others came along unexpectedly and went through with them. They weren't with me when I arrived at the portal wing, but arrived here. Hence, the split. Know anything about that?"

"Um, I wouldn't call it a split gateway . . . more side by side, but yeah, I might know a smidgeon."

"Bud, don't make me drag it out of you." Rigel straightened and glared at the pilot.

Marcus heaved a big sigh. "Dude, we're on the same side. Chill. This is huge for me to admit. You have got to hold it in strict confidence."

"Works both ways. This conversation never happened."

"The FJ Council chose Collinsville as the best place to manufacture the Pathfinders. You didn't know that?"

"Due to my Inner Circle connection, I'm not always informed in real time of current Jumper activity. Since the Pathfinders were banned by Presider Grassely, I knew the Freedom Jumpers were looking for a manufacturing site—didn't know it was in Wyoming."

"It's the least-populated state, yet Collinsville is big enough to have the materials we need. No one will pay attention to what's going on inside a big metal farm building, plus we plan to put a security barrier around it. Fortunate to get Trebo Luapa to help us."

"Trebo?"

"Yeah, helps to have friends in "low places"—a.k.a. Earth. Heh-heh. Trebo was like an older brother to me when I was Senior Superlative. His parents sponsored me. He was away at college most of the time I was there, but we've always kept in touch. He left Texas to purchase and manage the Wyoming property. Got a job there as an engineer, which made it easier for him to accept the Freedom Jumper offer. And eventually with a new portal inside the building he bought, no one will see anything suspicious."

"Hold it. A new portal? Meaning the one from the school to Gansarcal?"

"Yup, created by yours truly. You know what they say, ask a busy person. I still hafta move it from the school to the barn. Thing is, I'm a rocket scientist, know what I'm sayin'? Interested in machines, so I'm no expert in astrophysics." Marcus chuckled. "But I *am* the transportation man with good connections to Gansarcal, so who got elected to figure it all out? Me. Could never have appealed to the gateway specialists, since you might say what I'm doing is illegal, and it would have alerted my dear sister and Dr. Euse of our intentions. I really coulda used Meissa's help, but I didn't want to risk getting her in trouble. Anyhoo, we needed a new portal not on the radar. I tried to copy Biloxi, changing the coordinates and such, but I inadvertently reconfigured it. Trying to fix that mess, I screwed up San Diego."

"Way to go, Marc. Not a very bright move."

"Lighten up, man. The gateway from Gansarcal to the school is temporary. When the building is ready, I'll switch it over. Biloxi and SD are back to normal now, except gotta admit, I screwed over my sister, which I truly regret. But she's not a Freedom Jumper, so I couldn't say anything. As much as she bugs me, I hated to see her struggle. She kept fixing it; I kept breaking it. But then she wouldn't have gotten the promotion to team leader if I hadn't caused the first crash. So everybody wins. One day I'll tell her, after things calm down. Right now she'd have my head if she knew."

Rigel grimaced. "Aren't you worried you'll be caught and sent to prison?"

"Let me tell you, I sweated it for a while, wondering if I should try to create the Gansarcal to Collinsville gateway or not. Then I found a way to erase my bogus account before it could be detected. Had to have more than . . . nah, I won't go into the details. They'll never trace anything to me."

"Good luck there. You'll be visiting Gansarcal for something other than a vacation."

"Not messin' with astrophysics anymore. After I change the coordinates from the school to the farm building, I'm sticking to my main thang—travel is my game; improving it's my aim."

"Isn't that catchy. You really should be in advertising. I take it that's the infamous dock off starboard?"

"The one and only."

"What's the building for, besides a portal?"

"Small equipment storage for watersport activities. Let me give you the grand tour, unless you got more questions."

"One. How are you going to keep unauthorized D'Gnomans from detecting the portal?"

"I don't like to admit it, but you're looking at a genius. Yup, right before your eyes." Marcus laughed.

"Come on, Marc, quit messing around."

"By messin' around, man, I'm tellin' ya, I was so deep into digital dirt I wasn't sure for a while there if I was gonna put it all back together. But in the process I found a way to transfer the stealth tech of the new Pathfinders to Gansarcal."

"You found out about the Pathfinder's stealth technology?" Rigel raised his eyebrows in disbelief.

"Shouldn't take all the credit. Did have some FJ help from a couple members who worked on the latest PF. The portal is undetectable and untraceable. And it closes as soon as the traveler leaves the dock. There will be a keypad installed, which I haven't got to yet, that will serve two purposes: a lock for the shed and a separate password code for the portal. Those with permission of the Freedom Jumpers will have the code downloaded to their comm-cell. Your friends were lucky they didn't leave the dock. They wouldn't have gotten home."

"Okay, I've had enough." Rigel stood up, stretched his arms, and yawned. "Let's get on with the tour."

Marcus opened the hatch. The men descended the stairs to the tarmac.

"The lake was formed from a natural depression after water was pumped from an underground aquifer," Marcus said. "You probably know that."

"I do. But what strikes me is the sky. The triangular panels making up this dome are seamless. The sky touches the horizon as it would on any planet."

"Yeah, those clouds are computer-generated graphics, so when they're functioning, they'll appear to change shape, for example, from cumulus to cirrus, that sort of thing. Right now no one is in the control room, so they're static. Matter of fact, no one is around, period. Workers have gone home on the transporter to DG. That leaves the penitentiary on the far side, nowhere near here. So this would be a good time to show you the hotel and check out the Neptune Lounge."

"I'm down for that. Incredible amount of palm trees and flowering plants, etc., were in the budget. Now that I see them, wow, wouldn't know they're artificial."

"Remarkable it is. The pathways aren't in. You okay slogging through the sand to the hotel, old man?"

"I'm almost twice your age, but don't you worry, I can whip your butt."

"You ain't comin' close to my butt."

"I meant beat it."

"That doesn't sound any better."

"Beat you in a race. Damn it, it's been a long day. Where's that lounge? If nobody's around, how you gettin' in?"

"Nothing's locked up. We'll pay for what we drink, if there's anything there *to* drink. Might not be stocked yet." Marcus took off running, with Rigel not far behind.

Both men were out of breath by the time they got to the Coral Reef Resort and Spa.

"Not bad. You surprise me for a man your age."

"Knock it off, Marc. You'll be my age one day. Let's hope you're in as good a shape."

The wide, palm-lined portico led to large doors resembling clam shells covered in glittering gems in a paisley pattern. As they approached, the doors whisked apart. The resort was aptly named, as the lobby made one feel immersed in a vibrant coral reef. Sculptures of orange, yellow, red, and purple coral, complete with scores of tropical fish, lined three walls.

"Wow, this is really beautiful," said Rigel.

"Yeah, the huge coral sculpture in the middle has water jets set to Caribbean music. Take a little salsa, mix in some reggae, add some calypso, and you got beats like no other." Marcus swayed and rotated his shoulders. "Makes ya wanna dance, party, spend mo' money. Hey, Elvis, turn on the fountain, will ya?" he called in a loud voice. "Where are those dudes? You never did tell me how you knew about my Elvis Presley and Otis Redding droids."

"You're the genius. You tell me."

"Ha, got me there. Wait. Oh yeah, your friends, Nancy Leopold and whoever was with her, correctamundo?"

"Right on, sonny-boy."

"I should probably tell ya I got Otis and Elvis here as lookouts. Well, they're also part of the entertainment package. They're around here somewhere, patrolling the premises. I've asked them to let me know if they see Meissa lurking about. I hate to say this, but Meissa found out about Trixie and wants to know how she stayed on Earth. She didn't gather anything useful from the Bayer inventory. I wouldn't put it past her to seek Harold and Erma out whether she had permission or not. She might even meddle with Trixie and Nancy, as well."

"Euse told me Meissa uncovered the truth and that she'd denied Meissa's request to visit. Don't think she knows about Nancy." Rigel threw Marcus a piercing glance. "How serious a threat is your sister? You say she doesn't know about the vaccine?"

"She is super set on gaining access to Harold and Erma about the gateways. Even though they're working now, she still wants to talk to them. How much she knows about the nepial gland research, I haven't a clue. She's awfully smart, though, and probably suspects Trixie's lifetime on Earth is related to the gland. She knows whatever it is, it's highly classified, and she hates that sort of thing. Not sure how far she'd go to get what she wants. I mean she's not a murderer or anything."

"Yet how many family members and people next door have said, so-and-so was such a nice person, can't imagine him hurting a flea. Then their darling is caught red-handed in some horrendous act."

"Guess I'd keep my eye on her. And you know who else I'd keep my eye on? Betel G. Euse."

"I had breakfast with her this morning and she sounded almost threatening. She was a school chum of Trixie's and seemed all caring about her when she asked me to go to Collinsville. But she seemed on edge that night, and today she actually questioned if I'd had the vaccine."

"Folks are saying she's visibly pulsating, changing her mind constantly on decisions she's made, shouting commands at co-workers, criticizing the recovery team and about everyone else."

"She's got a lot on her plate, and she's mentioned retiring. That decision's weighing on her mind as well."

'I'm just sayin', I wouldn't make excuses for her." Marcus placed his hand on Marcus's shoulder. "Keep your eyes open."

"Thanks for the advice, bud. Inform me right away if you hear anything more."

As they headed toward Neptune's Lounge, Marcus's comm-cell let out a high-pitched screech.

Rigel stopped in his tracks, squatted, and covered his head, as if expecting an attack from above. "What is that?"

Marcus glanced at his cell. "A distress call from the Sassy Sistas. They were helping Meissa with the Bayer inventory. They're still at the archives because I haven't picked them up yet. Something must be wrong, so the tour has to end, my friend. Gotta fly."

CHAPTER 17:
WHEN GOOD GHOULS GO BAD

Meissa couldn't get over the feeling something was missing from the Bayer inventory. She'd been fuming over the partial line entry ever since it occurred. The droids had opened a bin containing assorted dolls. Under the column heading "Item" was the entry "doll." The next column was "Description." Every doll had a description. Except one. Why had the droids not completed the description?

Marcus had explained away the omission as no big deal—simply bad air causing a glitch. No mistakes were made, he assured her. Still, she was certain the database error was Marcus's fault. He had acquiesced too quickly to her request for help. He always gave her a hard time whenever she asked for his help, but not this time. Was he looking for something too? She couldn't imagine what it would be or why. His work with machines, both transportation and robotics, had nothing to do with either Harold or Erma Bayer. The inventory was complete, and there had been no other incidents. So whatever it was he wanted had to be in the bin marked M19K71.

The more she thought about the possibility of Marcus having an ulterior motive, the angrier she got. With her mind in a whirl, Meissa couldn't concentrate on work. She glanced at the clock on the wall. It was only mid-afternoon. To get anything done was useless, so to ease her suspicions, she would have a little dialogue with her brother's androids. She should go down there anyway to make sure no bins were omitted before the inventory was officially closed out and Marcus retrieved his droids. As she left the office, she told her coworkers she was leaving for the archives and would be gone the rest of the day.

Meissa grabbed a Scrambler to the archive building. Inside, she threw the nasty-looking sentry a glare, whizzed by him without showing her ID, stomped into the elevator, and growled for the lowest level. Inside the basement storage room, the androids were standing dormant, their jobs done—Marcus had not picked them up yet. "Wake up, you stooges!"

The females came to life, raising their heads and opening their eyes. Frowns replaced smiles when their guest was recognized as Meissa Shining.

"Greetings, fiend," replied Saffron defiantly.

"Friend," corrected Sojourner.

"Friend or fiend, we'll get beaned," added Sagan.

"Shut up. Did you take anything from M19K71 and not return it?"

"No, boss."

"We're at a loss."

"Looking for the sauce you lost?"

Meissa scowled, tapping her foot impatiently. "Let me rephrase the query. Where is the toy you retained?"

"We kept no toy."

"Stealing would not bring us joy."

"We speak to annoy. Oops, did I say that?" Sagan covered her mouth with her hands. "I was getting into the rhyming thing."

"Figures. You are annoying and you are liars. I. cannot. find. the answers. And it is driving me wild!" Meissa kicked each Sista in the knee. They crumpled to the floor, screeching and flailing their arms, one after the other. "I've got more important things to worry about than some dumb missing toy. I hardly think it would be related to my own problems anyway. You can have it."

"She is a mean fiend," said Saffron

"Told you we'd get beaned," said Sagan.

"I am signaling Marcus. He'll be steamed," said Sojourner.

"See if I care." Meissa stormed out of the basement, erupted out of the elevator into the main hall, and was abruptly stopped by the sentry.

"Halt!"

"What? I have done nothing wrong. You're talking to the head of a very important department."

"Name's Thadd Verra."

"I don't care what your name is. What do you want?"

"Ya *will* care when I tell ya what I heard as ya thundered past me earlier. Notes were streaming from yer brain like the exhaust velocity from a rocket. Amazed ya didn't achieve lift-off. First rule of Anger Management 101: Don't let yer guard down. Ya flunked real nice."

The tension in her body was ready to snap. "What did you hear?"

"Not sayin', but I offer my most humble assistance." Verra bowed deeply. "We'll have ta take this tête-à-tête someplace else. Meet me at midnight, Meissa. At the AI recycle depot. And don't let anyone know."

"Are you bonkers? I'm not meeting you at the depot, especially at midnight."

"With what I got, yer'll want ta scratch my back, an' I'll scratch yers."

"No, thank you. That's obscene." She dashed out of the building. How'd he know her name? Her badge, of course.

Meet me at midnight, the creepy watchman had said. Meissa was home trying to recall what she'd been thinking when she'd entered the National Archives this afternoon. What had that man heard?

He was right about flunking anger management. Two gateways had gone down, and she hadn't understood why. Now they were miraculously back up, but for how long? She didn't know that, either. Nothing like this had happened before. What had changed? She desperately wanted to interrogate Harold and Erma Bayer—there wasn't any better source than the originator. Would Erma be able to offer clues as to what possibly could go wrong with an established gateway? And Harold, for why their daughter, Bellatrix, had lived so long on Earth? She was certain it had something to do with the brain's nepial gland. That information wasn't part of her job, but it intrigued her. What she'd do with the knowledge, she hadn't decided yet, probably leak it to the public. Then authorized travelers would say, "You mean I wouldn't have to worry about death while on Earth if there was a way to avoid it?" It would be fun to watch Presider Grassely explain that one away.

Dr. Euse had denied Meissa visitation, so she'd have to figure out some way to get to the Bayers without her boss knowing. Meissa knew where they had been moved at the time of their arrest, but she'd not ascertained their current mental state. Perhaps they were in protected nursing care. After all, they were near the end of their lifespan.

Solving problems had been easy for her until these gateway issues emerged. She had a new job, but she wasn't doing very well at it so far. She worried about the abduction of Harold and Erma Bayer and the role the government played in it.

To top it off, the inventory database error still bugged her. No shocker that her stress level was through the roof. She'd be hearing from Marcus soon enough, after kicking his lovely androids. Craters, that was the first time she'd ever taken physical abuse out on anyone, even mechanical beings. But wasn't it better to take her anger out on some*thing* rather than some*one*? Those droids weren't in any pain, and it sure felt good.

"What's becoming of me, Flekk? You got any answers?" she asked her Bengal cat.

Waking from a nap, Flekk yawned and stretched her long body. "Answers to what?"

"I don't know." Meissa heaved a sigh. "What if I released the Bayers from their pen captivity on Gansarcal? Wouldn't that be a hoot? I'd like to see the Presider deal with that one."

"First, he'd have Dr. Euse fire you."

"Yeah, wouldn't want that. I need this job if I'm going to replace Euse one day. But I really want to shout, here I am! Look what I did! I did it for you, the people! You deserve to know your favorite scientists are alive!"

"You go, girl! More power to you!" Flekk sat back on her haunches and paddled her two front paws to show her enthusiasm.

"The idiot at the archive's front desk stopped me today. Must have heard my jumbled thoughts on the Bayers. As surely as there are three moons orbiting D'Gnome, I've broken my confidentiality oath, even though I didn't utter a single word. I was careless, and I'm sure he read my mind about the Bayers being alive. He wants to meet me at midnight at the recycle depot. I don't think I have a choice. He'll blackmail me, unless I deal first. What do you think, Flekk?"

"Check him out. Do a background check."

"I can't even remember his name. Maybe I'll search for National Archives security guard and see what comes up in their personnel directory and look for a schedule of who worked when. Thanks, Flekk. It's nice to be able to talk to you."

"No problem, but right now this beautiful body could use some nourishment."

"Okay, fine." Meissa reached down to stroke the soft, multi-colored spotted fur and scratch behind Flekk's ears before heading to the kitchen.

As Meissa sat at the table, she called up a screen to begin her search. Why midnight? He wouldn't want to discuss such sensitive information in a place full of security cameras, probably with audio, especially if he were going to blackmail her. It was asinine, but she would go.

Her search brought up Luke Wersalkky. No facial hair in the picture, so it must be an old photo. She really didn't get a good look at his face—he wore a cap pulled down over his forehead, and the bushy beard obscured his facial features. No criminal record anyway. Married, with a wife and two teenage boys. A family man couldn't be too dangerous.

With that settled, midnight couldn't come soon enough. With several hours to go, she worked herself into a nervous frenzy. She knew she could call for help easy enough if he threat-ened her, but what kind of a deal could she make? She poured herself a hot bath, added some calm-ing lavender scent, and soaked, hoping the answer would come if she relaxed.

The robot recycle depot in the daylight was scary enough; in the dark, it was downright gruesome. Meissa's school chums used to tell horror stories about giant robots, ready to strangle anyone who made it past the gate. The place was haunted, and brain-computer interface experiments used to be done there. Brainwaves floated around trying to enter your head like a worm through your ear, classmates would declare. Some kids, like Mar-cus and his reckless friends, would dare each other to climb the fence, run in, grab proof, like a loose metal hand or foot, and run out before get-ting caught. Meissa never partook so didn't really know if the harrowing stories of escape were true. She'd rather have been reading than doing some-thing stupid like that.

Outside her front door, a Scrambler hovered with warm, ambient lights glowing inside and out. On her approach, the door slid up. It was chilly out, and Meissa welcomed the warmth of the ship.

The recycle depot was outside the city limits, but in a rocket taxi, she only had a minute to de-cide to turn back. "We have reached your destination. Please take your belongings with you," cooed the soft feminine voice. Ah, well, have courage, she told herself. You're an adult, not a scared child. She asked the Scrambler to wait for her return and exited. As she stepped out into the night, a tall, foreboding gate announced the entrance to the repository. Gargoyles, one perched atop each post on both sides of the gate, looked down on her: Make one wrong move and you're dead, they seemed to say. No wonder kids were frightened. Would she have to climb the rusted iron bars like her childhood friends used to do? The guard never gave her directions besides meeting him here. A prickly sensation spread throughout her body; she shivered and shoved her cold, clammy hands into the pockets of her jacket.

Behind the gate, in the darkness, two bright green lights bobbed six feet above the ground moving toward her. Meissa squinted. Was that a security machine roaming the grounds? Nothing illuminated the yard. This was insane. As she turned to run, a raspy voice called out, "Ah, the shining one, ya came. Come in, come in." The iron gates creaked open.

She looked back at the Scrambler, then took a few tentative steps inside. "Yup, I'm here. What's with your eyes?"

"Babe, the betta to see ya with."

"Yeah, right."

"Yah, really, thar infrared lenses. The betta to see in the dark. Cool, huh?" He blinked, and his eyes disappeared for a split second.

"Tell me what you heard and how much money you want."

"Whoa, yer no fun."

"I'm not here for fun, Mr. Wersalkky."

"Mr. Who?"

"Luke Wersalkky. Your name. I searched the employee database."

Between fits of laughter, the large man spit a sunflower seed's shell onto the ground. "Mr. Wersalkky is back at the archives moppin' floors. He unfortunately let his guard down when I hinted his wife was my lover. He don't remember much now. Database must not be updated." He chuckled, his gold tooth glinting in the dim glow from the Scrambler, and spit again. Another shell bit the dust.

"Okay, I'm leaving."

"Hey, I told ya my name. Thadd Verra. Not gonna hurt ya, so cool yer jets." He spit upwards, this time the shell pinging off the gargoyle. "Bull-seye!"

The name did sound familiar. "Please stop that. I can't stand spitting of any kind."

"That's all I got. Rest's in my pocket. Want some?" Thadd Verra dug deep into his pants pocket and held out a handful. Meissa shook her head. "Yer loss." He shoved them back inside.

"What do you want, Verra? Wait, are there cameras? Should I be worried we're being watched?"

"Nah, no worries. Nobody cares 'bout the graveyard. Come on. Got somethin' ter show ya. Foller me."

"No worries, then, we can talk here. I'm not going in there." She could see massive arms sticking up from the ground like tree trunks. Probably something from a mass production factory line. She knew they were scrap, but they looked like they could mash her into mush. "I don't have all night. What do you want?"

"Whoa, babe. Not so fast. Yer mad about that bitchy boss not lettin' ya see the scientists who lived."

"You know about them?"

"Oh, yuh, I know. See, I got connections at the pen. Dern't worry, yer secret is safe with me."

"Why do you want to help me?"

"Stroke a luck, eh? Ya managin' travel and all, and me in need of special permission to Earth. Duh, we can hep each other. Now, here's how I see it. Ya got good reasons to visit the Bayers, but they ain't gonna cooperate easy. Ya gotta be tough. Make 'em talk. If they dern't, ya gotta threaten 'em, kidnap 'em, be tough."

"You said that. How tough do I have to be if they're old and weak?"

"Thar not as bad off as ya think. Thar'll be stubborn. Threaten 'em where it hurts, ooh, ooh, with thar own kid. That'll git 'em talkin'."

"How do you know about their kid?"

"I know a lot, then again I don't know much." Thadd Verra rubbed his forehead with the fingers of both hands.

"I don't know if I can do this. I don't want to threaten or kidnap them. I just want information."

"Ya want that thar info or not? Ain't gonna be easy, but yer young, kinda, and strong. Used ta gettin' yer way, I bet."

"I am, but why do you need to go to Earth?"

"Got a dyin' friend. Want ta see her before she expires."

She didn't want to ask how he knew someone on Earth—he couldn't possibly have been a Senior Superlative. She couldn't imagine any other way he would have gotten permission to travel, but she really didn't want to know the details of his life. There was no way he'd let his guard down, as she so carelessly had. Rearranging his memory was out of the question. If he helped her, she'd have to give something in return. An unrecorded trip to Earth wouldn't be hard to do. She didn't believe he had a dying friend, but whatever his reason, she really didn't care, if he could give her what she wanted.

"Agreed. I'll get you to Earth and back. You get me to the Bayers."

"Deal." He reached out his hand to seal the agreement, but Meissa stepped back and offered her elbow instead. "Look, ya ain't gonna hurt nobody, but ya gotta have someone to keep watch if ya end up kidnappin' 'em. Got the right good thing fer ya. Let's go shoppin'. Babes like to shop, ain't that right? Thar's a section of the yard fer reject robots and androids, old school, but thar'll serve yer purpose."

"If I go any farther, there will be no more spitting and no more calling me babe, got it?"

"Ba—bummer, yer no fun."

"I know. Keep tellin' yerself that." Meissa wasn't sure if she should trust this coarse specimen of a human, but her better judgement seemed to have taken a dive. How else was she going to get what she wanted? Finding the answers she needed would give credit to her good name, which would bring her closer to her ultimate goal of Intergalactic Research Director, which would . . . that was it. That's what she wanted. Director of the Institute. The Inner Circle. A chance of making policy for the entire planet. Power.

"Okay, let's do this." She flipped on her comm light.

"Now yer talkin', but turn off dat light. Ya don't want ta show yerself ta the graveyard demons. Heh-heh. Plenty of moonlight if ya let yer eyes adjust."

Meissa flipped off the light and noticed that the moonlight gave the junk an even eerier glow. Shivers crawled up her spine.

"See dat buildin' up ahead? Gots robots and androids not yet ready for primetime recyclin'. If a droid might has a little life left, it gets thrown in thar."

A long, rectangular, shadowy shape hung in the distance. She sighed in resignation and followed Thadd Verra down a rocky road, through piles of artificial body parts as high as her shoulders, twisted wires heaped like giant nests, towers of circuit boards haphazardly stacked like dominoes, ready to topple at the slightest breath, and—WHIZZ. Something black streaked across her path. She screamed. "What the hell was *that*?" It was all she could do not to grab hold of her accomplice. She might have, if he hadn't smelled like a decaying carcass.

Thadd Verra guffawed. "Ah, that's Oleo chasin' his dinner. He my pet weasel. Oleo! Git over here! Meet our new friend."

"No, thanks. He can keep on doin' what he's doin'."

"Yeah, he's too fer gone. Yer'll meet him another time."

Inside the storage building, Thadd flipped a switch. Gadzooks! Here was a massive army of bodies, complete with faces ogling at her from every direction. Meissa rubbed the goosebumps from her arms and tried to slow her heartbeat. Have courage, have courage, she repeated silently, over and over.

"Hello, comrades!" called Thadd.

Meissa half expected them to salute, but nothing moved and silence reigned. Her voice strained, she squeaked, "Let's just pick one." She scanned the bodies nearest her and recognized one android as having belonged to her brother when he first began refurbishing androids. "How about that one?"

"Fine choice. Was recently in conversation with Miss Janis J. Know she'll work for ya." He picked her up, hauled her over his shoulder, and headed toward the door.

Meissa felt like a ghoul robbing the graveyard, preying on corpses. Thank the stars, we're out of here. She had never felt so awful.

Now that they'd gotten what they'd come for, Meissa agreed to open a private link for them to communicate from now on. No more midnight meetings. Working on a scheme to meet the Bayers while they exited this terrifying tomb kept her imagination in check.

Thadd stayed inside the gate. Meissa wasted no time jumping into the waiting Scrambler and high-tailing it back to the safety of her home. If all went according to plan, they would meet again on Gansarcal.

CHAPTER 18:
WHAT'S IN A NAME

Rain pounded the windshield. The wipers slapped back and forth, making it difficult for Nancy to see as she drove down the highway to the dance studio. Dark clouds filled the sky, obscuring the setting sun, making it seem later than 7 p.m. Tonight was the beginning of their ninth year of tap. At every recital she'd be so nervous, she'd get cotton-mouth. Maybe this would be the year she'd not have such stage fright. So far she'd said that every year! Yet she absolutely loved tap dancing and performing. When she took her place on stage and the music started, it was all smiles, despite her nerves. So many great memories. So many fun dances. "Mama Mia" was her favorite. Or maybe the Mary Poppins medley. The freedom of "Let's Go Fly a Kite," as they danced around the stage with kites held high, the tails swirling behind them, filled her with joy.

A sharp bolt of lightning lit up the mountain to the south. A clap of thunder right afterwards made her jump. The car swerved—she was hydroplaning! She let up on the gas, which was enough to straighten herself out. Had she been going any faster she could have lost control. The online safety course she and Ted had taken to get a discount on their car insurance had covered hydroplaning, but when it actually happened, it made her heart race. Turn which direction? Into or away from the skid's direction? She thought it was into the skid and don't hit the brake. Well, she had let up on the gas which slowed her down. She told herself to quit daydreaming about dance. She wanted to get to class in one piece.

Nancy parked as close to the front door as she could get and made a run for it, banging open the door to the common room full of parents, young dancers and their siblings as she hurried inside. Charlene was already there, talking with Milly. She tossed her dance bag on the floor and kicked off her wet street shoes. "Charlene, you finally brought some rain . . . and your cast is gone!"

"Freedom!" She lifted her atrophied forearm high as a winning prize fighter would in the ring. "It feels so good to have that thing off."

Joan was the last to arrive. "Oh my gosh, it's pouring out there! Sorry, I'm late. Marcus is here. He gives me fever, know what I'm sayin'?" She sat on a bench to change into tap shoes.

"We see it. Steam's rising from you like a—" Milly raised her eyebrows and shook her head. "I don't know."

"A fever." Charlene grinned.

Joan looked down at herself. "Well, I'm wet and hot, but I love a rainy night!"

A dozen chattering teens in black leotards and colorful shorts poured out of their assigned room. Jasmine was there and welcomed them. She was back for a fifth year of teaching the adults. During the day, she was a journalist for the *Tribune* and taught dance at night. She was in her late twenties, thin, and wore her light brown hair in a loose bun. The adults spent twenty minutes talking about Jasmine's grandfather, the summer, and the upcoming talent show. They were noisier than any gaggle of girls. Finally, Jasmine managed to squeeze in a question about Charlene's tap experience.

"Started tap when I was three and danced through high school. I don't care to say how long ago *that* was."

"You'll be fine. It's like riding a bike. You never forget."

"We'll see. I wasn't very successful the last time I rode my bike. Crashed and broke my wrist. Got the cast off yesterday."

"At least it wasn't your ankle," Jasmine replied. "You can still tap with a broken wrist. Anyway, nice to have you in class."

"Thank you."

"After class you can tell me your size and I'll get the costume ordered. Since Joan needs a name for the program, what are we going to call ourselves?" Jasmine pulled a notebook and pen from her dance bag. "Go ahead, let 'er rip."

On her way to the floor, Nancy literally let it rip. "Oh geez, I have never done that before. Excuse me." She frantically waved her hand in front of her red face. "Can't ignore that one and hope no one notices."

"First time for everything. Can't say I haven't let off a silent but deadly one myself," said Milly. "I cut a loud one in a yoga class when my rear end was up in the air. I was so mortified I never went back. From then on I practiced yoga in the privacy of my own home from a DVD."

Jasmine, laughing, broke in, "Okay, moving on. What should we call you wild women?"

"I forgot the beano, but I did remember a name . . . Hoofing Heifers."

"What? First you fart, then you call us heifers?" Milly said. "What is *wrong* with you?"

"I'm sorry. Hoofing Heifers sounded funny. I wasn't serious. Don't count that one."

"How about Jalapeño Hotties?" Joan shimmy-shook her boobs. "We looked spicy in that sparkly black dress from 'Proud Mary.'"

"That's a good one," said Milly. "But since Tina Turner sings 'Proud Mary,' we should call ourselves Tina's Girls. I can hear the emcee: 'Tina's girls don't do nothin' nice . . . and ee-zay, they do it nice . . . and rough! Watch out 'cause these girls gonna burn up the stage!'"

"Yeah, like that. I'll add it to the list," Jasmine said.

"Listening to y'all, I don't even want to say what I came up with," cried Charlene. "It's lame."

"Nope, except for Hoofing Heifers, we're not ruling anything out," said Jasmine. "Whadaya have?"

"Toe Tapping Tootsies. Lame, huh?"

They all made funny faces but assured her they really did like it.

"Charlene, we goof off more than we dance," said Joan, "Shoot, it takes us an entire year to learn a routine, when kids can whip out three, four, or more for one recital or competition. But this tap class is more than physical exercise—it's psychosocial, which is good for us. So I hope we haven't scared you off."

Nancy clapped her hands to get attention. "Okay, okay, Joan's right, but I have one more. I promise it's a good one."

"It'd better be better than heifer," Milly chided her.

"It is." Nancy drummed the floor with her hands and leaned to her left. "Thunder down under! Just kidding! What about Dancing Divas?"

Charlene said, "Aren't divas like opera singers or something?"

"They are, but a diva is also a temperamental person, like me—moody, bitchy, and irritable. I'd be unbearable, except for my great sense of humor, which none of you seem to appreciate. I looked it up. A diva is also confident and knows she's good at what she does. That's us!"

"Well then, let's take a vote," said Jasmine.

The newly named Dancing Divas rose from the floor in one fashion or another. The class reviewed a few basic steps in the form of a warmup for Charlene's benefit, and the hour was over.

The dancers said goodnight to their instructor and gathered in the common room to change shoes. "When's your birthday, Charlene?" asked Joan.

"April 1st. Why?"

"All our birthdays are in the fall—September and October—so we celebrate them with a combined birthday get-together. Hmm, April. I suppose we can let her join, ya think, girls?" Joan laughed. "I'm teasing. Put October 19 on your calendar. It's a Friday night."

"What are y'all doing?"

"It was my turn to pick, and I suggested we go see *The Music Man* at the high school," Milly said. "My granddaughter plays the mayor's wife, Eulalie Shinn. It's the Drama Club's first production of the year."

"Oh my word! *The Music Man* is one of my favorite musicals!" Charlene said. "I'd love to go. I even have a refrigerator magnet with a Harold Hill quote: Make today worth remembering."

"I should have said something earlier. I forgot about our birthday bash," said Nancy. "Hope you can make it."

"I reckon I can. My social calendar is pretty slim right now." Charlene chuckled. "Well, goodnight, Divas. I had fun tonight."

Everyone said their goodbyes. The rain had stopped, and Nancy drove home feeling good. She *was* a diva.

CHAPTER 19:
THE TIMES THEY ARE
A-CHANGIN'

Here it was mid-September. Two weeks had gone by, instead of the couple of days Nancy had said she'd need before calling her mother. Somehow she had to get Trixie to Collinsville. Since this would be no ordinary visit, it would be best if Ted were away. At this point, she could not fathom telling him anything about what she had learned. The soonest opportunity for Ted's absence would be a month from now, when he'd be on an elk hunt near Hoback Peak in the Bridger-Teton National Forest in western Wyoming. She always backpacked in with him to their favorite campsite. They called it their "grove of pines." Ted would have to go alone this year, but she didn't like that idea much, either—it was grizzly bear country.

Before she could bring up the subject, Ted had come up with the solution. Over dinner, he said, "By the way, I've been meaning to tell you, Trebo asked if he could join our Hoback hunt. He doesn't have an elk tag, but he's interested in big game hunting and wants to explore the area with someone who knows his way around. I said I'd talk to you about it."

Holy moly, here was her chance to bring up her mom's visit. "Actually, that would be great. I'll stay home and Bo can go."

"Are you sure?" Ted frowned. "You love the fall aspen colors and the Tetons. What gives?"

"Well, I've been thinking about arranging for Mom to visit. You're not that crazy about her anyway. If Bo goes with you, I can stay home and not worry about you hunting alone."

"What's wrong with you going there?"

"Nothing. I'd like her to come out one time before she's unable."

"You think she'll come here after all these years?"

"Maybe. I haven't talked to her yet. When I was a kid we used to visit Dad's family here. I can't explain it. I feel like maybe she's waiting for an invitation."

"She doesn't need an invitation, but if you feel she needs to come, then go for it. Hoback won't be the same without you, honey, but Bo really wanted to go and felt like he might be intruding."

"Tell Bo it's perfectly fine with me. Promise that on your way home, you'll stop in DuBois and bring me a chocolate Kahlua pecan pie."

"Promise."

Win-win for everybody.

Normally, a phone call to her mother would not cause abdominal muscle spasms or raise her blood pressure. She didn't have to make the call for Rigel—she could have told him no. But she had to do it for herself, because there were too many questions and not enough answers. This was worse than any stage fright she'd ever experienced.

Rigel hadn't said how long he needed her to stay. Knowing Trixie, she'd say fish and family stink after three days. Ages ago she had learned that quote was attributed to Ben Franklin and not her mother. But what about strangers, Mom? You're a stranger to me now. Auk! She couldn't say that!

Hi, Mom, I know where you're from, and I'm okay with it. Yikes! She couldn't say that, either. She had no idea where to start, but she had to get this done before Ted got back from the hardware store. She didn't want him around to hear this conversation. So she picked up her cell phone and told herself that whatever happens, happens. Sitting in her recliner, she held down the home button. "Call Mom."

"Hello, Nancy, so good to hear from you!"

"Hi, Mom. How are you?"

"Better. I've taken a new medication, and my bad headaches are gone."

"That's so good."

"What's new with you?"

"Actually, quite a bit, Mom. I've been talking to Rigel O'Rion. Do you know him?"

Several seconds of silence ensued before Trixie said in a soft voice, "I do."

Good thing Nancy was sitting down or she would have fallen to the floor. At her mother's answer, everything Rigel and Milly had said was true. There was no more doubt. When her mother didn't add anything else, Nancy barreled on, "That explains a lot. I know where you're from, and I'm okay with it." Had she really said that? Yes, but she did not want to make her mother angry, thereby making her uncooperative. Nancy would definitely grill her mother when they were together, but not on the phone.

"Yes, well, I'd rather not discuss it on the phone," Trixie said.

Had she heard that right? Could her mother read her mind from California? Calm down. It was only a coincidence they had thought the same thing at the same time.

"In that case, would you be able to come out around the 16th of October? Stay a few days? On the 19th, the high school is putting on a production of *The Music Man*. It'd be a chance to see the inside of the school. I don't think the theater has changed since you were there. Ted will be gone hunting, so we'll have the house to ourselves."

"I'd like that, sweetheart. I've been meaning to tell you for so long, but I didn't know how."

"I understand the difficulty. I've learned a lot from Rigel and Milly McGilly."

"Oh my, I remember Milly. Her parents were wonderful sponsors. I suppose you know about that too."

"I do."

"Well, make the arrangements, but remember, fish and family stink after three days, so no more."

"Yes, Mom, but we won't count your travel days, okay?"

"I can manage that. I'll pack a few things."

They discussed preferred flight times, the weather, how Ted was, that sort of thing, and that was that. The middle of October was probably not as soon as Rigel would have liked, but it was the best she could do.

Gathering her thoughts after the dreaded phone call, she felt it hadn't gone so bad after all. Except when Nancy offered to arrange flight assistance, Trixie had responded, "I am perfectly capable of flying without help." Nancy had meant she could arrange for someone to meet her at the gate and whisk her to the next gate with one of those electric carts. Denver International was a big airport, and getting to the gate for the smaller aircraft to Collinsville was a long way. But, gee whiz, could she fly? Was this some extraterrestrial trait in her DNA? She understood Rigel got around the old-fashioned way, once he arrived. She was overreacting, that was all. Still, she couldn't get flying off her mind and recalled a repetitive dream when she was a fifth grader, starting a new school, of soaring above the kids on the playground, arms spread wide, then landing smoothly on her feet, impressing her classmates. It felt real. But dreaming of flying and *actually* flying, unless you're in an aircraft, were two very different things.

Her mind was churning again. She recalled Bob Dylan's "The Times They are A-Changin'." No kidding. And changing fast. If her mother really was from D'Gnome, what does she use for identification? Even though she doesn't have a driver's license, she must have some form of ID. It must be fake. Her mother is not only an alien, but an *illegal* alien. A criminal! "There's an awful lot I need to know about you, Mrs. Bellatrix Bayer Herschel," she mumbled. Her breathing was shallow, her heart racing, palms sweating. Crap, when did she become prone to panic attacks? She knew the answer: after Rigel showed up. Breathe deep. Inhale through the nose . . . exhale out the mouth . . . inhale . . . exhale . . . relax.

CHAPTER 20:
GETTING TO KNOW YOU

When Nancy made her mother's plane reservations, she chose Tuesday, since it was the cheapest air fare, but forgot it was also dance night. She sent a group text to let the class know she would not be there. Joan had also sent a group text to say that her ex-husband had died in a single-car accident. He'd been thrown from the vehicle. She was in Des Moines, Iowa, with her two daughters for the funeral and to help them with final affairs. She would miss Tuesday but should be back by Friday for their annual birthday bash.

Ted offered to go to the airport with her, but she had wanted to talk to her mother alone. Nancy was grateful to Milly and Rigel for helping her accept her mother's situation, but she still couldn't quell the feeling that she was meeting a stranger. Twenty minutes, the time it usually took to get from the airport to the house, was not enough for all she needed to say, but if she drove slowly and took a roundabout way home, it would be enough to get the important stuff out of the way, like, thanks for coming, Mom. I love you. And why did you not tell me about this?!

Unlike Denver, with close to 150 gates, Collinsville International Airport had four. Nancy had gotten a guest pass to meet Trixie in the secured area. The jetway door finally opened, and passengers streamed into the terminal. When there were a few stragglers left, it occurred to her that maybe Trixie had changed her mind and beamed herself off the plane. That's ridiculous. Still, it was a huge relief to see her mother walking unassisted down the jetway, the last passenger off the plane. Nancy studied the woman wearing tan polyester slacks and an untucked blue-flowered blouse under an open white cardigan. She had one arm pressed against a large leather purse hanging from a long strap across her body. She looked like any other older woman. Nothing alien about her. She was looking down at her feet, watching her steps, but when she glanced up, her face broke into a broad smile, showing perfectly white teeth. Her once-vibrant freckles were hidden in deeply-lined creases, which deepened even more as she smiled.

Parted in the middle, her blunt-cut auburn hair framed hazel eyes. Nancy knew she didn't inherit her mother's hair, which still showed no sign of grey and stayed straight as a stick, even in humidity. Nancy's hair frizzed at the slightest hint of moisture in the air. She *had* inherited her mother's hips, for sure, and who knew what else. She held out her arms for a hug. Oh yeah, the arms. The flappy, floppy upper arms. Thanks, Mom, Nancy thought, returning the smile.

"So happy you're here!" Nancy said, as they embraced.

"I'm happy to be here, too, sweetheart."

"Baggage claim is around the corner. I parked across the street from the terminal, so it's not far, if you want to walk, or you can wait by baggage claim, and I can drive around to get you."

"I'm not an invalid—it feels good to walk after sitting so much today. I'm relieved to be here, to finally get it over with, telling you everything, that is."

"We'll have plenty of time. Ted leaves tomorrow morning, then we can talk our hearts out." Nancy took her mother's hand as they waited for the luggage to arrive. In a few minutes a warning buzzer sounded. The metal belt creaked and began snaking in and out of the baggage claim area. Trixie's bag was one of the first out, and Nancy grabbed it when her mother pointed to it. "You have just the one?"

"Yes. I didn't bring much."

Nancy drove the shortest way home. There wasn't any point getting into an in-depth discussion about family life—there wouldn't be enough time, no matter which route she took. Instead, she asked, "How is your garden growing?" Trixie's love of gardening, both flowers and vegetables, was another thing she could attribute to her mother. Nancy had become a Master Gardener four years ago. And reading. Her mother loved to read, as did Nancy. Gardening and reading, two activities relished by a recluse such as Trixie.

"Oh my stars, I can hardly keep up with the weeds. Freezing ten quarts of strawberries this week about did me in."

"Too bad you couldn't have brought some. I haven't tried growing strawberries." There was a pause in the conversation. "Mom, I wasn't going to bring it up until tomorrow, but what if you had died and I'd never found out and then something happened?" Nancy tried to keep her voice from sounding hysterical or accusatory, but it was hard.

"You are so like your father, wanting to get straight to the point. No beating around the bush. I have struggled with this your whole life—when to tell, what to tell. I tried telling your father many times, but he always thought I was joking. My biggest regret is not telling you, but I couldn't muster the courage. I was scared back then, and I'm scared now, because what I have to say will sound unbelievable."

"You don't have to be afraid anymore. I love you, Mom, no matter what."

"I love you, too, my precious daughter." Trixie sniffed and pulled a tissue from her sweater pocket.

Nancy sighed. She knew they were both under a lot of stress over this whole D'Gnome thing. "Actually, one more day won't hurt." Nancy glanced at her mother. "At least for tonight, we'll have to act like nothing has changed."

"I can do that. So how is the community garden coming along? I suppose it's late in the season for Wyoming."

"It is. We have a waiting list for plots, so we're looking for a location to expand. Hope to have that ready before this spring. We weren't going to talk about it anymore, but I can't stop believing I've made a sharp U-turn from a typical American life to being part D'Gnoman. What does that mean?"

"There's no reason for you to change your life from the way it is now—you're perfectly normal. D'Gnomans' brains are capable of higher functions, that's all."

"Yeah, Rigel talks about telepathy a lot. Can you do that?"

"I can, but intrusion into someone's mind without their permission is an invasion of privacy, and privacy is respected. D'Gnomans don't use telepathy unless both parties drop their defenses. If we stopped vocalizing altogether, we'd lose the ability to speak. Besides, if I listened to your thoughts all day, I wouldn't be able to hear myself think!"

"Ha, ha." Nancy giggled nervously.

"While I'm here we'll see how much telepathic skill you have. I'll teach you how to block intrusions. One day it will come naturally to you and you'll choose when to drop your shield."

"I'm already feeling overwhelmed by this. Thank goodness we're almost home. When we moved into this neighborhood, none of this was here, just open fields. Now there are several new streets, houses, an elementary school, and restaurants. Well, here we are." Pulling into the garage, she turned to Trixie. "Thank you for coming, Mom."

Trixie reached over and touched Nancy's hand. "Don't worry, we'll get through this together."

Ted was in the garage, loading gear into his pickup for his hunting trip. He opened his mother-in-law's car door and extended his hand. "Hello, Trixie, you're looking well. How was your trip?" Trixie lifted her legs out and took his hand to stand. Ted gave her a perfunctory embrace, then grabbed her carry-on out of the backseat.

"Thank you, Theodore. The flights were smooth, except for a little turbulence coming into Collinsville. Something smells delicious," she said, as they walked into the house.

"That would be Nancy's venison stew."

"Ah, yes, Nancy said you're leaving tomorrow to restock the freezer."

Early the next morning, Ted left with his next-door neighbor, Trebo, for his elk hunt, leaving mother and daughter to do as they pleased. Rigel was in town, but they'd meet him and Milly on Thursday. Nancy wanted to keep Wednesday open for her mother to reacquaint herself with Collinsville. Plus, they had a lot to talk about. Friday evening, if all went well, Trixie would join Nancy and her dance classmates to observe their combined birthdays at the high school's production of *The Music Man*. This week could turn out to be both a comedy and a tragedy.

Her mother drank coffee from a mug with "I need chocolate NOW!" on the side. Nancy didn't own a coffeemaker, but Trixie insisted that instant decaf was perfectly acceptable. Having cleared the breakfast dishes, she joined her mother at the dining table with a refillable water bottle.

"Are you comfortable here? We can move to the family room," said Nancy.

"No. I prefer a stiffer chair for now. We can move after I finish my coffee."

"Okay, tell me more about Dad."

Trixie took a sip of coffee and a deep breath. "At first, I tried to tell him where I was really from. He claimed I was joking, because UFO sightings were common back then."

"They were?"

"Yes, but there were as many explanations as there were sightings—a weather balloon, the military testing some high-tech aircraft, whatever. The unidentified spacecraft would not have been from D'Gnome. By the time I arrived in Collinsville, we had a better way to travel."

"I know. I went through a portal with Milly and two other friends. We intended to go with Rigel, but something went awry, and we were separated. He arrived on D'Gnome; we arrived on Gansarcal. We didn't stay long. Thankfully, Milly knew how to get us back."

"Rigel." Trixie had a faraway look in her eyes. "I haven't seen him in so long. He, Saiph, and I were best friends back then. Have you met Saiph?" She refocused on Nancy.

"Huh-uh, but I know she's Rigel's sister."

"How is Rigel?"

"Well, you'll find out tomorrow. He's here, staying with Milly."

"I had a feeling he was here." At Nancy's sharp glance, Trixie held up her hands. "In my defense, it was a snippet I accidently picked up on our way home from the airport last night. Thoughts have volume, and yours was a little loud when Rigel entered your mind."

"That's an understatement." Nancy groaned and covered her ears, as if to shut out her mother's words from her brain.

"That won't work," she laughed. A full laugh, a different laugh than the ones Nancy had known lately, like she was finally getting into her element. "I'm glad you've found a medication to help your headaches."

"Did Rigel tell you why I've been on Earth so long?"

"He said your father created a vaccine to reduce the swelling of a gland we, or Earth folks, don't have, and that you got it right before you left as a teenager."

"Yes, it was an experiment. He didn't know how long it would last. It would be a lifelong study. I would not return to D'Gnome. The vaccine contained a booster should the first dose lose its efficacy. The booster kicked in right after your father died. Grandpa didn't know how long the first booster would last, so he gave me a booster pill should I need it. The last several years the headaches have been getting gradually worse. I took the pill recently, when I couldn't handle the pain anymore."

"So it wasn't a medication from a doctor."

"No."

"At least you're feeling better."

"Yes, and since I wasn't returning with the rest of the students, the question was, how do you explain the disappearance of an Earth Study student?"

"Fake her death?"

"Yes! Did Rigel tell you that too?"

"Mom! No! I was kidding. You're supposed to be *dead?!*"

Trixie nodded. "News feeds went out that I had, immediately after completion of the Earth Study stint, joined a mission to seek new worlds. The spacecraft soon experienced an on-board explosion. The fire was quickly put out, but not quickly enough for me. I died from smoke inhalation and poisonous gases. Fortunately, I didn't feel a thing." Trixie chuckled. "*Unfortunately*, there was no body to recover, only ashes."

"Mom! How can you joke about that? This is disturbing." Nancy was sure she would have remembered if Rigel had said her mother was supposed to be dead. This was beyond her comprehension.

"I know this whole situation is overwhelming."

"Yes, you *would* know," Nancy said, a tad too sarcastically.

"We don't have to finish. I can go home right now."

"No. I'm sorry, Mom. This is hard for me."

"I know it is." Trixie placed a reassuring hand on her daughter's hand. "Are you all right?"

"Yes, but just when I was going to say nothing surprises me anymore, you lay that one on me. Holy mackerel!" Nancy said, good-naturedly.

"Oh good, you're not upset."

"I wouldn't say that, but I'll get over it." Nancy wondered what their relationship would have been like if all had been revealed years ago. "I still can't get over how we're talking about this. It's unreal." Nancy shook her head in amazement. "Tell me more, but first, do you need a refill?"

"No, thanks. I limit myself to one cup a day. So how could you have gone to Gansarcal?" Trixie asked. "There's no portal. Or there never used to be. Of course, I've been away from D'Gnome most of my life. But *why* would you go there? It's a barren rock, like Earth's moon, except for the massive prison dome."

"You'll have to talk to Rigel, but we did. There is some sort of vacation resort being built."

"Galaxies galore, I have a lot of catching up to do! I'll be curious as to what Rigel thinks of your separation."

"We'll meet him tomorrow at Milly's apartment. Finish telling me about Dad."

"Let's see, we got a little off topic, didn't we? I tried to tell him; he wouldn't believe me. When I insisted I was telling the truth, he accused me of dipping into the Mitchells'—Milly's parents'—liquor cabinet."

"Had you?"

"Certainly not!"

"Just checking." Nancy grinned, and her mother's laugh was musical. "I am so glad we're having this conversation! So how did you two meet before you fell in love and eloped? I can't believe I've never asked."

"We met at the homecoming pep rally and bonfire the night before the big football game. It was at a small lake north of town. I had walked away from the raucous school crowd and saw Jim sitting alone on the ground, strumming his six-string—an ethereal melody floated to me on the night breeze." Trixie paused a moment, then refocused. "He played several measures repeatedly, as if studying the notes for a song he was writing. I sat behind him so he wouldn't see me. I wanted to listen and not disturb him, but I was so drawn to his music that I pulled out my pocket flute and experimented with a few notes in accompaniment. He turned around and smiled. My heart absolutely melted."

"That is so romantic!" They were two teenage girls talking about a new boyfriend, but Trixie's mood suddenly changed.

"I found out through my father that falling in love was a side effect of the vaccine. That was a surprise even to him and his fellow researchers. Otherwise, D'Gnomans don't have the inclination, hormones, whatever, for amorous relationships with people from Earth."

"Really? I wonder about Milly and Rigel. They seem to have something going on."

"We'll have to interrogate him and find out. He must have had the vaccine. I've been gone so long, I don't know what's been happening on DG. Anyway, I was young, carefree, and happier than I'd ever been, so I blew off my parents' instructions and the code of ethics I had signed. I didn't think it applied to me since I wasn't going back. And who could argue with true love? I knew the story of my homeland sounded outrageous. But I could never have taken Jim to the school portal to prove my origins. Even if I could have, I would have been worried I'd frighten him away. What was I to do? Any demonstrations of preternatural power I was certain would scare him too."

"I see your point. I admit I didn't take it very well when Rigel and Milly tried to tell me. I actually passed out from the stress that was building in me. What is preternatural power?"

"Mental powers that would be considered out of the ordinary here, such as precognition, telepathy, clairvoyance, let's see, what else, psychokinesis." Trixie counted on her fingers.

"Psycho what?"

"Kinesis. Moving objects with brainwaves alone, which I can't do. Not every D'Gnoman can achieve psychokinesis, but all of us develop telepathy early on."

"That's what Rigel used when he unlocked a door at the school. He called it kinetic energy. Wow, that's cool. You can't fly, can you?'"

Trixie smirked. "No. We don't have superpowers like flying or swinging from building to building, like in the movies."

"Oh, thank goodness. And your blood isn't green?"

"Where in the world did you get that idea? Rigel, I bet."

"Yeah, he has a weird sense of humor."

"I remember him as rather quirky, playing jokes on people. He was funny. I liked him, not in a romantic sense, mind you. He was more like the brother I didn't have. Anyway, I gave up trying to tell Jim. I figured he would learn sooner or later, and I'd deal with it then."

"What did you tell Dad about your family?"

"Well . . . " Trixie hesitated. "For all he knew, I was an exchange student from Stavanger, Norway. I told him my family had disowned me when I decided not to come home after graduation. It wasn't like we had money to march off to another country. And I refused to make an international phone call, especially when they never called me. I left it at that, and we never spoke much about them again. Oh, what a tangled web we weave when first we practice to deceive." She was near tears.

"You did what you thought was best." Nancy tried to lighten the mood by saying, "Hey, you want to take that tour around town now?"

"No, I came here to tell you your legacy. When you asked questions about your grandparents, I said they lived too far away and couldn't afford to come over. In truth, I knew they could show up at any time.

"Before I left home my senior year, Mother told me not to be surprised if she popped in for a visit one day. She had no inkling when that would be, several years at best. She was working on a device she called a Pathfinder, which could bypass the established portals and take you anywhere.

"Most importantly, she warned me to trust no one. There was no 'except this person or that person.' Then, later, when I had a husband and a child to worry about, I became wary, looking around every corner. I did not know who or what I was looking for, but mainly I didn't want to draw attention to my family."

"So that's why you were such a recluse. Lately, I've been wondering about all this, you not going out much, no one ever coming over. I couldn't have sleepovers, that sort of thing."

"Yes, but no matter where we lived, we always took the bus to the library."

"I loved the library and still do. Why was it you'd go there but not other places?"

"Crowds bothered me most. I always felt safe at the library. But I was most fearful of my parents materializing at home, in front of someone, without notice. That's what could have happened with the Pathfinder and why we never had guests over."

"Materialize. A shimmery sort of separation and then your body becomes solid again? Kind of like when I went through the portal?"

"Exactly. And how would you explain that to guests? Bending space-time, or beaming people through a cosmic tunnel will happen to Earth scientists one of these days. It's why the D'Gnoman government is so protective of our travel.

"Anyway, one night when your father was working late at the gas station, Rigel and Saiph came to our house. All I could hear was my mother's last words: *Trust no one.* I was afraid to let them in, even though they were both my friends, but I also heard Rigel's telepathic message to me: My parents had drowned in a rafting accident, and their bodies had not been recovered. I was devastated. I never got to talk to them before they died. I told Jim I had received a phone call from the authorities, not that my two friends came to the door. Again, I was digging myself deeper with lies." Her hands covered her face as she slumped.

"I'm so sorry, Mom. I didn't know."

"It's okay, sweetheart. It wasn't your fault."

An image popped into Nancy's mind. "I remember that night. We lived in a grey, two-story house. I had a stuffy nose and was looking out my bedroom window. There was a streetlight on the corner, and I saw two people walking toward our house. When I heard you crying, I was frightened. I imagined they were burglars trying to break in. Finally, Daddy came home and tried to calm you. You started whispering, fearful you'd wake me up, although you probably knew I was at the top of the stairs! The next day you and Dad told me my grandparents had passed away. I never mentioned the visitors I saw. For years after that I had recurring dreams about two people crossing the street under the streetlight, then fading into the darkness, yet still lurking outside our door. And now I know why Rigel seems familiar to me. I saw his face! What a relief. I *knew* I knew him from somewhere."

"You have an extraordinary memory."

"Not really. We hadn't lived in that house very long—new house, new school, traumatic event happened. Makes it easy to compartmentalize stuff like that."

Trixie gave her a pitiful look. "We did move around a lot."

"Why did we?"

"You might have thought it was because I was always on the run, afraid someone was watching me, but in reality, it was your father's jobs. It was one thing or another. He never had any high-paying work, so he tended to change jobs frequently. We couldn't always afford the house we were renting, so we'd move. He was such a good auto mechanic, but he also wanted to play his guitar and sing. There was a little wanderlust in him too. Yet he worked hard and provided a good living for us."

"Then what made you stay in San Diego?"

"I'm sure you remember Grandpa Herschel died shortly after Grandma."

"Yeah, I told Milly and Rigel it was a real love story."

"It was. I believe Grandpa died of a broken heart. They had Jim rather late in life, and as the only child, he inherited their property in Collinsville including the gas station. He didn't want to live in Wyoming so sold it all for a very large sum of money. We bought a house. Of course, we didn't have today's exorbitant housing prices. He found a mechanics job he liked that fit his schedule, so we stayed."

"Wow. I never realized he changed jobs so much. Guess I was wrapped up in my own kid world. There's so much I didn't know."

"And there's so much I want to tell you, but I don't know where to begin." Trixie had tears in her eyes again.

"At the beginning." Nancy handed her a soft tissue.

"You know what? This would be the perfect time to show you the holo-drive of family photos and videos my mother gave me before I left home. Can't get any more beginning than my child-hood."

"A holo-drive?"

"It's similar to a flash drive, except you don't have to plug it into a computer to see what's on it. Wait a minute. I'll show you."

She went to her bedroom and came back with a three-inch long, naked doll with long, wispy, rainbow-hued hair.

"Where'd you get a troll doll? It looks like the ones I collected as a kid."

"Holo-drives come in all shapes. Mother could 3-D print anything she wanted. I have no idea why she picked this. Let's move to the family room. We can sit together and watch." They left the kitchen and made themselves comfy on the sofa. "Mother and Father have a copy at home, well, DG. When I say DG, I mean D'Gnome. Their troll has orange hair. Mother asked me which one I wanted. They were the same, she said, except the hair. I wanted the bright rainbow colors.

"I brought it with me, knowing I would finally show it to you." She held the small rubber doll out for Nancy to see, then pulled the ends apart. From the head section a metal circular piece protruded, from which a three-dimensional video of a toddler flowed and appeared in front of the women, a little over an arm's length away. The visual area covered the size of a 20-inch screen.

Startled, Nancy pressed back into the sofa. "Whoa! That's freaky!" She saw a child chasing a ball over a manicured lawn under a gargantuan tree, the base as big as a kid's wading pool. What looked like thick ropes twining around each other formed the trunk, which rose up twice the height of the stone house. As the trunk narrowed near the top, a canopy of green leaves and huge white flowers branched out like an umbrella.

"Why are you so astonished? Holographic technology is already being used on Earth," Trixie said.

"Yeah, well, I've never seen it right in front of me. This is awesome! That's you!" Nancy pointed at the moving 3-D image.

Trixie nodded. "I was about three then."

"This is so cool. You are adorable! I have never seen pictures of you as a child."

"Well, here you go. Mother filled this with hundreds of still images and videos."

"Your house is beautiful. The black and brown swirls of stonework are really unusual. Love the pretty blue front door and matching flower boxes. Of course, you'd have flower boxes and a field of flowers for a yard. Looks like a gnome home I've got in my backyard. Is that where the planet's name came from?" Nancy was serious, but Trixie laughed.

"Our early ancestors lived in caves in the mountains. D'Gnome means 'cave dweller.' This is my parents' house, and those are my mother's flower boxes. You're looking at the traditional stone home of those in the outback. We didn't live in the city. My parents commuted to work."

"These early D'Gnomans weren't little men and women in pointy hats, were they?"

"No, funny girl, but the idea of the garden gnome protecting the environment could have been started by someone from DG. I haven't looked into that particular folklore."

"You really taught me a lot, and I haven't thanked you enough. My love for gardening comes from you. I'm always getting asked about my flowers."

"Your grandmother always said the world can never have enough flowers."

"I wish I could have met them."

Trixie sighed. "You said nothing could surprise you . . . but they might still be alive."

"Holy cow! Harold and Erma? My grandparents?" Nancy had tried so hard to accept everything that had been thrown at her, but the fastballs kept coming. She looked at her mom in disbelief.

"When you were in college, they popped into the kitchen unannounced, exactly like Mother said they might. But I had been told they'd drowned, so I was as shocked as you are now when I saw them standing there. That was over thirty years ago, and I haven't heard from them since, so they could be dead or alive. I don't know for sure."

"Would Rigel know?"

"He might. I plan to ask him. Are you okay?"

Nancy messaged her temples. "I'm really not sure. I'm trying to stay calm and dance on, metaphorically speaking. It's what we say to each other in dance when we start freaking out about tap steps."

"That's sound advice."

"Let's finish the pictures, then we can go for a drive."

Nancy spent the next hour watching in astonishment the life her mother had left behind. Momentarily, she forgot her grandparents could be alive and listened to her mother's commentary. "In my wildest dreams," Nancy said, "I could not have imagined we'd be watching you as an ordinary child in such an extraordinary place. D'Gnome has three moons! That's amazing! At first I thought Milly and Rigel were nuts, but looking at these incredible pictures—" Nancy shook her head.

"I am grateful to them for smoothing the way." As they got to her teenage years and Trixie was preparing to say goodbye to her parents, she reached out and touched the image. It paused, hanging in mid-air. The picture showed Erma holding out two trolls as if to say, Which one do you want? "I was getting ready to leave for the

Senior Superlative Earth Study Program. Do I need to explain it?"

"Rigel told me a little about the program, but I wondered why they let kids come here."

"Young people were not to interfere but to watch and learn, to see where D'Gnomans had once been and to appreciate their own planet. When they became future leaders of commerce, technology, medicine, education, and other industries necessary for a civilized society, they would not repeat mistakes made by those from Earth.

"As part of the application process, seniors selected topics related to their chosen location. Saiph and I chose Collinsville. She was going to write her thesis on the availability of rural medicine and its effects on the state. I wanted to explore the cowboy culture, rodeos, the whole bit. I wanted to ride a bronc!"

"Yikes! Did you?" Nancy was blown away—this was her mother speaking! She couldn't imagine her mother wanting to participate in such a dangerous sport.

"Not a bronc, but I learned to ride a horse. I was more interested in having fun, while Saiph was the dedicated one. She wanted to be a doctor. I was smart enough to be anything, I just couldn't decide."

"With my genetics, I should be a genius or something. What happened?"

"Don't denigrate yourself. You're smart. You graduated with a degree in finance. There was nothing wrong with being a CPA."

"I know. I enjoyed my career but enjoy retirement more. I was fortunate to retire early, and as much as I wanted to get out of the office then, I still volunteer part time at the Senior Center during tax season. So far it hasn't interfered with gardening classes."

"I'm very proud of you. I've always been proud of you."

"You talk about regrets—I regret leaving you alone in San Diego."

"You know I insisted on staying put. Walking to and from the bus stop keeps me in shape. I could call the senior bus that would come right to my door, but I like walking. And you can't beat the weather. I wouldn't like the cold and snow."

"Or the wind."

"That's true. I think this troll picture is the last one. Thank goodness, because my rear end is getting sore from sitting here—I need to stretch. After that was taken, I soon left for Collinsville."

They turned back to the screen. "Hey, look." When Nancy touched the tiny, triangular icon on the belly of the orange-haired troll, the image of the troll receded into the background and a text document opened. Despite a sore behind, she had never seen her mother move so fast. She scrolled through a few pages. It looked like gobbledygook to Nancy.

"Mother must have told me about this embedded file the day she gave the troll to me, but I was so excited to go to Earth that lots of what she said I probably didn't retain—in one ear, out the other." Trixie touched the X in the upper corner of the document to close it. It disappeared, leaving the picture of Erma holding the trolls. "Now if you don't mind, my voice is getting hoarse, so I'd like to lie down for a bit before we go out." She slid the lower body half back onto the upper half of the troll, the picture disappeared, and it looked like an ordinary toy again. You could not see where the two pieces merged. She took the troll with her and left the room.

In twenty minutes, Trixie was back and ready to go.

"What was that document?"

"Instructions for creating the Pathfinder. The prototype, anyway, since it hadn't been fully tested when I left at seventeen. I hadn't noticed it before, but I've looked at these only once after I first got here, then merely scrolling through them. Let's not mention this to anyone, okay?"

"My lips are sealed. Let's take that drive around town. We can keep talking in Mrs. Teal." At Trixie's furrowed brows, Nancy said, "My car. I call her Mrs. Teal. Be nice to her or she might stall on us."

"Whatever you say, sweetheart."

CHAPTER 21:
AROUND TOWN

Trixie was most excited to see Collins High School. "I'm pleased the main building is still here. I figured they might have torn it down by now."

"They've replaced windows but can't change much else, because the old part is on the National Register of Historic Places. It's also my favorite. Reminds me of a gothic cathedral. I absolutely love it."

Trixie recalled Milly's childhood home address. Cresting a hill overlooking the older section of the city, the yellow leaves of the cottonwoods glowed in the sunshine. "Lionel and Ruby Mitchell were wonderful people and took such good care of us while we stayed with them," Trixie said. "I suppose they don't live there anymore."

"No, I believe Milly said they moved to be near his relatives in Mississippi. They wanted a warmer climate. Her mom passed a few years ago, and I think her dad's in a care facility there now."

"Oh, sorry to hear that. Their house hasn't changed much, except the cottonwoods are much bigger. They're glorious with their fall color!"

"Downtown hasn't changed much, either. Grandpa's garage is still there."

"Really?"

"We'll drive by. They're revitalizing the old town. Kind of like Old Town in San Diego—well, not quite, but they're keeping it historical, yet modern. Fixing up some of the buildings and converting others to unique eateries, breweries, and galleries."

A short while later, Nancy drove past the gas station that her paternal grandparents used to own and that her dad worked part-time at as a teenager. Trixie smacked her chest. "Oh my goodness, it looks the same. Even the sign. Whoever owns it now did a great job restoring it."

A few more blocks away, Trixie said, "There's the Rialto! Many good times at *that* theater!" Nancy pestered her mother about how many make-out sessions went on there. "None of your business! Goodness, so much of this town is the same, yet so much is different—I could be in another world."

"Technically, you are." Nancy realized her mother must have struggled, too, with her new reality of living in the United States. Nancy lifted and dropped her shoulders as she sighed loudly.

Trixie looked at her daughter. "What was that about?"

"Nothing really. I'm beginning to grasp what you would have gone through to live here."

"I was welcomed and treated kindly everywhere we moved, but I always felt like an outsider. I knew I was different. I didn't want that for you, which is one reason I never told you."

The rest of the morning went quickly, with all the exclamations of how sprawling Collinsville had become. Even Nancy was amazed, she'd said, at how fast the city had grown in the eleven years they'd been here.

"At least you have room to spread out. There's not a hillside in Southern California that doesn't have something built on it. One day I feel it's all going to come crashing down."

"I hope not. I'm getting hungry. Where do you want to go for lunch?"

"How about Kentucky Fried Chicken?"

"Mom! We don't have as many choices as San Diego, but tell me what you're hungry for, and I'll make some suggestions."

"I brought a coupon with me. What's wrong with Kentucky Fried Chicken?"

"Nothing." *Everything.*

"Oh, but you're thinking 'everything,'" Trixie said teasingly.

"Yes, I was. I just thought we could try a nicer restaurant. And, dang, I have got to learn this blocking thing."

At KFC, Trixie asked Nancy to park toward the back of the lot, away from the restaurant. "While we're cocooned inside the car, for fun, let's try a few minutes of telepathy. I'll tell you more about your father, then we'll go in."

"Okay, what do I do?"

"You'll be able to focus better at first if you close your eyes and hold my hands."

"I remember Rigel said hello to me one day. I was hardly aware it happened."

"Because your mind was unguarded. This should be the same. It will come easier if you don't fight it. Close your eyes, try to clear your mind, as if you are meditating."

Nancy reached for Trixie's hands. They felt soft and warm. "I've never meditated, but fire away."

After a few moments, Trixie asked aloud, "Did you hear me?"

"No. Maybe I'm not any good at this."

"My stars, Nancy, it's your first try. What have I taught you about quitting? You'd think I was talking to a five-year-old instead of fifty-five. Now try again. I'll add more to give you time to hone in."

. . . Saiph and I were leaving for DG . . . red brick house . . .

"How was that?"

"Freaky! I picked up part of it. You said something about leaving for DG and a red brick house." Nancy was flabbergasted.

"That's a good start. I said it was the night before Saiph and I were going home, back to DG that is. Jim pulled up to the Mitchells' house in his old pickup."

"How come I don't have that prickly feeling, like I did with Rigel?"

"Rigel may have sent a fear factor with his message to wake up your receptors."

"That sounds scary."

"It was harmless. Now relax and clear your mind." Nancy was trying very hard not to be alarmed by the harmless fear factor statement and to convince herself telepathy was nothing out of the ordinary. She closed her eyes again and concentrated on her inner being—she guessed that's what you'd call it.

I peeked through . . . saw a tall, thin man with . . . and black-framed eyeglasses saunter to the front door. He was so handsome . . . been a movie star. James Allen Herschel rang the doorbell . . . made him wait.

"Mom! I heard you! You made him wait?" Nancy kept talking audibly, because it did not come naturally for her to respond any other way.

"A little bit! I can't say I wasn't doubting myself. This was not the arrangement my parents had planned. I would go to college, get a job, and try my best to stay out of trouble. My stipend cash wouldn't last forever. In case of emergency, if I couldn't get ahold of the Mitchells, I was to contact my parents' friends who were sponsors in Fort Worth. They also knew I would not return to DG. I met your father and fell in love. My stomach was in a knot the day we eloped, yet I felt such exhilaration I was going to burst! Talk about conflicting emotions, but love won."

Her voice was animated, and Nancy saw her as a young girl. "How'd you manage getting away without anyone knowing?"

"The Mitchells went out to eat on Saturday nights. I said I wasn't feeling well, nothing serious, so they let me stay home alone. I left them a note that I was eloping and called Jim."

"How?"

"How what? I called him on the telephone." She rolled her eyes.

"I'm joking. I'll stop." Nancy reached for her mother's hands. Not that she needed them to listen—it felt nice to hold them. She closed her eyes again.

I opened the door and threw my arms around his neck. I'm nervous, and scared, and happy. Everything rolled into one. I was running away with the man I loved, no matter the consequences, and there would be consequences, or so I thought.

Trixie abruptly let go. Nancy could feel a difference, like a door had slammed shut. She opened her eyes. "Oh, Mom."

"Did you get all that?"

"I think so," she said with watery eyes. "I miss Dad. I didn't get to say goodbye or tell him how much I appreciated him or how much I loved him."

"I miss him too." Trixie squeezed her daughter's hands.

It's amazing what touch conveys: understanding, assurance, love. But then Nancy saw the near future, and the same emotions rushed through her as they had her mother—fear, joy—and sick to her stomach. "How am I going to tell Ted or should I tell him?"

"It won't be easy. I can be there if it'll help. You also have friends to back you up which I didn't have. He's pretty much outnumbered. He loves you and will accept you as you are."

"Glad you're so confident."

"Come on, let's go eat."

After receiving their chicken and coleslaw and selecting a table, Trixie asked, "Should we do the rest of the story telepathically?" Trixie asked. "You did really well in the car. The distractions from people and noise will be good practice."

Unsure if she could multi-task, Nancy finished eating. She kept her eyes open and did not hold hands. She sipped her drink and fiddled with the straw's paper wrapper in an attempt to look natural, instead of what might look like a staring contest.

Jim was much more mature than the other boys, which is why I was attracted to him. We became the best of friends. The complications of my being Norwegian did not matter to him.

This time Nancy broke the connection. "When you said Norwegian . . . Are you a U.S. citizen?"

"DG officials provided required documentation for us to enroll in school, including birth certificates from our 'host' country. I eventually became a naturalized citizen."

"Good to know."

"How was communication in here?"

"If you're focused on what someone is saying, you block out those around you, whether it's normal conversation or not. Can you speak Norwegian?"

"I used to, but I don't remember much anymore."

"How 'bout D'Gnoman? I haven't heard Rigel speak it."

"I can speak the language, but I prefer not to."

"Just say hello."

Trixie looked nervously around and whispered, "Eetah. Hello."

"Eetah. That was cool. Suppose there's no Rosetta Stone for that."

"A what?"

"Language-learning software. Sorry, I was being silly again. What did the Mitchells do when they found you had run away?"

"I had graduated. There wasn't much the Mitchells could do—I was eighteen, Jim had turned nineteen. They knew Jim and his family. He was a good guy, not some hoodlum."

"Did the Mitchells get in trouble with D'Gnome officials?"

"They weren't prepared for my sudden desertion, but I doubt they got in trouble, because they continued to host students. When Jim and I got married in Las Vegas on our way to California, I mailed the Mitchells a post card telling them I had married my star."

"You mean Dad?" Or did she mean an actual star?

"Of course I meant Dad. Who do you think I meant?"

"Alpha Centauri? Is that a star? I don't know, I was kidding. I knew who you meant. I'm still uneasy over all this. Makes me nervous and I say stupid things."

"I understand this is hard for you, but good grief, Nancy, your dad was always a star in my eyes, someone I admired and loved."

"Me too. I'll stop with the jokes."

"I think that's enough telepathy for now."

"I still want to hear more about your early life with Dad."

"Maybe another time. All I'll say is he loved us very much."

"I was a lucky girl who had two great parents."

"We were both lucky, except he died too young."

Nancy was misty-eyed again. "Lick your fingers and let's go."

They scooted out of the booth. Nancy took her mother's hand and briefly picked up a wisp of memory that she guessed Trixie did not mean for her to detect: *And it's my fault he's not here.* Nancy did not question her as they left the restaurant. Her father died of a heart attack—that was a fact—but Nancy wondered why her mother blamed herself.

Nancy could tell Trixie was getting tired, but she perked up as the two approached the art museum on their way home. "Milly's daughter, Lilly, is a professional photographer and runs her own portrait studio, but she has two scenic photographs included as part of an exhibit by local artists. She's also had several scenic photographs published in state and national magazines," Nancy said.

"Milly must be awfully proud of her. Since we're here, let's stop. I would love to see the photos. Milly was also artistic. Her father made a wooden easel with one side a chalk board and the other with clips for holding paper to paint. Watercolors plastered the refrigerator. She pretended the easel was part of her classroom and dolls were her students. It's no wonder she became a teacher."

Having already passed the museum, Nancy drove around the block. Entering the parking lot, she recognized Milly's shiny, burnt-orange car. "Mom, did you know they were here? I mean, how far does your telepathy reach?"

"What are you talking about? Know who's here?"

"That's Milly's car. I'm guessing she's showing Rigel Lilly's photos."

"Cross my heart, I had no idea."

Inside the spacious hall, Nancy paid the entry fee before pulling her phone out to text Milly. She wasn't sure if Milly had her cell phone with her, but the two-story gallery was large enough that they could miss each other. Her mother placed her hand over Nancy's hand, nodded toward the sign to Please Silence Your Phone, and said, "You won't need to call. I feel him. They're around the corner."

As Trixie and Nancy walked through a wide archway into the first gallery, Rigel was already rushing toward the pair. Feet spread apart, hands on her hips, Milly stood in astonishment at having been left in the cold so suddenly.

"Trixie!" Rigel rushed to the friend he hadn't seen since they were teenagers.

"Rigel!" The two hugged, stepped back at arm's length, never letting go, drank each other in, and embraced again, rocking side-to-side. "Nancy said you were here, but I'm not sure I'm prepared for such a shock. My stars, it's wonderful to see you! I don't have the words to describe how happy this makes me!"

"Me, too, my dearest friend. When Nancy said you agreed to come, it was all I could do to wait it out. And now here you are!"

Milly walked over to Nancy. "Hey, what's going on here?"

"When they're done lovey-doveying, I'll introduce you. At least no one else is around while they're causing a scene."

"Heck, you don't need to introduce us. Holy red hair, this is your mother!"

At that, Trixie turned from Rigel and held out her arms to Milly. "Do my eyes deceive me? Is this the little girl who soaked her head in a bowl of Jell-O?"

"Lord-a-mighty, you can't let that go either. Neither could my mother, God rest her soul. Amen." Milly reached into the hug and the two laughed.

"I can't believe this!" Trixie lightly slapped her cheeks. "You're all grown up now."

"And then some." Milly looked back and forth between Trixie and Nancy. "I've known Nancy for ten years and never made the connection! You two look so much alike."

"Okay, you three, knock it off before they call security. Let Milly show Mom Lilly's photos, since we're here. We can carry on this reunion at my house. We'll have a pizza party."

Trixie, wiping tears from her eyes, nodded. "That's a marvelous idea. I would love to see the photographs!" She took Rigel's arm as they returned to the exhibit.

Nancy's phone, still in her hand, vibrated. "It's Charlene. I'll call her back when I get home," she said to Milly.

Milly leaned close to Nancy and whispered, "They don't have some romantic connection, do they?"

"I'm pretty sure not."

"Pretty sure is not positively sure."

"Positive. After we look at Lilly's pictures, let's drag them apart and get out of here."

CHAPTER 22:
THE GIRL NEXT DOOR

Milly, with Rigel riding shotgun, pulled in behind Nancy and Trixie and parked in the driveway. Everyone entered the house through the garage and gathered in the family room. The furniture, floor lamps and end tables were made from aspen wood, the sofa and loveseat upholstered in a pattern with bears, elk, and leaves in brown, green, and maroon. An iron grate with a buck mule deer and the Grand Tetons' three main peaks in the background protected the gas fireplace. It was the log cabin décor Nancy loved, but without the log cabin.

"You guys mind if I invite Charlene over for supper? Her husband is hunting with Ted, so she's home alone."

"More's the merrier," said Rigel. "Wasn't Charlene one of the ladies who went through the portal with you?"

"Yup," said Milly. "She lives next door."

"I'd love to meet her, but be careful not to mention D'Gnome," Trixie warned.

Nancy returned Charlene's call. "Hi, saw you called while we were at the art gallery."

"That's all right. Remembered your mom was in town so didn't leave a message. Had something to show you, but it can wait."

"Listen, Milly and Rigel are here. Remember him?"

"Milly's friend at the World of Arts show."

"Uh-huh. We ran into them at the gallery. We're having Domino's delivered. You're welcome to join us." At Charlene's hesitation, she added in a sing-song tone, drawing out the "ert" in dessert, "Domino's lava cakes for dessert. Know you love them."

"Lava cakes? Bless your soul. What can I bring?"

"Yourself is all we need."

"I'll bring veggies and dip."

"Perfect. Come when you can. We're not eating for another hour."

Forty-five minutes later, Charlene knocked on the door bearing a colorful platter full of petite carrots, celery sticks, red bell pepper strips, and a mix of cauliflower and broccoli florets, with a bowl of ranch dip in the center.

"Hey everyone. Thank you for inviting me."

"Thank you for the veggies. They look yummy." Nancy took the loaded platter and set it on the coffee table. She introduced her mother. "And you know Rigel."

"Yes, I do. Hey, Rigel. And who's that cozying up to him?"

Milly stood up and held out her hand. "Milli-cent McGilly, howdy-do." Charlene giggled and shook Milly's hand. "Now git out the way, the pizza man's right behind you. This one's on Rigel. Git up and pay the man. I know you don't tip on . . . oh, shoot, just tip the man proper."

The group moved to the dining room, and when there was nothing left but pizza crumbs and a bit of broccoli, Nancy reverently placed the three cardboard boxes on the table, each sheltering two round, dark chocolate cakes, sprinkled with pow-dered sugar and filled with decadent chocolate pudding. Nancy and Charlene might be the polar opposites in fashion, but they knew a chocoholic's fix when they saw one.

Nancy placed each cake on a dessert plate, along with a fork, as she served them to her guests. She and Charlene ignored the niceties and used their fingers, as the cakes were meant to be eaten, moaning with each morsel, caressing the center with their tongues, and practically hav-ing an orgasm licking the warm filling from their fingers. The goofy pair expected laughs, but each audience member reacted differently. Trixie frowned. "You girls are being silly. Now stop that." Milly laughed and said, "I do not know you." Rigel choked. "You keep that up and I'm heading home to D'Gnome."

Charlene coughed spastically. "Excuse me. Inhaled wrong." She reached for her Diet Pepsi and croaked, "Did you say D'Gnome?"

Rigel looked at Trixie guiltily. To Charlene, he said, "Home. I was gonna go home if you kept up those finger-licking antics."

"You said something afterwards that rhymed with home. D'Gnome."

"No, I didn't."

Charlene grimaced. "Yes, you did. I don't mean to be difficult, but this afternoon I was unpacking some boxes I'd been holding back and came across a document of my husband's stuck in a book. There were multiple references to D'Gnome."

"Huh." Rigel took a swig of his beer. "Never heard of it."

"Not sure I believe you, but supposedly D'Gnome is an exoplanet in the El'o-el'ay Galaxy. Not as large as the Milky Way or Andromeda galaxies but within the Local Group, whatever that means."

Milly barely managed to squeak out, "Say what?"

"Tell us about your document, dear," said Trixie.

"Well, I've only lived here a few months. I was feeling homesick, which is why I hadn't unpacked everything. I kept hoping the move wasn't permanent. But I know it is. And, Miss Trixie, I adore your daughter. She is the sweetest person on the planet and has made me feel welcome here."

"Charlene, that's very nice of you. She *is* a sweetheart."

"Quit it, Mom." Nancy popped the last of the cake into her mouth.

"Thanks to Nancy, I feel Collinsville is my home now, which is why I started unpacking the last few boxes of books. Before Bo left with Ted, he gave me a topographic map of where they were camping. He pointed out the mountain peak, the river, and even a town named after John Hoback. So when I came across *John Hoback—Mountain Man,* I opened it up, curious as to why so much was named after him. That's where I found the papers. I'm sure he was hiding it from me. I never would have opened that book otherwise."

"What's in the papers?" Rigel asked.

"Stuff like string theory and wormholes." She shrugged her shoulders. "Portals to intergalactic communities . . . something about radio astronomy being out of date. A bunch of calculations, equations. I didn't understand any of it."

"I wouldn't worry about it. Maybe Bo's writing a sci-fi novel and those are his notes," said Milly. "He stuck 'em in a random book and forgot about 'em."

"I thought of that, but seems like I would know if he was writing a novel. All I know is I suddenly had an uneasy feeling come over me, like something was eerily amiss. Mainly, Nancy, because your name is in it. That's why I called you."

"My name?" Nancy asked incredulously.

"On the last page, Bo wrote in the margin: 'They are here. They *do* exist.' He drew a smiley face next to the note. I suspect he wasn't referring to the M&M's commercial with Santa Claus. Under the smiley face was your name and Ted's, with 'DG mom' scribbled below that."

"Holy cow," said Nancy, frowning.

"Y'all are squirming in your chairs. I see the strained looks y'all are giving each other. I feel like I've infiltrated your secret society by mistake, and y'all don't know what to do with me. What is D'Gnome and why did you deny saying it, Rigel? That's very weird." Charlene drummed her fingertips on the table.

"I'm weird, like you said. Ask Milly. She knows how weird I can be."

"Uh-huh," Milly said. "You got that right."

"Do you have the papers with you?" asked Rigel.

"I brought them, thinking I could talk to Nancy after you two left. Bo's out of cell range or I would have called him. I probably wouldn't have paid any attention to them, except how did he know your name? The book was in a box sealed by the movers, so your names would have been written *before* we got here."

Charlene retrieved the document from her bag and shakily handed it to Rigel. He scanned through the pages and asked, "What's your husband's name?"

"Trebo Luapa."

"My stars," said Trixie, clapping her hands together, startling everyone. "There were some Luapas who were sponsors in Fort Worth. Isn't that where you're from, Charlene?"

"Close enough. Sponsors of what? You all seem to be in on whatever this is. You're acting odd, and it's freaking me out."

"Nothing to be freaked out about, but it looks like we're in for a long night," said Nancy.

"What are you *talking* about?" Charlene shoved her chair back, stood up, and took a step away from the group. "Why would you *say* that?"

"Alrighty then, let's move this party to the family room and get comfortable." Nancy got up to gather the paper plates and napkins to toss in the trash. "Help yourself to drink refills."

"I feel a sense of déjà vu," Milly whispered to Nancy. They made eye contact, and Milly gave her a meaningful smile. *At least I'm prepared, should Charlene pass out like you did.* O-M-G, she had heard Milly, although Milly had practically thrown the silent comment at her.

"Sponsors of what?" Charlene repeated, as she sat down on the carpeted steps leading to the second floor, farthest away from everyone.

Nancy was thankful her mother took charge, easing Charlene into what would be knowledge hard to swallow, if she could at all, and not storm out, telling them they were all insane. "The Luapas I knew hosted high school exchange students. Their names were Harvey and Gilda. Do you know them?"

"Harvey and Gilda were Trebo's grandparents!"

"They were friends of my mother and father," said Trixie.

"That's cool, but I wouldn't think they'd have anything to do with this." Charlene indicated the incriminating paper. "What is it about?"

"Hmm, cosmic tunnels, space travel. Are you sure he isn't writing a book? Looks like research to me," said Rigel.

"I've never seen him writing for any length of time. He likes science-fiction movies and books, though."

"There you go," Rigel said in an end-of-discussion tone of voice. Nancy figured he knew more than he was willing to share. He handed the document back to Charlene.

But Charlene wouldn't let it go. Nancy could relate with all the questions. Charlene kept speculating on what the notes meant. How old were they? Maybe they were from his college days. But then why was the Leopolds' name in the margin?

"Trebo could have learned our name from the real estate agent, who, as you know, happens to live across the street. He knows Ted is into big game hunting, and if Bo had mentioned it, he could have given him our name. Bo may have pulled the Hoback book off the shelf when he got back home to Texas and jotted it down on the papers so he wouldn't forget."

"Maybe," Charlene said.

With the revelation of Charlene possessing a document relating to D'Gnome, a whole new dimension had been opened. There was a slim possibility that Trebo had met Ted when he was in Collinsville house hunting. No matter how you tried to explain it, Nancy had the same question as Charlene: Why was her name on that paper?

I know why, Rigel said, looking at Nancy. *Don't ask me now*. Oh, yeah, he can read her mind. Then it dawned on her, she had read his! Yikes! Her newfound skill was hit or miss until she got more practice. Nancy tried to grasp any other information that he wasn't spilling, but she couldn't. Of course, Rigel could select what he wanted her to hear or not.

"I was bothered at first," said Charlene, "but the rationalizations seem logical, so no big deal, right? Yet why was I picking up such bizarre vibes from y'all in the kitchen?" Her friends shrugged.

"Isn't it something, Charlene," Trixie said. "You live in Wyoming and I'm visiting from California, and we find we know someone in common from Texas. It's a small world after all."

"Or is it two small worlds," said Milly. Everyone looked at her sharply. "She's got to know sooner or later."

"Know what?"

Trying to protect Charlene from the outer space mumbo-jumbo hadn't worked, so Nancy and her cohorts had no choice but to explain the circumstances. They told her about the existence of D'Gnome. That Rigel and Trixie had traveled through an intergalactic gateway, the sort of cosmic tunnel Bo noted, from Ghanwik City on D'Gnome to Collinsville. That Nancy was not an alien, or star person, please. That Trebo's family lineage had been student sponsors for the Senior Superlative Earth Study Program.

"Y'all are joshing me, right? I've never heard such hogwash!"

"Charlene, it's not something you can explain very easily," Trixie said. "I came to Collinsville to finally tell Nancy. She is learning about D'Gnome for the first time, like you."

"Well, actually, I freaked a few times. But I'm right there with you. Still having a hard time digesting it. I know now, though, it's true. Everything they're saying."

"Think about it. Why else does Trebo have a paper with notes about some of the science we've talked about?" Rigel asked.

"Why in hell, excuse my French, did Bo lie to me? He lied to me about this move, about his job, about his involvement with you people." Charlene looked from Rigel to Trixie and back. "Who is this man I married?"

Rigel smiled. "I believe, Charlene, that Trebo had a legitimate job offer. At the same time, he's also helping a D'Gnoman named Marcus Shining with a project here."

"How do you know?"

"I haven't met your husband, but I know Marcus. Harvey and Gilda Luapa were Senior Superlative sponsors, but when they retired, Trebo's parents became sponsors. Marcus spent his senior high school year with Trebo's family in Ft. Worth. It makes sense that he would be the person Marcus would contact for a project between the two planets, because they go way back. Trebo was someone Marcus could trust."

Charlene scanned the group sitting around her and frowned at Milly. "Are you also one of them, Milly?"

"No way. And I'm shocked you didn't faint dead away, like Nancy did when she found out about D'Gnome." Milly poked at Nancy.

Charlene fanned her face. "It is awful hot in here, but I don't think I'm going to faint. I'm too stunned to faint. Mother always said we Bowie women could take anything in stride. Although not sure she would have been prepared for something of this magnitude. This isn't a cruel joke, is it? I really haven't known any of you all that long."

"No, Charlene," Milly said. "My family has sponsored D'Gnoman students for generations, like Trebo's family. He would have been bound by an unbreakable vow, as were all sponsors and their adult offspring. Since Trebo was not an active sponsor, he probably felt he had no reason to tell you."

"I can relate," said Nancy. "I have absolutely no idea whatsoever how to tell Ted. Same as Bo would feel about you."

"That doesn't exonerate him. He's in a new business that is so far-fetched I can't even describe it, and he didn't tell me! Ah-h-h!" Charlene shot off the steps with her hands in an imaginary strangle hold—presumably around Trebo's neck—and began pacing.

"That may be why he hasn't told you. It would be mindboggling to the average person," Rigel said.

"I'm not average, I'm his wife, for God's sake!" Charlene turned on Rigel as if his neck were next.

Trixie stood up and moved to put her hand on Charlene's shoulder. "Charlene, when Theodore and Trebo get home, we'll enlighten them both—kill two birds with one stone."

"I get to kill Bo," snarled Charlene.

"I was speaking figuratively," Trixie chuckled. "Let's not worry about it now. It's almost midnight." She covered a yawn with her hand. "We'll discuss it more tomorrow. If you'll excuse me, I'm going to bed." She left the room.

"We're gonna roll too." Rigel stood and took Milly's hand to pull her up. "Need to recharge our batteries."

Charlene's expression turned from anger to exhaustion. "Please, don't tell me you're a robot. I've seen ones in Japan that were difficult to distinguish between human or machine. I am at my mindboggling limit for today."

"We are much more sophisticated than mere robots, Madam."

Charlene's knees almost buckled to the floor before Trixie caught her elbow and gave a sarcastic "Thanks" to Rigel, the comedian.

"So much for my strong southern constitution," Charlene muttered.

"It *is* morning," Milly reminded her friends. "We do need sleep, so we better get going." Milly nudged the big man toward the door.

"Under no circumstances am *I* going home alone in the dark," Charlene said. "Major and Minor have auto feeders and waterers. They'll be fine until tomorrow."

"I've got an extra new toothbrush, or I can slip over with you to pick up a few things for the night. How about we all sleep in and get back together here for brunch tomorrow, say nine-ish? Is that too early?"

"No matter when I go to sleep, I still wake up by six," said Milly. "So nine-ish works for us. Goodnight." Rigel waited for Milly to move through the door, then closed it behind them.

"I still don't get what you all are talking about or why you'd make up something like this," said Charlene to Nancy after they'd run next door to gather toiletries, pajamas, and a change of clothes for tomorrow. "I am physically exhausted, but doubt I can sleep after all this."

"Me, either. Let's get ready for bed and we can talk some more. I'll tell you what happened after the World of Arts show that made me believe. We're in this together now."

CHAPTER 23:
THE KEY

Nancy set the lower oven to warm for her no-crust quiche made with fresh mushrooms, spinach, onions, ham, and Monterey Jack cheese. Charlene pulled enormous cinnamon rolls out of the upper oven as Rigel and Milly walked into the kitchen.

"Mm-mm. It's my turn to faint from the heavenly aroma in here. Dang, girl, that smells delish!" Milly set a bright yellow bowl on the counter. "What time did you get up to make those?"

"To tell the truth, they were frozen. All I did was put them in a pan and use the quick-rise method on the bag." As Charlene placed the hot rolls on a wire rack, Rigel reached for one and she whacked his hand away. "Hey! I'm fixin' to frost 'em. Hands off."

"All right, all right!" Rigel held up his hands. "It's good to see you smiling, Charlene."

"Nancy and I stayed up way past after y'all left and talked. It helped. What's in the bowl, Milly?"

"I made apple salad."

"Perfect." Nancy set a stack of plates and the food on the black and white granite-topped island for her guests to serve themselves buffet-style.

"This is for you, Trixie." Rigel held out a small book. "It's your mother's diary. It was found not long ago and given to me to give to you."

Everyone stopped what they were doing and looked at the pair. Trixie slowly took the book and carefully flipped through the pages. "I don't know what to say. Thank you. I'll look at it some other time." She left the room and returned a few minutes later.

During the meal, the friends kept their conversation light. Trixie shared that Nancy had inherited musical talent from her father—she was an accomplished flutist and had the voice of an angel.

"You sing?" Charlene exclaimed.

"You got talent?" teased Milly.

"Mom's exaggerating. I haven't played flute since high school. I sing everywhere but in public. And hell yeah, I got talent—I can tap dance."

Rigel revealed a few memories from the year he spent with Milly and her family. "Remember, Mill, when you climbed high into that big tree in your front yard and couldn't get down? Your mother called the fire department!"

"I've been petrified of heights ever since! What crazy stuff have you done, Charlene?"

"My word, I've got y'all beat on both crazy and heights. Back in high school, Bo and I climbed a water tower and painted a heart on it ten feet high. Told me one day he was going to marry me."

"Oh my gosh, you didn't get caught?" Nancy was shocked Charlene would have done something so daring.

"No ma'am, but they removed the ladder. The tower was repainted, but if you look closely, the heart's still there!"

"So you two were high school sweethearts?" Milly asked.

"You could say that. But we separated during college, dated other people, and then Bo went off to Colorado to get a masters in civil engineering. We didn't get back together until after he came home."

"Well, you got us beat," said Milly. "I'd never climb a water tower."

Nancy kicked them out of the kitchen while she loaded the dishwasher. Charlene was grilling Rigel when she joined them in the family room. "There are so many questions to ask, it would take a lifetime," she said. "Why hasn't NASA discovered D'Gnome?"

"They will. NASA's transiting exoplanet survey satellite is already finding new uninhabited planets in other galaxies. Technology is advancing faster than you can keep up with, let alone comprehend even a smidgeon of what's happening at facilities around the world, a lot of it kept under wraps."

"Bo told me about a recent survey—I can't remember who they asked—but 85% of the respondents said they'd make a one-way trip to Mars. I found that hard to believe, but if D'Gnome became public knowledge, we wouldn't have to worry about Mars. Why not tell people you're here?"

"Charlene, certain people know we're here. They are mostly sponsors who act as contacts for D'Gnomans and assist them in many ways if needed, but they are bound not to speak of DG. These are the trusted partnerships cultivated since our first interaction with Earth's humans.

"There's a clandestine group called the Freedom Jumpers, who don't believe our government is doing enough to reach out to Earth. They want to create a peaceful plan for contact in the future, so maybe our two worlds can become one, so to speak. It will be necessary, as your astronomers search the skies.

"But neither population is ready for a meet-and-greet. People here can't get along with the different cultures and religions that exist now. What would happen if extraterrestrials showed up on Earth, or vice versa? It will take a coordinated effort to avoid widespread hysteria.

"And as for Mars . . . humankind's nature is to be curious . . . seek knowledge . . . explore the unknown. There will always be a Mars or some other planet or moon. The universe calls to us."

Charlene was persistent. "But I know. What about me? I'm not a sponsor."

"Through Trebo and everyone in this room, you are a part of that partnership I spoke of," said Rigel. "D'Gnomans also have the nifty ability to delete memory. Do you feel you need to run to the police?"

"No, oddly I don't. The last thing I want to be is a viral sensation or labeled irrational. But can you really erase a person's memory?"

"To be honest," Rigel said, "memory isn't really deleted, more like rearranged. I should have called it memory modification. A modified memory—although rarely—can resurface in a dream, or more likely a person may experience a current event that triggers a recall. Or I can bring back your memory of Elvis right now, if you want me to."

Charlene sounded skeptical. "Bring back Elvis?"

"Not the man. Even we cannot bring back the dead, but I can restore your memory of the dock on the bay where you saw a likeness of him."

Charlene looked at Nancy. "Is this what you were telling me last night?"

Nancy nodded. "Yup."

"So you remember going to the World of Arts at the high school with Joan, Nancy, and me?" asked Milly.

"Yes. I loved the Taiko drums. I've actually seen a performance in Tokyo. Nancy said afterwards we ended up sitting on the dock of a bay. I saw Elvis Presley. I don't remember the dock or Elvis."

"Well, it happened," said Milly. "And you said you smoked weed."

"I did not!"

"Oh you did, sister. Told us not to tell your momma. Of course, we don't know your momma, so that secret is safe with us," Milly said.

"Maybe a little, but that was before the kids were born!"

"Uh-huh. Anyway, Rigel was there when we returned to the stage, and when that guard started coming at us, he did his hocus-pocus and, boom—" Milly's fists bumped and opened to jazz hands. "Memory gone, at least for you and Joan. Personally, I think it would be helpful if Rigel restored the excitement of our group encounter."

"Should I? Have y'all ever had your memory restored?"

"It's up to you and no, I haven't," said Nancy.

"Nope, never had the pleasure," said Milly. "But I'd say go for it."

Charlene looked at Trixie for confirmation. "You'll be fine."

"Okay, then do it."

"Your scientists are working on coding the brain as we speak. We don't need wires anymore to connect, which sounds terrifying, but it's not," Rigel said. "I'm simply going to rearrange a miniscule portion of your hippocampus. You won't feel a thing. It's easy for me to do when a person doesn't know it's coming, but since you're expecting it to happen, you might subconsciously interfere, so think of something other than what's happening at the moment. Close your eyes."

Rigel placed his fingers on Charlene's temples. Thirty seconds later, Rigel asked her to open her eyes.

Nancy and Milly had been sitting on the edge of their chairs, leaning forward. "How'd it feel?" Milly asked first.

"I didn't feel anything. I thought of how much fun we have in tap class and the exuberant applause we'll get from our show-stopping 'Proud Mary,' that is if I don't slip and fall. Then again I learned a wonderful life lesson from dance as a child . . . if you fall, get back up. Make your stumble part of the dance and keep going. That's what I was thinking when Rigel woke me."

"That's cool," said Nancy.

"Do you remember what happened after you met Joan at the high school the night of the World of Arts?" Rigel asked.

"She pulled me backstage. There was darkness and then . . . Sweet peaches! I saw Elvis Presley!"

"Yes, you did!" Milly and Nancy answered simultaneously.

"Jinx." Nancy good-naturedly punched Milly's arm.

Milly punched back. "And Otis Redding too."

"That's right. Joan knew a lot about him. Now I have one more question. Did this traveling thing really happen or not? Y'all say it did, but you must understand how outlandish it sounds."

"Oh, we do," Nancy and Milly agreed and punched each other a second time. "Jinx."

"Maybe, Rigel, you hypnotized me into *thinking* I saw Elvis. Hypnosis I could believe. Although I can't comprehend why you'd do that." Charlene entwined her fingers and cracked her knuckles. "How do I know it's real? Can we go there again?"

"No, Miss I-Have-One-More-Question, we can't go there again," Rigel answered amiably.

"We have two portals in the restoration test phase to ensure they are fully functioning. Could be the Collinsville gateway is unstable, for all we know."

"There might be a way to Gansarcal if I had the key to Mother's Pathfinder," said Trixie.

"You have a Pathfinder?" Rigel looked surprised.

"Yes, I do."

"What is a Pathfinder again? I'm sure you said, but there's been a lot going on in my head these last two days," said Charlene.

"The Pathfinder is a handheld device Nancy's grandmother, my mother, created," Trixie said. "It works the same way a gateway works, by bending space-time to create a shortcut between our two worlds. The Pathfinder is a portable gateway. It can take you anywhere you want to go on this planet or DG and between our two planets. All you have to do is think about your destination."

"I know the Freedom Jumpers have access to the device but had no idea you possessed one. I've never used a Pathfinder. And you have one? Here? Stars, I haven't felt this giddy since I was a teenager commanding a space mobile for the first time."

"Rigel," Milly admonished. "Chill."

"Sorry, Mill, it's like your favorite candy dangled in front of you, slightly out of reach. Because of my dual role in government—I work for the government and the Freedom Jumpers—I can't take the risk of getting caught with one. But this is different. On Earth it wouldn't be traced."

Ignoring the agitated man, Trixie addressed the women: "There is a key in the center, and if you hold it and focus on where you want to go, a picture appears on the key's surface to confirm your desired destination. Then you plug it in and off you go. It can take up to four people. I have it with me, if you want to see it."

"Need you ask?" Rigel grinned.

While Trixie retrieved the apparatus, Charlene briskly rubbed her palms together. "Mercy, this is like a good horror movie. It's exciting despite the underlying terror."

Trixie returned with a circular gadget about the diameter and thickness of a luncheon plate. It was divided into four sections with grips, each a different color, with a round depression in the center.

"Here it is. After you've drooled over it, we should get some fresh air and not waste this beautiful fall day." She placed the tool into Rigel's outstretched hand. "It may be out of date."

Rigel turned it over and over. "This is an original." He looked at Milly. "It's like a classic car. In mint condition. Hardly been driven. It's beautiful."

"It looks like an old Simon Says game my kids played with," said Milly.

"Your grandparents used one like this, Nancy, when they visited me."

"I apologize for the unnecessary sorrow I caused you back then, when I sent you the message that your parents had drowned," said Rigel.

"I do not hold you accountable. I understand the powers at play." Acknowledging the others' curious expressions, Trixie added, "What Rigel is talking about is that he and his sister were sent to tell me that my parents had drowned in a river rafting accident. Nancy was eight. Years later they visited me for the first time with the help from Freedom Jumpers, who provided disguises and were able to move them to the near side, where they could use the Pathfinder."

"The near side?" Charlene asked.

"Of the moon. I know, sounds outrageous, but that's where they were imprisoned. During their visit, they told me they *were* floating a river in D'Gnome's wilderness, testing the Pathfinder, which was illegal. They were caught essentially jumping without an authorized portal. They were arrested and sent to the penitentiary on Gansarcal."

Nancy was hearing this part for the first time and sat in stunned silence.

Trixie continued, "Nancy was at CSU. Her father was at work. I was alone in the kitchen. Needless to say, I was traumatized, as I believed they were dead. They showed me how the Pathfinder worked, and from our kitchen we jumped to Mount Rushmore and back. Not the crowded visitor areas but up behind Washington's head. Before they jumped back to D'Gnome, they left me a Pathfinder, which I immediately hid.

"Over the years, I tried to tell Nancy's father several times about my homeland, but he teased me about it and would not believe me. I gave up trying to convince him. Then I had the Pathfinder, and I could have easily shown him, but I was too afraid I would frighten him away. So, I said nothing, did nothing.

"Two years later, good ol' Harold and Erma—sorry, my parents—materialized in our kitchen again . . . in front of Jim. Nancy had started her new job and had moved out by then. You can picture the scene. I had to explain that it wasn't a magic trick, that they were from another planet. That sounds so silly, doesn't it? See? Even I have a hard time hearing the truth sometimes. He eventually accepted who they were that night, but the next morning he got out of bed, said he wasn't feeling well, and suddenly collapsed. I called 9-1-1 and performed CPR until EMTs arrived, but they couldn't revive him. I tried, Nancy, I really did." Trixie burst into tears.

Nancy rushed to her mother and held her. "Is this why you blame yourself?"

Trixie nodded, tears flowing freely. The dam had broken.

"It's not your fault, Mom."

"I have to take some responsibility. I was so afraid I'd lose him that I kept putting the truth off, but I lost him anyway. And you expected me to tell you? And lose you too? I couldn't do it."

"Are you sure we shouldn't leave?" asked Charlene.

"No," said Trixie. "I consider you all family." She blew her nose on a tissue. "But I hear you asking an obvious question: Could I have taken him to D'Gnome for care? It happened so suddenly, and I wasn't thinking straight. Even with our advanced medicine, he was beyond help.

"I was so angry when they reappeared a few months later that I threw the key at Mother and told her I didn't want to ever see it again. I never wanted to return to D'Gnome and would die in San Diego." Trixie frowned. "I haven't seen them since."

"You don't have the key?"

"Rigel! Is that all you can think about?" Milly slapped his arm.

"I apologize, Trixie. I do not mean to be insensitive."

Nancy also was crying, holding her mother and gently rocking her. Comforting her. The whole room grew heavy with sorrow before Trixie pulled away from her daughter and straightened. "This would be a good time for that fresh air."

"Y'all, I'm not sure how to say this," Charlene said, pulling a tissue from the box Nancy had given Trixie and dabbing her eyes, "but I might have the key."

"The key to what, dear?" Trixie wiped her eyes and blew her nose again.

"The key to your thingy, whatever you called it. Besides unpacking books yesterday, I also cleaned out our desk, which hadn't been cleaned and organized for years. It used to belong to Gilda and Harvey. I found something that would fit the center." Charlene pointed to the Pathfinder. "It had a picture of a kitchen, which I imagined was part of a child's puzzle, one that identifies parts of a house. I threw it back in the drawer, thinking I'd eventually find the puzzle."

"You're full of surprises, aren't you, Charlene?" said Rigel. "You think that's what she has?" he asked Trixie.

"My kitchen would have appeared last as we returned home from Mount Rushmore. And it hasn't been used since. Why would you have it?"

"Didn't you say the Luapas were friends of your parents? Perhaps Erma gave the key to Gilda for safekeeping, knowing Gilda could get in touch with you easier than she could. The desk must have a concealed cubby. She hid it in there and it got jostled open during our move from Dallas."

"I can't think of a better explanation." Trixie shook her head and pursed her lips. "All those years in her possession and Gilda never contacted me."

"We may never know why, as she died not long after Bo and I were married. Harvey passed three years later. I'll go get it. I should check on our dogs anyway. Who wants to go with me?"

"I do!" Milly shot her hand up.

Nancy looked at her mother. "Go. I'll stay here with Rigel."

"We'll be right back!" the women called as they ran out the front door.

After lavishing love on Major and Minor, Trebo's golden retrievers, Charlene led the group upstairs to the office.

"Ooh, look at this desk, what a beautiful antique!" Milly stroked the polished surface.

"Thank you. It's where I found the key."

Nancy bent down to look closer at a frame setting on the desk and read aloud: "You cannot discover new oceans unless you have the courage to lose sight of the shore. That's a nice saying."

"Trebo gave that to me before we left Texas. I thought he was trying to boost my spirits and instill courage in me to let go of Texas and discover a whole new world in Wyoming." Charlene picked up the picture and scrutinized it. "Instead, was he trying to tell me the new ocean wasn't the sagebrush sea, as he referred to Wyoming, but a fifth dimension? Now I'm mad all over again." She dropped the frame face down onto the desk. "Let's see if I can find that key thing. Luckily I kept it, because I was really on a roll with the garbage." Charlene rummaged in the drawer. "Here it is." She held it up for her friends to see.

"Didn't you say it had a kitchen on it? That's a waterfall," Milly said.

"It did, but 3-D things can show two different pictures, depending on how you tilt it."

"Yeah, but usually the pictures are related," Milly contended. "I have a bookmark with an African daisy that blooms and closes and blooms again, but it doesn't turn into a green bean."

"All I know is it feels oddly warm, which I hadn't noticed before," said Charlene. "What if it's a D'Gnoman creature wanting to get out?"

"Shut up. Let me see it." Charlene dropped the piece into Nancy's outstretched hand. She examined it closely. "I swear it's humming. Here you take it!" Nancy pitched it to Milly.

Milly barely made the catch. "The thing is vibrating!" She threw it at Charlene. "It's gonna hatch!"

"Crapola, Milly!" shrieked Charlene as it bounced off her chest. "I don't want it!" Barely scooping up the key before it hit her new hickory floor, she lobbed it toward the ceiling as all eyes followed.

"Someone better catch it. Don't let it fall and break!" Nancy yelped, and when no one moved, stepped up to snatch it, tossing it from hand to hand like a hot potato. "Get something to put it in, Charlene! The waterfall is pulsing. It's freaking alive!"

Charlene snatched a tote bag off the doorknob and opened it wide. Nancy chucked in the frightful gadget. "Let's get out of here!"

"Don't have to tell me twice," Milly said as she took the lead down the stairs.

"Step on it! I don't want this thing in my house." The women raced out the front door and Charlene slammed it shut.

Running across the rocks between the driveways, Charlene's foot slipped out from under her. The bag swung in the air, as Charlene fought to keep her balance. Nancy yanked the bag from her hand. "I'll take it." She overtook Milly and flung open her front door.

Back inside, the women moved as one unit into the family room, where Rigel and Trixie were still deep in conversation. "Here! It's alive!" Panting, Nancy tossed the bag to her mother.

"Girls, don't be silly." Trixie pulled out the key.

"It's got a heartbeat!" Milly said. The other two women stood by her side, ready to run. The waterfall glowed and pulsed between blue and green.

"This should have had my kitchen on it. Were you thinking of a waterfall when you picked it up?"

"I wasn't," said Nancy.

"I did not think of no waterfall. Oh, shoot! I hate when that happens! Double negatives are a pet peeve of mine. I'm so scared, I'm losing my mind!" Milly cried.

"I wasn't thinking of no waterfall, neither," added Charlene. "I swear it had the kitchen picture when I put it back in the drawer. When I took it out today, the waterfall was on it."

Trixie held the key while she showed it to Rigel. "It's certainly not alive, girls, so calm down. But from its behavior, it urgently wants to go to this place."

"I recognize this waterfall," answered Rigel. "It's on Gansarcal."

"Nancy told me Gansarcal has a resort there," Trixie said.

"It was inevitable being so close to DG. Cassini Falls is in the rainforest zone. There aren't any structures completed in that dome yet, but the water features are in. When finished, the place will be open with new and improved Scramblers ferrying vacationers."

"I have missed a lot, haven't I?" Trixie looked at Rigel wistfully. He didn't reply.

Nancy became the spokesperson for her bewildered friends clustered in the corner. "What's a Scrambler?"

"Part of our public transportation system," Rigel said.

"Can we get some of that fresh air you talked about earlier, Mom? Will the key behave if we leave it?"

"The key is inert until it unites with the Pathfinder which it senses is nearby, although I have never seen it act this way. I should stick close to it for observation. Tell you what . . . it's already after 2 o'clock. I'm getting hungry. Why don't you girls go pick up some sandwiches for us. I haven't nearly had enough time to chat with Rigel. There is so much I want to catch up on."

"We can take my car," Charlene offered.

"My car's already in the driveway." Milly grabbed her jacket off the aspen log coat rack standing near the door and dug out her keys. "I'll drive."

"Don't leave me!" cried a pleading voice.

"Who said that," squeaked Milly.

Rigel held out the key, rocking it back and forth. "I did. Come to Gansarcal. Ple-e-ase!"

"It's talking!" cried Charlene.

"You are naughty, Rigel," Trixie chided, laughing. "Don't play tricks. Nancy will bite your head off, and she's got two backups. Help me up, I need to stretch."

"That was you? Don't know where you're sleeping tonight but it ain't my house."

"Now that's cold, Mill."

"Humph. Let's go, Divas," Milly said, then grumbled as she marched to the car, "Never in my born days would I have foreseen our tap class so mixed up with star people."

Charlene opened the front, passenger door, and looked at Nancy over the roof of the car. "We left so fast we didn't ask them what they wanted."

"I'll call 'em." Nancy climbed into the back seat. "Too bad Joan's missing all this fun. Wonder how she fared at her ex's funeral yesterday."

"She's supposed to text us whether or not she'll make it to *The Music Man*," said Charlene.

Milly slipped into the driver's seat, put the car in reverse, and stomped on the gas. "Let's blow this fruit stand!"

Nancy's seat belt locked as she was thrown forward, stopping her from hitting the back of the front seat. "Holy smokes, Milly, *we* might not make it to *The Music Man*."

CHAPTER 24:
THE SUMMONS

Rigel and Trixie walked to the picture window and watched the dark-orange sedan tear off down the street.

"Let's hope they take their time getting lunch—we haven't had much of a chance to speak alone. Earlier, when the girls went to get the key, thank you for making me feel better about my guilt over Jim. Seeing you has brought so many memories flooding back of you, Saiph, and Bet. Poor Saiph always had her little brother hanging around when we were at your house. You were an inquisitive kid. 'Whatcha doin'?', you'd always ask. Saiph would yell, 'Get out of here!' and you'd scamper away. Remember that?"

"You three were mean to me. *That* I remember."

Trixie chuckled. "When our gang would go to Discovery Island, that play park on the shores of Lake August?"

"Stars, I haven't thought about the lake in a long, long time."

"There was an old Star Cruiser marooned for children to climb on. Saiph would be babysitting you. We'd pretend to be space pirates and tie you up. You hated that, but you'd escape, since you weren't really tied up, and we'd chase you. We *were* kind of mean back then, weren't we?"

"Ah well, I seemed to have turned out okay, don't you think?" They both laughed.

"You have! How are those other two?" Trixie asked.

"Both still alive and kickin'. Saiph has retired from her pediatric practice and volunteers at the Ghanwik City Hospital as a grandmother holding preemies and other sick babies. She was going to come instead of me, but she's laid up with a knee injury. She sends her love. Bet asked me to come, since Saiph couldn't. She's considering retiring soon—she's been the director of the Intergalactic Research Institute for four decades."

"I had no doubt about Saiph becoming a doctor. But, wow, that's quite an achievement for Bet. She was kind of a goof-off like me."

"Well, she takes her job very seriously now. Believes you might have information on the creation of the gateways or your father's nepial vaccine research. Biloxi and San Diego crashed, and no one knew why. So the head of the task force decided you or your parents might have information on how to restore them. It's a complicated story, but the good news is they're back up now and no cause for concern."

Trixie's brow wrinkled. "It's ridiculous to think I'd have any knowledge about my mother's or my father's work."

"That's what I said, but it was worth a try. I really wanted to come and see how you were doing."

"As you can see, I'm fine. How are you?" Trixie smiled mischievously. "I've picked up a certain connection between you and Milly. Fess up, little brother."

Rigel laughed. "Trixie girl, there is so much you should know and too little time. I'm guessing you must have suspected back in high school that an unknown side effect of the vaccine was your ability to feel a romantic attraction to Earthlings."

"Yes. Also my father confirmed it on his first visit to me. But at the time, I was young and hadn't thought it through. I paid the price for recklessness, that's for sure. I was so fearful for Nancy as she grew up."

"She's a feisty one. Nearly beat me up when I said I wanted to meet you. Loves you very much."

"Thank you, Rigel. Now back to Milly."

"All right, already. Milly's another feisty one like Nancy. Probably why they're such good friends. Her husband died about ten years ago. Besides her daughter here in Collinsville, she has a son in Savannah."

"Get to the point, Rigel. Did you get the vaccine?"

"Select members of the Freedom Jumpers received it, including me."

"I knew it!"

"Yeah, well, I've always admired Milly. During my stint as Senior Superlative student liaison, I was frequently at William and Milly's home. She was a loving, caring person whom I was attracted to, but she was married with children, had a successful life, and I wasn't going to interfere. Then routine blood work showed an above normal testosterone level, and I was pulled as liaison from the program fifteen years ago. But I felt the booster kick in the minute Bet suggested Milly could help me with Nancy."

"So, are you in love with Milly?"

"You could say that."

"Say what, yes or no?"

"Yes, head over heels. Are you happy now? I said it."

"Oh, Rigel!" Trixie hugged him.

Women. Rigel smiled at Trixie and shook his head. "Let's sit down until the girls get back." They sat together on the love seat. "You know, I wanted to see you directly without involving Nancy. But Bet, instead of waiting for the San Diego gateway to be fixed, decided we could better contact you through Nancy. I was concerned you might not like our butting into your family affairs."

"This weight has been pressing on my subconscious for so long that I knew the time was coming I would have to tell her. I am a thousand times grateful for what you did. The hardest thing I had to do in my life and someone else had to do it for me. I've always been a coward, despite my father's encouragement—'You're a pioneer! Brave and courageous! Go where no woman has gone before!' He said that to me when I left DG, but I can't remember when I last felt that way. My parents . . . Are they still alive?"

"I believe so. I have not seen them, nor do I know their health status, but unless something's changed recently, they are still living on Gansarcal. Freedom Jumpers have been their lifeline."

"Oh my heavens, I wasn't sure if they were alive or not. My mother and father. I've missed them so much! With the key acting like this, I have to trust they have been unable to contact me any other way. The key has been waiting for this moment. Do you think it's my parents summoning me to Gansarcal?"

"I honestly can't say, but contemplate this: the Pathfinder's possessor directs the key—that'd be you. Now the key is directing the possessor. What if some nefarious person has remotely accessed your Pathfinder and programmed it? With the gateway malfunctions, your parents' names have hit the gossip feed. Even though they're back up, the general public is still chattering about what happened to your family. Could make someone with extremely good hacking skills discover data they shouldn't, despite the high level of security. You could be in danger." He pondered the notion that Meissa had gained control.

"It's been so long since I left that I have been letting my guard down, but danger from what or whom? Is Nancy in danger? I knew I shouldn't have come."

"Yes, you should have. She needed to know the truth."

"I know. I'm always doubting myself. You can't imagine what it's been like, always wondering if I'd be found out. I wanted to protect my daughter, but it doesn't look like I'll be able to."

"She's strong like you. She'll handle anything that comes her way. I honestly don't know what our government would do if word got out that you were alive, or somehow the information leaked."

"If something happens to me, Rigel, you must promise to keep Nancy safe."

"Of course I will."

"I still need to see my parents. None of this makes sense, does it? You can't remotely control the Pathfinder; although, there probably have been plenty of upgrades. I am actually unaware of how it works anymore."

"I'm no expert either, but someone has activated it, and it's not you."

"It may have detected a physiological characteristic similar to mine—perhaps something in Nancy's DNA triggered it."

"But Nancy wouldn't have known about the waterfall."

"True. Then it has to be my mother or father trying to communicate, Rigel." Trixie sighed. "Even before I left San Diego to come here, I've had a sense it was time to go home."

"Gansarcal is not home to you."

"Close enough. My parents are there. Whatever this is, I don't want to get those girls involved. We could go to Gansarcal and be back before they get here with lunch. I need to know why this thing came to life. Don't you see? Something's not right. I *feel* it."

"And you want to charge into the unknown? Of course you do." Rigel grinned. "That's the Trixie I used to know. Fearless!"

"It is!" Trixie said. She scooted to the edge of her seat and leaned forward, as if ready to leap. "It will be a grand adventure, like my father said!"

"We could be entering dangerous territory. Meissa Shining, the team leader assigned to recover the gateways, was given a high security clearance. According to her brother, Marcus, she has already discovered that Harold and Erma are on Gansarcal and that you're in San Diego. Now that the gateways are up, she wants what no one has been allowed access—your father's research on the nepial gland." He had no proof that she was up to no good until Marcus had told him Meissa beat up his androids, the Sassy Sistas. She had a serious anger problem. "Marcus indicated that Meissa would stop at nothing to get what she wanted, including abduction."

"Of my parents? All the more reason I need to go! We've got to go to Gansarcal. I am sure Mother and Father are calling me." She stood up and reached for Rigel's hand. "Well, are you coming?"

Seeing Trixie so animated, Rigel capitulated. "Sure. Fine. Better I go with you for protection. Otherwise, knowing you and your newfound confidence, you'd use the Pathfinder the minute I was out of sight and go alone."

"Seriously?"

"Seriously. Plug the damn thing in."

CHAPTER 25:
WHERE'S MOM?

Half an hour later, with sacks of sandwiches in hand, Nancy called out for Trixie and Rigel. No answer. "I suspected they were up to something. She seemed all too willing to get us out of the house." Nancy spun past her friends to the kitchen, threw the sandwiches on the counter, then ran upstairs to the bedrooms, down to the basement, and out to the backyard. "They're not here."

"Let's not jump to conclusions," said Charlene. "I'm sure they'll be back soon from wherever they went."

"First of all, they don't have a car. My mom can't drive."

"Rigel can. Better check the garage," said Milly.

"Mom would not have gone anywhere without leaving a note." Nancy looked into the garage anyway. "My car's still here. And they wouldn't have gone for a walk. But they *would* have used the Pathfinder knowing they could be back before us. And I don't see it lying around. Do you? There's one place they'd have gone. That place with the waterfall. Something's happened or they would be back by now. We've got to go get them."

"Go get them from where? Gansarcal? Are you out of your ever-lovin' mind?" Charlene's eyes were as wide as moon craters.

"Yes and yes! That's where the waterfall is that was on the key. She probably wants to see the new resorts. I'm pretty certain it's where they would have gone. Not D'Gnome, but the moon, especially if she thinks her parents are there."

Milly sat down at the table with her Diet Pepsi. "Cool your jets, missy. Just because the key had a waterfall, doesn't mean that's where they went. The Pathfinder can take you anywhere. Any. Where. Maybe they're in Florida, for all we know, checking out Space Mountain at Disney World. If you had a Pathfinder, you wouldn't have to pay those high prices to get in."

Charlene huffed and sat down next to Milly. "I reckon we should think this through. Throw their food in the fridge and let's eat first. Unless you want it, Nancy, I'll take Trixie's Diet Pepsi, since you got sweet tea. Can't see this go to waste."

"No, take it."

"I'll drink Rigel's." Milly shook her head in disgust. "I swear I'm gonna give this poison up, next I'm telling myself at my age why not indulge in things you enjoy. I'm a regular see-saw, up-down, yes-no."

"My mom still drinks it," Nancy answered absentmindedly. "The key was acting freaky. That I know just looking at my mom. What if they're not here by the time we finish eating?"

"Then I'll agree something's wrong. Darn that Rigel!" Charlene unwrapped her sandwich. "All we know is the waterfall was on Gansarcal."

"And the key wanted to go there. So that's where we'll go. But how?" Nancy placed her palms together, resting her chin on her fingertips in contemplation.

"Be cool. I've got a plan." Milly unwrapped her sandwich and dug in. "Mmm, this Italian club is good. Let's eat. I have a funny feeling we'll need the nourishment. I was bringing treats to the drama kids this afternoon anyhow—now I have even more reason."

"What's your plan?" Nancy took a bite of her Philly cheesesteak.

"We'll go to the school and use the portal. Problem solved."

"How are we going to get into the school? You can't waltz through the front door anymore and go wherever you please." Nancy took a long drag on her sweet tea.

"Ah! That's where you're wrong," Milly said. "Granted, we'll have to stop at the office, but you forget Willy taught at the high school for thirty-odd years. Everybody knows me. My pineapple upside-down cake is famous . . . wait, no, that was the elementary school's annual spring fling cake walk. No worries. I always volunteer for the grandkids' high school band soup suppers. Not to mention the school secretary is a friend of mine."

"Okay, I see us getting to the office, but then what?" Nancy bent to pick up a piece of steak from the floor and dropped it onto her wrapper.

"My granddaughter is in the cast of *Music Man*, remember? Tomorrow is opening night. We're going. Anyway, Elizabeth told me they were staying after school today and ordering pizza for their final dress rehearsal. I volunteered to bring the cast and crew cookies for dessert. Cookies will be our excuse to get into the school, then back-stage."

Nancy nodded. "That's a possibility."

"But then we have to get through the portal," Charlene added. "Rigel said it might be unstable."

"Nah," Milly said. "I know Rigel better than anyone. That's his way of keeping us from doing what we're doing. If you recall, the problems were with Biloxi and San Diego. He doesn't want us using it without him. Like we don't know what we're doing."

Charlene smirked. "We don't."

"He's been using it fine," Milly contended. "To DG anyway. We'll figure it out."

"We'll have to. I can't wait anymore. They obviously thought they'd be back before us. They're not, so something is wrong." Nancy took another bite of her steak sandwich.

"But we need to be D'Gnoman, and we're not!" Charlene choked on her drink.

Milly pointed her finger at Nancy. "One of us is, or partially anyway. Maybe enough to get us through."

Nancy shrugged. "I did detect something when we were there with Rigel. I guess we'll find out when we get backstage. If I can't pull us through, I'm not sure what we'll do."

"Hit a concrete wall and fall to the floor, I suppose," said Charlene, chuckling.

"See?" Milly said. "Charlene's gettin' into it. If we did it once, we can do it again."

"All right. We'll do it. Let's hope it's newly updated to your choice of D'Gnome or Gansarcal and that if we seriously concentrate, our combined energy will take us in the right direction. We'd have to block everything out except the dock on the bay and hope that gets us there. Then we find the waterfall. How big can a biodome be?"

No one could answer that. The crew chowed down for a few moments, silently considering their next move.

"One thing is for certain: we don't want to end up on D'Gnome." Milly wadded her sandwich wrapper into a ball. "We'd have no idea how to get to Gansarcal from there."

"I'd hate to be arrested or murdered or worse." Charlene shivered.

Milly gulped. "What's worse than murdered?"

Charlene scrutinized her perfectly manicured French tips. "Hmm, let's see . . . your fingernails yanked out one by one?"

"You both have good points. If we arrive on DG, I can drop the Bayer name. We could beg for asylum. Rigel's sister would help us."

"Maybe," Milly said. "I am trying to remember if Rigel said anything else about what was happening on Gansarcal, besides the resort under construction."

"I recall a brief mention of a prison." Charlene took one last sip and chucked her ice into the sink.

"No one is living there yet," continued Milly.

"Except criminals." Charlene cracked her knuckles.

Nancy leaned back on the granite countertop. "That key was acting peculiar. Mom wasn't certain if her parents were still alive, so could someone other than my grandmother influence it?"

"Let's hope not." Charlene wiped off the table with a paper towel. "Honestly, I'm not sure I can do this."

"Well, I've got to find out. You guys don't have to come with me."

"Forget about it, Nancy." Milly straightened up, feet apart, fists at her waist. All she lacked was the cape. "Divas! We're in this together. One for all and all for one! We can *do* this!"

"Whoa! Do what? I hate to be a stick-in-the-mud." Charlene grimaced. "Before we go gallivanting off to la-la-land, let's talk about what we will do when or IF we get there."

"We'll take it one step at a time, as Joan would say," said Nancy. "I wonder how she's doing? Her daughters didn't have a very close relationship with their father, but all the same, it's a sad loss."

"Yes, it is. Hope she can make it Friday to the play," Milly said.

"I hope *we* make it to the play," said Charlene. "Okay, Divas, one more thing, and then I promise I'll zip it. I'm still leery about using the gateway. How did we get to Gansarcal instead of following Rigel? Gansarcal didn't exist to us; therefore, we could not, I repeat, could not have been *thinking* about it or using our combined energy. The Path-finder works that way, but I don't believe the school portal does."

"I did let go of Rigel's hand," said Milly.

"But then we shouldn't have gone anywhere. I mean this was supposedly a gateway straight to D'Gnome, the planet, not the moon. What if someone or some*thing* drew us to Gansarcal?" Charlene again examined her manicured nails.

"Stop it, Charlene, you're freaking me out! We've got to go before I lose my nerve." Milly tossed her balled-up wrap into the open trash can. "Score!"

"Okay, fine. Then we're outta here." Charlene slam-dunked hers. "Nothing' but net! We can't lose!"

Nancy pitched her wrapping at the container. It bounced off the rim, scattering crumbs.

Classes were out when the women parked at the high school. Small clusters of students were milling here and there on the expansive lawn.

"Look confident. We don't want to look guilty and have the security guard question us," Milly said, as the women, each holding two dozen bakery-bought, frosted sugar cookies, walked up the wide sidewalk to the front doors, which stood open. They breezed past the guard, as he briefly glanced at the boxes covered in plastic wrap.

When they got to the office, Milly stuck her head in and called, "Hey, Christine! How you doin'?"

Christine, hunched over a keyboard, looked up, lifted her hot pink eyeglasses to the top of her head, and grinned. "Well, look what the cat dragged in. Hey to you, Miss Milly! What'cha got there?"

"Cookies for the *Music Man* cast. Can we take 'em back? Elizabeth said they were ordering pizza, so I told her I'd donate dessert."

"Miss Milly, you're the kindest! It's the end of the day, so don't bother signing in. You go on and say hello to Elizabeth for me."

"I will. Thanks, Christine!" Milly texted Elizabeth that cookies were in the building. They hadn't gotten far before they saw four teenage girls in blue jeans and black sweatshirts with CHS Drama Club under white comedy and tragedy masks. The shirts were in varying degrees of style, with cut-off sleeves, shortened hems, or slices of neck missing. The actors oohed and awed over the orange, yellow, and red frosted treats. Elizabeth, thin like Milly but half a head taller, thanked her grandma and her friends. The young people returned to the drama classroom. The young-at-heart dashed backstage. The hallway door shut, leaving them nearly in the dark, except for the dim light of the exit sign.

After their eyes adjusted, Charlene whispered, "Hey look. They've taken down the curtain rod and painted the wall black."

"Good," said Milly. "Nothing left to fall on our heads."

Nancy stood to the left of her two cohorts. "We discussed this on the way here, but to reiterate: When I feel the force field, I'll tell you. We've got to hold each other tight."

Nancy moved slowly along the wall. "I feel it, but let me double check." She progressed farther. "I've lost it. Wait, I feel it. Egads, this is hard. You guys stay here. I'm going to start from the other side and move toward you." Again, the field was active, dead, active. The dead zone was only a blip but noticeable. She shook her head in consternation and wiped her sweaty palms on her jeans.

Milly tapped the wall. "Got it! There are two portals. Has to be. That's why Rigel went to D'Gnome and we went to Gansarcal. Rigel was in the lead, which means he would have gone through the one nearest you. We went through the one closer to where I'm standing."

Nancy's face brightened as she painstakingly moved back and forth to be positive of what she felt. "That's got to be it. Milly, you're a genius!"

"We'll see about that when we get to the other side. Rigel must have known, yet he didn't tell us. He's no better than Trebo."

"Don't get me started. Let's get this over with. My heart's about to leap out of my chest." Charlene took a deep breath and cracked her knuckles.

"Okay. Since these portals are so close together, I say we concentrate on the dock on the bay. Even if we don't have to, it might help. So concentrate on the dock and we go together. No hesitation."

"Dear God, I can't believe I'm doing this. I never even said goodbye to my family," whimpered Charlene.

"Keep your voice down. We're not gonna die," Milly assured her. "Go on, Nancy. Do your thing."

The women stood quietly in a huddle, arms embracing each other. They scooted to the left, then scooted to the right. "Positive this is the one. Remember, no hesitation and don't let go. TO THE DOCK ON THE BAY!" Nancy leaned into the wall and they were gone.

CHAPTER 26:
STRANGER DANGER

The Dancing Divas arrived calm, cool, and feet first, unlike the heap of bodies reminiscent of their last trip to Gansarcal. "We made it. High five, Divas!" Nancy held up her hand.

"Sweet peaches! We're alive!" Charlene said, slapping Nancy's palm.

Milly raised her face and hands to the sky. "Praise the Lord!"

"How are y'all feeling? Understand I didn't take it so well last time," said Charlene.

"I'm good." Nancy gave herself a cursory once-over. "How 'bout yourself?"

"Yes, ma'am, I'm good. Possibly the second visit isn't as disorienting. Milly?"

"I seem to have everything intact." Milly wiggled her fingers.

"Okay. Before we start searching for Mom and Rigel, we should take note of landmarks. Make sure we can get back to this place." Nancy pointed to her left. "That must be the hotel Rigel was talking about. Never saw it last time."

"We were a little preoccupied then," Milly said.

"I don't see anyone outside the hotel, so hopefully we're alone," said Nancy.

Charlene looked ahead off the end of the dock. "We are not alone. Three shadowed figures are moving in the brush, back behind the palm trees, straight ahead. The vegetation surrounding the palms is super-tall there, so they're hard to see."

Milly squinted. "All I see are orange flowers— they're pretty." She held her hands to her eyes, fingers curled like binoculars. "Shoot, you think you got high-powered vision? Rigel said sometimes our biochemistry changes."

"Don't know for sure. I only see shadows behind the trees. You see them, Nancy?"

"No. Is it Mom and Rigel? Are they coming this way?"

"Um, they just broke through the brush. They're heading this way, but it's not them," Charlene said.

"Are they friend or foe?" asked Nancy.

"How would I know? Oh, there they are! Dang, that's a lot of bling—can't be the enemy."

"Yikes, I see them. Well, we can't stand here forever. My mother's the reason we're here. I'll take the lead. These people may be friendly . . . or not. Anybody got a weapon? Bear spray, mace, anything?"

Charlene pulled her crossbody purse over her head and swung it in circles like a lifeguard's whistle on a lanyard. "I could knock someone upside the head or strangle 'em with the strap."

"Whoa." Milly took a step back at Charlene's gleeful aggressiveness. "All I have is my cell." She pulled the phone out of her jacket pocket. "I don't like carrying a purse. I could throw the phone, not that it would do much damage, or gouge their eyes out with my car keys. I saw that once on a self-defense show."

"Either way, we've got your back," said Charlene.

"Who's got 'er back? I say we *go* back," Milly said. "I didn't mean that. I'm letting nerves get to me. I didn't have time to get nervous last trip, because I thought Rigel would be with us."

Considering Milly's suggestion, Nancy hesitated for the briefest of moments before continuing toward the beach. At the end of the pier, she stretched her frame tall as a grizzly bear on its hind feet. "Show no fear, Divas!"

"Stay calm and dance on!" shouted Milly. "Hooey, that made me feel better already."

The group stepped to the ocher sand and stopped to assess the situation as their perceived adversaries approached.

"I can't read their minds," said Nancy.

"I discern no weapons. They do not appear to be dangerous," determined Charlene.

"They do not appear to be human, Captain."

"Geez, Milly, how can you make a Star Trek joke right now?"

"Heck, if Charlene has superhero eyesight, maybe I have an enhanced sense of humor.

Although I was hoping to leap tall buildings in a single bound. No more fear of heights!"

"Actually, she's right. They're not human," Charlene said. "They're robots."

"Are you sure? They look awfully human to me." Nancy peered into the distance.

"Yes, ma'am, I'm sure. Humanoid robots, very lifelike. Look how they're maneuvering through the sand. It's not natural."

"Ha! They're skinny. Unless they have death rays for eyes, we can take 'em." Milly stood with karate-chop hands at the ready. "I was a yellow belt when I was twelve. I still remember some of it." The robots shuffled closer in their short, tight, strappy dresses, their shoulders bare, as well as their feet. "Huh, they look more like hookers than fighters."

Nancy's shoulders relaxed. "On second thought, we should stay close to the portal, in case we need to get out of here fast. Let them come to us."

"Hello, hello, hello!" sang the newcomers in three-part harmony.

Charlene was first to address the trio, who were now within six feet. "Stop right there! Who are you?"

"We are gynoids, female androids. But we prefer the generic term androids," said the tallest one, in glittery blue, with ebony skin and long, brown hair. "I am Sojourner."

"Not ordinary androids, chic androids," said the red-bedazzled one, bald as a cue ball, with ivory skin. "I have loaned my luscious locks to a friend." She brushed her hand atop her smooth head. "I am Saffron."

"Would an ordinary robot have these sexy curves? I think not," said the shortest of the three in green-sequins, with matching green hair and skin. "Last check, I was still Sagan."

"Anyone who can sing like that can't be very harmful," said Charlene.

"Or maybe it's like a scam," said Milly. "They lure you in all innocent-like, then, shazam!" She clapped her hands together and the other two flinched. "You're toast!"

"Yikes!" Nancy exclaimed. "That didn't occur to me."

The blue android said, "We are here to greet you."

The red android said, "We are here to meet you."

"We will not toast you," assured the green one.

"Then you must be the welcoming committee," said Charlene. "Would you please direct me to the nearest restroom?"

"And then a piña colada would be nice," said Milly.

"We have no piña coladas," said the first.

"What is a restroom?" asked the second.

"Do you need a room to rest?" asked the third.

"I have to go to the bathroom."

"Is a restroom necessary to get to the bathroom?"

"Or do you need a room for baths?"

"We have no need for baths."

"Never mind. I can wait." Charlene looked at her buddies with raised eyebrows.

"Who *are* you?" Nancy asked.

"We call ourselves the Sassy Sistas," the three chimed together.

"Hey, we've got a name too! We're the Dancing Divas. Although we don't feel much like dancin'. And we're missin' a diva, but I'm Milly. That's Charlene. And this is our leader, Nancy."

"We know who you are," said Sojourner.

"You are in danger." Saffron indicated Nancy.

"Major danger from a stranger," confirmed Sagan.

"I am afraid there are unprincipled D'Gnomans about."

"What is this world coming to, Sistas?"

"These are discombobulating times."

"You *must* leave Gansarcal."

"Return before it's too late."

"Or you will be fish bait!"

"If I could use the restroom first," said Charlene.

"Me too," said Milly.

"We're not leaving." Nancy crossed her arms. "We are looking for a man and a woman who would have arrived earlier today."

"Yeah, a tall black man, six-feet-two, neatly trimmed goatee and mustache, muscular body, like he works out every day, and dark chocolate eyes that would melt any—"

"Quit it, Milly," said Nancy. "She's describing Rigel O'Rion. We're also looking for Trixie Bayer Herschel, an older white woman, five-feet-six, hazel eyes, straight light-reddish hair, blunt cut. Have you seen them?"

"We saw them briefly."

"They flew the coop."

"On the wings of a dove." Sagan gazed up at the sky.

"They're dead?" cried Nancy.

"Of course they're not dead!"

"Who said they were dead?"

"We meant they fled."

"On the wings of a dove."

Stop!" commanded Nancy. "I'm getting dizzy listening to you go round and round. Saffron, is there a single-user mode? I want one of you to answer at a time."

"From Nancy Renee Herschel Leopold, also known as Nannycakes, or Honey, or Gertrude, we are allowed to accept the command," said Saffron.

"Gertrude?" sang Milly and Charlene in not so harmonic two-part harmony.

"Ted calls me that sometimes; I don't know why. And I don't know how they know that."

"Our roundabout speech pattern was coded to annoy our programmer's sister. Your request has been applied. We cannot promise to sustain the language change, as we have been experiencing unexplained glitches lately."

"Thank you, Saffron. Now, what happened to Trixie and Rigel?"

"Our instructions are to send you back through the portal," replied Saffron. "Have you heard from Marcus, Sojourner?"

"He is not answering my call."

Nancy crossed her arms. "You didn't answer my question."

"We have already engaged in excessive blabber. You must return to Earth." Saffron pointed toward the small building at the end of the dock.

"Did you say bladder? Because mine is pretty full," said Milly.

"Too much blab-ber," said Sojourner, emphasizing the letter B.

"Excessive idle chatter," said Saffron.

"Stop this jibber-jabber and go home." Sagan's hands mimicked talking mouths.

"No. I am here for my mother, and unless you incapacitate us, we are staying."

"Marcus informed us that you might be obstinate. Confirmed and moving on," said Saffron.

"Um, would this Marcus be the man involved with my husband in a business those bastards are running behind my back?"

"Charlene, we have no knowledge of your husband nor of his business dealings. Marcus is our programmer, when we need programming that is, and he has placed us here to watch the portal. We were to contact him in case you or his sister, Meissa Shining, appeared. We have not seen her, but now you are here, and we are unable to reach him. Please, if you won't take the portal, then come with me." Sojourner turned in the direction from whence she had come.

"Wait. You said you saw my mother and Rigel."

"I will tell you what we know," said Sojourner, "then you must cooperate. We are certain they did not arrive through the portal, as we have been watching it closely, but we saw them fly overhead on the dove. They did not stop. We have not seen them since."

"I assume this dove is not like ours, which are this big." Charlene cupped her hands.

"Our dove is an enormous, domesticated bird, strong enough to carry two adults and a toddler. They are kept in a coop near the soon-to-be Oasis Resort in the desert biodome," said Saffron. "They are becoming accustomed to their new habitat before tourists arrive."

"Are you serious?" said Charlene, flabbergasted. She looked up, as if to spot more in the sky.

"Since I seem to be in some sort of danger, I am going to assume that my mother is not here for a joy ride and simply lost track of time. She's in trouble, isn't she?"

"We have no information on her current status. You must follow me." Sojourner began walking away.

"Stop," Nancy pleaded. "Please, tell me what's happening, and then we'll go."

"Meissa Shining is interested in finding your grandparents," said Saffron. "What she would do if she finds them, we do not know. Our instructions are to contact Marcus if she or you shows up. That's all."

"My grandparents?" Nancy sat on a dock step, shaken. "My mother wasn't sure if they were alive or not."

"They are missing from their home on the dark side. Their new location is a mystery," said Saffron.

"We suspect Meissa is here somewhere," said Sagan.

"These Shinings sound like a pile of horse dung, and one is associated with Bo."

"I know," Nancy said. "I'm sorry I dragged you into this."

"Don't be. Technically Bo dragged me into this. Wait 'til I get my hands on him. Maybe I can take down his partner right with him."

"Let it be, Charlene. It'll be payback time soon enough." Nancy looked up at Sojourner. "Please continue."

"Whatever Meissa is planning, she is operating under a short timeframe. In two more days, labor crews will return. She has a volatile nature. That is all we know. You are here, and we cannot reach Marcus," said Sojourner.

"Our beastie is cooked."

"Well done!"

"Silence, you two," admonished Sojourner.

"We need to find my mother. If Meissa has taken my grandparents, I am certain they are at a place called Cassini Falls. And that's where Mom and Rigel went. Don't you have police? Where are they? My grandparents have been kidnapped. Why haven't the police been notified? Where is everybody?" Nancy was going stir-crazy, jerking her head from side to side, wringing her hands. Which direction? Where to begin? Panic was close to setting in. Her friends tried to soothe her.

"We did not make it clear enough," said Sagan, "You are in the midst of a big government secret when it comes to these scientists. Hush-hush. No one is coming to anyone's rescue."

"Go," said Saffron. "We can talk while we walk. Marcus will erase any intelligence I have if we don't get you out of here. I'll be an A, not an A-I." She laughed at her joke and led the way.

"Marcus is our friend and a friend of Rigel O'Rion; therefore, you should consider him an ally," said Sojourner. "We were to be on the look-out, in case you tried to use the portal again. Here you are, as predicted. If we could not get you to return, then we were to protect you until Marcus arrived. We surmise your mother is safe with Rigel."

"None of that matters if Miss Meissa catches you. Being the first hybrid, she will cut you to pieces purely for fun." Sagan, who was in front of the Divas, stopped suddenly and turned. "Like this!" She drew an imaginary line from her neck to her pelvis, then placed her fists together and pulled them apart, as if ripping open her midsection.

"Okay, that's all I need to see," said Milly. "In case you don't know, a yellow belt isn't a high rank, and that was fifty years ago! Who am I foolin'?"

Saffron shook her head. "I cannot solve your query. If you are referring to a yellow belt in the martial arts, I would not fret. You are stronger than you think."

"Rigel said something about us being stronger, but I don't feel any different." Milly bent her elbow and checked her bicep. "Humph, does this look like a big muscle?"

"Not really. Maybe we should go back," said Charlene. "Especially if this Meissa could be dangerous."

"She has no history of violence," said Sojourner.

"Until she kicked in our knees," said Saffron.

"There is that. She's a rat," said Sagan.

"It's three against one," said Nancy. "If we're supposed to be physically stronger here, we can take her if we have to."

"You can test your strength later. March!" commanded Sojourner. Past the beach, the thick plant life was meant to be a natural barrier to conceal maintenance buildings from guests. Branches whacked the women's faces until they learned to step back from one another.

"What the cuss, isn't there an easier, safer way?" asked Nancy.

"We have been instructed to use the shortest route," said Sojourner. "It may not be the best, but it is the shortest."

One by one they reached the clearing and trooped into a one-room storage building for gardening tools, with barely enough space to spare for six people, human or not.

"Crap! I can't see," Nancy said. "Where's the light switch?"

"There is no hardware to control illumination," Saffron said. "The motion sensors don't seem to be working, but the vocal command is 'Russ!' It's DG for the word 'lights.'"

Nothing happened. "What's wrong?" Nancy asked.

"The new voice recognition software does not acknowledge artificial intelligence," said Sojourner.

"Why didn't you say so? Russ!" yelled Nancy. Darkness. "Turn on the stinking light! What's going on?"

"The bulb must be out. Lumos!" called out Milly. "I knew that wouldn't work without a wand, but it was worth a try. I'm a big Harry Potter fan."

"Y'all appear eerily green and shadowy to me," said Charlene. "That's so bizarre."

Milly jerked her leg and hip-bumped Nancy. "Move over, Nancy, you stepped on my foot."

"I did not—you stepped on mine." She bumped back.

Charlene entered the fray. "Something hit my shin!"

"I felt it too! Something's in here!" Milly shrieked.

"Don't be playing games with us, Sistas. We are in no mood," said Nancy.

"I don't feel anything," said Sojourner.

"Neither do I," said Saffron.

"Our newly replaced lower extremities may not have pressure sensors," said Sagan.

"True, but we do have the ability to think."

"I think we need a lantern."

"A light would be right."

"Yes! My cell has a flashlight. It's in my pack." Nancy yanked the cord off her shoulder, but before she could get if off, Charlene said, "Here, take mine." She pulled it out of her handbag, but the pass was incomplete, and it dropped to the floor. "Nobody move! Don't you dare step on my phone!"

"Oww-oooh."

"Did you hear that? It sounded like the howl of a wild animal. I'm gonna pee my pants!" Milly sounded frantic.

"More like a wounded dog. Is there something in here? I've also gotta pee bad," admitted Charlene. "We're so crowded in here, I can't see the floor."

"Whatever it is, it can't be dangerous, or it would have attacked by now," Nancy grumbled, as she dug out her cell and pressed the flashlight icon. The Divas' eyes followed the white light as it scanned the room.

The beam landed on a shaggy, chestnut and white animal. He wore a royal blue collar, with an onyx square tile embedded in the middle. "Look everyone!" said Charlene. "It's a cute, little cocker spaniel. Are you what's been bothering us? You don't bite, do you?" She held out her hand as an offering.

"Insolence!" the dog yelled, which made the human women scream. They climbed each other like there was an escape hatch in the roof.

"First, Madam, I am *not* an *it*. I am a descendant of royalty, a *Cavalier King Charles* Spaniel. I am not a lowly *cocker* spaniel. Secondly, handsome, yes, but *cute* I am not! Little? Agreed, I barely reach your kneecap, but I am gallant, brave, and *fearless!* I only bite in battle, *comprenez-vous*? I also speak several languages."

"That dog talks! I'd heard rumors, but never believed it. Now I've seen it. I'm gonna die having seen it all. There is nothing I haven't seen that tops this. This tops everything. That's a good thing, I mean dying, having seen it all? I can't take much more." Milly crossed her legs and squeezed her eyes shut.

"What the eff? Okay, my nerves are shot. This is nuts," said Nancy.

"You speak? Shut the front door! I mean my dogs speak, bow-wow, but not the English language. Am I dreaming?" Charlene rubbed her eyes.

Sojourner laughed, "Charlie, how did you get in here?"

"The door was open."

"That's it! Open the door!" The door flew open at Nancy's command.

"Watch out! Don't trample me to death," yelled the royal pooch.

Milly beat them all to the bushes, with Charlene tossing facial tissue to her friends on the way to a squat.

"Stop! You are not to be out there!" yelled the Sistas. But there was no stopping the Divas.

CHAPTER 27: WHO'S IN CHARGE?

Well, well, well. Who'd have guessed it would be so easy? Caught with your pants down . . . literally." A woman with short, spiky blue hair, wearing black leggings and a matching short, silver-studded leather jacket, stepped out from behind a large fan palm.

The women frantically zipped up their pants, kicking sand like cats to bury the discarded tissue.

"I've been examining our gateways for irregularities. Happened to take a second look the other day. Found a new, illegal gateway from our largest moon to Earth. 'Course I haven't found the culprit yet. Your guess is as good as mine why a podunk town like Collinsville was chosen as a portal, but it certainly brought in some foul-smelling bait." She let loose a throaty cackle and looked around, as if expecting others to join her.

"You must be Meissa Shining," Nancy said. "You're obviously not the smart twin."

"Shut up, bitch. I see the resemblance." Meissa began pacing back and forth. "I found out about the nepial gland vaccine that's keeping your mother alive. I talked to your grandfather about it, but he wouldn't cooperate. I suspect your grandparents' befuddlement is all an act, because they sure knew how to contact their daughter when given the chance. Can't communicate to Earth on the far side, so Thadd had the brilliant idea of bringing them to the near side so they could call their precious Bellytrix. He figured we could lure her here, and they'd think twice about not cooperating.

"After they sent the message to Bellytrix's—illegal by the way—Pathfinder key, I let Thadd lock them up in a place you'll never find. Precisely as expected, Belly showed up. Maybe they'll be more willing to talk once they find out she's here. And now look—here's their granddaughter. Bright stars above, you're the caramel sauce on my sundae. I'll add you on top of the two nuts I'm holding in the desert dome." Meissa cackled again.

"Screw you." Nancy glowered at her rival and lunged. Charlene and Milly each grabbed an arm, holding her back.

While Nancy struggled to get out of their clutches, Charlie charged Meissa's faux-leather legging like a missile. "You demented witch!" He bit, let go. She reached for him and missed. He bit again. He darted around her, making her spin like a top trying to capture him, but she couldn't.

Sojourner stepped forward. "Out of the way, Charlie!" A thin rope sprang from her index finger, and she wrapped the offensive visitor in a cocoon, like an orb weaver with her prey. "We've been up-graded," she said, when Charlie flung her a quizzical look.

"Tim-ber!" called Sagan, as Meissa toppled like a tree.

Saffron inspected the package squirming on the ground and pulled apart the fine silky rope enough for a menacing face to appear. "Let her access oxygen."

"You will regret this!" Meissa shouted.

"Stop yelling or we will redo the rope," warned Saffron. "What say you, Messy? Want to die by suffocation?"

Meissa lunged upwards. "BOO!" The androids toppled backwards but were caught by the Divas. Meissa strained but could not break the bond.

"Our friends weren't the only ones needing the loo." Charlie lifted his hind leg over Meissa's bound feet.

"I'll soon have you squealing like piglets. Don't think I'm here alone," Meissa warned. "I've got plenty of backup."

"Looks like they've abandoned you, and you're the piggy at the moment," said Charlene.

"Oink, oink," added Milly. "Up top," she said to Charlene for a high-five. "Yeah!

Nancy frowned. "Can one of you keep her quiet?"

Saffron aimed her index finger at the squirm-ing figure and sent an electrical current through the air. "New and improved." She chortled. "It's temporary. Unknown how long she will be out."

"Brilliant," Charlie said. "Now that we have attained some proper decorum, please forgive me for startling you in the shed—it could not be avoided. Allow me to introduce myself. I am Sir Charles, at your service." He curtly bowed his head, one paw forward. "My friends call me Charlie, so please, call me Charlie."

"How do you do. I am Charlene. I love dogs and have two furry friends, Major and Minor, back home."

"There's the British accent you wanted, Nancy," Milly said, before addressing Charlie. "I'm Milly. I'm a cat person myself. No offense."

"None taken."

No such niceties from Nancy. "He knows who we are."

"You are correct, Nancy Herschel Leopold, granddaughter of our esteemed scientists Harold and Erma Bayer." Charlie turned to Milly. "You, lovely lady, are Millicent Mitchell McGilly, the Mitchell ancestral lineage going back to the first arrival of D'Gnomans on Earth. And this canine-lover is Charlene Luapa, who has more recent connections to DG. According to Marcus, there should be a fourth traveler, a Joan Castillo, but she either did not come or . . . let us not contemplate the 'or'."

"She didn't come. How do you know about us?" Milly asked.

Charlie shook himself. "Pardon me. I am in much need of the groomer. I have been stationed here for weeks on end as sentry to the portal, watching for the likes of you. Or worse." Charlie growled at Meissa. "I was assigned to this post by Marcus Shining long before the Sassy Sistas got here. Marcus suspected you might try the portal a second time. Rigel O'Rion assured him it wouldn't happen again, but, alas, he was proven wrong."

"This Mr. Shining seems to be everywhere," said Charlene. "What's the best way to get rid of a pest like him?"

"Charlene! He is a good man," said Sojourner. "He cares about everyone, even his androids."

"When his sister left us crumpled on the floor in a dingy basement, he repaired us and brought us here out of harm's way," said Saffron.

"Although 'harm' now seems to have found her way to Gansarcal," said Sagan.

"Yes, and if I had been the one to enforce the command to send you birdies home," said Charlie, "I would have had you all on the last train to Clarksville, no question."

"You mean Collinsville," chuckled Charlene.

"If I had been given the chance to speak, yes, that's where you'd be right now. But I was commanded not to speak for fear of frightening you to death." Charlie scratched his side and shook himself again. "Marcus let the Sistas greet you instead of me." Charlie huffed.

"Well, you did a good job scaring the daylights out of us," said Milly, "but we're not dead. So let's get truckin'."

"Thank you, Milly. I've got to find my family." Nancy looked around apprehensively, searching for anyone lurking about.

Saffron nodded her head toward the abhorrent lump on the ground. "First, let's get her inside the shop."

Nancy appealed to her cohorts. "We'll have to drag her. She's too heavy to lift."

"Did you not know you have super strength here?" Charlie asked. "Some of you may have additional aptitudes, like you, Charlene. You will be able to see things others can't. And you, Nancy, are half DG. I sense great ability within you."

"What about me?" asked Milly.

"Have a go at it—take her into the shop yourself."

Avoiding the wet spot Charlie so adeptly left, Milly dragged the cocoon as if it were a five-pound sack of potatoes and heaved the bundle of joy through the door. "That was amazing!"

The women lifted each other, Nancy having a harder go at it. She was unnaturally strong, but didn't seem to have as much strength as the other two. When Milly uprooted a small tree, Sojourner broke the pandemonium. "Stop! Destruction of property is taboo."

"If you're caught—"

"You'll be turned into stew!"

"Apologies. You asked us to speak normally, but sometimes our speech short circuits and we revert to baloney," said Sojourner.

"It will pass," said Saffron.

"Or we'll kick his ass," added Sagan. "I am referring to Marcus, in case you are wondering."

"Oh, I like you," said Charlene. "I'll be right there with you, missy."

Milly plugged the tree back into the ground. "This isn't real anyway. It's fake. I don't see anyone else around, so now would be a good time to identify any extra talents, like what Charlene has. How about flying or leaping tall buildings. I'd even take a short building." Milly bent her knees and propelled herself into a standing long jump. She landed farther than she expected. Astonished, she said, "O-M-G! Did I do that?" Milly tried again and vaulted over everyone.

"For crying out loud, if you can do that, then I should be able to fly." Nancy rotated her arms in large circles as a warmup. "My upper arms are like the wings on a jumbo jet." She ran a few steps, arms outstretched, took a leap of faith, and landed a face plant in the sand. Sputtering, she ran harder the second time. Same thing. "Third time's a charm." But there was no charm. No flight. Merely sand in her face, in her shirt, in her jeans.

"After this flight debacle, I am reminded of an important factor in your defense. Superpowers will be good for nothing if sand gets in your eyes. Be mindful of that," said Charlie.

Next, Charlene took a stab at leaping and flying. She dove over Milly, tucked and rolled like a stunt woman, and landed on her feet. "Shut my mouth!" she said.

"Hey, don't get greedy," said Milly, hopping like a boxer eager for the knock-out win. "You already have an extra power."

"I hate to break it to you ladies, but now that Meissa and her cronies are here, this is not going to be all fun and games," Charlie growled. He sat on his haunches and scratched behind his ear. "You'll have plenty of opportunity to plow people down. Any word from Marcus, Sojourner?"

"He has not responded to my messages."

"So who's in charge?" Nancy said. "The Sistas, Charlie or this no-show Marcus?"

"Sir Charles is in charge," said Saffron, "until Marcus gets here."

"Then what's the plan?" Nancy crossed her arms and grimaced.

"Plan A—return travelers home—failed," said Charlie. "Plan B—wait for Marcus in shelter near portal—scrapped. Therefore, on to Plan C. We will head to the Coral Reef Resort. It has the closest comfort accommodations required by our visitors."

"If Meissa's got minions, like she said, you got a plan for them?" Charlene asked.

"We'll fight 'em off." Milly punched and kicked the air. "It's all coming back to me now."

"No Plan C, either," said Nancy, "unless it includes finding Cassini Falls."

"We will fight if we have to. You are strong women, mentally and physically," he said. "No more wasting time. Move it!" He barked a dog bark, which made everyone jump.

They had gone a hundred yards or so, when Charlene stopped. "About this fighting, will it be intuitive? I mean, we have no training, except maybe Milly."

"We are about to find out." Nancy pointed ahead. "That looks like a tram coming. Trams carry people."

Shaped like an Orca whale, minus its pectoral fins, the hover bus was covered in plumeria flowers in shades of pink and purple. It slowed to a stop and settled to the ground in front of the Coral Reef Hotel. In a few moments, the hover bus moved around to the back of the hotel and disappeared out of sight, leaving five people standing outside the grand front entrance. The troop walked down the wide portico lined with palm trees until the concrete intersected with a paved recreational path, then moved across the path onto the sand toward the Divas.

"Here they come," said Nancy.

"I know diddlysquat about who might be working here except this is a non-work day for regular personnel," said Charlie. "I know the hover bus runs through the three biodomes and will eventually shuttle guests from here to there and back again. Could be on a test run. I can't say."

"If it's being tested, why are there passengers?" asked Charlene. "I can see the people. I presume they're people and not androids. I swear they look like prisoners! They even have numbers on their chests."

"Heck, we're close enough that even I can see the florescent yellow jumpsuit one is wearing. The other four are in similar garb, wearing hunter orange." Milly was using her hands as binoculars again. "Seems to bring things into better focus when I do this."

"Searching my database," said Sojourner, "the yellow designates a prison crew chief. The orange jumpsuits are prisoners."

"They are humans," said Saffron. "If androids should commit a crime or fail in our duties, we are sent to the recycle depot, where our innards are brutally torn apart and thrown into piles, as if we were ordinary trash."

"We have no rights, which bites," said Sagan.

"Marcus said the biodomes would not be built should there be a possibility of the prison population mingling with vacationers. The resorts aren't open yet, so they are nothing more than a work crew," Charlie said.

"You don't know that for a fact," said Milly. "You just said you knew diddlysquat about this place. I say we jump 'em. Hiiiya!" Milly jumped into a Kung Fu fighter stance.

"We will do nothing of the kind," said Sojourner. "They are most likely gardeners, laborers from the penitentiary on work-release to maintain the grounds."

"If Meissa somehow got a message to her associates about her predicament, they could be on a reconnaissance mission. Oh god, I don't know how to fight," Charlene said.

"You'll be okay, Charlene," said Charlie. "You don't see a little weasel running around, do you? If Oleo's here, then so is Thadd Verra. He probably has contacts within the pen. I wonder if he's working with Meissa."

"Don't say that, Charlie," said Sojourner. "We will act as if nothing is out of the ordinary."

"It would be most useful, Nancy, if you read their minds as they get closer," said Saffron. "They may give away more than their spoken words."

"I'm not very good at telepathy and don't speak D'Gnoman except for 'hello,' which Mom taught me, but I'll try. What if they hassle us?"

"You'll toss them aside like that hapless tree back there," said Sagan.

"Don't worry, Divas. I have more spider silk in me." Sojourner twirled her finger, as if drawing tiny circles in the sky.

"And I'm a stunner." Saffron pointed and blew on her index finger, like a smoking gun barrel.

"What was it I had?"

"You sing, Sagan. Your song is that of a siren and will put them into a hypnotic daze," said Sojourner.

"We hope," added Saffron. "Nevertheless, stay behind us."

"There you go, mates," said Charlie. "I give you the battle plan in as few words as possible: we shall wing it!"

Nancy looked at the spaniel. "That figures." Then her eyes widened in astonishment, as the two women and three men neared. "I hear them! The woman in yellow leading the group is repeatedly sending a silent warning to the others: *'Do not engage. Do not engage.'* It's not English, yet I understand it."

"You are translating D'Gnoman. You're bilingual."

"Big stinking deal. I wanted to fly."

The advancing quintet mumbled as they passed single file:

"Eetah."

"Eetah."

"Sheezim bogo."

"Yomi."

The last prisoner grunted. Milly responded with, "Wanna dance?" He grunted again.

"Milly!" Nancy kicked sand at her.

"Hey!" Milly cried. "You don't have cannibals here, do you? Sounded like they were saying 'eat her, eat her, she's my burger, yummy.'"

"You're letting your imagination run wild," said Saffron. "It was a friendly greeting. No one is going to eat you."

"Not yet anyway."

"Sagan! Stop that." Saffron shook her finger at Sagan. "No one is going to eat you."

"Yeah, all they said was hello, have a nice day, and goodbye," said Nancy.

"Very good, Nancy. Most definitely gardeners," said Sojourner. "The administration would only allow the best-behaved prisoners to be on work release. So we have nothing to worry about."

"Which means," said Charlene, "they will find Meissa."

"I doubt they are gardeners." Nancy grimaced. "Meissa's shrieking was heard throughout the dome. Bet they're rescuing her."

"Disagree. No guests are allowed. Workers may assume we are trespassers, but they do not have authority to confront us," said Saffron.

"I pity them when they come unexpectedly upon Ms. Shining," said Milly.

"Whether landscapers or Meissa's pawns, we need to move on, and this sand is slowing us," grumbled Saffron.

"Sistas, I will lead the Divas to the hotel. We will meet you there."

"Sorry, Charlie, we are not leaving anyone behind, but that gives me an idea." Nancy squatted and pointed to her lower back. "Hop on, Sojourner. Riding on my back will make it easier for everyone."

"Not really," remarked Charlene but signaled Saffron to jump on.

Sagan, smallest of the three androids, hopped on Milly. And they were off to the races. Charlie was relieved to be covering ground swifter now, but he had never heard so much wailing in his life! Less than two hundred yards to go and they would reach the safety of the hotel. He had difficulty keeping up but managed to reach the strip of paved recreational trail where the Sistas had been dropped to the solid surface, albeit somewhat shaken.

"What a ride!" said Sagan.

"I am all shook up inside," said Saffron.

"Should we hide?" asked Sojourner.

"You sound like me."

"And I sound like you."

"Who am I?" Sojourner cocked her head to the side.

"What's going on?" Nancy looked at Charlie as if he had the answer. Panting, his tongue hanging out, he made bug eyes back at her.

"They're wonky," he replied.

"Oh shoot."

"Cannot compute."

"Reboot."

The Sistas performed their chicken dance and were back to normal.

Barely out of breath and in awe of their lung capacity and strength, the Divas stood at the end of the portico, in wonderment of the Coral Reef Hotel, with its huge, clam-shaped doors glistening with jewels. There was no breeze. The tall palms lining the entryway stood at attention, their fronds motionless as if to say: This is the calm before the storm.

"Listen up, troops," commanded Charlie. "We need to get inside . . . oh jolly good, here comes the slimy little weasel. Whatever you do, don't look at him. Ignore him!"

No one listened to Charlie. The little bugger commenced his weasel war dance, prancing and dancing and flipping on the path like a gymnast.

"Don't you see?" Charlie begged. "His antics are meant to distract his prey so much they become immobilized. Then he goes in for the kill."

"But he's so cute!" Charlene clapped her hands together under her chin.

Even Nancy agreed, "It's fascinating. I've never seen a weasel in the wild."

"He's too small to kill us." Milly bent down as if to get a closer look.

The Sassy Sistas stood enthralled, as well, until Sagan said, "Unless he has rabies!"

Charlie charged at the weasel, barking ferociously. The vermin raced off. Everyone snapped to attention. "That was Oleo. He's as slippery as his name implies. He is the sidekick of Thadd Verra, DG's biggest con artist. Verra is chiefly brawn and no brains, but he's smart enough to stay out of the reach of authorities. If Oleo is here, Verra is here. A special permit must be obtained for travel to Gansarcal. I know from Marcus that he is definitely on the no-fly list. I don't know why he would be here, but you better start listening to me. When I say don't look, you don't look. When I say run, you run.

"It's not a good sign when Oleo shows up, so RUN!"

CHAPTER 28: ESPIONAGE AT YOUR SERVICE

The Coral Reef's front doors split open automatically, as three humans, three androids, and one canine blasted into the lobby. The women stopped short and stared slack-jawed at colorful coral and fish sculptures surrounding the walls. The walls were teal near the floor, blending the colors of the seas, ending with deep blue near the ceiling. Another large coral sculpture erupted from the middle of the room with water jets dancing to spicy salsa music.

"Wow!" said Milly. "I'm beginning to think we *are* in Vegas."

Charlie's surveillance found the room deserted, except for two illustrious androids who needed no introduction. He asked the Sistas to keep their eyes open for any unusual movement and called to the droids at the concierge's desk to lock the doors. The Elvis Presley impersonator droid sauntered over to the group standing near the fountain.

"We cannot lock the doors, Charlie," answered Elvis. The red and blue crystals on his high-collared, split-front white shirt sparkled in the lights from the ceiling. He wore the same white bell-bottomed pants as he had when the Divas first saw him on their last visit to Gansarcal Bay. "But I will stand guard like a hound dog so the Coral Reef does not turn into a heartbreak hotel." Elvis grinned. "Thank you, thank you very much."

"Oh my god, I love you!" Charlene clutched her hands to her heart. "My momma loves you! One of the first memories in my lifetime was going to the drive-in movie and watching you on the big screen. Momma would fill a grocery bag with popcorn, and the butter would soak through the paper. I am salivatin' at the memory."

"You salivatin' over hot, buttery popcorn or hot, buttery me, you sweet thing?" crooned Elvis, sidling closer to Charlene.

"Both!"

Nancy, once again, was the first to focus. "That's not really Elvis, Charlene."

"I know it's not, but he is a great look-alike. Can't you have even a smidgeon of fun?"

"Not when my family may be injured."

"You're right. I apologize. This is all very difficult to comprehend."

"I understand." Nancy smiled reassuringly at Charlene. "I have to admit that being on another planet—or a moon, I guess—is enough to make you forget everything, including why we're here." Nancy stepped back and took another moment to appreciate the beauty. "It is impressive, isn't it?"

She addressed the two male entertainers: "Hey, you got something with a layout of this place? We're looking for Cassini Falls."

Otis Redding strode over from the concierge's desk, his polished dress shoes clicking on the stone tile. He also wore the same blue double-breasted jacket as when he met the Divas on the dock. His shirt was open at the collar. Both men were tall, but Otis eked out an extra inch over the six-foot-tall Elvis.

"You could access maps on your personal device if they worked here, but they don't," Otis said. "You can't conjure a hologram, either, without some practice. You will have to take a seat over there." He pointed to an area with several comfortable chairs surrounding a low table. "The table has a touch-top and will bring up a menu with maps of the resorts, plus entertainment and dining options, although none of that's available."

"It won't hurt to look at the schema, but we are not going anywhere until we hear from Marcus," said Charlie.

"You may *never* get through to him," Nancy said. "Then what?"

"Don't be cross. I'll come up with something."

While the Sistas strutted like peacocks, making their observation rounds, the Divas settled into the cushy chairs and studied the diagrams. Charlene invited Charlie to share her seat. "Thank you for not scooping me up like a puppy without asking. That is so undignified," he told her.

"Hmm, we are in the oceanic biodome." Nancy pointed to a *You are Here* label. "Pretty amazing."

"I guess I know a bit about this place," said Charlie, sitting with his head held high. "As you can see, the biodomes form a triangular pattern and are connected to each other with corridors by which guests may traverse from one resort to another. That big dome in the middle of all this is the operations center: computers, power generators, air circulators, water purifiers, everything to keep this home-away-from-home sustainable. You probably should note the emergency exits to the escape pods, should they be needed."

"Lord, I never thought of emergency exits. For what?" Milly said.

"Escape pods? To where?" Charlene asked.

Before Charlie could answer, Otis, back at the concierge's desk, shouted, "Yo! Sir Charles! We have a situation."

The women looked up from the map. "Doesn't look like an emergency, so no need for escape pods yet," said Nancy.

"You stay here, I'll go see what it's about," said the cavalier spaniel.

Charlie jumped down and trotted to Otis. Otis tipped his head to the side and bobbed his index finger toward the floor.

"What the bloody hell," said Charlie.

"Hello, dawling."

"Aurora? What are you doing here?"

"My name is Sylvia. Not SYL-vee-aw, but Syl-vee-AW, as in awesome. Awesome spy, that is."

"Rubbish. You are Marcus's house cat who riles me to no end. How did you get here, and why has your bit of fuzz morphed into a black . . . what is that? A shaggy mullet?"

"Thank you, dawling, I will take that as a compliment." Sylvia purred. "As a Sphynx, I rather stand out among cats. I wished to be incognito, and Saffron was kind enough to lend me her wig. Your brown and white 'do could use a new 'do. You look a trifle rag-tag for one of your rank."

"I admit I have been away from the groomer for some time. More importantly, incognito for what? Again, how did you get here?"

"Overheard Marcus say interstellar beings might arrive on Gansarcal and tapped you as guardian of the gateway. Miffed I was not invited. As I found it difficult to resist the intrigue, I recently hitched a ride as a stowaway on his last run."

"Won't he miss you?"

"He's not home, dawling."

"Stop calling me that."

"Oh, all right. What a party-pooper you are. You will come to appreciate my undercover work, dipsy-wipsy, when I tell you what's happening in the other domes."

He let out a low growl. "I could have you running for dear life, if you keep it up."

"Me-ow."

Charlie didn't get the chance for a chase. Three interstellar beings sprinted past them. The women must have expected the doors to open automatically, like the front entrance, because they collided into the brass-plated doors. Boom-boom-boom. One after another bounced off the solid surface. Foul language erupted, along with slapping and kicking, but nothing made a difference until Otis butted in. "If you're goin' to hit somethin', hit the manual override button on the wall to your left."

"Don't assist them!" Charlie cried out, but the brass doors whisked apart and the beings disappeared.

"Oops! You won't like that. Your charges are out of sight and in the sights of some rather repugnant scoundrels." Aurora/Sylvia licked her paws and cleaned her face and whiskers.

"They've been warned of the dangers. Wouldn't have been able to stop them anyway. How many scoundrels?"

"Maybe a dozen or more. Hard to tell if some are hiding. Convicts obviously. Headed by Thadd Verra."

"Meissa Shining is here also. Are they working together?"

"Haven't seen her but heard a mention of her name. A team was rescuing her from some thugs. Would you and your associates be the thugs?"

"We would be the thugs, yes. Marcus improved the Sassy Sistas with remarkable skills. Last saw Meissa stunned and spun into a cocoon up to her chin."

"I doubt she's in that condition any longer. Bad Thadd and his crew have ways into all regions of this place, and how fortuitous for them today is a non-workday. Everyone is gone who matters."

"Aren't you a fountain of knowledge."

"I told you, I'm a spy. It's my job. Get this, Meissa is holding the Bayers behind Cassini Falls in the rainforest. There's a huge storage room back there."

"Nancy asked about the falls. That's where the Earthlings will be headed."

"We will need all the womanpower we can get. I suggest rounding up the Sassy Singers."

"Sistas. They are the Sassy Sistas. And neither you nor they are coming with me."

"I will. You need my espionage services."

"No, I don't, Aurora."

"Sylvi-AW! And you said the Sissies were upgraded. We'll need them. Yoo-hoo! Sissies!"

"Don't push me."

"Too late. Sissies! Come here, dawlings!"

CHAPTER 29:
A SPY IN THE RAINFOREST

When Nancy hit the manual override button, a small square the size of a soda cracker embedded into the wall, the women scrambled through. The door from the hotel lobby sealed shut behind them. They stopped short. "Holy cow!" Nancy said. "This is gorgeous."

Computer-generated images projected onto the curved walls created a lush, leafy-green rainforest. Woody vines twisted and knotted through the treetops, swaying softly as they crawled to the ground. Macaws and other brightly colored birds flew overhead or perched on tree limbs. Gibbons swung through the branches.

"Are those monkeys real?" asked Milly. "They look real. Hope they stay up in those trees."

A recorded voice cheerfully interrupted the birdsong and screeching monkeys. "Welcome to the rainforest. You may hike the paved trail or enjoy a bicycle ride. If neither mode of transportation is to your liking, please exit the corridor to the nearest hover bus station, although your experience will not be as immersive. Enjoy the jungle!"

"Somehow that doesn't sound as inviting as it should," Charlene said. "Look at this bike rack. It's an anaconda slithering in big humps. I hate snakes."

"I love snakes!" Milly stroked one of the silver humps.

"Seriously?"

"No. I hate them. Any snake, even the harmless garden variety. Haven't got the bikes stocked I see. Bet you're happy about that."

"I was hoping they *would* be here to see what their bicycles looked like. They may not be like ours at all."

Nancy shuddered. "I can't stand worms, let alone snakes. Hey, guys, after Charlie got up to see what Otis wanted, we said we'd go straight to the falls, since the key indicated Cassini Falls. I am positive that if Mom and Rigel are able to break Meissa's bonds, they would also head to the falls."

"Yeah," said Milly. "We'll knock the heck out of whoever gets in our way."

"That's right. Let's leave before Charlie or those sassy tag-alongs try to stop us." Nancy took off running, then suddenly stopped halfway through the passageway. It took Milly and Charlene a few more steps before they halted. "If we get close to those doors at the other end, they might open and we'll be completely exposed, so stick to the side of the tunnel as much as you can. Hopefully the sensors won't see us. Before we go, thank you for being here with me. I love you both."

"We love you too," said Milly.

"We wouldn't be here if we didn't," said Charlene, opening her arms for a group hug.

Nancy wrapped her arms around her two friends, squeezed, then broke away. "Since we haven't encountered anyone so far, I'm certain Thadd and Meissa are waiting behind the doors down there. Harold and Erma are likely in there somewhere, probably being guarded. Let's stay together if we can. If we get separated, we'll meet at Cassini Falls in the back of the biodome."

Toward the end of the passageway, at what Nancy estimated to be a safe distance from setting off sensors, she stopped and plastered herself against the wall, gesturing for the other two to follow. No one spoke as they inched closer to the end. Finally in the corner, they clung to each other, waiting, hardly breathing. Listening and hearing nothing but the sounds of the rainforest, Nancy loosened her grip and said, "Charlene, you need to take a look and see what's out there."

"Oh sure, why me?"

"You have the best eyesight," Nancy said.

"Y'all could see people out there as well as I could."

"Then let's vote. Who thinks Charlene should give it a look-see?" asked Nancy.

Milly and Nancy raised their hands. "Majority rules—it's you. Congrats." Nancy smiled and patted Charlene's back.

"Gee, thanks."

Nancy smacked the manual open button. Charlene scrunched her eyes closed, inhaled deeply and exhaled slowly. "I am strong. I am brave. I am—" The doors closed before she could look out. "Woo." Charlene rotated her shoulders.

"That's okay," Nancy said. "Probably no one's out there. Try again. Take a quick peek."

"Easy for you to say." Charlene straightened her spine and shook herself. "Stay calm and dance on, Charlene. You can do this." She leaned out before Nancy hit the button and the door opened. "Egads! It opened." Charlene rapidly scanned the area before falling back into Nancy. The doors shut again, blocking their view.

"It's spooky quiet in there, but there's plenty of light. I didn't see anyone or anything emitting heat, but they could be hiding. I don't have x-ray vision. Some vegetation has been planted. Otherwise in the center there's a bunch of huge, round columns made of what looks like steel connected with beams. From the map we looked at, it's the treetop-themed rooms of the hotel. Looks like a giant jungle gym. No pun intended. I could see the waterfall at the very back."

"The doors don't open without a reason," Nancy said. "If anyone is in there, they've learned we're here."

Milly shifted from one foot to the other. "Now I wish I had a stun gun like Saffron's."

"Welcome to the rainforest," an artificial voice announced. "You may hike the paved trail or enjoy a bicycle ride. If neither mode of transportation is to your liking, please exit the corridor to the nearest hover bus station, although your experience will not be as immersive. Enjoy the jungle!"

"Someone else is in here or that recording wouldn't have come on!" cried Charlene.

"Have no fear, we are here!" sang the Sistas in that glorious three-part harmony from the opposite end of the corridor.

"Oh geez, it's the Sassy Sistas and Charlie." Nancy grimaced. "Some other strange-looking creature is with them."

"It's a cat," said Milly. "I'd know a cat anywhere."

"We can't escape them so they might as well join us," Charlene said. "I, for one, am glad to see them. The Sassy Sistas, with their upgrades, may come in handy."

"Maybe, but we're so close, it's hard not to rush to my family. Now we've got to wait for them."

"Keep the faith," said Milly. "Your family will be okay and so will we. Remember, your mom's with Rigel. He'll protect her. And Meissa's not gonna do anything with your grandparents while we're here."

"We are glad you are unharmed," called Sojourner.

Nancy beckoned with her hands. "Stay to the side and squeeze in close to us so the doors don't automatically open."

"I recall recently having squeezed in close to you, and it didn't go so well," said Sagan.

"Good grief, we'll be fine!" said Milly, but her eyes were on the shaggy, long-haired cat, whose body seemed out of proportion with the skinny, white legs. "Who's this?"

"Please, let me introduce Aurora, an ordinary house cat who resides with the elusive Marcus Shining," answered Charlie.

"Beg your pardon. I am far from ordinary. I am a spy and my name is Sylvi-aw, accent on the third syllable, dawlings."

"You've got to be kidding me," said Nancy.

Swallowing hard, Charlene asked, "What else talks in your society, Charlie?"

"That's it. Cats and dogs. Apes, if they hadn't all left for another planet."

"Lord-a-mighty," said Milly. "Wish my Cinnamon could meet you, Sylvi-aw. She'd be jealous of your beautiful rhinestone collar. She's not nearly as long-haired though. I'd be brushing cat hair 24-7. That's more hair than even a cat lover like me could manage, but look at those cute pink ears and blue eyes peeking out from all that hair. Bet you're all fuzzy soft. Come here, sweetie." Milly bent to pick up Sylvia, but all that came up in her hands was a ball of black fur, leaving the naked, wrinkled, white Sphynx behind. Milly screamed like a banshee and threw the hairy handful into the air, the commotion knocking Nancy into the door opener. Once again, a gaping hole appeared ready to swallow whoever passed through.

"I've been exposed!" Sylvia hissed loudly. "How can I be an effective spy when my cover's been blown?"

"We've *all* been exposed!" Nancy cried. "Forget it. I'm going in." She stepped out of the passageway into the rainforest biodome, or what would eventually be the rainforest when it was completed. The others followed Nancy. As they moved into the dome, the door slid closed behind them. She looked back to make sure everyone came through and saw Saffron scoop up the wig and refit it onto Sylvia.

Huge columns, each five stories high, connected with crossbeams, were scattered throughout the central area. She could hear the splash of the waterfall in the distance.

There was a large pond on Nancy's left. A creek flowed from it along the outer edges of the dome. On either side of the creek were giant ferns. Pink and orange flowering bushes dotted the greenery. The creek, Nancy surmised, fed into the waterfall's splash pool, picking up again on the opposite side. To her right she could see the creek disappearing into a small cave, which probably hid a recirculation pump. Again, sand was everywhere.

"Lights are on, but nobody's home," said Sagan, laughing at the ancient joke.

"Oh, they're home," said Nancy. "We've got to believe someone's around, if Meissa says she's got Mom and Rigel tied up in the desert zone. There's got to be some structure around Cassini Falls

that's holding my grandparents. Do you see anything, Charlene?"

"There's an emergency shelter built into the
rock behind the waterfall," said Sylvia. "You can't
see it from here. Your grandparents are there."

"How do you know?" Nancy asked.

"I'm a spy, remember?" Sylvia yawned and
stretched.

"Are they okay?"

"That I cannot say. I did not see Meissa bring
them to the shelter, but there is an android guard
outside that wasn't there two days ago. There
would be no need for a guard if someone wasn't
in there."

Milly, at Charlene's shoulder, said, "If Meissa
and her henchmen are in here, what are they
waiting for? It's not like they can't see us."

"They're waiting for us to move away from the
doors, so we won't run back inside," said Nancy.
"I'm going to the falls. You can come with me or
go home."

"I'm staying, but what's that big, black lump
floating in the pond? What if it's Rigel?" Milly
wrung her hands. "Charlene, look closer. Don't
tell me it's Rigel or Trixie, either."

"In case it could be one of them, we'll look, but
we're not taking any more time," said Nancy.

"It's not emitting heat, so it's probably not a
body," Charlene said.

"Unless it's a dead body! What if they killed
him and dumped him in the water? He'd be cold
and dead!"

"God, Milly, simmer down. I'll check it out." Charlene moved closer. "I can't tell . . . what the—" She scrambled backwards. "Eyes! Eyes! No way am I going over there alone. Y'all are gonna come with me."

All three women tip-toed closer, until Milly stopped. "Do we need to get closer? If it's not Rigel or Trixie, what do we care?"

"You were the one wanting a closer look." Charlene threw her arms up in frustration.

At that moment, a long, black beast with three bright green eyes in its bulging forehead and short spikes down its back surged forward. With its mouth agape, a purple tongue unfurled to lasso the leg of the nearest victim. "Awk!" yelped Milly. "It's a crocodile!"

The women screamed and ran back to the Sassy Sistas. The creature slid back into the water.

"No! It's a croc-a-doodle!" Sylvia convulsed into laughter, knocking her mullet sideways. She clawed it back into place. "It attacks every hour or so. Live ones are endemic to D'Gnome. I should have told you, but it was too funny to see your reaction."

Nancy thought she saw movement in the bushes on the other side of the pond, but turned her attention to Charlie when he thumped his tail.

"While you ladies were going bonkers, I've been thinking that someone needs to find Rigel and Bellatrix."

"I'll go," said Sylvia. "A spy works better alone anyhow. If they are in the desert zone, it won't be hard to spot them. I'll report back to you."

"Thank you, Sylvi-aw," said Nancy. "I would appreciate that." She couldn't believe she was talking to a cat.

"I'm off. Adios, amigos." Sylvia disappeared through the open corridor to the desert biodome.

"Don't say anything, but there may be people or something in those bushes over there." Nancy surreptitiously pointed to the pond.

"Is it Rigel?"

"Milly, if it was Rigel, he'd be meeting us, don't you think?"

Milly crossed her arms and nodded.

Oh god, I'm going to die. I knew it. And I never got to tell Bo goodbye," Charlene cried.

"Stop it. We've got our strength. We're not going to die!"

"You've got us too," said Sojourner.

"We'll protect you," said Saffron.

"So don't be blue," said Sagan.

"Good to know." Nancy ran her fingers through her hair. "I think we should follow the stream away from the pond, over there by the cave where it goes into the ground. I don't want to go through the center and be sitting ducks," said Nancy, leading the group around the hotel framework. A tiny, bright yellow and black frog jumped out of the foliage along the stream and landed on Nancy's arm. She squealed. "What is that?" She brushed it off, only for a blue one to take its place. She flicked it off, too, but there were more jumping out of the bushes.

"It's a dart frog. I remember it from the zoo with my grandkids. I don't know about the pretty blue ones, but the yellow ones are poisonous!" Milly brushed her arms, legs, and torso in a preemptive move to keep the frogs from landing on her.

The frogs were smaller in length than the second knuckle on a pinky finger, but they had the Divas dancing like marionettes gone wild.

"They look freaking real," said Nancy. "Something's disturbing them or they wouldn't be jumping out like this."

"The croc-thing was animatronic, now these are real. So what's real and what's not real around here?" asked Charlene. "I don't like this."

"I'm real, chick-pea," said a gravelly voice behind them. A muscular man in a bright orange jumpsuit, number 6001-7664, stepped out of the foliage—the same foliage the frogs were vacating. He smashed a blue frog on his bald head before flashing a toothless grin, then wiping his hand down the front of his uniform. "Welcome to the jungle."

Behind him were five other men and women in orange and yellow jumpsuits.

The Sistas and Divas shrieked and scurried back to the croc-a-doodle.

CHAPTER 30:
KNOCKED SENSELESS

Nancy allowed herself to cower for a brief moment before she said, "Good grief, what is *wrong* with me? The way to get to the waterfall is to confront these guys. Sistas, stay out of the way so you don't get hit. Come on, let's go."

The Divas stepped cautiously back to Charlie, who had stood his ground. The prisoners were guffawing and slapping their hips and thighs at something Charlie had said as the women approached. They heard Charlie say to the lead prisoner, 6001-7664, "Where's Verra? It's barmy he'd leave an underling in charge."

"I don't have to answer to you, you mangy mutt."

"And proud of it. But I'm a lover not a fighter, and if you let these women and their three android friends pass, I won't unleash them on you. If you don't cooperate, I'm warning you—those boots are gonna walk all over you." Charlie growled and bared his teeth.

"Ooh, I'm scared of your little threat." Number 6001-7664 kicked Charlie in the ribs. He went flying, yelping, into the ferns.

That was enough to kick the anxiety out of Charlene. She tossed her shoulder bag aside and yelled, "We got this!"

"You bet your sweet ass we do." Nancy yanked off her drawstring backpack.

"Stay calm, girls, we're gonna dance all over these deadbeats!" Milly balled her fists and bounced up and down on her toes.

The Sassy Sistas attended to Charlie while chaos broke loose.

"I want the orange ones! Gig 'em, Aggies!" Charlene shouted with her fists high in the air, thumbs up. She wasted no time in wiping the grin off the man who had kicked Charlie with a well-placed, strong uppercut. The thug was a few inches taller than Charlene and more muscular, but he was knocked senseless. She opened and closed her fist a few times, cracked her knuckles. "Who's next?" she yelled, then charged at a short, skinny man running away. He got nowhere before Charlene tripped him, and he fell on his face. She grabbed him by his collar and crotch, swung him back and forward into a steel post. He slithered, unconscious, to the ground.

Nancy punched 204-2861, a woman with long, tangled brown hair and bushy eyebrows, in the stomach. She doubled over, and Nancy finished her off with the club of both fists to the back of her head. She turned to a shorter, bald man next to her and gripped his arm, flipped him over her shoulder with a "Hiiiya!" and slammed him to the ground. She wiped her hands on her jeans.

Looking around, Nancy saw Milly kicking and punching and . . . "Who you callin' bitch, bitch?" Milly head-slammed her attacker against a post. Her assailant was out for the count.

"Don't mess with Texas!" screamed Charlene, as she gut-kicked another prisoner.

Nancy counted five orange and one yellow jumpsuit sprawled on the sand. Milly and Charlene were still engaged in fighting. Where were these idiots coming from? She got her answer when a ruffian dropped from above and knocked her to her knees, her glasses slipping to the ground. She was gifted a bloody nose before Charlene picked the thug up and smashed him to the ground.

Charlene pointed to the metal structure and shouted, "I'm goin' up!" She leaped to grasp the first girder on one of the towers, and swung herself up. She now had a drone's view. Nancy was picking up her glasses when Charlene shouted, "Nancy, behind you! SING!" to which the Sassy Sistas, who so far had left the sass to the Dancing Divas, broke out in song: "Stop! In the name of love, before you break my leg."

Nancy grunted loudly while jabbing an elbow to the goon's stomach. She stomped on his instep, straightening him up enough to break his nose with the heel of her hand, and—for the *coup de grâce*—belted him one in the groin with her knee. He rolled around like a curly fry.

Above the "think it o-o-ver" emanating from the singing droids, Nancy called out, "Thanks, Charlene!" All the while, the Sistas' song and dance moves added an odd entertainment value to this circus.

More orange jumpsuits were descending from the rafters. They must have plastered themselves to the uppermost beams, which is why no one saw them. Charlene stayed where she was to warn her friends. "Over there, Milly! Nancy, on your left!" Charlene also had her hands full engaging those she could reach from her perch in the rafters, knocking them to the ground, swinging naturally through the structures like a monkey. As each adversary bit the dust, Saffron was there. "Haven't I been go-o-od to you?" ZING! "Haven't I been swe-e-et to you?" ZAP! The ones Saffron couldn't get to, Sojourner deftly gift-wrapped, singing, "I've tried so hard, hard to be patient."

The Sistas' singing ceased when Charlene lost her grip on a beam after being kicked from behind. She fell to the ground, barely missing the steel girders. Her breath knocked out of her, she lay motionless. After several seconds she rolled into a fetal position and moaned. Sagan and Saffron rushed to her.

Sojourner, air punching like a boxer in the ring, kept her eyes on Nancy and Milly. The pair tag-teamed the woman who had jumped to the ground after pushing Charlene. Nancy was clearly panting but managed to shout, "Don't be flip with me, you loser," while landing a left jab. POW! The loser fell into Milly's arms, and she was all about using that yellow belt she'd bragged about, "You goin' down, sucker!" And just like that, she was right where Milly wanted her. Sojourner moved in for the bind.

Waiting for more attacks, their backs to each other, Milly and Nancy turned to find Charlene struggling to stand. "Winded." She gulped a few breaths and yelled, "But I am woman! Hear me ROAR!" Then she doubled over into a coughing fit before croaking, "I'm fine."

Charlie ambled, limping slightly, out of the bushes.

Charlene squatted and rubbed his soft, albeit rumpled, fur. "Are you all right?"

"A tad stiff. No broken bones. I've been watching for Thadd and Meissa, but haven't seen either. Apparently saving the best scum for last."

"You got that right. Delightful to see you again." Meissa grinned.

"Where did you come from?" Nancy asked, frowning. She looked around but saw no one else in the vicinity.

"I knew you'd have super strength, which is why I recruited so many, but I reckoned you wouldn't know how to use it, or you'd eventually tire. We underestimated you. Kudos."

Charlene, Milly, the Sistas, and Charlie gathered around Nancy. "We don't want your kudos," Nancy said. "Why would you do this?" Scattered like confetti, she indicated Meissa's bound and unconscious comrades.

"This was Thadd Verra's idea. I wanted the formula for the serum, and he knew how to get it.

Or I thought he did. Harold and Erma wouldn't cooperate. I warned them this would happen, but they didn't seem to care. The precious vaccine was more important than your mother or you, I guess. Too bad, so sad. But I've got one more weapon, and he'll knock all of you out cold."

Bringing up her family made Nancy angrier than ever—as tired as she was, a newfound energy coursed through her blood. "Leave her to me!" Leading with her left shoulder, she rushed and threw her arms around Meissa's waist, tackling her to the ground. Back on her feet, Nancy threw a flailing Meissa into the pond for a hard landing on the croc-a-doodle's back. "Do your thing, Sistas."

But the Sassy Sistas couldn't get to Meissa before she rolled off the croc into the shallow water and, choking, managed to struggle upright. She grappled with her balance and sloppily waded forward. Closer now, Saffron stepped up, pointing her finger, but only sparks flew. "Out of juice, are you, sassy-frassy?"

Meissa splashed to the bank, but Sojourner's web gun petered out. Meissa picked off the sticky strand as she advanced. "No more spidey-thread? Too bad."

"Not so fast, prissy-missy." Sagan broke into a lovely aria from "Queen of the Night" from Mozart's *The Magic Flute*. Whatever her siren's song was designed to do, it was not working on the humans. Meissa performed a jig and laughed in her face. "What's wrong?" Sagan asked her other Sistas.

"Your skill was not so much a hypnotic trance as muscle paralysis," explained Sojourner, as Sagan earnestly upped the volume, trying to neutralize the dancer. "Affects a certain receptor in the brains of men."

The melody abruptly stopped. "Only men? That's not fair!" Sagan stomped her foot in frustration.

Sojourner patted Sagan's arm. "Marcus intended your siren's song to affect males to spare Rigel's female friends. He knew we would have to deal with his sister and her companions, but, at the same time, could not risk immobilizing the Divas."

"I suppose that is logical reasoning," said Sagan. "Oh! Heads up!"

From the top of the nearest column, stiff as a four-by-four post—THUD . . . splat—Bad Thadd dropped to the ground in front of them, knocked out cold. Next to him landed his sidekick, Oleo, dead as a door nail.

"Poor little weasel," said Milly. "He couldn't take the fall."

"I did that!" yelled Sagan. "I did that! Whoo-hoo! My song knocked him out, and Bad Thadd fell to the ground like a dropped dumbbell."

Charlie jumped up and down. "Jolly good job, Sagan!"

"Goes to prove, dumbbells like him don't belong on the Penthouse floor," said Charlene.

Meissa booted her motionless partner. "You big lummox. You left me back there alone, and now this. Why can't you do anything right?"

"What?" Nancy scoffed. "Your lummox flummoxed?"

"You and I aren't done," sneered Meissa. In a swift move, she kicked at Sojourner's knees.

As Sojourner went down, she screeched, "Stop, you fool!"

"You better think—" Before Saffron could say more, she also collapsed onto her buttocks.

"You better think about what you're trying to do to me!" yelled Sagan.

"What do you think you're doing?" Nancy shouted. "No one treats my friends that way!"

Charlene spared Sagan's stabilizers by kicking the back of Meissa's knees. She grunted and collapsed, rolling to her side. "There. How does that feel?" Meissa threw her an angry look but didn't respond. Charlene kicked her to her stomach and sat on her thighs. Milly reined in the ankles, while Nancy pulled the cord from her hoodie and tied Meissa's wrists behind her back.

Nancy slapped her hands together as if brushing off dirt. "You three hurt bad?" she asked the Sistas.

"Damage is slight," said Saffron.

"We're all right," said Sojourner

"But what a fight!" said Sagan.

"You're not kidding! I can't believe we fought like that. All of you were amazing! Thank you from the bottom of my heart." Nancy crossed her hands over her heart.

"Leave us," said Saffron.

"Go find your grandparents." Sojourner pointed to the waterfall.

"We'll call authorities to clean up the scum," said Sagan.

"We're taking her with us. If my grandparents aren't in the shelter, she'll know where they are."

"Then I will inform Otis and Elvis that the Sistas are in need of repair. Maybe they've heard from Marcus." Charlie swiped at the onyx screen in his collar and said, "Send message to Coral Reef front desk . . . Chums, I'm heading your way. Please open the doors to the Coral Reef passage from the rainforest."

"Will you also look for the spy cat?" asked Milly. "Seems we should have heard from her by now."

"Right-o. I'll keep an eye out. Good luck, Divas." Charlie moved slowly toward the corridor leading to the oceanic zone.

Nancy and Charlene retrieved their bags they had thrown down before the fight broke out. "Thank you again, Sistas! You too, Charlie, and get some rest!" Nancy called out as the Divas turned away.

"Nancy, before I go anywhere, I'm sorry, but I've got to get the sand out of my shoes," said Charlene.

"Good idea, we don't need blisters." Nancy plunked down to the ground.

"I'm awfully thirsty." Milly smacked her lips and stuck out her tongue. "Imagine there's anything to drink in this shelter?"

"No idea, but I've got a water bottle in my backpack if you don't mind sharing."

"Don't mind," said Milly. "I'm dyin'."

Nancy dug in her pack and passed the bottle. Although she offered Meissa a drink, she refused. With the bottle back in the bag, they emptied their shoes.

"If I sit here any longer, I'm not going to be able to move at all," Milly said.

"Nap's done, missy." Nancy yanked Meissa to her feet. "Time to get this over with."

CHAPTER 31:
CASSINI FALLS

Prodding their captive to keep moving, Nancy glanced at the two friends beside her, as they slugged through the sand. No one was talking. She wondered if they were as tired as she was. The fight had taken more out of her than she'd expected and guessed that having some DG blood in her made the difference. She would never admit that out loud with Meissa in the audience, and hopefully Meissa wasn't reading her mind. She didn't act like she was. She looked rather dejected.

They had been skirting piles of construction material and machinery. As they turned back toward the creek, they came across the end of a boardwalk. Nancy stepped onto the forest green composite decking. "Looks like they stopped here but intend to continue once the hotel is finished," she said.

"At least we can move faster now." Charlene massaged her tense neck muscles.

"Praise the Lord, I could use a break from this awful sand," said Millie.

It wasn't long and they were at a suspension bridge that crossed the waterfall's splash pool. The boardwalk continued past the waterfall a short distance, then ended. Standing on the bridge, the cold water misted the women as it cascaded down a cliff. Cassini Falls, completely enclosed within the biodome, was taller than the present hotel structure. She estimated it to be several feet wider than her outstretched arms. Waist-high railing deterred—although would not *prevent*—anyone from jumping into the splash pond. No vegetation grew anywhere on the grey rock wall.

"So where is this shelter, Meissa?" asked Nancy.

"If you can't see it, that's not my fault. I'm getting wet. I'm leaving." Meissa started to walk off. Milly stopped her.

"Well, it's gotta be back there somewhere," said Nancy.

Charlene was already scoping out a way to get behind the waterfall. "We can cross the creek here—the rocks will work as stepping stones. I can see the front of a building built into the rock wall."

Standing on the decking behind the waterfall, protected from the mist by a clear barrier, Nancy banged her fist on the steel door and shouted for her grandmother. No one answered. She listened carefully for sound behind the door and cleared her mind, in order to pick up any telepathic messages. She shook her head. "I get nothing." Neither the biometric scanner nor the alpha-numeric keypad was of any use to her.

She turned to Meissa. "Open it."

"Make me."

"Oh, you shouldn't have said that." Nancy reached out to clout her on the head, but Charlene caught her arm. "That'll make her more stubborn."

"I don't care!" Nancy shoved Meissa, and she fell backwards. "It's her fault we're here. How can you be such a monster? Why would you hurt old people to get what you want? That doesn't make sense to me!"

"Let's break it down," said Milly.

Meissa screwed up her face at Nancy. "They're not hurt. And that's a life-lock door. You couldn't break it with all the strength in the universe. It's locked and I don't have the key."

"You better have the key or I will absolutely beat it out of you. I've had it." Nancy circled Meissa sitting in the sand.

"Did someone say key? I got a brand-new key." An android of average height and weight, with long, bushy, brown hair approached the group from the other side of the façade. She was dressed in sandals, navy bellbottom pants, and a loose-fitting multi-colored long-sleeved shirt; several strands of beads hung from her neck. "Hey, Miss Meissa. Who ya got with ya?"

"They're nobodies, Janis J. Do not speak to them."

"I do not like to be told what to do."

"Janis J, I pulled you from the AI recycle depot because you were the most intelligent of them all. That's why I wanted you to guard this door. Please, do not let them in."

"I ain't going ta outright give 'em the combination. I'll make 'em work hard for it. Before they figure it out, your rescue party will have arrived."

"I doubt there's any rescue party," said Milly. "We pretty much flattened the dimwits helping her."

"They won't be escaping their bonds before prison security rounds them up," added Charlene.

"Who's the hippie?" asked Nancy.

"I am Janis J, the prototype her lousy brother dumped for his harmony hags."

"Ignore them. It's you and me," implored Meissa. "Friends look out for each other."

"Never got any help from my friends," said Janis J. "Seems we're at a stalemate, chick." She turned to the three from Earth and with a snap of her fingers whipped up a hologram featuring a lengthy equation. "Simple math, really. A second grader could do it. If you solve it, I'll give you a clue for the first key code and so on and so on." She hummed softly to herself.

Nancy glared at Meissa. "Try to run and you will lament the day you were born."

"Not going anywhere, girlies. You proved you'd overpower me. I plan to sit back and enjoy the entertainment. By the time you get it figured out, I'll have reinforcements here." She scooted away from the group. "Getting comfortable."

Nancy turned to the screen and grumbled, "A second grader on what planet?"

"Who's the math guru?" Charlene's head snapped back and forth between the women on either side of her.

"Not me." Milly poked her finger at Nancy. "You were the accountant. Any higher math I've had is like muscle—if ya don't use it, ya lose it."

"My job didn't require this stuff. Couldn't come up with the answer without a scientific calculator."

Charlene slapped her thigh. "I have a calculator on my phone. But guess where my phone is?"

"Why didn't I think of that? I've got mine." Nancy dug in her pack. Charlene and Milly leaned in close, reading the hologram as Nancy punched the numbers into the calculator. "The answer is two."

"You've got to be kidding me—that long string equals two?" said Milly.

All three gaped at Janis for confirmation.

"Yup."

"So two is the first number in the combination," Nancy said.

"Nope."

"Then what is it?" Nancy wadded her hair with her fists. She was reaching the end of her patience.

"I'll give you a hint: Here I stand broken-hearted, had it once and now it's parted."

"O-M-G," Charlene chuckled. "Bo says, 'Here I sit broken-hearted, tried to poop but only farted.'"

"That's it! The number two is poop!" Milly danced. "We got it. She had to poop and when she did, it left her body, ya know, parted with it. Put in P-O-O-P, Nancy, see if that works."

"Wrong! Man, you people are gross." Janis J held her mid-section and groaned. "If I could puke, I would."

"You're a piece of junk. Tell me or I'll knock your head off."

"No, you won't. You need me. Meissa doesn't know it either."

Nancy kicked the door. "If it's not the numeral two and it's not number two, then it stands for something else," she growled. "Like twins? Second place? Second fiddle?"

Janis J waved her index finger with each idea. Nancy was in her face. "Tell me."

Charlene put her hand on Nancy's shoulder, but she shook it off.

"Two as in double, a double-wide," suggested Charlene. "You used to live in a double-wide mobile home, then you sold it."

"That's the most ridiculous idea I have heard so far, except the poop thing. If you keep this up, 'Dialing for Dollars' will have found me."

"Duh, I'm a teacher—I should know better. It's the second letter of the alphabet," said Milly. "Except I don't see how you had it, then lost it."

"Now you're getting warmer."

"Okay, B is the first letter in the combination," said Nancy.

"Hot as Hades. This is so much fun. Let's do another one."

"No! Tell us!" Nancy punched the air.

"Can't, crybaby. Here's another equation." Again, she snapped her fingers.

"Might as well let her finish. What else can we do? The quicker we get this over with, the better," said Charlene.

Nancy cleared her calculator. "This one's longer than the first."

"It's fifteen," came a nearby voice.

No one paid attention to which one of them said fifteen, but Charlene counted on her fingers. "O. B-O. Here I stand broken-hearted, had it once and now it's parted. You had B-O until you showered?"

"Charlene, dear, androids don't shower." The fourth Dancing Diva, Joan, had a grin so wide it would have cracked a stone statue.

"Oh my god! How'd you get here?" Nancy turned to stare at Joan, as did Milly and Charlene.

"It's a really, really long story, but I know you're here to rescue your grandparents, so I'll save it for later. This is Marcus Shining, the guy I told you about."

BAM! Marcus stumbled backwards covering his face. Charlene had decked him in the nose as fast as a lightning bolt strikes the ground.

"I'm bleeding. What the hell. Why'd you hit me?"

"Because I don't like you."

"You don't know me."

"Doesn't matter. You got my husband mixed up in some ludicrous space project. He's lucky he's not here. I wouldn't've left him upright. I might not even-ah left him alive!"

"Whoa. You're Charlene. Pleased to meet you. Trebo tells me you're a wonderful—"

"Shut up." Charlene turned to Joan. "*This* is the Marcus you're dating?"

"Yeah, but I didn't know he was involved in all this until a little bit ago. Sounds like you've got some splainin' to do, Marcus sweetheart."

"Okay, okay, we're wasting precious time," said Nancy. "Concentrate. She said the clue was something she had, then lost, or it parted."

"She farted," said Milly.

"No, I said *Bo* farted." Charlene rolled her eyes.

"Man, you Earthlings are re-e-al weird. You're givin' me the kosmic blues."

"Give me the damn code," Nancy demanded.

No one noticed Charlie trot up until he barked. "ARF! Down here! Trixie and Rigel have been found. They're safe, but Milly, you need to come with me."

"You said they were safe. What's wrong with Rigel? Something's wrong. I know it," Milly said.

"Trixie is fine," said Charlie, "but Rigel was bitten by a rare type of scorpion. Sylvia is treating him with an antivenom, but he needs medical assistance. Trixie wanted to take him to D'Gnome, but he would not leave without seeing you first. Hopefully, I convinced him to stay put by telling him I would bring you to the desert."

"Oh my god, oh my god, where is he? I have to see him."

"Follow me."

"Wait! I want to go with y'all," Charlene said. "No offense, Joan, but I don't want to be near this man. And Milly shouldn't be going off by herself. Charlie, honey, I don't mean to hurt your feelings. You'll be with her, of course, but I'd like to go too."

"Don't be daft. You're welcome to come. Follow me." Milly and Charlene ran after Charlie, who appeared to have recovered from his earlier abuse by the prisoner.

"Hey, where's Meissa?" Nancy spun in all directions.

"Leave her be. She won't get far," Marcus said. "We've called the police. They're sending guards from the prison."

"So you're the missing-in-action Marcus, huh?" Nancy threw him a quizzical sideways glance.

"Suppose I am. I regret not having taken my sister's obsession with the glandular research more seriously, but I haven't known for all that long. If I had, I could have prevented this."

"Ya know, would love to hear more, but I've got an urgent situation. I am positive my grandparents are behind this door. They could be starving or dying, and we can't get it open! Janis J has the combination, but she won't give it to us."

Marcus acknowledged the android. "Hey there, Janis J."

"Screw you, man. I was your first. Didn't I give you nearly everything that an android possibly could? You dumped me anyway for those worthless harmony hags. I'd been around too long, learned too much, became too independent. You didn't like that, did you?"

"That's not true. I was immature, hardly getting started. I will always remember you as my first and most talented. I apologize for rejecting you. Listen, I have a proposition to restore your confidence in me. I will make you a headliner. You'll be a Janis Joplin. Not Janis J. How 'bout it?"

"Why not. I have nothing left to lose. Promise?
"Promise."

"Far out!" The android tossed up another equation.

"The code, Janis. This woman needs the code to get into the building," Marcus said.

"No, we've got the code," said Joan softly. "What she had and lost was love. She's spelling her lover's name. Ms. Joplin, it's Bobby McGee, isn't it? He was your lover, but you parted ways."

With a huff, Janis admitted, "Yeah, I let him slip away up near Salinas."

"Hate to interrupt this sentimental journey, but I really need to know if my grandparents are in there. Is that the combination or not?"

Janis bowed her head. "It is, but you won't find anyone worth beans. Those two have gone ga-ga."

Marcus smiled at the droid. "Janis, would you please return to the Coral Reef. Check on what Otis and Elvis are doing. They have a habit of straying from their duties. Keep them in line for me, will you?"

"Gladly. My job here is done. Later, chick-a-dees."

Nancy, with a shaky finger, punched in B-O-B-B-Y-M-C-G-H-E-E. "It didn't work. You said it was Bobby McGhee. What's wrong? Get her back here. She keeps stringing us along. I'm gonna tear her apart, limb by limb."

Joan stepped up. "You spelled it wrong. Delete the H."

Nancy tried again. The heavy door rumbled sideways, unhurriedly revealing the contents it had been hiding.

CHAPTER 32:
SUNRISE

Standing outside, not knowing who or what might be waiting for her inside, Nancy peered into the dark room, while Joan and Marcus stayed close behind her. "Grandma and Grandpa, are you in there? Anybody here?" she yelled. When there was no answer, she ventured over the threshold. Bright white lights flickered on, illuminating a cavernous room with floor-to-ceiling storage shelves as far as she could see.

From the back, she saw an elderly couple shuffle forward, gripping each other for support. These people are my grandparents, Nancy thought, the famed Harold and Erma Bayer. She could hardly believe it. Looking as if they were simply heading to the beach, Harold clutched a folding chair under one arm. He wore a Hawaiian print short-sleeved shirt and tan linen loose-fitting pants. Erma matched his pants and wore a white elbow-length blouse embroidered with colorful flowers. She was heavier and more stooped than her taller, thinner husband. Both had long white hair tied in pony tails. "Where's Janis J?

Janis J?" Erma called, breathing heavily. "Janis J?"

Marcus spoke, "I sent her to the Coral Reef."

Harold squinted at Erma. "Sent who to the reef?"

Coughing, Erma cried, "Can't remember."

"Here, my sweet, sit down." Harold unfolded the chair.

Nancy cautiously stepped closer, afraid to upset their delicate mental state. "It's all right. We're going to get you out of here."

"No one else around, eh? Just you three?" Harold whispered.

"Yup, nobody else. I'm Nancy, your granddaughter. And these are my friends, Joan Castillo and Marcus Shining."

"We are alone, Harold," Marcus said. "All clear."

"Son of a gun," Harold straightened and said in a booming voice. "Can't mistake that beautiful face and unruly red hair. Come here, child!"

Nancy worried Harold was confusing her with Trixie. There wasn't much difference, merely a younger version before them. Erma cried out, "It can't be! No! It can't be Nancy Renee! I'm hallucinating. Harold, tell me the truth."

"You're not hallucinating. It's your granddaughter."

Nancy ran toward their open arms. Emotions crashed into the cold, stark room with wave after wave of love so strong Nancy couldn't breathe.

When the hubbub subsided and Nancy reluctantly let go, she stepped back to take in the family she had never known. "Are you hurt? My gosh, it's cold in here and you're wearing flip-flops!"

"We're not hurt." Harold gestured in the direction of the shelving. "There is plenty of sustenance. We weren't in any danger, at least not from starving. This is an emergency shelter built deep into the natural hillside. From our estimation, it's capable of housing a hundred people for two years. In the back are beds and blankets, showers, an infirmary, everything."

"Where is Trixie?" Erma asked.

"In the desert, with her friend Rigel O'Rion," Nancy said. "Mom's okay, but Rigel needs medical attention from a scorpion bite. He's being treated with an antivenom, but we shouldn't stay here much longer. Are you strong enough to come with us?"

"This old body's still got some fight in it now that you're here." Tears fell down Erma's face.

"Why did you separate? And why is Rigel O'Rion with Trixie, when she should be here with you?" asked Harold.

"A neighbor of mine had the Pathfinder's key. Charlene Luapa. It was in the desk she and Trebo got from his grandparents."

"You mean Gilda and Harvey Luapa?" asked Harold.

Nancy nodded. "Yes. They, I mean my neighbors, recently moved from Dallas to Collinsville. It might have fallen out of a hidden cubby, because she'd never seen it before."

"Moons above, thought I'd never hear that name again." Harold smiled and stroked Erma's back.

"Charlene was at my house when Mom brought up the Pathfinder. So we went to get the key. Rigel recognized the picture on it as Cassini Falls. They sent me and my friends out to pick up sandwiches and when we got back, they were gone and the Pathfinder was missing. When they didn't come back, I figured something was wrong. Charlene and I, plus my friend Milly, who . . . I never thought of this before, but you would know her parents, the Mitchells. Good grief, this is a small world—or two small worlds, as Milly once put it. Anyway, we came to rescue Mom and Rigel. And now you too!"

"You cannot imagine how glad we are you're here. The key finally worked. We had tried over the years but never received a response," said Harold. "Now we know it was locked up in a secret compartment."

"Oh my . . . Gilda. So long ago." Erma's voice trailed off. She slumped in her chair. Nancy kneeled and put her arm around her grandmother's shoulders.

"Let me get this straight." Harold wrung his hands together. "Trixie used her old Pathfinder and left you behind in Collinsville. Then how, in all the planets, did you get here?"

"I used the high school portal."

Erma looked at Marcus, "How nice of you to accompany Nancy."

"I didn't. Joan and I arrived via my Pathfinder."

"I am part DG, at least enough to get me and my friends through the portal." Nancy hesitated as her admission sank in. "I'm D'Gnoman," she repeated, astonished, as if she'd seen a meteor streak across a dark sky.

"That you are, my child, that you are," said Harold, grinning. "Good to hear the Gansarcal portal is up and running."

"I still have to move it from the school to the barn, but I'm working on it," said Marcus.

"You'll get 'er done, son, no doubt about it," said Harold. "You're smarter than your sister, who calculated that kidnapping us was the answer to getting the nepial gland vaccine."

"Harold!" Erma scolded and cleared her throat. "You shouldn't talk that way."

"It's okay. I don't know what's come over her," Marcus said.

"I will say, she's more self-destructive than harmful to others," said Harold. "And her comrade—how she got involved with him is a mystery—but Thadd Verra has reasons of his own for his actions. Someone should have looked into him a long time ago, instead of letting him go about his business in that recycle depot. Sorry state of affairs, that is."

"It's a sorry state for both," Erma said. "Meissa's mind is very complex. We need to help her."

"We'll deal with her if we have to. Next time she won't get away. Janis J said you were ga-ga. What did she mean, Grandma?"

Erma smiled. "Your grandfather has been pro-active in our survival. Being the mastermind that he is—"

"Wait a minute. Stop that," Harold grumbled.

Erma blew him a kiss. He blushed, a crooked smile lighting up his face. "Harold knew all along the government might try to mentally incapacitate us, so he was already prepared with an antidote to shield our brain from manipulation." She coughed. Marcus retrieved a cup of water from a nearby faucet and handed it to Erma. "Thank you, love."

"I can take it from here, sweetheart." Harold kissed the top of Erma's head. "We had been taking the drug for quite some time to build up tolerance, not knowing when our deception would begin. The government is frustrated because they can't stop us from working on a coordinated effort with Earth. Incapacitating us was one way, in their strategy, to keep information from leaking."

"So, we're not ga-ga," Erma giggled. "And neither is Meissa. Most things come easy for her, but she has difficulty processing her failures." Erma took a deep breath. "She can't see failure as a stepping stone to success."

"While my twin can be obnoxious, I doubt she would seriously harm anyone," said Marcus. "Although I am shocked she's gone this far. She escaped moments before we obtained the key code from Janis. We assume the police will pick her up for participating in the prison outbreak."

"Mr. Shining," Harold said, "Do you know what happens when you assume? Makes an ass out of you and me." He chuckled, then addressed Nancy and Joan. "We don't have a D'Gnoman word that makes it sound so funny—ass, you, me. You should not assume Meissa has been arrested. She's long gone by now, especially if that Thadd character is with her. He's as slippery as that weasel of his."

"Well, the weasel croaked in the rainforest," said Joan with a grin. "Thought I'd throw that in."

"What about Bad Thadd?" asked Erma.

"Last we saw he was out cold and should be rounded up with the rest of the vermin," Marcus answered.

"Poor man," said Erma. "He needs help, as well."

"We better get going." Nancy stood up from her crouched position next to her grandmother. "Oh, ouch, my knees are sore. Give me a minute to loosen up, then we can go."

Joan suggested they gather a few supplies before they left. Nancy held open her drawstring backpack, while Joan filled it with water and random packages of food.

Marcus's Pathfinder was traceable. Erma's smaller device had a detection blocker and would be the safest and fastest way to travel to avoid anyone still in the rainforest. The mini had four telescoping arms to transport as many people. It did not need a key like the older model. Joan volunteered to stay behind so Harold, Nancy, and Erma could go first. "I am excited to sample a few of these packages. I know you have to leave, but I want to verify I can read the language. Is this goulash with ground beef?"

Harold responded, "Correct, my dear. You may like it better heated, but it's safe to eat straight from the package. You should try the real thing when it comes fresh off the food printer. People of DG long ago ceased raising animals for food and now consume cultured cells from a laboratory. Doesn't sound very appetizing, but you'd be surprised. Grown, preserved, and packaged all in one place. Very efficient and environmentally friendly. The replicator, a much more advanced version of your 3-D printer, will produce whatever form you want, with an unlimited array of ingredients. Although we still grow fresh fruits, vegetables, and grains in limited quantities, the printer will replicate all those things so you can create a recipe or pick a meal off the menu."

Erma grimaced. "No one wants to stymie an enquiring mind, dear, but—"

"Of course. There are more pressing matters to resolve," Joan said. "I understand. You guys go on. I want to investigate this stuff. Not every day you get a chance at tasting future food. Probably less fat and sugar. I thought you might have pills to fill you up."

"Pills were such a fad. Not nearly as satisfying. I will have to sho—"

"Harold!" Erma coughed and took a sip of water. "Is your brain finally pickled?"

"Okay, okay," he said. "Stop the chit-chat and take hold of the Pathfinder. You've got to see Trixie. We both want to see her."

Erma held out the small unit. Four short antennas protruded from the disk. Harold helped Erma to her feet.

Marcus planted a solid kiss on Joan's lips. "I'll be back for you soon. In the meantime, please don't go thinking your muscle and wit will get you by. Thadd Verra is dangerous and could still be around, should he escape the police. If my sister returns, try to keep her engaged until I can get back. I want to talk to her. If you need to escape, your enhanced brain will allow you to use this." He handed her his Pathfinder.

"God, Marcus, take a breath. I can handle a little alone time."

"Right. My Pathfinder will get you back to Collinsville. You know how to use it. Also put this on." He unsnapped the comm-cell from his wrist. "It's voice activated. Say 'Call Charlie.' He'll be with us and will know what's happening. Keep him apprised. Leave the door open, in case a new code generates and we can't get you out. I don't have Janis J's computer brain to hack the combination."

"Go!" Joan laughed. "I'll be okay!"

"All right. Take hold, Nancy." Marcus gripped the fourth and said, "To the desert dome!"

Nancy felt a sense of heavy pressure all over her body, unlike the tingling sensation of the

school portal. She lost her breath, then everything went dark. Next thing she knew, she and
her three travelers were standing in the cool desert sand. The landscape was barren and flat,
vast and lifeless, except for a wired enclosure in
the distance with giant doves parading back and
forth and a pod of people sitting on the sand. Next
to them sat a diminutive, dark-haired spy cat and
a ratty-tatty Cavalier King Charles Spaniel.

CHAPTER 33:
DARK SHADOWS

Dark shadows encroached into Meissa's mind. Doubts. Fears. Failures. Stupidity. The list went on and on. She had no idea what she was doing or where she wanted to go, except to go home, crawl into bed, and forget this whole thing ever happened.

Maybe that pile-of-parts Janis J had been trying to help her after all by distracting the Earthlings so she could sneak away. She hadn't gone far for a reason. There was an underground tunnel from the shelter to escape pods. Thadd planned to use a pod to get them back to D'Gnome unnoticed, so they wouldn't get caught. Caught? Was she to go into hiding the rest of her life? You're just now realizing you're a criminal? You should have realized that when you met Thadd Verra at midnight in the AI recycle depot. Now you have no choice but to continue this disaster.

Crashing through ferns and flowering shrubs was the man himself. "Thadd! You made it. Thank

the stars you're here. I was beginning to worry."
Was she worried? She truly didn't care anymore.

"What have I told ya? Ol' Thadd knows what he's doin'. Lucky that droid run outta rope. Woulda had ter think of some other way to git here."

"Cut this off, will you?" Keeping her eyes on Thadd, Meissa half-turned to show her wrists still tied.

Thadd drew a knife with a five-inch blade from a leather sheath attached to the belt holding up his baggy, worn blue jeans. "Shucks, never got to use this." He ran his thumb lightly over the sharp blade. Meissa flinched. One whack and Meissa's hands were free. He sheathed his knife. "Ya see them people leave the shelter?" he asked.

"No, but they had no reason to hang around. I'm sure they've gone to the desert to get Bellatrix."

"Let's go then. With the tunnel, we can get to 'er first and take 'er hostage."

"Too much time has passed. That's not going to work now." Meissa pounded the sandy soil with the heel of her boot.

"You doubtin' me, babe?"

"No. Purely the timing. And, please, I beg you, don't call me babe. I've asked you over and over."

"Aww, old habits die hard. Whatever ya do, don't doubt Bad Thadd. I can take on them Earthlings. Hafta take out the droids first, though."

"The androids weren't with them."

"Well then, that'll make it easy."

She was skeptical, but to appease him and to give her time to figure out what to do, she said, "If we can hold Bellatrix, the Bayers will surely give me the serum formula."

"Okay then, we're wastin' time." He pulled Meissa to her feet and marched off toward the shelter.

The massive door was open. A path of partially-emptied, single-serving packets led to the woman who had arrived with Marcus earlier. Riled to see anyone still inside, Meissa sneered. "How many of you creeps are still crawling around here?"

"Just me. Not exactly crawling yet, but if I keep this up, I will be." Joan laughed and waved at the discarded containers littering the room. The Pathfinder sat on the floor out of Joan's reach.

"Don't be cute. I was rescued after all."

"I see that. Amazed you're here, Verra. You were unconscious when Marcus and I kindly stepped over your carcass. Should have finished you off to ensure the cops swept you up." Joan leaned nonchalantly against the condiments shelving.

"Before cops arrived, Thadd recovered from his fall. That's how strong he is."

"Oh, he's strong, but he didn't have the pleasure of Sojourner's thread or Saffron's stun gun. What happened to you, Meissa? You are a respected astrophysicist. Your brother loves you. You could have talked to him before you got involved with this vile mutant."

"Watch it, lady." Verra took a menacing step forward.

"Hey, Thadd. How do you pronounce your name? Is it Tad like tadpole, or Thad like thump, the sound you'll make if you come closer?"

Verra raised his fists and slowly advanced. "Yer askin' fer it. Kiss tomorrow goodbye."

"Meissa, keep your goon in check, please. I can help you if you don't run."

"You ain't callin' the shots, babe. Yo, what's this?" Verra raised his big foot and crushed the Pathfinder. The unit shattered. He lunged.

Joan was quick with the hot sauce. It hit Thadd's bulging eyes. "Aye-e-e-e!" He covered his face. One swift kick to his privates was all it took to bring him down, writhing and bawling like a baby. Joan whooped in astonishment at having toppled the man twice her size. She picked up Erma's chair and smashed it over Thadd's head, leaving him unconscious.

"Meissa, I am in no mood to play games, especially since your buddy demolished a device that did not belong to me. Thadd's out of the picture, so listen to me. Do you hear? Listen to me. We can help you. We're going to see your heroine, Erma Bayer. If you don't want to talk to me, you can tell her all your troubles."

Meissa backed into a shelving unit and slithered to the hard floor. She mumbled, "I made a fool of myself in front of her. How could I have done that? What is wrong with me? All I wanted was to be accepted. People wouldn't believe me if I told them about a vaccine. I needed proof. If I had the actual formula or showed them Bellatrix was still alive, I would be famous."

"What are you muttering about?" Joan sat down next to Meissa and offered her a coconut cream pudding. Meissa batted it out of Joan's hand. "Suit yourself." Joan picked it up, tore off one end, and sucked. "Mmm. Light and refreshing. You should treat me nicer. I might be family someday, Sis."

"Sis? You're dating my *brother*?"

"Uh-huh."

"And why is my brother attracted to you, bitch? Because he got a shot that very few people have access to. It's a side effect of the nepial reduction drug. Otherwise, D'Gnomans would never have starry-eyed relationships with your kind."

"I sort of know about that."

"How? How do *you* know about the vaccine? You're a crummy Earthling!" Meissa screamed and beat the floor with her fists.

"Oh, it's very recent. Had a little download. Actually, a massive download. A brain-computer interface with that old songster droid of your brother's, Otis Redding. Man, if I don't know everything there is to know about D'Gnome, including you, Sister. Although Marcus told me about the vaccine and that your heroine was Erma Bayer."

"Screw him. He doesn't care about me. I recently found out about the Freedom Jumpers and that my brother is one of them. Yet he never asked me to join. They all know about the vaccine. What have I done that warranted no invitation? How do ordinary citizens find their way in? Must have to have the right connections. Friends, that is. Well, there's my answer. I don't have any friends or, obviously, a relative that matters."

"I'll be your friend."

"Shut up. You make me sick."

"Hey, just trying to help."

"Well, you can't. I wanted to be famous like Erma Bayer. Really make a difference with finally getting our people to know what the government was doing behind their backs. Come to find out that's what the Freedom Jumpers were planning, but planning ain't doing. I believed I alone could do better. Get it done. Now no one will know my name."

"Oh, they'll know your name, but for all the wrong reasons."

Meissa hung her head between her knees. She couldn't cry. She felt heavy, like her body was filled with lead.

Thadd rolled onto his back and moaned.

Then, from outside . . . a heavenly aria . . . in German. Thadd stiffened with muscle paralysis.

"Hallo-o-o!" called Sojourner, barging into the shelter along with her two Sistas.

Sagan's siren song ended when she saw Thadd Verra immobilized.

"We aren't the only ones who have been upgraded! Otis and Elvis are certified mechanics." Saffron performed a deep knee bend. "Our stabilizers are as good as new!"

"And Saffron and I have been reloaded." Sojourner whipped up a web to bind Thadd. "Charlie messaged us you were here."

Joan tossed the pudding package and got to her feet. "You arrived just in time."

"Sistas, I smell duplicity."

"Hypocrisy."

"Trickery."

"You mean her?" Joan indicated the troubled woman leaning against the shelves with her arms around her knees.

"She's the one. What should we do with her?" asked Saffron.

"I'd like to smash her knees."

"What has gotten into you, Sagan?" said Sojourner, feigning disdain. "On second review, I like that idea!"

"Hold your horses, girls. We'll need her knees to get her to the desert dome. Got some important people to meet. Come along, dearie. And you, too, Sistas. There's a shortcut using an underground utility tunnel from the shelter, with connections to each of the dome corridors. There's an actual map engraved on the wall. Guess if you can't pull a map out of thin air, you got a hard copy." Joan chuckled. "The door's over here. It will be much easier for you three to maneuver using the tunnel, plus we'll miss any excitement lingering in the rainforest proper. Get off your keister, Miss Meissa." She didn't move. "Look, this is your chance to redeem yourself. If you don't cooperate, I'll make sure you don't go anywhere but to jail. I said get up!"

Joan sent Charlie a message on the comm-cell: "Charlie, we're on our way. Me, the Sassy Sistas, plus Meissa Shining. Also need a cleanup in Aisle 4, Chili Peppers and Hot Sauces."

Meissa had completely let her guard down. She questioned her motives. She really was in over her head. How could she have been so foolish? Thadd Verra was a security officer at the National Archives, with a nice family, until she found out the truth, but by then she couldn't find any other way forward. After their first meeting at the recycle depot, Verra appeared to be quite charming and even funny. He convinced her that she could get what she wanted with his help. What was she to do now? She grudgingly followed Joan into the tunnel.

Falling in behind Meissa, the Sassy Sistas marched to their own tune, goading their captive along with a military-style cadence:

"Let's go, Shining."

"Get a move on."

"We must get there before it's dawn."

"Pick your feet up."

"While you can."

"For your knees we have a plan."

"Tee Hee Hee."

"Tee Hee Hee Hee."

"We are off to the big blue sea. That's where we're going, right, Joan? Gansarcal Bay, after we rescue everyone. Back to the portal to send you and your friends home?"

"Can't promise anything, Sagan. All we can do is try."

CHAPTER 34:
SUNSET

Nancy did not like the feeling of traveling with the mini-Pathfinder. Materializing in the desert biodome, she felt stiff. She circled her arms and touched her toes. "That was a little intense."

"It does take some getting used to," said Harold. "The mini's for short jumps. Not meant to get you to Earth. Nothing harmful, though."

Nancy pointed to Trixie, Rigel, Milly, and Charlene, approximately a football field's distance away. "There they are!"

At Nancy's shout, Trixie scrambled up. "Mother! Father!"

"Trixie!" Erma clutched her heart and sank to the sand.

"My brave, beautiful daughter!" boomed Harold, holding out his arms.

Trixie rushed to her family, stumbling several times.

"Sir, this is a long-awaited reunion—" Marcus said.

"Thirty-five years," said Harold.

"I gave my Pathfinder to Joan. Trixie has her old Pathfinder, but it can be traced if I take it to D'Gnome. I'd like to use your mini-PF to take Rigel to Saiph's house. She can treat his wound without having to admit him to a public hospital. Will you be okay until I get back?"

Harold glanced at Erma and said, "Go do what you need to do."

"Yes, sir." Marcus grasped the small device and walked toward the cluster sitting around Rigel.

Rigel reclined on his elbows with pain in his eyes. Milly held his swollen foot in her lap. Charlene sat next to Milly, with Sylvia and Charlie on either side of her. They looked up expectantly as Marcus approached with the mini-Pathfinder in his hand.

"I don't need to read minds to know what you're thinking, Marcus Shining. You are not leaving me behind. End of story," said Milly.

"What do you think, Rigel?"

"Let her come. She should be safe enough at Saiph's."

"Has Joan contacted you, Charlie?" Marcus asked.

"Got a message she's on her way, with the Sistas in tow, along with Meissa."

"Meissa, huh? Guess that will have to wait. Got to take care of Rigel first. Thank you, Sylviaw, for your quick action. You saved his life."

With that note, Sylvia clawed off her mullet wig. "Then I declare my work here done. Spy business is brutal. Please, call me Aurora. Marcus, much appreciate if you would return my undercover accessory to Saffron. I can't wait to get back to my cushy, comfy, and calm life."

"Not yet you can't," said Charlie. "We've got a cleanup in Aisle 4, remember?"

"I am not putting that wig back on."

"You don't have to, Aurora. I like you exactly as you are."

"Really?"

"Really. Wrinkled skin and all."

"That's purr-fect. I like you too. Ratty fur and all. Pals?"

"Pals."

The Sphynx, with her tail held high, a small curl at the tip, and the Cavalier King Charles Spaniel, tail wagging, sprinted away.

"They look like a happy pair," said Charlene.

Marcus laughed. "Quite a change. It'll be interesting to see how they are when we get home. They've always fought like cats and dogs."

"I don't exactly want to crash the party over there, so if y'all are leaving, I'll go check out the doves and wait for Joan." Charlene clambered up and brushed the sand off her jeans. "Bless your heart, Rigel. I hope you have a speedy recovery."

"Thanks, Charlene. See you 'round."

While holding one extension, Marcus offered the mini-PF to Rigel who grasped an antenna. "Have a hold, Milly," Rigel said. He held Milly's hand, while she gripped the third with her other hand. They disappeared—sucked into the atmosphere, like a genie into its bottle.

Yesterday, Nancy's new understanding of her mother had brought them closer together. Today, she felt a huge sense of elation at meeting her grandparents. In such a short amount of time, she had gained so much, yet standing here, watching her family, she felt a foreboding sense of loss.

Understandably, her grandmother, for the second time today, was blinded by tears. Erma had fallen to her knees and now rocked back and forth uncontrollably sobbing. Trixie cradled her mother in her arms the best she could. Harold, on his knees, tried to soothe his lifelong love and his long-lost daughter. Nancy dropped down next to him and entwined her arm in her grandfather's.

"I'm not much help. Suppose we should let them have their moment," Harold whispered to Nancy. "Erma has carried such heavy guilt about their last visit with the key and all."

When her crying abated, Erma locked her hazel eyes on Trixie's. "My dearest Trixie, I am overjoyed to see you. I am so sorry for letting you go. The Presider was depraved for using you as an experiment and cutting our ties. I missed you so much and deeply regretted jumping when James was home. There are not enough words to describe how remorseful I am."

"Mother, all was forgiven long ago. I had a wonderful life. Look at Nancy. She is so much like you. The second I saw the key, I knew it was you and Father. I didn't hesitate to come. I missed you, also, and love you with all my heart."

"I love you, too, my precious child." Erma smiled and gazed at Nancy. "And my beautiful granddaughter. How I longed to see you, to hold you, play games with you."

Nancy smiled. "I love you, Grandma, and so incredibly happy to be with you." She reached out to lay her hand on her grandmother's hand.

Erma covered Nancy's with her free hand. "I can't be happier than to be surrounded by my beloved family."

"Mother, what has made you so weak?"

Erma swatted dismissively at the air. "Oh poo, it's just my heart. There's nothing stopping old age, even in our society, but I was determined to hold on until I saw you. You'll be preparing me for the stars soon enough, but this ol' gal's got a little spunk left in her. What is important is we were finally able to get a message to you. We have Meissa to thank for that."

Trixie hugged her mother. "You are a courageous woman, and I want to follow in your footsteps." Erma's face lit up. "I brought the troll holo-drive with me to Collinsville to show Nancy. I never had the courage before. So many wonderful memories, thank you. I will cherish them."

"Did you find the documents?" Harold asked.

"Documents? Plural? I found one, yes. The Pathfinder instructions."

"That and in the cake on your sixteenth birthday, you'll find the vaccine formula. Keep the troll safe. There are two. Marcus has the orange-haired one. If any data was completely destroyed, a foundation has been preserved on the troll holodrives. One would not have to start from scratch. Our most current data is stored on external drives with the Jumpers."

"I left the troll at Nancy's. It'll be safe there," Trixie said and looked at Nancy. "It's in the nightstand drawer."

"Don't worry, Grandpa. We'll keep the troll safe." Nancy squeezed his hand.

Nancy happened to look over at Charlene, who was talking to the doves, when Marcus arrived from Saiph's. Harold, too, had seen Marcus arrive and waved him and Charlene over to join them. When the group reunited and Charlene was introduced, Nancy said, "I see Milly won the battle to stay with Rigel. She can be stubborn when she wants to be."

"You're not kidding," Marcus said. "I agreed to go back for her in a little while. Meanwhile, Joan, the Sassy Sistas, and Meissa are on their way here."

"Sit down. You are family, and we need you here with us," said Trixie.

"That's right." Erma patted the sand. "Please forgive our deplorable accommodations, but sit your patooties down. Make yourselves comfortable while we wait for Joan and company. You must be the Charlene Nancy mentioned who had the Pathfinder key."

"Yes, ma'am. It was in a desk bequeathed to us by Harvey and Gilda Luapa, my husband's grandparents, after their deaths."

"Ah, I'm sorry to hear of their passing. The Luapas were good friends," said Harold.

"Thank you. We do miss them."

"Many years ago, Erma gave Trixie's Pathfinder key to Gilda, in hopes she would one day give it back to Trixie. Even though it took more years than we expected, we are fortunate it worked out in the end."

"It saddens me to hear about Harvey and Gilda," said Erma. "You know, Charlene, Ft. Worth was my team's first gateway city. At the time, Harvey Luapa was a well-known planetary scientist." She cleared her throat. "Excuse me. Would you grab me some water, Marcus, dear? There's a care station near the doves." Erma swallowed hard and continued, "There were only a few families who went back generations to our first visitations which is why we selected the Luapas as future student hosts for the Earth Study Program. I got to know Gilda through Harvey. She was so much fun to be around; we became best of friends. I loved her to pieces. Go on, Harold. I can tell you want to say something."

"Well, I don't get a chance to brag much about your work, my sweet, and here is a captive audience. Erma was a dreamer . . . but not the only one. It was she and her crew who organized the Freedom Jumpers and asked others to join, in hopes that our two worlds could live as one." Harold smiled. "Imagine the possibilities, she always said, didn't you, honey?"

"That's what drove our work. Possibilities. We started out as a small group wanting to travel more freely without government interference. Then it turned into much more, with an increased membership and a serious effort underway to make First Contact with Earth in a peaceful manner." Erma cleared her throat again.

"First contact?" asked Charlene. "Some people on Earth already know about DG."

"What she means," Harold said, "is when Earth's general population becomes aware we exist. Our people know Earth is inhabitable, but travel is restricted, except for a few elite groups. On the other hand, it is hard to comprehend what will happen when Earth's population suddenly learns another planet similar to Earth is reachable. We would be completely overrun."

"Come to think of it, Rigel did mention something about the need to avoid widespread hysteria. That would certainly be a problem."

Marcus arrived with a pitcher of water and papers cups for everyone. "Thank you, dear. This might surprise you, but our people first visited Earth hundreds of years ago. Civilizations back then weren't advanced enough for us to worry about reciprocal visitation." Erma sipped her water.

"If there was a threat from Earth, our government's answer would be to shut down the gateways. If that didn't curtail the immediate influx, they'd have no qualms about using destructive weapons," said Harold. "The Freedom Jumpers believe we could benefit each other if travel was done in a coordinated manner."

Nancy was taking it all in, but she looked at Charlene who looked a little pale. Nancy empathized with her. Her face had probably lost color, as well. She knew what her grandparents said was true, but it was still hard to accept.

Harold shook his head as if to clear it. "Enough of politics. Marcus, Erma and I want to convey our deepest admiration on hearing your Gansarcal-to-Collinsville gateway is up. How is the building in Collinsville going that Trebo purchased?"

"Excuse me. What about Trebo?" Charlene's head snapped up. "I know he's been working with Marcus on some project, but he bought *property*?"

"Why yes, Trebo's a major part of the plan. He bought eighty acres twenty-five miles outside Collinsville. All that's on it is a large metal building used to store hay and equipment but, with a few improvements, it will be used for producing the Pathfinders."

Charlene's face changed from pale to red. "I knew he was partnering with you on some project, of which I know none of the details, but he bought property and didn't tell me?" She glared at Marcus. "And you didn't tell me, either?"

Marcus shrugged. "Beg your pardon, but we've just met. My apologies."

Charlene turned her back to him with a huff.

"Since you are here, I assumed you knew." Harold looked at Marcus. "See there? Made an ass of myself. I didn't mean to upset you, Charlene. Trebo will tell you when the time is right."

She looked up. "The time was right however long ago this whole fiasco began."

"Yes, I suppose I won't argue with that." Harold nodded.

Charlene sighed. "I apologize for my outburst. It's not your fault. I came here with Nancy. Bo has told me nothing about D'Gnome. All this is very new to me. It's been overwhelming at times."

"I realize how you must feel," Harold said. "Trebo's assistance is important to our cause. With some work, a small farm might be a nice cover for our operation of building the Pathfinders. You know anything about growing sweet corn or tomatoes, Charlene?"

"All I've ever raised are three kids, Mr. Bayer. I am from a Dallas suburb. The closest I've ever been to sweet corn and tomatoes is the local farmers' market."

"Well then, we'll have to figure something out." Harold grinned, straightened his back, and clasped his hands together. "All right, people! Erma and I have bored you enough, except maybe Charlene. No one else has anything to say?"

"Hey! Look who I've got!" Joan called out loudly as she approached, leading a small parade. "She keeps popping up like a jack-in-the-box. Can't seem to get rid of her. Wants to tell all her troubles to Erma Bayer."

"Well, hello! That is a very good possibility," Harold replied with a wave.

Joan, Meissa, and the Sassy Sistas stood before the group sitting in the sand.

"This is as good a time as any to discuss our recent misadventure, eh, Meissa?" Harold said.

"Please, join us." Erma swept her hand in a semi-circle, but the newcomers remained standing.

"I don't want the vaccine anymore. I don't care about anything, including the gateways. I wish I could die."

Marcus scrambled to his feet. "Meissa, please, I need to talk to you."

"Too late for you, Bro. Way too late." She turned away from her brother who had taken a few steps toward his twin. "Stay away from me."

Marcus stopped and threw a pleading look at Harold and Erma.

"Meissa, this is not what we want," said Erma. "We value you as a brilliant soul. Yet those so labeled seem to be tortured the most. Harold and I knew all about that. We hold nothing against you, as we had those same labels and high expectations from ourselves and those around us. You and I constantly question whether we make the right decisions. We must accept our mistakes as learning opportunities and move on. Please, let us help you."

Meissa covered her ears. "I don't want your sermon."

Harold, who had been cradling Erma, shifted away from his wife and struggled to get up after sitting so long. He held out his arms to Meissa. "Then hear this, if nothing else. We sent our precious daughter away, not knowing if we would ever see her again, convincing ourselves it was for a good cause. Erma and I suffered from our decision to let her go. It has been thirty-five years since we held her. Erma and Trixie separated in anger. If you hadn't given us a chance to contact her, Meissa, Erma would never have known all was forgiven. We were able to share our love with each other today. *You* were the answer, not the problem. We can still work this out together."

Meissa stood solemnly, regarding her heroine. Here was the woman she admired. She had wanted to be like Erma Bayer ever since she was a little girl. Yet she didn't really know Erma, except that she had gone down in history as an eminent astrophysicist. What kind of woman was she? Someone like Meissa, herself, hungry for recognition? Erma had a family who loved her and she loved them. Meissa had blind ambition but nothing else. Her parents were off on a real mission, not the fake one invented for Trixie's youthful disappearance. Even her brother looked at her with loathing. Everyone thought Thadd Verra was vile, and now everyone would think the same of her. Her reputation was ruined. What had she done?

"I hate myself! I am a vile human being!"

"No, Meissa!" Erma cried. "You set the ball in motion. We will no longer be held in captivity like animals. Mistakes can be mended. You will be remembered for good things to come! Please, come here, child."

Harold stepped toward the distraught woman, again with open arms. "Please—"

"I should *never* have listened to Verra! It all went wrong!" Meissa screamed, a dissonance so harsh and deafening it sent the caged doves into hysterics, flapping and pecking at their metal confines, terrified, desperate to escape. Meissa felt the same. She, too, was terrified, shrieking unintelligibly, spinning and yanking at her clothing. How could she escape this body? This mind? Why couldn't she fly like the doves? She'd fly away, away from everyone, where no one would find her. She really did deserve to be alone. Who could love her anyway?

Harold looked troubled. "Seems I'm at a loss to help anyone today. She is having a breakdown, and nothing short of a tranquilizer will calm her." ZAP. Meissa collapsed to the soft sand.

"Solved it," sang Saffron.

"What the eff!" cried Nancy.

Charlene scooted away from Saffron, fear in her eyes. "Good lord, don't shoot!"

Joan knelt beside Meissa to check her pulse. "This day is getting more bizarre with every breath I take."

"I stunned her," said Saffron.

"She's not dead," said Sojourner.

"Or Marcus would have our heads," said Sagan.

"That's right, I would," Marcus said. "Everyone relax. Saffron has not gone rogue. She determined what was best for the situation and reacted. I wish I would have paid more attention to my sister, then we wouldn't be in this mess."

"When she wakes up, you can tell her. We would have tried to pacify her, but maybe this is for the best," Harold said. "Soon we will be discovered as missing. We must leave right away for D'Gnome to be well ahead of the authorities."

Without any forewarning, Trixie said, "I want to come with you."

"What?" Nancy stiffened.

"I'm sorry, sweetheart. Things have been happening so fast that I haven't had a chance to talk to you about my decision. I can't put this off any longer. I knew in my heart before I left San Diego that it was time."

"Time for what?" Nancy's palms were sweating, her breath shallow. She was nauseous. Great, was she having a panic attack right here? She deepened her breathing to get more oxygen to her brain. Sat up straighter to expand her lungs. Maybe she hadn't heard her correctly.

"Did you not hear me tell Mother I would follow in her footsteps?"

"Yes, but I thought that was something you were saying to comfort her. Gosh, Mom, I would have appreciated more of a heads up."

"I didn't know myself until this moment. I want to join the Freedom Jumpers."

"And do what, Mother?"

"Whatever I can. I don't know for sure, but I am positive I want to go. I hate leaving you more than anything, but it doesn't mean we won't see each other again. Don't be surprised when I pop in unannounced."

Despite the fear of losing her mother, whom she'd only recently found, the comment brought a smile to Nancy's lips. "That's what Grandma said to you when you left D'Gnome for your Senior Superlative trip."

"I did say that, by gosh." Erma pressed her hands into the cool sand and repositioned herself. "Wasn't it yesterday when you were a teenager?"

Trixie reached for Nancy's hand. "You have plenty of friends to get you through your dilemma with Theodore. I will be embarking on a journey I am ill-prepared for and that may be fraught with danger, but imagine the possibilities!"

"Galaxies galore! That's the little girl I carried," Harold said. "You're too big now, so get up off of that sand. You, too, granddaughter. We need to jump." He helped Erma up.

Nancy clambered to stand, and when she was upright, shook her head in resignation. There was no point in debating the issue. She remembered her mother in the car, full of life and enthusiasm, talking about her elopement with the love of her life. She'd never seen her like that. Now here she was again, full of energy. And possibilities. "Okay, fine. It's not like you need my permission."

"It no longer matters if Erma and I are tracked, so we will take Trixie's old Pathfinder to the spot on the river where we were arrested. We will be met there by a Freedom Jumper who will use an untraceable PF to move us into hiding.

We'll be gone from the riverbank before anyone can pick up on our arrival, and they won't detect our departure. When our disappearance from Gansarcal is discovered and leaked to the media, it will create quite a stir, since people believed we died on a rafting trip. Presider Grassely will have a lot of backtracking to do." Harold laughed. "Oh, how I've waited for this moment!"

"Is Mom going to be safe? Will there be a civil war starting or something?" Nancy was not sure her mother knew what she might be getting into.

"The forest floor is smoldering," Erma said. "No one knows what will happen. Depends on the Presider and senators. Citizens will want to know what else has been hidden from them. The Freedom Jumpers will do their best to keep peace."

"Your mother will be safe. You keep the mini-PF, Marcus, to collect your friend Milly." Harold reached up to clasp Marcus's hand. "Thank you for your devoted support of us, son. Keep your eyes on the stars and may you fare well."

"Peace to you, my friend. Erma and Trixie, we will meet again," Marcus replied.

"A copy of my will and other important documents, plus the house keys, are in my suitcase," Trixie whispered in Nancy's ear when they hugged goodbye. "Remember to keep the troll safe."

"Should I be worried about someone looking for it?"

"I doubt anyone knows about it. Mother asked me to keep it safe, so I'm asking you. Mother's diary is also in the nightstand. It's yours now."

There were more hugs and kisses, tears and promises between mother and daughter.

Nancy moved a few steps away from her family, as did Marcus, Joan, and Charlene. She gazed at her grandparents—found and lost again—as her grandfather held out the Pathfinder for her mother to grasp. Trixie said, "I love you, my dearest daughter."

"I love you too. Please stay safe."

Trixie took hold of the Pathfinder and they were gone. Not such a pretty departure, but rather harsh, like the collapsing of a tall building, its cloud of debris sucked up through a vacuum hose.

A huge gash had been torn in Nancy's chest, her heart ripped out and tossed into the garbage. To be whole one second and empty the next was excruciatingly painful. While she had briefly known Harold and Erma Bayer—famous scientists, just like Rigel had said—Nancy felt certain she would never see them again. And her mother, who she was just getting to truly know, may or may not come back.

Nancy sucked in a deep breath, forcefully blew it out her mouth, and turned to her friends, trying hard not to cry.

CHAPTER 35:
THIS AIN'T NO PICNIC

What will happen to her?" Nancy asked Marcus, indicating the motionless woman with blue hair.

"I don't know. She didn't get the vaccine formula, but I'm sure her name will be linked to the prison outbreak. The justice system won't take kindly to that. She is my sister, though, and I want to protect her. Regardless of our trials and tribulations, I love her. She's the only sibling I have. I wish I would have taken the time to understand what was happening to her. I'd tell her I was sorry for being a crummy brother."

"Can she stay here until we decide what to do?" Joan asked. "We could take her with us."

"She'll have to stay. She can't travel in her current condition. I honestly don't know what to do. I'd like to talk to her, but my first priority is to get Milly back from Saiph's. Then we will return you to Earth. I've got Erma's mini-PF to get me to D'Gnome to pick up Milly. If something happens here and you need to leave in a hurry, don't wait for Milly and me. My Pathfinder that Joan has will get you back to Collinsville."

"Funny story about your Pathfinder," Joan said, digging the toe of her shoe into the sand. "The PF had a slight mishap . . . I guess you could call it a major mishap. Bad Thadd smashed it to pieces. Good news, Thadd is finally out of the picture."

"Are you serious?"

Joan cringed. "It was my fault. I shouldn't have put it on the floor."

"Okay then, you'll have to stay on Gansarcal until I get back. Wait for me in the Coral Reef Hotel. Let me have the comm-cell, so I can keep in touch with Otis and Elvis."

"There's always the portal," Charlene said.

"Not a bad idea. Let's meet at the portal." Marcus pecked Joan on the lips. "I've got a lock on it now. In case I don't get back in time, here's the code." He whispered in Joan's ear. "See you soon." He strapped the cell to his wrist and pulled the mini-PF from his pocket, extended an antenna, and disappeared to retrieve Milly.

"What kind of goodbye kiss was that?" Joan looked down at Meissa's unmoving body. "So what's next?"

"We'll be off to the Coral Reef Hotel," said Sojourner. "Are you coming?" she asked no one in particular.

"Not yet," said Nancy. "I think we need to take a moment and gather our sanity. If it's okay with Joan and Charlene, we'll stay in the desert a little bit longer. Check on Meissa's vitals."

"I wouldn't mind catching up on what's been happening," said Joan.

"If y'all want to stay, I'll stay, but you, Sistas, cannot leave without a hug." Charlene hugged Saffron, then Sojourner, then Sagan. Joan and Nancy followed down the line, hugging each Sista.

"Our first hug, Sistas," said Sojourner.

"How was it?" asked Joan.

"Cannot compute exactly. I will need many more to define a hug. Preliminary findings show it similar to gratitude. I understand gratitude."

"Feels like friendship," said Saffron.

"Or family. See, Sistas?" said Sagan. "We *can* feel."

"We are grateful to you for more than once coming to our rescue. Thank you," Nancy said.

"Although," said Charlene, "you scared the devil out of me when you shot Meissa with your stun gun. Still, I consider you friends. Now scoot."

"Wait. Before you go, I've got an idea." Joan clapped her hands. "The Dancing Divas are participating in a talent show in a week. How about if the Sassy Sistas perform? Isn't that a great idea?" She appealed to Charlene and Nancy.

"We'd have to coordinate with Marcus," Nancy said. "Maybe he could bring Elvis and Otis too."

"Gotta include Janis! She could be the headliner, like Marcus promised her. It would be a fabulous show. Draw in lots of donors. We'll scarcely have enough time to advertise, but we'll get 'er done." Joan did a happy dance—a Broadway tap step. "You three go on. We'll figure it out."

When the Sassy Sistas turned to leave, Nancy sat down in the sand and dropped her daypack in front of her. "Come on, have a seat. I'm starving."

Charlene plopped down and placed her hand on Nancy's shoulder. "Hey, you all right?"

"Yeah. For a moment there, I was the happiest girl in the whole U.S.A., and now I feel like the absolute unhappiest. Everything happened so fast, my head is spinning."

"You still have us," said Charlene.

"We are family." Joan sat cross-legged on the other side of Nancy. "Milly would feel the same way if she were here."

"Thanks. You are all amazing women I am proud to call my friends."

"Sisters," corrected Joan. "And I thought you were starving. Open up that pack, Sister."

Nancy tugged the drawstring open and dumped the contents into the sand. She tossed out small water bottles. "Anything here good to eat?"

Charlene picked through the individual-sized packages. "Ooh, this stuff probably has less sugar and fat."

"That's what I said!" exclaimed Joan, sitting cross-legged. "I'm not hungry. Tried a bunch of different foods at the shelter. You two go ahead and enjoy."

Nancy ripped open a packet. "Tastes like chicken nuggets. Not bad if you like chicken nuggets." She passed the nugget bag to Charlene.

"Thanks." Charlene took a bite. "Ugh." She gulped her water.

"This isn't how D'Gnomans normally eat. Supposedly, when it's fresh off the printer, it's much tastier," said Joan.

Nancy rummaged through the pile. "No chocolate or freeze-dried ice cream?"

"Nope. This one's got a picture of pork chops," said Charlene.

"They're fruit-filled pork chops, to be exact," said Joan. "Although it's safe to eat, I wouldn't recommend that one unless it's heated."

"How do you know that?" Nancy flipped the bag over to see if there was English on the package.

"The easy answer is Harold told me. But you will not believe how I got encyclopedic knowledge of this place."

Nancy tossed the chops down and tipped over another package. "There's got to be something edible. Sorry, how'd you get so knowledgeable?"

"When Marcus and I got here, I agreed to a brain-computer interface with the android Otis. I literally received a language infusion, the history of D'Gnome, I mean everything straight to my brain. I swear, it was the strangest thing. Painless. No wires, nothing besides a buzzed feeling in my head."

"Oh my god! That's crazy!" Nancy dropped the chicken alfredo. "I've read about Earth's scientists working on brain-computer connections, but that is too freaking futuristic."

"Well, I'm proof it works. I know some about Gansarcal's biodomes. The temperature inside is regulated to a comfortable degree. The biodome's roof reflects ninety percent of the sun's radiation. Solar energy is harnessed for use during day and at night when outside temps drop by hundreds of degrees."

"Wow," said Charlene.

"Yeah, well, I don't know everything, and actually, Marcus told me about the biodomes. These ceiling panels block natural light. They are controlled by a timer, but with the construction, I don't know the schedule and didn't think to ask Otis or Elvis. Let's hope we're not plunged into darkness anytime soon."

"How did you even get here?" asked Nancy.

"And what in tarnation are you doing with Marcus Shining?" asked Charlene.

"Oh geez, where do I begin? Marcus is the guy I told you about that I was dating. Of course, I didn't know he was a star person. I'd still be processing that little tidbit if I hadn't had that crazy download. Anyway, I was in Des Moines with Aspen and Oakley. The funeral was Wednesday, yesterday, right? Then this morning, the girls wanted to meet some friends they hadn't seen in a long time. I ended up going to a fast-food place by myself next door to the hotel for lunch. I'm sitting there with a plate of nachos big enough to feed a family of four, when who walks in?" Joan sighed. "Anyway, he was there on business. I'd told him I had a funeral to go to in Des Moines, but he swore it was coincidence he was in Des Moines at the same time. He had flown in on his private plane. By the way, he owns a plane—did I tell you that?"

"No, go on," said Nancy.

"We talk, and he asks if I want to fly somewhere on the spur of the moment, for fun. Told me he could easily file a flight plan. Told him I couldn't just take off because I had driven out with Aspen and Oakley. I called them, and they were fine with driving home alone. But before we finished eating, this terrible alarm went off. I thought it was a freakin' fire alarm and was ready to grab my food and run. Instead, it was his comm-cell. He said it got louder with the urgency. I didn't know it at the time, but one of the Sassy Sistas was trying to contact him."

"So you're the reason they couldn't get ahold of him," Nancy said. "They kept trying, but he must have turned off his comm."

Joan shrugged her shoulders. "All he told me was there was trouble in paradise and he needed to pick up some friends. I don't know how to make this short."

"We're all ears," said Charlene.

"Okay. So we leave the restaurant. He drives a super-nice BMW Z4 roadster. He says he has to stop at a friend's house first. When he pulls into the garage, he kisses me and everything goes black. I thought he date-drugged me, because the next thing I know I'm sitting on the end of a dock. I didn't know how I'd gotten there, although it seemed familiar."

"Take a breath," chuckled Nancy. "I wish Milly was here to hear this."

Joan drew a deep breath, her cheeks puffing out when she exhaled. "Well, the paradise he was referring to, O-M-G, was Gansarcal! And the friends were you guys!" Joan rocked backwards, kicking her legs in the air, spraying sand, and shrieking. Sitting back up she grinned. "All of us here in this unbelievable place blows my mind! Am I dreaming?"

"Unfortunately, no, but we get it," said Charlene. "Freaking weird-ass shit. Pardon me. You know, I never used to cuss like this until this alien shit happened. See? There I go again."

Nancy got up and bent over, holding her finger under Meissa's nose. "She's breathing." She pressed the prone figure's shoulder, but there was no movement. "How much longer do you think she'll be out?"

"I'm guessing not too much more. You wouldn't think the stun would last longer than an hour," Joan said.

"Okay, we've got to clean this up and get going." Nancy dropped to her knees and began shoving the packets into her daypack.

"Hey y'all, I see someone coming," said Charlene. "Not a robot. A big human woman. Even from here she looks mean. If she has a weapon, our strength won't stand a chance. Remember what Charlie said about sand in our eyes? Put as much sand as you can in your pockets. It may be our sole defense."

"There wasn't supposed to be anyone else here. She's too far away to read her thoughts, but her body language is all about aggression. Maybe she's from security making the rounds," said Joan.

"Well, whoever she is, have no doubt; she'll be able to read our minds." Nancy shoved fistfuls of sand into her hoodie pockets as inconspicuously as possible. "Think of dance or something, not family. If she's a straggler of Meissa's, we don't want her holding family over our heads. I can't block. I never got that far with my mother. Keep your mind blank."

"I can block," said Joan. "Part of the download. I can also read, but not her. She's not letting her guard down."

"That's more than I can do, so you're in charge. When you decide something, Charlene and I will follow your lead. Got it?"

"Aye-aye, Captain."

"What about mind control?" Charlene whispered. "Can she make us do stuff against our will?"

"From what I got from Otis, not other D'Gnomans. Other mammals like us, sometimes. Keep thinking random thoughts or sing a song in your head, if you can't empty your mind."

With their pockets full of sand, they began picking up the food containers and shoving them back into Nancy's pack. "Hello, ladies." Scrambling to their feet, a tall, muscular woman, with at least twenty braids of fiery red hair cascading down her back, stood before them. The braids reminded Nancy of whips that could knock them all over with a snap of her head.

"How quaint—a picnic! I haven't been on one of those since I was a kid."

"If you're hungry, we've got—" Nancy was cut off by the newcomer.

"Ms. Leopold, I presume?"

"Maybe." Nancy stepped in front of her friends and surveyed the area to be sure there wasn't some sort of militia with her.

"Oh, I know who you are, and I couldn't care less. I am looking for Rigel O'Rion. Have you seen him?"

"Haven't seen anybody. Why?" Nancy asked.

"He works for me and skipped an important meeting. I have some information to share."

Nancy found it difficult to clear her mind. *Probably pointless to pretend we don't know him . . . clear your mind, think happy thoughts . . . our talent show will be a huge success. Everyone's a star.*

"Not everyone, but I am a star—a force to be reckoned with, and I am dying to explode something if you don't cooperate. I'll put you out permanently, like Meissa Shining lying here, only much worse. See?" She pulled out what looked like a small rocket launcher from inside her long, flowing blood-red cape.

"Holy crap!" said Charlene. The Divas staggered back a few feet.

"There'll be nothing left but dust, so don't try any super-strength tricks on me. Now, you will all accompany me to the Coral Reef Resort. That's where the party's happening."

Nancy was certain Meissa's eyelashes fluttered, but she hadn't moved otherwise.

"I love a party!" said Charlene. "I was a popular hostess of countless garden parties. Oh, get real. I hated it. I could never be as good as my mother or older sister. I was a fraud at my own debutant debut. The last thing I wanted was to be shown off like some prize. 'But the cotillion's tradition,' my mother said. God, I hated it."

"Shut up, blondie. We're not here for your pity party. We're here for my bash, and you're all invited. Get a move on. Don't want to be late." The heavily armed visitor herded the three women toward the oceanic zone's corridor. They left Meissa behind.

Nancy kept her mind racing: *How often should you replace running shoes? Not that I'm a runner. I'm a walker at home, but here I can run. Should I run? Stop, she'll see that as a threat.*

"Are you threatening me, Ms. Leopold? Going to run, are you, when I open these doors?"

"No, I'm a walker. Walk, walk, walk." *I've always had a hard time blanking my mind.*

"I'll blank your mind. You'll be like your grandparents." She raised her unarmed arm and slammed the button. The doors slid open. "Move!"

When the Divas hesitated, she turned to Charlene. "March!"

Nancy was taken aback when Charlene stiffened and marched into the corridor. She turned in circles, hands drumming an invisible drum. The Divas could do nothing but follow Charlene into the corridor.

Suddenly, Joan yelled, "Hey, Bazooka-braids! Take this!" She double-fisted sand into the woman's face. Charlene immediately recouped, and all three threw sand as if their lives depended on it. Temporarily blinded, it was Bazooka-braids dancing now. Joan punched a code into the wall. A door glimmered into shape, and the terrified women hopped through. It solidified, leaving Bazooka-braids to screech and cough to her heart's delight.

They had stepped onto a lift, which dropped them to the ground floor. "This way," said Joan.

Nancy was thankful Joan was in charge. She possessed an uncanny knowledge of the bio-domes, including passcodes, which the monstrosity outside must not have or she would have been after them already.

They hurtled helter-skelter into the catacombs. "Making our way to an exit," Joan called as she sped on. She slowed down, stopped on a large X, and yelled "Ell!" A square-shaped surface separated from the floor, lifting the women into darkness. The movement nearly knocked Nancy off balance, but she managed to hold on to Charlene and together they stayed on board.

"What'd you just say?" squeaked Charlene.

"Up. Ell means up in D'Gnoman."

"Where are we?" Nancy demanded.

"The landscaping shed. Across from the portal."

"The one without lights." Nancy knew where they were now. "Doubt anyone's been here to fix them. Lights! I mean Russ!" Yup, darkness as black as deep space.

"Hang on a sec." Joan fished for her phone and turned on the flashlight.

"My phone! Here's my phone! I dropped it when we first got here." Charlene blew on the cell, wiped it on her pant leg, and shoved it into her purse.

"Obviously the Sassy Sistas didn't know about this elevator or we could have used it and not had to run across the sand," Nancy said.

"What do we do now?" asked Charlene.

"Catch our breath. Gather our nerve. And one of us takes a sneak peek out the door," said Joan.

"Oh, sure, let it be Charlene. She has the best eyesight."

"No, no, remember, this is a democratic group. Let's take a vote," said Nancy.

"Forget it, I know how the last vote went. I'll go, but can't we punch a hole in the wall instead?"

"I suppose we could, but the sound could alert Bazooka-braids to our hidey-hole. Is that what you want?" Joan said. "You wouldn't be able to see anything anyway. You're going to have to go out there and peek through the oleander shrubs."

"Come on, y'all. I am *not* going out there."

"Where is a spy cat when you need one? I'll go." Nancy voiced the door open and crept to the shrubs several feet away, spreading the blossoms apart enough to see Milly and Marcus . . . and Rigel sitting on the dock steps, with his heavily bandaged left foot stretched out, crutches beside him. What's he doing here? Nancy frowned and ran back inside the shed.

"Good news! Milly, Marcus, and Rigel are at the dock."

"Rigel! What's he doing here?" Joan asked.

"Asked myself the same question. They don't know about Bazooka-braids. I say we hightail it to the portal while we have a chance and get back to Collinsville. Marcus is a big guy; he can take care of himself and Rigel. Any questions?"

"Nope, none," said Charlene.

"Once we're away from the shed, we will defer to you, Joan. You have a sense of this place that we don't have."

They huddled outside the door and crept to the thick oleander shrubs, spreading the branches to peek through. "Be ready to run on the count of three," Nancy said.

"That sounds so familiar," whispered Joan. "Run *on* three or one, two, three, and *then* run. Kidding! I knew what you meant."

"Oh god, they're like sitting ducks," Charlene said. "Where do you think she is?"

"We're not waiting to find out! One, two, three, RUN!"

Oleander branches scratched their faces; shoes sank into the soft sand with every step. Expecting the Divas to come from the hotel, the dock groupies didn't see them coming until Charlene yelled, "Hey! Over there!" She pointed to a tornado of sand and plant debris blowing from the hotel direction.

"Must be her," Nancy yelled as she ran. "She is really furious to be able to whip up a sandstorm through psychokinesis. We might not make it to the portal before her."

By some miracle, or as Joan put it, the energy needed for psychokinesis of storm magnitude slowed her down, they got to the dock first. "No time to explain. Crazy lady coming." Nancy pointed at the sand devil.

"Huh," said Marcus. "Wonder what's going on with the weather system. The architects did not plan to create storms."

"No, no. Not weather. Big red scary woman," Nancy yelled, as if they couldn't hear her. "We have to use the portal and go home. NOW. You can come with us or not."

Charlene and Joan both reached for Milly. "I'm not leaving Rigel," Milly said, wriggling out of reach. "He's recouping at my apartment."

"That's fine, sweetie. We'll take him with us. Come on now," urged Charlene. "We have to go home."

The sand settled and Rigel said, "Wait a minute. That's Dr. Betel G. Euse. Charlie messaged and said she'd seen you having a picnic in the desert and that she was on her way to meet us at the dock. She's a friend of mine."

"You don't get it. She's no friend and this ain't no picnic," Charlene said. "She threatened to kill us if we didn't cooperate."

"But we got away," Joan added.

"She's got big black, soulless eyes, the kind to better blow you up with," Nancy said.

"That's nonsense. Bet likes to make a grand entrance, that's all. What a show-off. We'll see what she wants." Nancy noticed Rigel's outward demeanor was very different from the apprehensiveness she detected. Marcus, too, looked nervous.

"You can see what she wants; we'll be seeing ya. Get up, Milly." Nancy reached for her hand and tried to pull her up from the steps. "We're going home."

Charlene reached for Milly's other side and yanked. "Yeah, have a nice visit, you two. We're leaving and taking Milly with us." With the two of them pulling hard, Milly stumbled away from Rigel. "If you want to protect her, you'll get your butt up on those crutches, Rigel," Charlene said, "and move out of the way."

But it was too late. Bazooka-braids was upon them. If they ran to the portal, she'd most likely shoot them. So the four Dancing Divas stood off the dock bunched together like cloves in a garlic bulb. Milly, not realizing the danger, tried to break from their grasp.

"Stop it, Milly," Nancy said.

"Why? What's going on?"

"Be quiet. Anything you say could set her off." Joan pulled Milly closer.

"Set her off? What are you talkin' about?"

"Don't argue with us if you want to live," said Nancy. She couldn't say any more.

Bazooka-braids held her cloak tight around her body. Her gun was not apparent. She bared her teeth into an unfriendly sneer. "Hello, Rigel. How are you and your friends?"

"Nice display with the sandstorm, Bet. What's up?" Rigel grinned.

"Oh, let me see . . . I have always liked you. Maybe more than liked, but our relationship always remained platonic, never more. I was okay with that until lately, when I discovered undercurrents of an unsavory kind. And you are a part of it. The underground society of Freedom Jumpers? Sound familiar? The first alarm went off when you said, 'Maybe it's time for a change.' Shouldn't have let that slip. You know the government, including those in the Inner Circle, want nothing to do with letting the vaccine become public or free up travel. You were a part of that circle, Rigel. Now you're a two-bit spy, a traitor!"

"Stars, Bet, I didn't mean anything serious by that comment. It doesn't hurt to reconsider ideas once in a while for their relevancy."

"We've been friends since practically the day we were born. And, you bastard, you used me! You might as well put a stake through my heart. How could you have done that?"

"Bet, that's not true. I didn't use you."

"You got into the Inner Circle because of me! That alone is enough. Your second mistake was not telling me about the new gateway. How long did you think it would take before I found out? Why would anyone conceal a new gateway, unless they were up to something illegal?"

"When I talked to you last, I didn't know anything about a new gateway."

"The third? You betrayed me by skipping golf and lying about going to your office. You didn't have office work to catch up on. You were all worried about your Earthling paramour. Don't think I didn't pick up on that. Three strikes, you're out, lover boy."

Rigel threw his head back and laughed. "Hells-bells, Bet! It was your idea to see Millicent!"

Oh-oh. Nancy could see mad Bazooka-braids didn't like him making fun of her. She pulled her arm out from under the cape. It happened so fast there was no time to run. BOOM! The little building at the end of the dock splintered into a million pieces, most of it blowing out to sea. At the blast, everyone screamed and covered their heads as pieces rained down. Chards hit their legs and arms but didn't penetrate the women's jeans or jackets. A few pieces of wood stuck in the backs of the men still sitting on the steps.

Unhurt, Milly cried hysterically and ran to Rigel, who wrapped his arms around her as the last remaining debris rained down.

Joan, Charlene, and Nancy clung together.

Charlene drew her hand away from her neck. "Oh my god, I'm bleeding!"

"Shh, hush, let me look." Joan examined the wound. "It's not bad. You'll be okay."

"We shouldn't run. Any movement we make could provoke her," whispered Nancy.

"She annihilated our way home!" Charlene pushed back. "And you're going to let her get away with it?"

"We couldn't take her if we tried, not with her being armed," Nancy hissed.

"You're right, little girl. Oops, your way home is broken. Now whatcha gonna do?"

Marcus stood up. "What is it you want, Dr. Euse?"

"Marcus, nice to see you here, as well. To top these last days at the Institute, I am being condemned for two gateway malfunctions. Know anything about those?"

Marcus looked at his shoes and didn't answer.

"You are both idiots," she said.

Joan peeled away from the bulb. "We hear ya, girlfriend, when it comes to men. Despicable pieces of fungi. Lowest of the low. Seems your gripes are with them, though, so if you don't mind, me and my peeps will head to the Coral Reef."

"No, you're all going to die. It's so hard to decide whether I pick you off one by one or blow you all away at once." Dr. Betel G. Euse laughed gleefully. Her back was to the hotel, but everyone else could see Meissa Shining striding toward them with her index finger to her lips. Relishing the frightened faces, Dr. Euse was completely caught off guard when Meissa seized her from behind, wrenching backwards the arm holding the weapon.

As soon as Dr. Euse began struggling with Meissa, Joan grabbed Milly. With Rigel's urging she offered no resistance and ran toward the landscaping shed.

Nancy heard Marcus yell, "Meissa! Stop!"

"Go!" Meissa yelled back. "Get him out of here!"

Marcus must have listened, because in Nancy's peripheral vision, she saw him heading their way, with Rigel over his shoulder. Next to the dock steps, Meissa had wrapped a red braid around Betel's neck when the blast went off. The Divas had almost reached the oleander. The powerful discharge was mostly absorbed into the moon's surface, causing sand and rock to spawn their own storm. Screaming and pushing through the shrubbery, they were showered with red sand and bits of rock. Nancy spread the branches so the men could scramble through.

"Oh Lord, it's raining bloody sand. I'm feeling light-headed. The lights are dimming." Milly slumped into the arms of Charlene and Joan, who sank to the ground with her. Joan examined Milly for any wounds but found none. "She'll come to in a minute. Or sooner," she added, as Milly moaned and opened her eyes.

"Am I still alive? What happened?"

"You blacked out for a minute. Bazooka-braids and Meissa are dead," said Nancy.

"I'm dead?"

"No, not yet. You fainted." Nancy brushed debris from Milly's jacket.

"I fainted? Oh lordy, where's Rigel?"

"I'm right here," he said.

"You ladies okay?" Marcus asked.

"Physically, we're fine; mentally, could be better," said Nancy hugging herself.

"Are you kidding me? Look at this awful, horrid gook!" Charlene scrubbed her fingers through her hair. "And I'm still bleeding!"

"Whoa." Marcus put his arm around Charlene. "We'll get you cleaned up. There should be a first aid kit inside here." He opened the door to the landscaping shed. "Russ."

"The lights aren't working," Joan said. "We've been here before. But first, let me pull those big splinters from your coat. You, too, Rigel." She pulled out the pieces sticking through the material.

"One of those went clear through," said Marcus. "Ouch, that stings!"

"Don't be such a wuss." Nancy yanked a chard from Rigel.

"Ouch! Still doesn't compare to my foot, though."

"Let's get everybody into the shed," said Marcus.

"There's really not enough room in there for everyone. I'll stay here with Rigel and Milly," said Joan.

Nancy and Charlene fished out their phones. Inside the dark building, they used their flashlights to scour the space for a first aid kit. On the back wall over a sink hung a red metal cabinet with a white cross. Next to it was a paper towel dispenser.

Marcus flipped a switch next to the cabinet and light flooded the room.

"Well, that sucks," said Nancy. "How'd you do that?"

"It's an emergency generator. Now, come here, Charlene, and I'll get you fixed up." Marcus opened the cabinet and pulled out disinfectant, a bandage, and tape. Charlene sucked air when Nancy touched wet towels to her cut, but Nancy assured her it didn't need stiches. When Charlene's neck had been bandaged, they went back outside.

"Yo, Marcus, could the blaster have damaged the biodome?" asked Milly.

"No. If so, we'd hear sirens going off," said Marcus. "These shields can withstand fighter jet missiles. A few, anyway. Her gun had a short range, and the impacts were taken primarily by the building and the ground, not the dome."

"What about Meissa and what's-her-name?" Nancy pointed to the crater near the dock.

"If we hadn't run when we did, we'd be there with them. I am so sorry about your sister, Marcus." Joan took his hand in hers and brought it to her lips to kiss. "Are you okay?"

Marcus drew in a long breath. "Yeah."

Nancy found it difficult to find the right words. "I'm sorry about Meissa." She wasn't sure what she could say about his sister. She was a good person, misguided maybe, but meant well...? Better to say less than the wrong thing, though. Then she realized what Meissa had done. "Meissa saved our lives, Marcus."

The others offered condolences, as well. "Thank you. We should get to the hotel. I can take care of my sister and Dr. Euse later. The authorities have loaded up the prisoners in the rainforest and are back at the penitentiary. They wouldn't have heard the explosions on the far side of the moon. But they may come back for a security check, so we should go."

"A part of the floor in the shed drops to the underground corridor. It'll be easier than traversing the sand," said Joan. "It leads to the Coral Reef. Think you can make it, Rigel?"

"I don't need coddling." Rigel limped a couple of steps. "Unfortunately, the wound is too fresh to put much pressure on it. Let me use you, Marc, as a crutch. You don't have to carry me."

This time there was no stopping to gaze in wonderment at the beauty of the lobby. The Sassy Sistas came running, waving their arms, to meet the distressed group.

"We heard the blast!"

"The blast left us aghast!"

"You can tell us what happened at last!"

"Euse blew up the portal. We were able to get away. Euse and my sister are dead," Marcus said.

"I feel sad." Sojourner frowned.

"I feel sad too," said Saffron.

"I don't think I like this feeling," said Sagan. This time there was no dance from the Sassy Sistas.

"I am beside myself with remorse. As a canine, I pride myself on my insight into human character. I should have sensed Dr. Euse's anger. Yet she appeared so friendly. I blame myself for not warning you properly." Charlie hung his head, with his tail between his legs.

Aurora sat on her haunches close to Charlie and delivered a mournful meow.

"I could not stop the Coral Reef from becoming Heartbreak Hotel," said Elvis Presley.

"What a sobering sight," said Janis J. "My loss of Bobby doesn't come close to the loss you are experiencing. I would give you a piece of my heart if it would help."

"Thanks everyone." Marcus let go of Joan's hand and thrust his hands into his pants pockets.

"Excuse me, Marcus," said Otis Redding. "I am very sorry for your loss. Meissa left a sound bite with me in case she didn't come back. Would you like me to play it?"

Marcus nodded. "Sure."

The droid replayed the recording: "My whole life I wanted to be like Erma Bayer. Smart, successful, respected. I worked to get in with all the right people, advancing my career. Or who I thought were the right people. Then I got a security clearance that showed me how much the government was keeping secret. I was nothing more than a naïve pawn. I became angry and helpless. I wanted to change how the senators governed. If I exposed the vaccine, it would show the world that I would not hide anything from them. I was convinced I could do it better by myself and everyone would adore me, but you can't achieve significant change alone. You must surround yourself with intelligent, caring people, like Erma did.

"I allowed Thadd Verra a trip to Earth, and he brought the scorpion back with him. It was a pet from a dying friend. I asked him to get rid of it. I don't know if it was an accident he left it here or not. He wasn't always lucid, but during a coherent moment he shared with me a heinous act that makes me angrier than ever at certain senators. If these are my last words, and I don't know that they will be, but if they are, I want someone to look into Thadd Verra's atrocious living conditions.

"It was Thadd's idea to capture the Bayers. I went along with it and I am sorry. Unlike Euse, I never would have hurt anyone. And I never leaked the existence of the vaccine. I don't know what happened to me. But I still want to be like Erma. And Erma was brave to have sacrificed her family for the good of the people. As I laid in the desert sand listening to Euse threatening to kill innocent people, I realized what I had to do. If necessary, I would sacrifice my life for the greater good. I apologize to those I hurt. Tell my brother I love him too."

Marcus blinked hard and wiped a tear from his cheek. "Thank you, Otis, but enough of this. It's time for you to go. Let's see . . . my Pathfinder's been destroyed. Harold took Trixie's. The mini-PF Erma gave me can't get you to Earth. The portal's blown up." Marcus ticked off on his fingers the avenues of return that were no more. "Hooey." He took a deep breath. "That leaves an escape pod from here to the Institute. There will be a staffer in the transport room—"

"I know what to do," piped up Joan. "I'll stupefy the staffer's frontal lobe. He or she won't know what's happening. We'll not panic. In other words, stay calm and dance on. Activate a portal to Collinsville. Anybody gets in our way, I'll whack their memory too."

"You can do all that?" asked Charlene, flabbergasted.

"It was quite the download."

"Nice meeting everyone," said Nancy. "Goodbye, Charlie and Sylvi-aw. Thanks for your help."

"I'm Aurora now. It was my pleasure." Aurora purred loudly and rubbed against Milly's leg.

"My pleasure, as well." Charlie leaned back on his hind legs and dipped his head in a salute.

Nancy returned a salute to Charlie. "Goodbye, Marcus." She hugged him briefly. "Remember, we are family. If there's anything we can do—"

"There's not. You guys be careful."

Milly, too, wrapped her arms around Marcus and said, "Meissa will rest in peace now; her soul's in His hand."

Charlene gently coaxed Joan away from Marcus.

"Come on, Joan," said Nancy. "We're counting on you to lead the way to the nearest pod. Goodbye, all. Thank you, again, from the bottom of my heart for your help. We will meet again!"

CHAPTER 36:
BACK TO SCHOOL

The Dancing Divas were back where they started—in the theater's crossover. Milly called to the school secretary on their way to the front door. "Bye, Christine! Kids loved the cookies. Maybe they'll save you some."

Christine waved. "You have a good afternoon, Miss Milly!" The Divas were past the office before Christine could get a good glimpse of the disheveled women. They marched out of Collins High like the soldiers they were.

Phones dinged as they walked to the parking lot. Nancy looked at hers. "Nothing from Ted. Of course, he only left yesterday. It's so weird today is still Thursday. I think."

"Yeah, it is," said Milly. "No need for you to text us, huh, Joan. You made it home from the funeral by way of—"

"Gansarcal," Joan snickered. "Not the paradise I was hoping for. The funeral seems so long ago."

"You all want to stay at my house tonight?" Nancy asked. "I'm not feeling like being alone. We can try to wrap our heads around all that's happened."

"We should have a slumber party and sleep on the floor in the family room and order pizza and lava cakes," said Charlene.

"Technically, we had pizza and lava cakes yesterday," Milly said.

"Oh god, you're right. Well, you two?" Charlene looked expectantly at Joan and Milly.

"I'm in," said Joan.

"As the oldest, I claim the sofa," Milly said, as she unlocked her car. "But I need a shower first. I'll drop everyone off and we can meet back at your house."

"Okay. We'll clean up and be back at my house by six. Bring your pj's. We'll order delivery of something or other." Nancy opened the car door and climbed in.

The Dancing Divas didn't fall asleep until the wee hours. Long after the sun had come up, blurry-eyed Nancy grabbed raison-cinnamon bagels, plain cream cheese, orange juice, and some hard-boiled eggs from the fridge. "I made the eggs for Ted to take with him, but he forgot, so we might as well eat them. Unfortunately, I don't have anything but instant decaf. We could go to Starbucks or McDonald's, if you want."

"Are you kiddin' me?" said Charlene. "I feel like I've been run over by a truck. I'm happy to sit right here and not move for a month."

"Ditto," said Milly. "This spread looks good to me. Then I'm going home and take a nap before tonight."

"Oh, a nap sounds so good." Yawning, Joan reached for an egg. "I suggest we set our alarms, in case we sleep into the night and miss the whole play."

"Good idea," said Nancy. "What time are we meeting?"

"How 'bout 6:30 in the lobby," said Milly. "I told Lilly I would be sittin' with you, since this is our annual birthday bash, although I invited her to join us. Brianna is drivin' up from Denver to watch her sister's play. They won't miss me. By the way—" Milly raised her juice glass. "Happy birthday to us!"

"Happy birthday to us!" everyone sang, clinking their glasses together.

"Your friendship is the best present I could ever have!" Charlene held up her juice glass again for another toast. "To friendship!

"To friendship!"

"One more," Joan added. "We made it back alive and in one piece—to life!"

"To life!"

Later that evening, at 6:30 p.m. sharp, the four Divas converged in the school lobby, looking to all the world as if they'd experienced an ordinary day. The only one missing was Trixie.

As they selected their seats, Joan lightly touched Nancy's arm. "Hey, I know you're missing your mom."

"You'll have to teach me how to block, since my mom never got the chance." Nancy smiled weakly.

"I don't need to read your mind to imagine what you're going through. Remember what we talked about last night? Whatever your role will be in D'Gnome's future, we will be right there with you. We are family."

"Did I hear family?" Milly asked.

"What, are you reading minds now too?" Nancy's smile this time reached her eyes.

"Heck no. We are family—one for all and all for one! Maybe we should change our name to the Four Musketeers, or Five. We can't forget Jasmine. Although we should not bring our teacher into this ET business."

Charlene leaned forward in her seat. "I'm on the end, and it's noisy down here. Did I hear y'all say we're gonna change our name? I don't care as long as it's not something like the Hoofin' Hussies or whatever that awful name was Nancy suggested. Although she did come up with Dancing Divas and I liked that."

"It was Hoofin' Heifers and there ain't no way we're changin' our name to that," said Milly. "All this hot air blowing around me, you're gonna wilt Elizabeth's flowers. Now hush."

"Love you, Milly," said Nancy. 'Love you, Joan, and you, too, Charlene."

"Come on, Divas." Joan stood up. "Group hug. Let's hug like no one's watching. I'm so thankful we're alive and well."

"All right, all right. Watch the bouquet," Milly said and hugged the hardest.

"WHOO-HOO!" they yelled together. Laughing, they settled into their seats.

Four days later, Ted called Nancy to say he had harvested a six-point elk. They would have lots of good meat. He and Trebo were spending the night in Jackson and would be home tomorrow afternoon. Nancy reminded him of the pecan pie and to buy another pie of his choice. She was inviting the Divas over for dinner when they got home.

Charlene had received the same call from Bo. She texted Nancy: Since boys are spending the night in a hotel, they will be plenty rested up. I say we don't put off the inevitable another minute.

Nancy replied with a Diva group text: Bo and Ted home from hunt tomorrow. You are invited to my house tomorrow night, 5:30 p.m., for dinner and a murder.

Charlene: I was kidding. Murder would send me to prison. Will try Nancy's idea of diplomacy first, and then think about murder. Could always escape to Gansarcal.

Milly: Leave me out of the murder, but I'm down for dinner and an escape to Gansarcal.

Could use a nice spa right now. Thanks for the invite.

Joan: Mind if I bring Marcus? He's here and I'm getting another fabulous massage later. You know where that leads! TMI, but think I'm in love!

Nancy: You go, girl! He's always welcome. Making two big pans of lasagna. Garlic bread, salad, and pie. Plenty to go around. Don't bring anything. See you tomorrow.

Bo and Ted hadn't been home more than a couple of hours when Charlene texted Nancy: Bo brought me a delicious-looking chocolate pecan pie. Do you think he is trying to pacify me for some reason? He's acting weird.

Nancy: I asked Ted to bring me one. Bo probably bought one for you, knowing you like chocolate. Pacify? He doesn't know that you've learned about DG.

Charlene: Is Ted acting any different?

Nancy: Nope. Throwing his dirty clothes on the laundry room floor as usual.

Charlene: Can't you read his thoughts?

Nancy: Why? Ted doesn't know anything, either. And I wouldn't go rummaging around someone's mind looking for something in particular anyway. Even if I could, it's like reading someone's personal diary without their permission. Wouldn't do it.

Charlene: Guess I'm paranoid about this whole thing. Hope I can eat pie. My stomach is churning.

Nancy: Mine too, but pretty sure I can eat the pecan pie. It's got chunks of chocolate. Could probably eat the whole thing no matter how I feel, it's so good.

Charlene: Have you decided how to bring up DG?

Nancy: No. Let's play it by ear.

Charlene: Ok. See you tonight.

Milly arrived at the same time as Marcus and Joan for dinner. Everyone was introduced—Ted to Marcus; Bo to Milly, Joan, and—

"I know Marcus," said Bo. "Hey, Bro, what a surprise to see you here. How's it going?" The two men shook hands.

"Bro? So you *do* know each other." Charlene glared at her husband.

"Yeah, I got to know Marcus when he stayed with my parents his senior year of high school," said Bo. "I was at the Colorado School of Mines for my graduate degree, but met him a few times when I went home to visit. We've stayed in touch over the years. Isn't that right, Marc? I don't think you've ever met my wife."

"Oh, shut up. I can't do this nicey-nice anymore. We know each other. Let's get this over with. If it weren't for Harold Bayer and the people in this room, plus Rigel O'Rion helping me understand your deceitfulness, I'd be ripping you a new asshole, Trebo Luapa." Charlene's face flushed bright red, and she was visibly shaking.

"Whoa, *what*?" Bo pulled his head back, his eyes big as saucers.

Nancy was shaking, too, at least inside. She looked at her hands. Was her nervousness apparent to anyone else? Scanning the people standing around her kitchen, Ted was the single one completely in the dark. How would he take it? Would he end up like her father, who had acted like he understood, then died the next day from shock? Nancy noticed he looked alarmed at Charlene's outburst.

"Stop! The lasagna has a half hour yet to bake and then it has to set for a few minutes, so let's all sit down at the table." Nancy made sure everyone had something to drink, then looked at her husband. "Ted, I don't know how to tell you this, but—"

"You're part star person. Aren't we all?"

"Aren't we all what?" Nancy wasn't sure she'd heard right.

"Made from stardust. I know all about you and your mother. Or some of it."

Nancy frowned. He wasn't in the dark after all. "You *know*?"

"Um, funny story."

"Mind if I tell it?" Bo looked at Ted.

"Go for it."

"I assumed Ted knew about his mother-in-law. One night over turkey tetrazzini—those freeze-dried meals are pretty good—I asked him if Trixie had *ever* been back to D'Gnome. He had no idea what I was talking about and wouldn't let it rest when I refused to say anymore. So I told him everything."

"Everything?" Charlene shouted. "You tell *him* everything and you don't tell *me*? Well, guess what, buddy? *I* know everything. Like you left Texas with an ulterior motive to build Pathfinders. Yeah, I know what those are. You bought land without my knowledge, even though we said we'd always discuss large purchases. How dare you go behind my back? Oh, and I've used the portal at the high school TWICE and went to Gansarcal. You know what that is? It's a moon and I almost got killed there. That's right. And you are a disgusting liar!" Charlene broke down, sobbing.

Bo quickly moved to his wife's side, got down on his knees, and looked up at her. "Hey. I'm really sorry. If you know everything, then you knew why I couldn't tell you. Confidentiality and all that. Unless you and I were actively sponsoring Senior Superlatives, D'Gnome was best left unsaid. I know we agreed to always discuss large purchases, but it wasn't our money that bought the place. I grappled with telling you because anything I said would sound . . . crazy." He shook his head in defeat. "You must see how hard it would be to explain."

Charlene hiccupped. "I suppose so. Nancy said the same thing about how to tell Ted."

"And now she doesn't have to," Ted said. "Although there seems a lot more to this than what Bo has told me."

"Oh, I assure you, there's plenty more where that came from," Nancy said. "Thanks for being so understanding. I didn't know anything about this, either, until the end of August. You won't die on me, will you? My dad had a fatal heart attack after he found out."

"No. Bo and I had a very long conversation. I can handle it."

"Damndest dinner party I've ever been to," said Milly, crossing her arms and grinning.

"Oh, before I forget," said Marcus. "Rigel sends his regards. His foot has another week, and it should be fully grown back. A little physical therapy and the old man will be running circles around me again."

"Regards? That's all he sent?" Milly scowled. "*Regards?*"

"All right, he sends his *love*. And he misses you."

"Humph. That's better."

"And . . . Marcus can't bring all the droids for our show," said Joan.

"Right. Will bring Janis Joplin and the Sassy Sistas. Otis and Elvis will have to stay at the Coral Reef," Marcus said.

"That's fine," said Nancy. "We'll take what we can get."

The timer buzzed and Nancy got up to take the lasagna pans out of the oven. She set them on the island and started the garlic bread on the griddle.

Ted wagged his index finger at Milly and Joan. "How are you two sitting there like this is old news?"

They both explained their relationship with the exoplanet. Milly told him that her family had served as a contact for D'Gnomans for generations and had sponsored students with the Senior Superlative Earth Study Program, like Bo's family. Joan said that while she had known Marcus for not quite a year, she had found out about D'Gnome and Gansarcal basically the same time Charlene learned.

"Cripes," said Ted. "This sounds more like a movie than real life."

"I wish it was, but it's not." Nancy kissed his head. "Let's eat while the lasagna's hot. Bread's done. Everything's on the island. It's buffet style, so help yourselves."

CHAPTER 37:
STAY CALM AND DANCE ON

Two hours before the talent show started, the Dancing Divas, carrying their costumes and dance bags, met outside Collins High. Trebo was there and Ted, too, to see for himself what he imagined only happened in the movies. Inside the school, performers and their guests milled about, but no one took notice as they slipped through the hallway door leading to the stage.

Joan and Charlene stood guard at each end of the crossover to make sure no one came into the area, as Marcus appeared with Janis Joplin and Saffron, one android in each hand. Next—and to Milly's complete surprise—arrived Rigel, with Sagan and Sojourner.

Milly screamed like she'd seen a zombie coming for her. Rigel grinned and hugged her to him.

"You guys, keep it down. You're gonna draw the security guard," whispered Nancy.

"Come on, we can't stay here." Joan herded them to a corner of the large holding room, where the acts would later line up. Marcus stayed with his droids, but Trebo, Ted, and Rigel left to take seats in the auditorium.

"Oh Lord, now I'm going to be too nervous to perform, knowing Rigel's in the audience," Milly said. "I can't do this."

"Yes, you can," said Joan. "You can do 'Proud Mary' in your sleep, Milly, and you know it."

"Doesn't matter. He'll be out there."

"You won't even see him with all the stage lights," said Nancy.

"I don't care! You're gonna hafta go on without me."

"Milly. Listen to me." Nancy held both Milly's shoulders and looked her in the eyes. "What do you always say when we question our ability to dance? Huh?" Nancy let go.

"I can't remember. I can't remember any-thing." Milly paced in circles, fingers on her temples.

"Stay calm and dance on, Milly! You got this!" said Joan. "We are going to freaking razzle-dazzle them out there!"

"We are! As soon as that music starts, the en-ergy flows through us, and we love it. You've said so yourself," said Nancy.

"I'm not sure I'll get over my stage fright, even when the music starts," said Charlene. "I actually feel light-headed thinking about it. I haven't danced in front of people in decades. And to make it worse, we go last. I'd rather get it over with quick."

"You did great at dress rehearsal last night. If you stumble, keep tapping. Make it part of the dance. No one will notice. We all mess up, so don't worry about it. Come on, we got this, Divas!" Joan repeated and slapped Charlene's back.

"Let's review the steps real quick. It will help all of us feel better," said Nancy. "We don't need music or shoes. We'll run through it once and then it'll be time to change. Jasmine's probably in the dressing room already."

"Fine. I won't even see him. I'm gonna pretend he's not there." Milly took a deep breath. "That's right. Stay calm and dance on."

"Ooh, we have 'Proud Mary' in our repertoire," said Saffron.

"Call it up, Sistas!" said Sojourner."

"One, two, three, four!" Sagan clapped each beat.

The girl group sang a cappella: "We're rollin'. Rollin'. Rollin' on the river."

"Okay, okay, start over." Nancy waved to stop the song.

"But skip all the slow stuff," said Joan. "We start when the trumpets come in on the rough stuff."

"Fast forward, Sistas!" said Sojourner.

The three androids shimmied until they got to the starting point of the Divas' dance. The trumpets sounded.

"Hit it!" Saffron grinned.

Not taking up as much room as they would on the stage, Divas performed their choreography. At the end of the three-minute routine, applause broke out from the other brightly costumed dancers filling the room. The Divas and Sistas bowed and thanked the small crowd.

"Yea! We did it!" Charlene held up her hand for a high five. Milly slapped it, and they both collapsed onto chairs next to the wall.

"Marcus, we've got to go change," said Joan. "Here's the program. Janis Joplin, as promised, is the headliner. She'll be followed by the Sassy Sistas. They'll come on stage at the same time, though. The Sistas will be in the background as Janis performs 'Piece of my Heart.' The Divas are the last act. There's a TV monitor over there so you can watch what's happening on stage."

"Before you go, have you seen Janis?"

"No." Joan looked around the crowded room. "Have you guys seen Janis?" she called to her fellow tappers.

"Here I am. Just snooping around a bit."

"Stay here. No more roaming. We'll be right back." Joan left Marcus and the androids to join the other Divas. They left the holding room to meet their instructor and change into their costumes.

"Welcome to UP's talent show! This is not a contest. Tonight, we are all winners! Everyone's a star! Congratulations to all our hard-working graduates and their dedicated mentors." The emcee waited for applause to die down. "Did you enjoy dinner and dessert?" More applause and whistles. "UP greatly thanks our generous donors to the silent auction. Be sure you peruse the numerous tables in the lobby loaded with fabulous gifts.

"And let's not forget the trip to the tropical island of Grand Cayman in the warm Caribbean! Bidding is open until 9:30. If you want to leave the auditorium to check on the latest bids, please, *please*, wait until an act is over before you move up and down the aisles.

"Hey! Let's get this show started so I can get in on the bidding. I could use a vacation to paradise! Seriously, folks, our graduates will be making a difference in our community, state, nation, the world, and maybe even the universe one day! There's a spotlight waiting for each and every one of them. But first, let the spotlight shine on the Rock-n-Roll Heavenly Band. You may have seen them performing at different venues around town. Show your love for these talented musicians. They volunteered their time tonight for your enjoyment.

"Now, please welcome our first act. A group of impersonators. They are actually androids, those fancy robots that look like humans. You've never seen anything like them, and they are right here on our stage! PLEASE WELCOME JANIS JOPLIN . . . AND THE HARMONY HAGS! Wait. I was told the girl group was called the Sassy Sistas. Who changed the prompter? Strike the Harmony Hags. Welcome to our stage, THE SASSY SISTAS!

". . . Folks, we have broken a record in fundraising. Collinsville, Wyoming, has the most generous people in the country! Thank you all so much. Our final act tonight was responsible for bringing our opening act together. Please welcome the Dancing Divas tap dancing to Tina Turner's 'Proud Mary.' WATCH OUT 'CAUSE THESE GIRLS GONNA BURN UP THE STAGE!"

Lessons from the Dancing Divas

Nancy: The universe is unlimited and so is your potential. Look up at the stars and DREAM BIG no matter your age!

Milly: Stay calm and dance on! YOU GOT THIS!

Sonia: When you're down, there's no place to go but UP! SMILE! You are smart and brave and beautiful!

Charlene: If you stumble, make it part of the dance, and KEEP GOING!

Sharon (Bellmer) Obert first dreamed of writing a novel in fifth grade when she discovered the Trixie Belden mystery series. At the same time, *Lost in Space* was her favorite TV show. One day she would combine mystery and outer space into an adventure like no other. Her dream came true with *Stay Calm and Dance On.*

Sharon lives very near the fictious town of Collinsville, Wyoming, with her husband, Paul, and lots of fairies, gnomes, and trolls.

Visit her website at **StayCalmDanceOn.com**
for more of Sharon's stories